A Box Full of
DARKNESS

ALSO BY SIMONE ST. JAMES

The Haunting of Maddy Clare
An Inquiry into Love and Death
Silence for the Dead
The Other Side of Midnight
Lost Among the Living
The Broken Girls
The Sun Down Motel
The Book of Cold Cases
Ghost 19
Murder Road

A Box Full of
DARKNESS

Simone St. James

MICHAEL JOSEPH

PENGUIN MICHAEL JOSEPH

UK | USA | Canada | Ireland | Australia
India | New Zealand | South Africa

Penguin Michael Joseph is part of the Penguin Random House group of companies whose addresses can be found at global.penguinrandomhouse.com

Penguin Random House UK,
One Embassy Gardens, 8 Viaduct Gardens, London SW11 7BW

penguin.co.uk

First published in the United States of America by Berkley,
an imprint of Penguin Random House LLC 2026
First published in Great Britain by Penguin Micharl Joseph 2026
001

Copyright © Simone Seguin, 2026

The moral right of the author has been asserted

Penguin Random House values and supports copyright.
Copyright fuels creativity, encourages diverse voices, promotes freedom
of expression and supports a vibrant culture. Thank you for purchasing
an authorized edition of this book and for respecting intellectual property
laws by not reproducing, scanning or distributing any part of it by any
means without permission. You are supporting authors and enabling
Penguin Random House to continue to publish books for everyone.
No part of this book may be used or reproduced in any manner for the
purpose of training artificial intelligence technologies or systems. In accordance
with Article 4(3) of the DSM Directive 2019/790, Penguin Random House
expressly reserves this work from the text and data mining exception

Book design by Nancy Resnick
Printed and bound in Great Britain by Clays Ltd, Elcograf S.p.A.

The authorized representative in the EEA is Penguin Random House Ireland,
Morrison Chambers, 32 Nassau Street, Dublin D02 YH68

A CIP catalogue record for this book is available from the British Library

HARDBACK ISBN: 978-0-241-79374-9
TRADE PAPERBACK ISBN: 978-0-241-79375-6

Penguin Random House is committed to a sustainable future
for our business, our readers and our planet. This book is made from
Forest Stewardship Council® certified paper.

For Stephen King,
who teaches so many of us not only how to be a writer,
but how to be a good one.

Someone I loved once gave me a box full of darkness.
It took me years to understand that this, too, was a gift.

—Mary Oliver

1

VIOLET

Long Island, New York
September 1989

When I wake in the middle of the night, I don't always see darkness. Sometimes I see fog outside the window of my old bedroom, the way it curled like smoke, and I can hear water dripping from the trees. Sometimes I see my daughter's face on the day she was born. I can often picture with perfect clarity our old kitchen in the house where I grew up, or the patent shoes I wore until I outgrew them and handed them down to Dodie, or the yellowing secondhand paperbacks I used to pilfer from Vail's bedroom bookshelf.

Other times, the faces of the people I've seen over the years appear in my mind: the girl in the stairwell at my high school; the man in the window of a neighbor's house, gesturing for me to come in; the woman underwater in the lake, still wearing her wool dress and straw hat. I never forget any of them, and I think somehow they know it. That's why they show themselves to me.

Why I can see them when no one else can, I'll never know.

For a moment, in the dark, it's almost peaceful to recall their faces. Then I turn my head and catch something from the corner of my eye, and for a moment I think I see—

But no, never. Not for years.

It doesn't matter how long it's been. I'm always afraid it's there.

And then I close my eyes and wonder what it's like to see nothing at all.

The day was clouding over as I took my equipment from the trunk of my car. Buckets, cleaning solutions, brooms, mops, gloves. The house stood a few blocks from the shore, a split-level that was dark and empty of life. My employer, Tess, had given me a key.

I stepped through the front door and paused, taking in the silence. The quiet of a house that is no longer lived in is somehow different from any other silence—a little like pitch-darkness. The place was tidy, dim, slightly dusty, the blinds drawn. From what Tess had told me, the elderly woman who owned it had died in a hospital, not here. That was something, at least.

The easiest place to start in a job like this is the bathroom—small, and just about everything must go. I started with the guest bath, leaving the upstairs bath for later. Then I moved to the cabinets and bookshelves in the sitting room, sorting rapidly.

I was a cleaner, but of a specialized kind. The company I worked for cleaned out dead people's houses, sorting and distributing their belongings. Some people died with no living relatives left to do the job; others were, for whatever reason, not on speaking terms with everyone they ever knew. Some isolated themselves, and others were genuinely loathed. When that happened, my employer would get a call from a landlord, lawyer, or other far-removed person, and Tess would send me.

A Box Full of Darkness

It was an efficient process. Since I had no connection to the person who had died, I could do the job without shedding a tear or feeling a pang of guilt. Throwing out the used toothbrush made me feel nothing. I didn't care that this woman had listened to Lawrence Welk records or had been prescribed antibiotics in 1981. I could toss out the old handmade Christmas ornaments. I could box up the family photos without being tempted to look at them, even for a moment.

I'd gotten into this line of work when my own mother died, alone in a rented apartment, far from the house where my siblings and I were raised. I'd wanted nothing to do with her belongings, hadn't wanted to touch her dresses or whatever items she'd kept of my father's for all those years. I had never even been to her apartment and didn't want to go now. So I'd found a service to empty it for me.

Tess was the one I'd hired. She and I hit it off. She always needed cleaners, and when I offered, she was willing to hire me even after knowing the dark corners of my history.

Now I cleaned for other people like me, and I never judged. Because I knew what it felt like to want to walk away from someone and forget.

At lunchtime, I tugged each finger of my rubber gloves to pull them off, then rooted through my bag for the sandwich I'd brought. I used the old woman's kitchen phone to call Tess, because the woman had died only a week ago and her phone line hadn't been disconnected yet.

"Good afternoon, this is Tess," my boss said when she answered. She was most likely sitting at her desk in her office, doing accounting and making schedules.

"Tess, it's me."

"Violet, hi. How's the job going?"

"Just fine, I guess." I looked across the counter to the sitting room, which was almost completely sorted. "This one's not too hard."

"Anything valuable?"

"Not much." We talked about scheduling the trash pickup, the charity pickup, the appointment with the secondhand dealer who would take items of value on consignment. I glanced at the ceramic salt and pepper shakers on the counter, the plastic napkin holder. I'd start on the kitchen this afternoon.

"Your ex called," Tess told me. "He said to tell you your daughter won't be coming to stay the weekend. Something came up."

I put down the crust of my sandwich. I'd been expecting that, though it still hurt. "Something always comes up."

"I know, Vi. He's being a grade A asshole. You should call a lawyer."

I shook my head, though she couldn't see me. "I don't need a lawyer." Lisette was fourteen, and the custody battle had been over long ago. I'd lost. Lisette visited me less and less lately, but whether that was her decision or Clay's, I didn't know.

"I'll help you pay for it," Tess said, because she was a good person, and we'd been friends for years. She also thought I needed money, which I didn't.

"There's no point," I said. "He'd just use my past against me, like he always does. You'd waste your money. Lisette will be an adult in a few years anyway."

"I don't care what Clay says. She isn't better off growing up away from you."

That was debatable. Even I admitted that. But I said, "I appreciate the vote of confidence. I really do."

"Find yourself another man, Vi. Get out there. A woman who looks like you—jeez. If I was single and had your legs, no man on Long Island would be safe."

I ignored that. Any man who knew exactly how damaged I was would run screaming. "Anything else?"

"Yeah, a weird one. I got a call from a man who was looking for you. He said he was from Daylight Landscaping, in Fell, and he was calling about the house."

Shock sent heat up the back of my neck and made my vision blur.

"Violet?" Tess asked on the other end of the line.

I braced my palm against the Formica countertop and closed my eyes. The landscapers had been hired years ago, and there had never been a problem. Not once.

Something was very wrong.

"Violet?" Tess sounded alarmed.

"I'm here." I cleared my throat, tried to sound even a little bit normal. "They called you?"

"He said you weren't answering your home line, and the answering machine didn't pick up, so he wasn't sure he had the right number. You'd left him the office number in case of an emergency, so he called here."

There couldn't be an emergency, not a real one. There was no one living at the Fell house. Unless the place had burned down. The thought gave me a jolt of panic. "What did he want?"

"You have a house upstate?" Tess's tone was curious, even a little suspicious. She'd seen me for years as a down-and-out former mental patient, not a person who owned property. Property big enough to need landscapers, no less.

"It's . . . my parents' old place," I explained lamely. "No one lives there. The landscapers keep it up."

"Huh." There was an unpleasant tone in Tess's voice. "You're full of surprises, Violet."

Her meaning was clear. Tess thought I had confided in her, told her everything, and she didn't like that I hadn't. Because she knew I'd spent time in a mental hospital, because I'd taken a job with her, she thought she knew the important things about me. But she didn't, and now she was catching on.

There went another friendship. I'd add it to the pile.

I fumbled around next to the old woman's phone and found a pen and a pad of paper for taking messages. "Give me the number," I said.

She recited the number, which was long-distance. I scribbled on the pad, then hung up with Tess. I left the pad and pen where they were and walked out the door to the small back deck, trying to gather my scrambling thoughts.

I wasn't going to call. The last thing I wanted to do was call. Whatever was on the other end of the line was bad—I already knew that. The landscaper wasn't calling with an idle question or a problem with an unpaid bill. I felt a sinister tug, like on a long-slack fishing line. The house in Fell was waking up, pulling on its strings. I wasn't going to answer.

My course of action decided, I went back into the house. I was annoyed that the call had come to me instead of to Dodie or Vail, that I was the one who had to deal with these things. Dodie was in New York, modeling for shampoo ads, and she was never home at her tiny apartment to take a phone call. And Vail? Our brother, the middle child, was in a cabin in the woods somewhere in Montana. He called me from a different number every year, and I'd had to track down one of his ex-girlfriends to get his latest number, which he might have changed again. Vail was extraordinarily good at disappearing when things got hard.

I would start on the kitchen of this dead woman's house and forget about all of it. I picked up my rubber gloves from the kitchen counter, turned, and froze.

A woman stood on the stairs, her hand on the railing. She wore a plum-colored dress from the thirties, and her dark hair was pulled back from her face in a classic style. When our eyes met, a chill of cold air whispered over my skin.

She didn't speak. In all the years I'd been seeing them, they'd never spoken.

"Okay," I said to her when I had found my voice. "I understand."

The woman turned and glanced behind her, up the stairs. Her free hand worried the fabric of her skirt, twisting it. She turned back to me.

I nodded at her, reassuring her again. "It's all right."

She was afraid of something. They sometimes were, especially when it came to the bedroom. She didn't want me to go upstairs and look. Sometimes, they were afraid of what I'd see.

It might be the birth certificate that revealed she wasn't who she said she was.

Or the divorce decree from the abusive husband she'd fled at eighteen and never told her children—or her second husband—about.

It wasn't just the women. The men had secrets, too. The letter from an old lover, dated twenty years after they swore they'd never see each other again. I'd once found an old photo, lovingly framed and hidden, of two men in the army, their arms flung over each other's shoulders as they posed for the camera, both of them smiling and happy. Whatever that photo meant had died with both of them.

The sight of this woman on the stairs wasn't a shock to me. All I felt was a weary kind of familiarity, the exhale of taking on another burden. I would remember this one, just as I remembered all the others I'd seen since childhood, the people no one else saw. Whatever secret this woman didn't want spoken would stay unspoken with me. It was part of doing this job, of being here to see the dead when there were no other living people left to do so. It was what made me who I was, and I had paid the price for it.

"I won't tell," I told the woman.

She didn't move. Maybe she didn't believe me. I felt my pulse heavy in my neck, my temples, a blood rush. I blinked, and when I opened my eyes again, she was gone.

It didn't take me long to find the item the woman was worried about. It was in her dresser drawer, half-hidden beneath her jewelry. She had lived alone, not worried that someone she lived with would see her secrets. And she had wanted the photograph in easy reach.

It was of a baby, a few months old, fat and smiling, lying on a blanket. On the back of the black-and-white photo the word *Thomas* was written in careful pencil. No last name, no date. No indication of who Thomas belonged to or what had happened to him.

I ran a finger over his little face and decided the woman had given him up for adoption. She was too young, and she'd given him away, said the story in my head. Thomas had been adopted by a nice young couple and had a great life now, with kids of his own. I couldn't bear to think of any other story for him, so I didn't.

I slid the photo into the back pocket of my jeans. When I turned around, I saw sitting in the middle of the bed, stark in the sunlight from the curtained window, the note with the phone number I'd left next to the old woman's phone.

I hadn't brought it upstairs, and I felt a surge of irritated anger instead of fear. The people I saw didn't move things around, didn't give me their bossy directives about my choices. What gave this woman the right? Who the hell did she think she was?

"I'm not going to do it," I said aloud, my voice a rasp in the chilly silence.

But I did. As if the woman in the plum dress had scolded me, I crossed the room and snatched the note from the bedspread, picking up the bedside phone. "You can pay the long-distance charges, then," I snapped, jabbing my finger into the rotary dial. "Serves you right."

"Daylight Landscaping, can I help you?" A man's deep voice answered the phone. "Henry speaking."

"My name is Violet Esmie," I said, trying to keep my voice steady. "I'm returning your call."

"Right. Thanks for calling me back, Mrs. Esmie."

Esmie was my birth name. I'd never taken Clay's name when we married. I didn't bother to correct him.

"What can I help you with?" I asked.

"Mrs. Esmie, I'm sorry to say this, but I have to terminate our contract."

My throat constricted. "What? Why? I've been using your company for years."

"Yes, and we appreciate your business. But unfortunately we won't be going back to your property. We will refund a portion of your last payment and—"

"I don't care about that. I care about why. Why are you doing this after all this time?"

Henry cleared his throat. "Mrs. Esmie, I'm going to assume you haven't visited the property recently?"

I could have laughed at that, but it would have had no humor in it. None of us—not Dodie, Vail, myself, or our parents, who were now dead—had been to the Fell house in eighteen years. We wouldn't sell it, we wouldn't demolish it, and we wouldn't go back. We'd just live with it weighing us down forever.

"No," I managed. "Not recently."

"My employees have concerns. They tell me . . . Well, they said they've seen some strange things. I wrote it off at first, because it was crazy, but then some of my guys threatened to quit if I sent them back, and I can't afford that. So I went to the property myself, and I can't write it off anymore."

He sounded embarrassed. He'd assumed I'd scoff at him or disbelieve him. Instead, I said, "What did you see?"

"I've been going over it and over it in my mind, you understand. I'm not the kind of person who sees things. I haven't even told my wife. It was just so strange. But I'm never going back there—I know that much. Nothing could make me go."

I had no time for this. "Who was it?"

Henry paused.

"It was a person, right? So who? Who did you see?" Was it Mom or Dad? I wondered. The thought of one of them wandering around the old house made me angry, but something told me that wasn't it. An icy shard of cold slid into my stomach, because if it wasn't them, it had to be— No. No.

Henry said, "Look, Mrs. Esmie—"

"*Who did you see?*" My voice was a hoarse shout as I cut him off.

"A boy," Henry said. "A little boy, about six or seven, standing in front of the house."

Something hard hit my knees. The floor. I'd fallen to my knees without realizing it. "Did he speak?" I asked.

"Mrs. Esmie—"

"*Did he speak?*" I shouted, my voice ringing in the dead woman's bedroom. "Just tell me. *What did he say?*"

Henry sounded frightened now. He wasn't the only one. My anger had turned into sick, nauseating fear.

"The little boy at your house," Henry told me. "He said, 'Come home.'"

2

VAIL

Montana

The door clicking shut behind me was a relief. There was nothing but the darkness, the rain, and silence.

I stood there for a long minute, holding the box of files, my overnight bag at my feet. I'd spent too many hours in airports in the last two days, seen too many people. California had too much sunshine. This was much better.

I set the box on the floor and brushed my sleeve over the lid, wiping off the rain. I unlaced my muddy boots and picked the box up again, walking steadily through the darkness, weaving around the few pieces of furniture in here without needing to see them. I set the box on my kitchen table and turned on the lamp there.

I scrubbed my hands through my wet hair, rubbed the rain from my temples. I needed a shave. The cabin smelled like pine, and the floor was cold against my damp socks. I was so completely alone here that I could die and no one would find my desiccated body for weeks. That was a selling point for me.

I got a glass of milk from the kitchen, the light from inside the fridge the only light I needed. As I turned back to the table, the blinking light from the answering machine caught my eye. I ignored it. Friends? I had none. Ex-girlfriends? No, thank you. My sisters? They had no reason to call me that I could think of. My parents? Thankfully dead.

Instead of walking toward the phone, I went back to the kitchen table, sipped my milk, and pulled my notes from the file box.

> Subject: Charles Zimmer
> Age: Fifty-six
> Status: Divorced, lives alone, two grown children
> Number of encounters: At least twenty, exact number not calculated
> Type of encounter: Home invasion and possible study
> First encounter: 1974

Twenty encounters at least, over fifteen years. It was an interesting case, though not a completely unique one. Charles Zimmer of Sacramento, California, was an investment banker, rich and good-looking, wearing crisp tan pants and a pressed white shirt to our meeting. He did not appear to be crazy.

His house was large, decorated in painful white, with floor-to-ceiling windows and icy air-conditioning. With my overgrown hair, beard, and red-and-black flannel shirt, I'd looked like a lumberjack who'd somehow wandered into his gated neighborhood.

"You don't look like you're from VUFOS," he'd said to me, looking me up and down. "I expected someone . . ." He trailed off.

"Nerdy," I supplied. It was true that VUFOS—the Volunteer UFO Society—was packed with nerds. I stuck out at meetings and conventions, just as I stuck out in Zimmer's living room. Not fitting in was a chronic condition of my life.

A Box Full of Darkness

Zimmer had shrugged, as if people like me rarely figured in his philosophy. "I suppose you're popular with the lonely housewives making reports."

"Most of the reports we get come from men," I replied. "Statistically. Like you, for example."

Zimmer's expression had soured, but the remark shut him up. "Let me show you around and we'll get this over with."

I read the next page of my notes.

Points of entry: Three doors (front, garage, back)
Time of encounters: Night (all)
Communication from entities: None
Physical encounters with entities: None (recalled)
Missing time: 30 to 60 minutes each time
Injuries from encounters: None
Other manifestations: Electronic disturbances, most often the clock radio

In the bedroom, where Zimmer said most of the encounters had happened, I took out my camera and shot pictures while Zimmer watched. He was starting to look uncomfortable now.

"Do you see lights?" I asked as I circled the room.

"Yes. They're blinding, right in my eyes."

I felt a physical shudder of revulsion at that, but I suppressed it. This wasn't about me. "And then the figures looking down at you?"

"Yes. Four or five of them." It was some kind of catharsis for him to admit this out loud. He'd likely wondered if he was losing his mind for the last fifteen years. "Have you seen this before? Tell me. What's going on?"

"Yes, I've seen this before." I paused at the bedroom window, looking down over the backyard. There was a pool there. "They're studying you."

"What the hell for?"

"There are a number of theories." The pool was empty of swimmers, baking in the merciless California sun. A faint breeze rippled the surface, then stilled again.

I stared at the pool too long, and Zimmer said, "You used to be an Olympic diver." When I looked at him in surprise, he added, "I researched you before I let you into my house, Mr. Esmie. Of course I did."

I looked back at the pool. "Your research has errors. I never got as far as the Olympics."

"Why did you quit?" Zimmer asked.

I ignored him and walked toward the bed, looking up at the ceiling. "You have a skylight."

"Yes." He was nervous again.

"I will never understand the architectural fascination with skylights. To me, their popularity is inexplicable. How long have you lived in this house?"

"Four years." Zimmer paused. "The last house—it had a skylight, too. But I've already thought of that. I had someone come and check it. It hasn't been tampered with. They aren't getting in through there."

Of course it wouldn't appear tampered with. They were too clever for that, but I didn't say it out loud. Zimmer was already frightened enough.

"What is it?" Zimmer asked when I was silent for too long. "Do you think it's a problem? What are you saying?"

I stared up through the pane of glass at the square of sky beyond. I imagined whatever hovered above being able to look down at you while you slept, taking in your slumbering figure with its large, eerily slanted pitch-black eyes. Watching. Until its long gray fingers reached out to touch the glass.

A Box Full of Darkness

"I'm saying I'd never sleep under a skylight," I said to Charles Zimmer. "But that's just me."

I set aside the spools of film I'd get developed tomorrow. I reorganized my notes. I could do this in the morning, but I was awake now, and I had nothing else to do. The investigations for VUFOS were my job, though it didn't pay. One of the worst things about me was that because of my trust fund, I didn't need money.

I sorted through the report I'd requested from VUFOS of other encounters they'd documented in the Sacramento area, looking for similarities to what Zimmer had told me. There were other encounters in the area, but the details didn't match Zimmer's, and none that moved from house to house. These entities were interested in Zimmer specifically and tracked him from place to place, a phenomenon that wasn't unknown in UFO research.

Another option, of course, was that Zimmer had some type of psychosis. That was always possible in these cases.

Several hours later, I noticed the blinking light on the answering machine again. I put my empty milk glass in the sink and reluctantly pressed the button.

There was only one message, and it was Violet's voice, though she didn't identify herself. "Vail, call me." She recited her number. "It's about Ben."

The message ended with a beep, and I stood in the dark. I could feel my hands opening and closing, opening and closing into fists.

After a minute, I picked up the phone and called Violet, using the number she'd left. I never had a need to write numbers down. I had no idea what time it was in Long Island, and I didn't care. Violet would answer.

"Vail?" my sister said when she picked up the phone. She sounded like she'd been drinking. "Is that you?"

"If you lied to get me to call you, I'll never speak to you again," I said, my voice thick. "Never."

"You think I'd lie about that? About Ben?"

That name, spoken out loud, was like a blow to my gut. I only ever heard it in the silence of my own head. I hadn't heard it spoken in years.

"I wouldn't lie about Ben," Violet said, making me flinch again. She had definitely been drinking.

"What happened?" I asked.

"The landscapers quit. They got spooked off the grounds. He's there, Vail. He's saying, 'Come home.'"

The breath hissed out of me, hot agony leaving my lungs. There was no question of believing. No one would lie about this, least of all Violet.

"Can you leave?" my sister asked me. "I'm in the middle of a job. I'd bail on it, but I owe her. The woman who owned the house, I mean. I want to finish the job, talk to my boss. I'll be there as soon as I can."

"I can leave," I said. "I'll get on a plane."

"Okay. I'll be two days, three at most. I have to talk to Lisette—"

I would be in Fell in twelve hours, tops. "It's fine. I'll come."

"Call Dodie," Violet said.

"You haven't called her?"

"No. I can't." Violet's voice cracked, only partly because she was drinking. "You do it, Vail. Please. *You* do it. You're our brother. *Do something.*"

I sucked a breath in deep and stared at the ceiling. Ben, my little brother who had disappeared when I was fourteen. Ben, who was still in the house where I grew up, where I hadn't been for two decades, where I'd had those dreams. Ben, who I thought might have been taken by aliens. Ben, who wanted me to come home.

Violet was still talking. "She never answers the phone. Will Dodie even come?"

"Dodie will come," I said.

Her laugh was bitter. "You're so sure. Then I guess I'll see you both soon."

We hung up. I stood in the dark, recalling the last phone number I had for my younger sister. I hadn't called it in months.

Where did you go, little brother? The question that had dogged me for years. *Where did you go?*

I'd bring my research with me. I didn't own much. The furniture had come with the cabin. I had a suitcase of belongings, maybe two. Nothing sentimental keeping me here. Nothing sentimental keeping me anywhere.

Where did you go?

Ben wanted me to come home. My ticket would be one-way, and I'd bring everything, because this trip was going to be long, permanent. Maybe I'd get an answer. Either way, I already knew I wouldn't be coming back here.

Exhaling a breath, I picked up the phone.

3

DODIE

New York, New York

Everyone hates first dates. The awkwardness, the sheer terror of rejection. The armor you have to put on, piece by painstaking piece, before you leave the house. The pinching small talk. Excruciating, really. Just awful.

I sat at a small table in a restaurant in the Lower East Side and made sure everything was just so. The cutlery wasn't spotted, the single candle was lit, the cloth napkins were folded into pleasant squares. I adjusted my posture to be straight enough to flatter but not so straight as to appear stiff. I didn't need to check my hair or makeup in my compact mirror because I already knew I looked good. I always did.

Tonight's first date was named Ethan Markham, and I'd never met him before, which was perfect. One of the other models at the agency, Nadia, knew him from the building she lived in. She suggested him to me because all the models I knew were aware I was dating, that I was looking. I put the word out. They might have thought I was a little pathetic, because it behooves a model to be standoffish with men, to make them chase her.

Nadia didn't want to date this Ethan Markham herself, and she didn't say why. It was probably because she was sleeping with a photographer in Hell's Kitchen while also seeing a man who claimed to be a movie producer and was almost definitely a liar. In other words, she was busy, so she sent him my way.

All I knew about Ethan Markham was that he lived in New York, was in no way involved with the modeling business, and was thirty years old. I knew that his voice on the phone was low and pleasantly nervous when he called to set up this date. He made no small talk and hung up as soon as possible. He also had a nice name, which spoke of a man who was conventionally handsome and probably a bit of a bore. That was fine with me, because after tonight, I'd never see him again.

I tapped my fingers on the table, impatient. My nails were manicured, my hands soft, because yesterday I'd modeled a watch for a jewelry company. Hand modeling was lucrative and hard to get. Many models disdained it, because since no one sees your face, you can't get famous. This was never something that bothered me, and my hands were exquisite, so I was in some demand.

There was murmured conversation in the dim corner of the restaurant, and then a man appeared at my table. "Dodie Esmie?" he asked, hovering just behind his chair, in case he had the wrong woman.

I pushed my chair back and stood, smiling. I hid my surprise. Ethan Markham was tall—over six feet—and lean, his limbs long. His dark hair fell in curls about an inch too far in need of a cut, flopping over his ears. He wore dark-framed studious-looking glasses and an expression that was serious and rather sweet. He held out a large, rawboned hand to give me a handshake, like an undertaker. His suit was navy blue.

"Hi," I said, shaking his hand. His skin was warm, which surprised me again. Everyone had clammy hands on a first date. Ethan's hand felt pleasant. Though his demeanor was solemn, his face was youthful, his jawline clean.

He dropped my hand quickly, pulling away. "It's nice to meet you."

We pulled out our chairs and sat, facing each other.

"You surprised me," I said to him after we'd given our drink orders.

He blinked at me. "Why?"

"Because you don't look like an Ethan. But honestly, I'm happy about it. Life is boring when everything is the way you expect."

A small crease appeared between his brows as he frowned. "I don't know what a Dodie is supposed to look like," he admitted. "I've never met one before."

I laughed.

"Did I say the wrong thing?" he asked. Before I could answer, he shook his head. "Wait a minute, I'm confused. What is an Ethan supposed to look like?"

"Blond, I think," I said. "A Wall Street type, maybe. Square chin. Lots of golf."

This seemed to throw him further into confusion. "I don't golf. Is that a problem? I've never been to Wall Street in my life. I'm sorry if I've let you down."

"Relax," I said. I reached over and touched his arm, which was a mistake, because my fingertip touched the inside of his wrist and he pulled away again, as if by reflex. It was a little bit like a come-on, which wasn't what I intended.

I pulled my hand back. I had to regroup, which I didn't usually need to do. "I only mean that you don't have to worry about the impression you make on me because it's just a first date."

Ethan looked surprised, and then the waiter came, and we were distracted by giving our orders. I ordered a caprese salad because it was delicious and because it always confounded people. It was a salad, which meant a model could order it, but it was also cheese. Perfect.

"I thought impressions were important on a first date," Ethan said when the waiter had left. It started to sink in for me just how earnest he was. His eyes were dark and handsome behind his glasses.

"They aren't important with me," I explained. "I'm very good at first dates. They're all I do."

There was a pause as he processed this. He was a man who didn't need repeated explanations. "You mean there won't be a second date?"

"There never is," I said, sipping my seltzer. I never got tipsy on dates; it ruined the experience. "Don't take it personally. In fact, you should find it freeing."

"My God, you're strange," he said, a note of soft wonder in his voice.

I took it as a compliment. I leaned toward him, lowering my voice. Maybe it was the candlelight, but I was starting to notice that beneath the nerdy awkwardness, his cheekbones were actually nice, and there was something kind yet masculine about his mouth. "Think about it," I said. "I haven't even asked what you do for a living, because it doesn't matter to me. You can volunteer it if you like, or you can make something up. You can be anything you want. I'll never know the difference."

He lifted one of his big hands and scratched the back of his neck, still taking me absolutely seriously. "Okay then, I suppose I'm a . . . CIA codebreaker?"

"Fantastic," I said. "Nadia likely told you I'm a model, so I'm not going to bother to lie. So I'll say that I was born in Madagascar, where my siblings and I were abandoned by our parents and raised among pirates and thieves. We had a little brother, but he was lost at sea, washed overboard in an instant during a storm. We never found his body. My father died on the other side of the world, and when my mother heard of our little brother's death, she drank poison. Quite tragic, really."

Ethan lowered his hand, and his expression slowly changed to one of comprehension. For the first time, he looked like he was in control of this situation, like he'd just unfolded a map of the place where he was currently lost. "I see," he said.

My mouth went dry, and I swallowed more of my drink. I didn't know what he saw, and I wasn't going to ask. When I lowered my glass, I smiled. "So, tell me, Mr. CIA. Do you know who killed JFK?"

He didn't kiss me at the end of the date, when he brought me to the door of my apartment building. Most men at least tried, but not Ethan. He didn't press me for a second date, either. This was the game—my game—but for the first time, I wondered if I'd done something wrong. Then I pushed the thought away.

Alone in my apartment, I washed the makeup from my face, and then, standing naked in my bathroom, I brushed my hair and twisted it into a braid. I had no job tomorrow, but the day after, I was booked for a shampoo commercial. I'd stand with my back to the camera, lean my head back at exactly the right angle, and do the upward swipe, my hands under my hair at the nape of my neck and sliding up. At the same time, I'd shake my head so my hair moved back and forth. My hair was glossy, dark, and long, and I was good at the upward swipe combined with the head shake. I'd nail it in one take, maybe two.

I was so very skilled at useless things. If my mother hadn't drunkenly fallen down a flight of stairs to her death several years ago, she'd be appalled at what I'd become. It was the only reason I ever wished she'd lived a little longer.

I dabbed moisturizer on my skin, put on an old nightshirt, and climbed into bed. It was late. I lay there, staring at the ceiling, hoping for sleep. When I'd put my hand on Ethan's wrist, I'd briefly felt his pulse beneath the warm skin. He really did have a nice face. I wished now that I'd succeeded in making him laugh, because I wanted to know what it sounded like. But now I'd never know.

I was dozing off when my phone rang on my nightstand. I picked it up without thinking. "Hello?"

My brother's voice. "Dodie."

"*Vail?*" He hadn't called me since my birthday, because he always called me on my birthday. He had never called me in the middle of the night.

Cold panic bloomed in my gut. This was something bad.

"We have to go back," Vail said, his voice gruff and pained. "To Fell."

My heart started a slow, hard, panicked beat in my chest. "No. Oh no. What is this, a joke? Absolutely not."

"You're going." The words were harsh, and I could hear the pain in his voice. "As soon as you can. Ben is—"

"*No*," I shouted, so loud that one of the neighbors would hear. "I won't go, Vail. I won't, and you can't make me."

"Would you be quiet for a second? Ben is there."

Under the covers, my knees drew up, an instinctive reaction. I didn't need details. I already knew enough. Too much. "Was it Violet? Did she see him?"

"No, but she's coming, too. As soon as she can. He's asking, Dodie. Ben is asking."

My eyes were stinging and dry, my throat thick. The words came out like molasses. "I have to, don't I? We all do."

"I'm getting on a plane in a few hours," Vail said. "I'll see you there."

I hung up, and there was a moment of silence before my phone rang again. Twice in one night? This was unheard of. I picked it up again.

"Hello?"

This time, it was Ethan's voice. "Dodie? I'm sorry to call so late. Are you all right?"

Was I dreaming? Had I fallen asleep hours ago? I couldn't think straight. "I'm fine." I was anything but fine.

"Oh, okay then. I'm sorry if I woke you, but I can't sleep. I keep thinking." He paused, and I could imagine the serious crease between his eyes. "I wanted to say I'm sorry."

My mind was a blank. "For what?"

"For whatever happened to your mother. And, I think, your little brother." He paused again. "I think that's what you were talking about tonight. I mean, I'm pretty sure. It seemed like it was important, and I didn't ask you about it, and I didn't tell you I'm sorry. And I am."

I made myself breathe, my hand gripping the phone. I'd told him a story, a stupid story, and he'd seen through it. How had that happened? How was everything slipping out of control?

"Okay," I managed, too stricken to bother to lie anymore. "Thank you."

"And I'm sorry I didn't kiss you," Ethan said. "I wanted to, and then I thought maybe you'd think that was all I had been after all night, and then I got too into my own head, and I didn't do it, and I missed my chance. My only chance, as it happens. And I tried to tell myself it was fine, that it was what you wanted, but now I don't think it was. And I'm never going to get another chance, so I regret it now. I should have kissed you."

I was leaving New York. As soon as I could pack my things, as soon as I could get out of here. This wasn't going to be a weekend trip or a vacation. It was the end of everything. The life I knew had vanished like smoke with one phone call.

I was going, and maybe I was never coming back.

"Yes," I said, staring into the darkness. "You should have kissed me."

"You have my phone number," Ethan said. "Call me if you need me, Dodie."

I hung up on him.

Then I turned onto my side in bed, and finally I started to cry.

4

VIOLET

The woman behind the counter at Rona's Burgers knew I was hungover. Probably because I was at a roadside burger place at eleven in the morning when they opened, ordering a hamburger and greasy fries.

"Rough night?" she asked. She was about sixty, with creases bracketing her mouth and eyes that had seen some things. I was the only customer in the restaurant, my car the only one in the parking lot beside hers. Past the lot, cars flew by on the highway.

"Rough few years," I admitted. "I need my burger to go."

"I hear ya," the woman said.

Two days of wine were taking a long time to leave my system. I'd worked extra hours to finish cleaning out the old woman's house, going in at six in the morning and not leaving until nearly midnight. Since no one lived there, my hours didn't matter. I couldn't have said why I did it, only that it was wrong to leave her hanging like that when she'd trusted me with her photo of baby Thomas. I couldn't let her down, even for Ben. Maybe because of Ben.

But I'd brought several bottles of wine with me as I worked, sipping through the day so I'd never be entirely sober.

A Box Full of Darkness

When the house was finished, I'd taken leave from my job, telling Tess I didn't know when I'd be back. There was no pay, of course. That didn't matter to me, which Tess had started to suspect. She told me she'd call in a replacement and she couldn't guarantee I'd have a job waiting when I got back. We left it at that.

It had been surprisingly easy. It was harder to call Lisette, who was at Clay's house, and tell her I was going away for a while. She was sullen, angry, and childish, even though she was fourteen and she hadn't wanted to stay with me in the first place. "So you're going, just like that?" she'd snapped. "You're *leaving* me?"

"I have to," I'd said. "My family needs me."

"You hate them!"

Had I said that? Where did she get it from? Had Clay told her that? I didn't think I hated Vail and Dodie, and besides, I wasn't talking about them. I was talking about Ben. None of us had ever hated Ben.

"Well, I'm going home for a while," I'd said, peevish with my own daughter as the wine headache gripped the back of my skull. "It has to happen, so deal with it. I'm not going far. I'll call you every few days."

"Don't *bother*," Lisette said dramatically, hanging up on me.

I was a bad mother. The courts knew it, Clay knew it, and I knew it. There was something missing in me, and I had never been good at it, never been able to do it right. But in that moment, I knew that Clay wasn't winning any awards, either. If my daughter was an asshole, it wasn't entirely because of me.

Still, I'd drunk most of a bottle of wine after that conversation.

During my next glass, I'd realized I'd referred to Fell as *home.*

When I moved out at seventeen, I got a job as a waitress in the restaurant of a Long Beach hotel, the kind that catered to tacky weddings and boozy work retreats. I was tall and reasonably good-looking, and when I wore my hair tied back, the right makeup, and the black uniform of the staff, I looked older than my age. I'd worked hard at the job, motivated by the fact it came with cheap shared lodgings that kept me away from Fell. I wasn't the strange girl with the missing brother anymore. Instead, I was just another server plating canapes and dodging ass grabs.

Behind the scenes, the job was a master initiation into drugs and alcohol, and I was an eager student. I'd gotten drunk fast, got high even faster, hoping that taking something—anything—would make me stop seeing ghosts. The line cooks taught me that a bump of coke gave you the perfect second wind to drink longer, a trick you could repeat until dawn. When I was blacked out, I didn't think about my parents, or my siblings, or the dead man I'd faced in an upstairs hallway my first week there, or Ben. *Ben.*

It worked at first. I spent a year in a blur of work and alcohol. My mind was never calm or sober enough to think about anything. The perfect solution. If it killed me, so be it.

Then, one night as I lay in bed, listening to one of my roommates throw up in the bathroom, I felt Sister's hand on the back of my neck.

I'd known immediately what it was. That struck me later—that there was no question, no *what was that?* I hadn't wondered, even for a second, whether I was imagining it. I never imagined Sister. She simply was.

Her icy fingers had squeezed me, and then she was gone. She hadn't needed to speak. She was reminding me that I hadn't escaped her, that I couldn't escape her. That she was watching. That she could still make me afraid.

I should have stopped then. I should have sobered up and begun a virtuous life. But I didn't.

My father was sober in very few of my memories, his handsome face red, his eyes bleary. Mom waited until after her youngest son disappeared, and then she started drinking with a vengeance. She was hardly capable of caring for herself by the time she mercifully died. The thought of both of them brought me such sick shame, such hatred of myself, that it also should have sobered me. I should have learned from the example they set, but I didn't.

Clay was on a corporate weekend with his coworkers when I met him. He was just good-looking enough, just charming enough, paid me just enough attention, that when he asked to see me after my shift, I said yes. We met in his room and split one bottle of wine, and then another. I remembered thinking, *He'll do.* He likely thought the same about me, and I didn't care. I felt nothing at all.

It was quick, and then it was over. He went back to his cushy job, I went back to work, and I didn't think about him again.

Everything that came after I found out I was pregnant was a series of dreary, predictable mistakes. I hadn't wanted to track down Clay, but I had to because I needed money. We'd married when we barely knew each other because Clay felt guilty and because his parents insisted on it. The marriage was a hopeless disaster that fell apart. After Lisette was born, I'd vacillated between depression and paranoid terror, which came over me whenever I remembered Sister's hand on the back of my neck. Now she wouldn't only haunt me—she would haunt my daughter.

Clay called me unstable, and he was right. The only thing I did right in those days was get sober when the doctor told me a baby was coming. I screwed up everything else.

Blunder followed blunder—a separation, and then a custody battle. Lawyers. And then the mental hospital. I had never forgiven myself for that. I had never forgiven Clay, either.

When I got the call about Ben, I'd allowed myself two long, blurry days soaked in wine like the old days, feeling sorry for myself, wishing all of this had happened to someone else. Then it was over. This morning, I'd winced through the headache and the rolling nausea, packed my car, and started driving.

The woman behind the counter was grilling my lone hamburger

while I waited, my temples throbbing and my eyes dry as sandpaper. The silence stretched too long, so I said, "Are you Rona?"

The woman made a scoffing sound. "Hell no. Rona was my mother. She started this place. She's been dead for fifteen years."

She was looking at what she was doing, so she didn't see me glance around, nervously wondering if I'd see old Rona lurking in the shadows of the walk-in freezer or hovering in the doorway of the bathroom. It was too early, and my head hurt too much, for that.

"My mother died, too," I said.

"Good riddance," the woman said.

I blinked. Her hostility was shocking and kind of refreshing. "Something like that."

The woman melted a thick piece of cheese on top of my burger, then flipped the whole thing onto a warm bun. It actually looked pretty good. "Where are you headed?" she asked.

"Fell." I was thirty minutes away.

The woman gave me an assessing look, her eyes narrowed. Then she said, "I can see it."

I wondered what gave it away. The hangover? My obvious misery? Fell was a weird place, bigger than a town, smaller than a city, a dot on the map of New York State. Most people drove past it or through it without noticing it, but it was a place where strange things happened.

Murders happened in Fell. Disappearances. Bodies turned up in weird places. People there died in "mysterious circumstances." They also lived in mysterious circumstances. Mysterious circumstances were, honestly, what defined Fell. It was hard to explain if you hadn't grown up there, but I knew more about Fell than I knew about any other place I'd lived, even though I made a point not to visit. Staying away from Fell was my attempt at *not* knowing the things that went on there. It hadn't worked.

Rona's daughter had obviously spent time in Fell at some point, and she hadn't liked it much. Most people didn't.

A Box Full of Darkness

Did I look like I belonged there? I didn't know what other people saw when they looked at me. Thick, dark, unstyled hair, dark eyes, the corners of my mouth turned down. I never looked particularly happy. My natural expression was very serious. Men thought I was good-looking, and they came on to me, but when I turned them down, they backed off. Something about me was intimidating, even a little scary.

So yeah, I looked like I belonged in Fell.

I took the grease-spotted bag of food to my car and left the parking lot. As I pulled onto the highway, I rolled down my window and ate my hamburger as I drove. My hangover was starting to dissipate. I was as ready as I could be for the sight of my beloved hometown.

Fell hadn't changed much over the years. It was still just shabby enough to escape notice, the downtown quiet on a weekday morning. I passed the WELCOME TO FELL sign, the Royal movie theater with the marquee letters that never stayed up, the library, the Milkshake Palace, newsstands, a laundromat. If I took a left to the east end, I'd encounter the Fell College of Classical Education, a dusty place that taught Latin and Greek to a couple hundred students per year at most. Mom had wanted one of us to attend Fell as an intellectual status symbol, but none of us had even set foot on the campus.

Just to spite her, we'd never gone to college at all. Vail had his diving career, which he quit before it could be a success. Dodie got by on her considerable looks and nothing else. I had partied until Clay and Lisette happened. Ambition was not in the Esmie siblings' blood.

Outside downtown, I took Number Six Road past the empty lot where a theme park had once been planned and then abandoned, past the motel where the pool was closed because a kid had died in it. All of that had happened after we left, but I knew that if I took the turn to the motel—where I had never stayed—I would see the pool closed and empty, dirt and leaves scattered on the concrete bottom. *Get out of my head,* I wanted to scream. *I don't want to know this shit. Leave me alone.*

I took the turn into our neighborhood, then our driveway, my hands going cold on the steering wheel. And then I was at the house.

The street was as empty as I remembered, gloomy and still. There were no kids, no one walking their dogs, just like in my childhood. The houses were spread apart, the windows dark. We'd been the only kids in the neighborhood while growing up, isolated in a place with no other children. Whether this part of town had ever been lively, I had no idea, but even now, it was one of the most silent places in my memory. There were no playgrounds, just chilly homes with ragged lawns and missing shingles, unraked leaves, and the occasional twitching curtain. The house across the street had been empty for my entire childhood, sinking into rot. When Ben disappeared, no one would have seen a six-year-old boy if he left the house. In this neighborhood, he could have vanished without a ripple.

I looked up at our house now, set far back from the street, with its slanted gables and dark windows, its deteriorating façade, its solitary rotting shingles like sore teeth. It had probably been a prestigious house when my parents bought it, or as prestigious as Mom's money could buy. Now it just looked sad, like a woman's wedding dress rotting away in her closet, important for one day and now worthless.

The grounds, at least, had been maintained until a few days ago. The inside of the house hadn't been touched in eighteen years, though I had paid the minimum to keep the water and electricity hooked up. I hadn't done it out of love. I had done it because it was easier to keep the house out of mind if the pipes never burst or the electrical never caught fire. If our parents' money kept the house standing, it meant none of us would have to come back.

And yet here we were.

A Box Full of Darkness

There were two cars parked in front of the house—a beat-up old Volvo and a shiny new Jeep. I weighed them silently, making an educated guess. The Volvo, I thought, was Dodie's, because she lived in New York and wouldn't want to flaunt an expensive car in the city. The Jeep would be Vail's, rented at the airport. Vail would hand money to the car rental company and drive off in whatever was handed to him without looking at the receipt.

So I was the last one to arrive. I paused when I got out of my car, listening to the hush of the wind in the trees, staring at the house I grew up in the way you'd stare at a face that you hadn't seen in a long time. This house was the worst place, the most awful place. The place I didn't want to be. And yet it was the next thing because Ben had asked, and where else was I going to go?

I strode up the long driveway, leaving my bags in the back of my car. I was wearing black jeans, a black sweater, and black boots that laced up the ankle. My hair was down and I wore no makeup. I wasn't a cleaner today. I wasn't a mother, either, or an ex-wife, or a former mental patient. I mounted the steps to the porch and swung the front door open.

The front hall was dim and smelled musty. There was a woven rug over the worn floorboards beneath my feet. A single lamp by the door, two coats on hooks, no art on the walls. My head spun for a crazy second as I oriented myself.

There was a curl of cigarette smoke lacing the stale air. "She's here," Dodie's voice said from a room down the hall. The living room.

"Um," came Vail's reply.

I strode toward the voices, letting my boots make noise on the wood floor. In the living room, Dodie was sitting cross-legged on a chair, her sneakers abandoned on the floor beneath her. Her hair—dark like mine, though her face was different, more elfin and less serious—was tied in a twist on the top of her head. She was wearing soft, wide-legged pants, cream-colored, with her delicate bare feet folded below the hem, and a garish tight tee of lime green with a rip along one seam. She held a plate in her lap and was lifting a cracker with something smeared on it to her mouth. A cigarette sat in an ashtray next to her, lazily lit.

On the sofa sat Vail, all six-feet-plus of him, long-legged and lean, his hair in too-long curls and a beard on his perfect jaw. His jeans looked years old, his flannel shirt only slightly younger. He was stretched across the sofa, taking up the whole thing, his booted feet crossed at the ankles and resting unapologetically on the old, dusty cushions. He was reading a magazine.

I paused in the doorway. When was the last time my brother, my sister, and I had been in a room together? I couldn't remember. Our mother had had no funeral, and her ashes had sat in the trunk of my car until I'd finally dumped them unceremoniously into Long Island Sound.

Dodie looked at me with a smile and amusement in her eyes, then stuffed the cracker into her mouth. Vail flipped the page of his magazine.

I nodded toward the cigarette. "Put that out," I said to Dodie. "This place is probably a fire hazard."

My little sister chewed her cracker and shrugged. "Help yourself," she said with her mouth full.

"Damn it." I crossed the room, tapped the ash off the cigarette, and put it to my lips, taking a long drag. The way it made my head spin was only slightly different from the way it was spinning already. "Want some, Vail?" I asked.

"I quit," Vail said into his magazine.

"So did I," I said.

"So did I," Dodie echoed.

None of us commented further. I stood in the middle of the room, smoking that sweet, sweet nicotine until the cigarette was a nub. Then I ground it out in the ashtray.

I looked at Dodie, who was licking a crumb from her lip. She wasn't wearing any makeup, either, but whereas my features were drawn in smudged charcoal, hers were etched in beautiful, precise lines. "Please tell me that cracker wasn't eighteen years old," I said to her.

Her eyes went wide with delight at the thought. "No, but that would have been *amazing*. Vail has been here long enough to do a food run. And I brought food myself, because I figured there was a good chance I'd starve otherwise."

At the sofa, Vail's boots hit the floor with a thump as he sat up. "Dodie exists on crackers," he said, his voice gruff as always. "She puts goop on them."

"It's pâté," Dodie said.

For the first time, Vail looked at me, and my brother's gaze met mine. I swallowed. The last time I'd seen Vail was three years ago, when he'd briefly been in Long Island on one of his investigations. I met him at a café, where we'd had coffee together mostly in silence. I remembered thinking how he'd filled out since his diving days, how he looked nothing like a boy anymore because he was a man. It had struck me the way changes do when you haven't seen someone in a while.

Later that day, long after he was gone again, it had also struck me that that one hour of near silence with Vail had felt more like a conversation than any real conversation I'd had in years.

I wondered if I looked different to him now than I had then. I probably did. My surviving little brother was all bone and muscle and healthy fat, beautiful. The trimmed beard made him look even more mature. He was in his prime physically, but he still had the shadowed gaze he'd had since he was a little boy.

We exchanged a wordless look, the kind I hadn't known since the last time I saw him, and then he lifted the magazine he'd been reading to show me. He had picked it up from a pile on a table. It had

Richard Nixon on the front as the issue's current news. "This is what we're dealing with," he said bluntly. "This house is fucked."

I nodded, rubbing my damp palms on the thighs of my jeans. "I agree. Can we do this drunk, do you think?"

"Can we, please?" Dodie asked.

But Vail shook his head, and I knew he was right. I was done with my moping in wine. We were here, in this hell house, for Ben. We hadn't spoken his name yet, but it echoed around the room anyway. We couldn't disrespect our little brother by being drunk for whatever this was.

"We're white-knuckling it," my brother declared. "Let the fun begin."

5

VAIL

The first thing I did when I arrived at the house, alone, was take the dust cloths off the furniture. The second thing I did was get a phone line hooked up. This had required a trip downtown to the offices of the phone company to get our long-defunct line activated. I had leaned toward the woman behind the counter, held her gaze, and given her twenty dollars. Through a haze of blushes, she'd promised an express hookup, with the bill to come to our address. I didn't even have to offer her a date. I thanked her and didn't bother to tell her that the bills would go in the trash.

I didn't need the phone line myself. I never talked to anyone. But Violet had a daughter, and she'd need to be able to reach her.

By the time Dodie arrived a day later—she'd apparently bailed on a photo shoot—I had already scouted the surrounding houses. My memories of this neighborhood weren't good—long days of unsupervised boredom, my parents shouting at each other, Ben disappearing. It was as fun as growing up in a Siberian gulag, and my sisters and I were as well-adjusted as could be expected as a result. I didn't have hopes that the place had improved.

To the left of our house, the old lady who had lived there when we were kids was gone, replaced by a family named Chatham, according to the mail I lifted from the mailbox next to their front door. No one was home, but from what I could see through the windows and based on the bike in front of the garage, there were two parents and a kid of about ten. This was surprising, because there hadn't been any children in the neighborhood when we were kids, as if childhood fun was against the law here. Whoever this kid was, he or she was probably lonely. In other news, the Chathams subscribed to *Newsweek* and got the JCPenney catalog in the mail. Nothing interesting there.

I went across the street next. The house here had been empty for as long as I could remember. It was aging back then, the windows blank-eyed with dust and dirt, the weeds overgrown. A wooden front porch had rotted away year after year as I grew up, a marker of time going by.

A place like that would usually be a magnet for neighborhood mischief—but there were no kids in our neighborhood except for us three. My sisters could not have been less interested. I had probably thrown a bottle at the house once or twice, but the place looked like a corpse, and the game wasn't much fun. I never asked why no one lived there. In Fell, people left their homes and never came back. Not much in this town had a tidy explanation.

But someone had been to this house in the last eighteen years. There was scaffolding on part of the deconstructed roof, and the lawn was churned into fossilized piles of soil, old rainwater filling the ruts left by construction vehicles. The rotted porch was torn out, and fresh lumber had been dropped on the lawn, then left to rot in turn. Three crushed, faded Coke cans sat in a pile of gravel. Someone had started a renovation—months, maybe years ago—and then abandoned it.

As I stared at the scene, I felt awake, alert, as if the phone call about Ben had pulled me out of darkness and thrust me under a bright light. Had someone bought the old, abandoned house from my childhood? Who was it? Why had they stopped their renovation so suddenly that they hadn't cleaned up their garbage or carted the lumber away? I'd find those answers, and soon. I'd done dozens of investigations for VUFOS, and I hadn't always followed their rule book. When it came to Ben, there was no rule book.

The house to the right of ours had belonged to the Thornhills when we were growing up, and apparently it still did. In my memory, they were a couple in their forties with no kids, who traveled a lot because Mr. Thornhill was some kind of—what—traveling speaker? Lecturer? The memory wouldn't come. I could only remember that Mr. Thornhill had round-framed glasses, and Mom had always felt sorry for them because they had no children, even though Mom didn't care about her own. Nothing else surfaced in my mind.

The Thornhills would be in their sixties now, and not only were they not home, their mail was piled on their doorstep. The geraniums in the pot next to the front door were black and sodden. I picked up the mail and flipped through it, then got distracted when I noticed the welcome mat. On impulse I lifted the mat, looking for a key.

There wasn't one. But a hunch trickled down my spine, and I turned to the long-dead geranium, lifting the rotting pot. Beneath it was a house key, sitting tarnished on the cement.

I put the key in my pocket and put the pot back down. Then I picked up the stack of mail and went home. The wind had picked up, and clouds were chuffing high in the sky, crisscrossing the sun. No cars drove by, and nothing moved. As I approached our house, a raven alighted on the roof, flapping its dark wings and making a throaty sound. Then it went silent.

It was habit that we'd take our childhood rooms, so I climbed the stairs and headed toward mine. My boots were loud on the floorboards.

Dodie had graciously allowed me to carry her luggage upstairs, but when I offered, Violet told me to go fuck myself. I heard her banging her suitcase through the front door, cursing. Dodie said something I couldn't hear that was probably scathing, and Violet sighed heavily.

The upstairs hall was dim and stuffy. The walls were blank—bare of photos, framed memories, or art. We'd always lived as if we rented this place, even though we owned it. My bedroom door was the first at the top of the landing. Next to me was Ben's bedroom, which had been an "office" for our father—who never did any work—and a storage space. We'd cleaned it out when Ben came, and after he'd gone, the room had become disused again. Beyond Ben's room were Violet's, then Dodie's, and our parents' master bedroom at the end of the hall.

I opened the door of my childhood room. In here was a twin bed with a faded red blanket—my feet hung off the edge when I slept in it—and a dresser with chipped navy blue paint. Next to the window was a bookshelf, empty of books, that was leaning distinctly to the left after all this time. My suitcase was against the other wall, next to the stacked file boxes that contained my VUFOS files, taped shut for the trip from Montana.

The room was shoved in the back corner of the second floor, which gave it an odd shape and a slanted ceiling. When I was ten years old and five feet tall, I'd continually banged my head on that ceiling. Now I was thirty-four, over six feet, and eighty pounds heavier. I had no hope of getting out of this without a concussion.

I dropped onto the bed, making it creak. My boots left tracks in the dust on the floorboards. We'd never had a maid service clean the inside of the house, so there was dust everywhere, settled into the fabric of the dust cloths I'd pulled from the furniture. But as I sat with my hands dangling between my knees, I stared at the disturbed dust on the floor, thinking.

Downstairs, Violet was saying something about the phone line.

Dodie waited too long, then asked in a stilted tone, "How is Lisette?" She obviously had no interest in the answer. She might have needed to recall Lisette's name. We Esmies were bad with children. Violet was a bad mother, and Dodie and I would never have children at all. We'd used up all our skill with children on Ben.

I looked down at the scuffs on the floor. When I'd walked into this house alone two days ago, my first thought had been: *It isn't as dusty as I thought it would be.*

It was dusty, yes. But for a house that hadn't been occupied—or entered—in eighteen years, it wasn't dirty enough. There were no mouse droppings or ceiling leaks. No nests or dead rodents. No burst pipes. No mold. The electricity was on—Violet must have been paying the bill—and the fridge hummed in the kitchen. The furnace was still in its place in the cellar, silent but functional. When I turned on the kitchen tap, a burst of brown water had come out, and then it had run just fine.

I'd watched the water and thought, *Eighteen years?*

The air hummed in this house, a low-level vibration I felt at the back of my neck. Had it always been like this? Was that why I'd had such strange, vivid dreams when I lived here?

The figures standing over my bed. The light shining in my eyes.

After Ben arrived, he'd sometimes come into my room at night, and I'd awaken to find him curled next to me, his little body like a furnace against my skin as he slept. I'd brush my hand over his soft brown hair, and he wouldn't wake.

I exhaled, because for a moment I could almost feel it again, Ben pressed next to me. My gaze fixed on the closed door of the closet.

Had I looked in this closet after he disappeared? I thought I had, but I couldn't exactly remember it. I must have looked here, because it was one of Ben's go-to hiding places. He'd slide into the back corner, his arms around his knees, laughing breathily and not very quietly into his hands. There were so many games he liked to play. We'd looked everywhere for him that day and in the days that followed—from the attic, accessed only by pull-down stairs that Ben couldn't have reached, all the way down to the cellar, which was really a crawl space just big enough for the furnace. In all of that searching, I would have looked in the closet.

I stared at the door, my skin prickling. I thought I heard— Was that a sound?

I stood, strode across the room, and flung the closet open.

There was a box of old junk, a hanging coat that had fit fifteen-year-old me. Untouched dust on the floor. Nothing else.

I peered into the gloom, searching for a trapdoor or a hidden passage. A wardrobe that led to Narnia. Somewhere my little brother could have gone.

We'd been so frantic—Violet, Dodie, and me. Hide-and-seek was Ben's favorite game, and we liked to humor him. They'd hidden, and I was It. It was my job to find them. I'd found Dodie and Violet, and then we'd all looked for Ben.

We never found him.

The snow coming down soundlessly out the window, the silence. The heavy air. The panic as we searched and searched.

It hit me all over again, square in the chest. He'd been so excited. I'd failed him—I was supposed to find him, and I hadn't. I still hadn't. I was still staring into this closet, looking for his hiding place. Where the hell had he gone? Why hadn't he been able to come out? *Where did you go, little brother?*

When they came home, our parents had looked, too. And then the police looked. The house had been searched, every corner and nook, for the little boy who had disappeared. He'd gone on a winter day with fresh snow on the ground, and there were no tracks leading to or from the house, no car tracks. Wherever Ben went, logic dictated, had to be somewhere in this house.

A Box Full of Darkness

Come home.

"I'm here," I said out loud to the empty closet, the silence, the dusty floor. "It's me, Ben. I came. We all came."

No one answered me.

I closed the door.

6

DODIE

I could hear Violet's voice downstairs in the kitchen, her tone low and tight with concern. She was on the phone with her daughter. *Yes, I'm here. Call if there's an emergency. No, I don't know how long I'll be here. I'll call you again soon.* I stretched my legs out on my childhood bed and stared at the ceiling, listening. Violet sounded so *parental*. When had my sister become a parent?

Eventually, she hung up. Water ran in the hallway bathroom and a toilet flushed. Vail's heavy footsteps pounded down the stairs. If I had to guess, I'd say he was going to the living room to see if he could get a signal through the rabbit ears on the TV. More steps on the stairs, then a drawer opened and closed in Violet's room as she put her clothes in her old dresser.

I absorbed it for a moment, the sounds of my siblings in the house. In my life in a tiny New York apartment, I was used to the sounds of people all around me, but these weren't strangers. I knew that Violet was likely brushing her hair right now, wrestling its thick length back into a fresh ponytail. I knew that Vail had left a mess of splashes on the bathroom counter. I also knew that in ten minutes, he'd have the TV working. Vail was good with technical things.

We had no plan here, because what's the plan, really, when you've come to find your long-dead brother? No one makes a plan for that. We weren't children anymore, and we'd never been happy in this house except when we were with Ben. And yet I felt something shift inside me, subtly moving behind my rib cage as I breathed the dusty old air of this house and stared at the flowered wallpaper of my childhood room. This place was familiar, and except for the dust, it felt more and more like I'd never left. Time bent in and touched itself, like a circle. The house knew me. It knew my strangeness.

I sat up, ignoring how my feet had rumpled the bedspread, and looked at the wall, sighing. I'd been—what—fourteen when I was last here? A juvenile idiot. I'd liked to cut photos from magazines back then and pin them to my bedroom wall. The magazines were shoplifted, because our parents never gave us any money and I was very good at stealing in those days. A skill I had let rust with disuse over the years.

The photos were still there, the last ones I'd had up when we left the house for good. What did young Dodie like to pin to her walls? No handsome movie stars or singers. There was an ad for Pond's cold cream, another for Camel cigarettes. A tourism ad for St. Maarten, featuring a photo of a beautiful beach. A photo of a Christmas tree—not ours, of course—with presents under it. A catalog page featuring a pair of shoes that I probably wanted to either buy or steal. The pictures on my walls had changed constantly, an endless gallery of things I wanted, thought I wanted, or simply liked looking at. When I stopped wanting something, I threw the photo of it away.

In third grade, I'd been invited to a birthday party, one of the few times such a thing had happened. I'd gone, saddled with a shiny wrapped gift that I'd had to beg my mother to buy, and as I passed by the formal sitting room at the birthday girl's house, I'd spotted a framed family photo on a side table. It was of two parents and three children on a ski hill, posing with wide smiles, their cheeks a healthy blush of red.

I'd dutifully played the silly birthday party games, waiting for my chance. At a moment when the cake had come out and no one was paying attention to me, I'd murmured about going to the bathroom and slipped down the hall to the sitting room. Stealthily, I'd taken the framed photo from its place and slid it into my coat, which was hanging from a hook by the front door. At the end of the party, I'd walked out with the photo with no one the wiser.

I'd put the picture on my dresser. It cheered me in a way I couldn't explain to see those five strangers smiling at me every morning and night. I didn't pretend they were my family—I no longer even remembered the people's names—but the photo gave me comfort. We had no family photos of our own, so the picture of another family was a reminder that this life somehow existed, that there were people who lived like this, took pictures like this.

Eventually, my mother noticed the photo. She lost her temper at my theft, screamed at me, then threw the picture away. Her reaction was really quite satisfying. Worth it, even though I had to sacrifice the picture.

Now I opened my dresser drawers and rifled through the old T-shirts, the now-tiny underpants. An early bra, two soft triangles of embarrassed cotton. I'd left these behind because they were too small for me even then, and I couldn't wear them anymore. In the end, we'd lasted two years in this house after Ben vanished before Mom couldn't take it anymore and we left in a hurry, like thieves.

I found a crusted mascara, a half-used lipstick I'd probably swiped from Violet. Except for the odd pictures on the wall, this was the room of any sad girl in a bad movie.

From under the bed came a soft sound, a faint thump. The sound of something rolling, then stopping.

A Box Full of Darkness

My hand stilled in the drawer. I closed my eyes as my breath tightened in my throat. For a second I could smell dampness, mold, and dirty water. A rotten smell that permeated my nose and went all the way up into my skull. I could taste the damp in the back of my throat, taste the cold as the water rushed up, rising and inexorable, ready to pull me into its filthy depths, to pull me under and stop my breath—

From downstairs came the shrill sound of music from the TV, blasting through the house. The opening of the local news. Vail had gotten the TV working. The sound receded as he turned the volume down.

I opened my eyes. There was no water, but the smell—I could swear I smelled it. Taste its foulness in the back of my throat.

I could go downstairs and watch the news with my brother. Or I could stay here and look under the bed.

I wasn't going to look under the bed.

I wasn't going downstairs, either. Instead, I walked to the bed, pulled the covers back, and got in, fully clothed. I slid under the cool, musty sheets and lay my head on the pillow. Everyone knew, because it was a law of the universe, that whatever was under the bed couldn't get me here. It had no power. This was the only place I was safe.

For all my childhood, this had been the only place I was safe.

As a newscaster's voice rang downstairs in the living room, I pulled the blankets over my head, turned over, and closed my eyes.

7

VIOLET

Self-sufficiency was in the nature of the Esmie children. Though we grew up in a big house and had money—with the money for us children locked in trust funds—our parents never employed any help. Rooms got dusty until one of us cleaned them. When your pile of dirty clothes became unbearable, you did your laundry yourself in the semi-functional washing machine. Our parents were almost never home for meals, so we each perfected the art of single-serve nourishment—an egg or two, or a bologna sandwich, or slices of toast.

Sometimes, when I got tired of timing my own soft-boiled egg, I ate at the home of my only school friend, Alice McMurtry. Alice was a sweet girl with glasses and pimples on her receding chin. She and I swapped notes in class and snickered about boys. Looking back, it was remarkable that I had a friend—everyone thought I was strange and disagreeable, and I couldn't argue the point. But Alice either didn't mind or was so desperate for friendship that she found me sufficient. When I went to Alice's house, Alice's mother would always make us something delicious—gooey grilled cheese or bowls of homemade soup. I loved eating at Alice's because I didn't have to make whatever it was, which made it taste better.

When we were twelve, Alice was found dead on the path running alongside the train tracks, the one we sometimes walked when we wanted to take the long way home from school. I vaguely remembered the days after she died—wondering what had happened to my friend, getting my only answers from the rumors going around the halls. Had someone hurt her? Was she murdered? Had she died in pain? I remembered spending an hour in the library, scanning the local newspapers for news of Alice and finding nothing. Even in Fell, wouldn't a murdered child be news?

I'd walked by Alice's house in the next neighborhood, a thirty-minute walk away, determined to talk to her parents, then balking at the last minute. I'd lived in a fog of confusion that added to the loneliness and pain. In an often invisible childhood, it was the most invisible I had ever felt. No one noticed that I was upset and confused. No one told me anything.

I finally lucked into answers when I eavesdropped on two teachers gossiping over cigarettes outside the gym doors. There had been an autopsy—I couldn't even imagine what this entailed, my friend pulled to pieces—and Alice hadn't been murdered after all. "Heart defect," one teacher said. "Poor kid."

"Just one of those things," the other teacher said.

"True. But it doesn't make for much of a story, does it? What a letdown."

When Alice's parents put their house up for sale and moved out of town, I wondered if they agreed.

No one cared that I spent my school days in agony, wondering if I'd see Alice standing in a doorway or waiting for me when I glanced out the window. I lay awake at night, wondering if I'd have to see my dead best friend, just like I'd seen all the others I wasn't supposed to talk about. When I talked about the dead people, everyone thought

I was mentally ill. The only people who didn't think I was crazy were Dodie and Vail, but I rarely told them about the things I saw. When we were in the house, someone might be listening.

I walked into the kitchen now to see Vail standing at the counter, his back to me as he stared out the window at the view over the rear of the property. The toaster was on the counter. He'd made his own breakfast, then cleaned the dishes. I felt a pang of familiarity at the sight of it, as deep and moving as pain that took my breath away for a second.

Then I got out the bread and put two slices in the toaster. I fished in the cupboard for the peanut butter we'd bought yesterday to make my own single breakfast. Vail didn't speak, his only acknowledgment of me in the change of air in the room, his silent awareness.

There was a near-full pot of coffee on the counter, my brother's only concession to anyone else living in this house. I poured myself a cup and said, "I'm going into town today."

"Yeah?" Vail was wearing his ancient jeans and a thick navy blue cable-knit sweater with a tee under it. After his years as a diver, wearing next to nothing, it seemed he liked to layer up now, as if he'd been cold all that time.

"There must have been a police report," I said, not having to explain what police report I might be talking about. "I remember police here. Lots of them."

Vail nodded, still looking out the window. "Uniforms. Some guy sitting me down on the living room sofa and asking questions. Hanna? Manna?" He pressed his fingertips to the spot between his eyes. "I can't remember his name. I remember thinking it rhymed with *banana*."

I shook my head, smearing peanut butter on my nearly black toast. "I don't remember a banana man. One of the cops was Bradley Pine's dad. I remember that."

Vail groaned. "Bradley beat me up twice in high school. I hated that kid."

I focused on my toast, unwilling to admit to Vail that I'd had a wild crush on Bradley Pine, the big football jock, in high school. I'd been obsessed with him, and he'd had no idea. He'd looked through me like glass. "Anyway, if there's a police file, the Fell PD will give it to me to read."

"Do police departments do that?" Vail asked, glancing at me for the first time.

I shrugged and took a bite of toast. "They will," I said with my mouth full.

He nodded, as if this made perfect sense. "What's in those woods behind the house?" he asked, changing the subject.

For a second, I scrounged in my brain for an answer. As a mother, you feel like you have to have an answer for every single question that's asked of you, no matter how outrageous. Then I remembered that I wasn't a mother right this minute, and I didn't have to know anything. "I have no idea," I said.

Vail grunted. We'd never been the kind of kids who would wander the woods, exploring and playing imaginary games. Our dreary neighborhood didn't exactly invite it. I loathed uncertainty, Vail would rather read books, and Dodie simply didn't give a shit. She was one of the least curious people I knew.

So the tangled trees and brush that extended behind the house weren't mapped terrain. We didn't hang out back there, which had baffled the adults after Ben disappeared. They were all certain that he must have wandered in that direction, wanting to play, and met some kind of accident. I remembered being asked, over and over, where we usually went back there, if Ben might have gone to a spot he remembered. No one had believed me when I'd answered that as far as I knew, Ben had never been to the woods in his life.

"They searched, remember?" Vail said, following my train of thought. "Like he would have just gone into the trees by himself."

"Stupid," I agreed. The adults had all thought this was plausible because they didn't know Ben. He didn't go exploring because he was an Esmie. He was one of us. He preferred to be wherever we were.

Even if Ben had gone into the woods, which he hadn't, what did they think had happened to him? Was there a cliff to fall over, a well to fall into? It wasn't the Mojave Desert. There were no fairy-tale wolves. If a little boy wandered into the trees and got cold or scared, he could simply turn around and come home.

"I'm going to go back there today," Vail said, looking out the window again. "I'm going to see what's there."

I nodded, popping the last of my toast into my mouth and washing it down with coffee. "Take Dodie with you."

He gave me a glance that was both scathing and amused. "She's asleep."

"It wouldn't kill her to get out of bed."

A smirk crossed Vail's lips, the big-brother kind of smirk that promised trouble for his little sister. "You know, I think I'll do it, if only for the entertainment value."

"I'll bet it's wet back there," I said with some relish. "Muddy. Buggy. Somehow cold and sweaty at the same time."

"Perfect," Vail agreed. "Let us know how it goes with the police."

"I will."

"And let me know if Bradley Pine has been longing for you all this time and finally wants to marry you."

I had a second of shock, then I dropped my coffee cup into the sink without bothering to wash it. "I hate you so much."

"If I catch sight of him, I'll break his fucking nose," Vail said jovially. "It'll be fun."

I didn't bother to answer. I just banged out the door.

8

VIOLET

After so much time away, it only took minutes to feel like I had never left downtown Fell. Maybe the place truly hadn't changed much, or maybe Fell would always be mapped out in my brain because I had dreamed of it so often over the years. I parked at the end of Sidewinder Street and walked, feeling the familiar cracked sidewalks beneath my feet, just like I had when I'd walked here as a teenager.

Fell wasn't a remarkable town. It did not boast a lively downtown or a fun central hot spot. To walk through Fell was to take in low-rise rental apartments that had seen better days, thrift stores, corner video rental shops, secondhand record shops, and an abundance of laundromats. The Royal movie theater sold tickets for two dollars and rarely showed first-run movies. I passed a pawn shop, a bait-and-tackle shop—though Fell was not located on any body of water—and a hair salon with faded photos of old hairstyles taped to the windows.

I bought a newspaper in the magazine shop on the corner. I stared longingly at the cigarette display at the counter as I paid, but I resisted the impulse. Then, tucking my newspaper under my arm, I crossed the street to Scooty's Treats and bought myself a Creamsicle. Scooty's was a special occasion when we were kids, mostly because with all the ice cream treats being kept behind the counter, we couldn't steal them and had to actually buy them. That made it stand out. When Ben came along, we'd bought him Creamsicles whenever we had the money.

I wasn't in a hurry to complete my errand. For the moment, Fell had sucked me back into its clutches like it always had, and it made me curious. What *was* it about this town? Or was it me?

I passed a bus stop with someone sleeping on the bench, a bike repair shop with a rusty bike wheel propped outside the door. The chill air whispered under my collar and down my neck. *Welcome back*, it all said. *Where did you think you were going?*

I reached the Fell police station, located on a dead-end street and surrounded by a flat parking lot. Six police cars were parked in a precise line outside the front door, so maybe it was a quiet day for crime. The station was squat, made of ugly concrete with streaks of pigeon shit on the walls. I pushed through the glass door and walked to the front desk, inhaling the smell of old sweat mixed with janitor closet.

The uniformed policeman at the front desk could have been forty or sixty. It was hard to tell with the serious bags under his eyes. A cheap office divider had been placed behind his desk, so anyone entering couldn't see the rest of the room. The cop regarded me with weary disinterest as I scraped the last of the Creamsicle from its stick with my teeth. I'd never seen anyone more in need of a nap.

"Hi," I said. "I'm looking for Detective Pine."

The cop blinked his bagged eyes at me and didn't move. "There's no Detective Pine."

"There was twenty years ago. Did he retire?"

The cop looked back down at his magazine, not bothering to answer.

I spotted a trash can by the door, threw out my Creamsicle stick, and came back to the desk, wiping my hands on my jeans. There was no one else standing at this desk, and no one else behind it. It could have been a library. The Fell police station wasn't a very busy place. "Look," I said. "I have information on a case that Detective Pine worked on. The Ben Esmie disappearance."

The cop showed not a flicker of recognition, but he said, "You'd have to talk to Detective Canner about that one."

Canner. That was Vail's banana man, I guessed, if you made the stretch that *Canner* rhymed with *banana*. "Where can I find him?" I asked.

"He's dead now," the bag-eyed cop said. "Have a nice day."

I shrugged. "No problem. I'll just go see Detective Pine at home in Evergreen Heights."

Evergreen Heights was the neighborhood adjacent to Fell High School. I knew the Pines lived there—or used to—because I had seen Bradley enter a house there after school once. It was a coincidence, I swear.

Bag Eyes gave me a second, sharper look, and I knew he was re-evaluating me as a local. "What did you say your name was?"

"I didn't say, because you didn't ask. My name is Violet Esmie. I'm Ben Esmie's big sister."

There was the briefest whisper of hesitation, and I knew that Bag Eyes was familiar with my name. Had he been one of the uniforms crosshatching our property that winter day, looking for my little brother? It was possible, though I didn't remember him. What I remembered from that day was deep, sickening fear because Ben was gone. Just gone. It was like he'd been switched off, a radio signal cutting out.

It was different from the dull, churning unease I'd felt after Alice McMurtry died, when I didn't know what had happened to her. The fear I felt after Ben vanished was the kind of fear I wouldn't feel again until I watched Lisette sleeping in her crib, her sweet face relaxed, her long lashes touching her cheeks. I'd stared at her, and I'd thought of Ben, all the things that might have happened to him, and then I'd gone to the bathroom and been sick with terror.

Bag Eyes pushed his chair back, making it crack. Or maybe that sound was his knees. "Wait here," he said curtly, then left the desk and disappeared behind the divider.

I waited. What was he doing? Talking to someone back there? Making a call? Shuffling around in silence, hoping I would go away? I pictured him with his back to the divider, arms flattened, eyes wide, holding his breath.

Finally, he came back. He pulled out his chair and sat in it again, giving no indication of where he'd been. "You know the Pop-Top Diner around the corner?" he asked.

I gave him an icy stare without answering, because of course I knew. It was a look that I'd taught both Vail and Dodie from an early age. It said, *I will not dignify that with an answer.*

"Right. You do." Bag Eyes nodded. "Go there, get a booth, and wait fifteen minutes. Detective Pine will be along."

I almost heard it in my mind then, like a real sound—the *click* of this town opening to me. Everywhere else I'd been in my life, I was no one, but now I was home.

In Fell, I wasn't an ex-wife, a bad mother, a mental patient. I was an Esmie kid. I had stolen from the store around the corner and had snuck onto the bus when I wanted to go somewhere and had no fare. I had grown up across from an abandoned house, and my best friend had died next to the railroad tracks. Fell was frightening to the strangers who came here, but it wasn't frightening to me.

"Fifteen minutes," I said to Bag Eyes. "If he isn't there, I leave."

He nodded, and I saw a glimmer of curiosity in his deadened face. He wanted to know what I had to say, why I'd come back after all this time. "Fifteen minutes," he said. "He'll be there."

9

VAIL

Dodie took forever to get dressed, and when she finally came downstairs, she was in a terrible mood. She was wearing baggy cotton pants, belted and rolled up at the ankles, a black tank top, and a cardigan she'd buttoned to the neck. She was carrying an ancient pair of brown boots.

I looked her up and down, amused at the tangle of her dark hair tied on top of her head and the scowl of her perfect brows. "Those are my pants," I said.

"Shut up," she snapped. "If I'm going to ruin clothes on this little errand, I'll ruin yours instead of mine."

I grinned. "Did you have fun going through my bag? I haven't unpacked it yet. In order to get to those pants, you had to touch my underwear."

"I did *not* touch your underwear."

"You did. You so did."

"Can we just get this over with, please?" Dodie dropped the boots forcefully to the floor, making a satisfying clatter, and shoved her feet, clad in wool socks, into them. "Ben isn't back there. We both know he isn't."

"He isn't," I agreed. "But I want to know what *is* back there."

"We've never wanted to know before. Because finding out entails walking through the muddy woods like a couple of lunatics."

I shrugged. "We're not kids anymore, Dodie. We came here for answers. We won't get them if we don't look. And I want to get out of this house."

My little sister stopped arguing, because I knew that she agreed. The house was oppressive, and it wasn't just because of the Miss Havisham decor, the dust cloths, and the curtains drawn over the old windows. It was the gloom of every minute of our miserable childhoods winding its way around our necks and down our throats, pulsing behind our eyes. Just making breakfast in this kitchen, like I'd done so many times alone as a kid, brought back bad memories.

Dodie laced her boots, grabbed a banana from the kitchen counter, and followed me to the back door, making sure I could hear her loud, dramatic sigh.

We started across the lawn behind the house, heading for the bank of trees that were losing their leaves in balding splotches. The air was heavy and damp, and my boots were already wet in the grass. I took a deep breath, filling my lungs. It was Fell air, but it was still fresh, familiar. It carried the scent of rot and faraway gasoline. The aroma of my hometown.

Just behind my shoulder, Dodie took a bite of banana and spoke through a mouthful because she knew that would drive me crazy. "How did you get the phone hooked up?" she asked.

I gritted my teeth at the sound of her chewing. "I asked the phone company to do it."

"So fast, though," she said with deceptive calm. When Dodie bothered to notice things, she really noticed them. "Does one of your ex-girlfriends work there? Did you seduce her and break her heart? What did you promise her, Vail?"

She was, as usual, skating close to the truth. I'm not a good person. If I'd had to sleep with the woman at the phone company to get what I wanted, I would have. I'd never feel bad about it, even for a second. At least she'd get a bit of excitement for her end of the deal.

"I never promise women anything," I said, which was the truest thing I'd ever spoken in my life.

Dodie laughed.

"What do you care about the phone anyway?" I asked her. "You don't have anyone to call."

"Just my agency," Dodie agreed, tossing her banana peel into the bushes. "It's for the best that they can't reach me now. They're furious that I canceled on the shampoo people at the last minute. I'm not in their good graces."

We walked for a few minutes in silence, stepping through the thick underbrush and dodging low branches. My body started to wake up, the old athlete in me stretching and roaring, ready for activity. I never missed my old diving career, but my body liked to move, as if I was born to swing something heavy, like a hammer or a sword. "I should have been born a medieval knight," I said as we made our way forward.

"You would have made a good one," Dodie agreed, as if this was a normal thing to say. "How is the UFO business?"

"Full of liars. Though, to be fair, some people are legitimately crazy, which spices things up a bit."

Dodie laughed again, the sound ringing in the damp air. "You've just described New York City."

I grunted. "So you plan to go back to the modeling thing?" *When this is over,* I didn't add. Whatever *this* was.

"For now. Until I decide to buy a yacht, put on a caftan, and sail to Greece, where I will find a man as beautiful as a statue to wait on me hand and foot before giving me nightly ecstasy."

"That's an image I didn't need in my head." The trees had closed behind us and the house was no longer visible. We weren't far from civilization, but if you turned in a circle, all you'd see was trees. I paused, feeling the light sweat on my skin under my layers, thinking about which way to go.

Dodie stood by my shoulder, hunched into her cardigan, looking vaguely miserable. "How did you sleep last night?" she asked me.

I looked at her more closely. She wasn't just grumpy, she was tired. I should have noticed sooner. "Fine, I think," I said slowly. "I don't really remember. Didn't you sleep?"

"Of course I did," she said, a little too quickly.

"No, you didn't."

"I'm just making conversation."

"Want to trade bedrooms? You look tired."

"I can manage. Thanks for the compliment." She looked around. "The Thornhills are that way." She pointed. "School was somewhere there. There was a house over there with an old lady in it. She's probably dead now. That's all I know."

"Impressive," I said.

She picked up on my sarcasm immediately. "Stuff it, Vail. I only learn what I need to learn, and nothing else. It's how I save brain space for other things."

"Other things like shampoo."

"Says the man whose area of expertise is how to jump into a body of water."

Ouch. "Who owned the house across the street when we were kids?" I asked her.

"No one," she replied. "It was empty."

"Someone attempted a renovation sometime since we left, then gave up."

She shrugged.

"The Thornhills aren't home," I said. "They haven't been home for approximately ten days." I knew this from the newspapers and mail I'd picked up from the porch.

Dodie's eyes lit up, and our gazes locked.

"No," I said. "Not today. We're supposed to be looking for Ben."

"Fine, you joyless drip. Where to now? It's your expedition."

"You're the one with a map in your head, even though it's faulty."

"You're the one that dragged me out of bed."

We could bicker like this all day. We *had* done it all day, plenty of times. "The faster you pick a direction, the faster this is over with."

"So pick a direction, then. I'm cold."

I turned and took a step. Dodie's heavy sigh behind me said I'd chosen wrong.

"For God's sake, we'll go the other way, then."

"Well, you've *picked*. So I guess we'll go this way, since apparently, that's what we're *doing*."

I pushed branches out of our way, but I let them snap back a little hard, so she yelped behind me.

"You really slept normally?" Dodie asked after a minute.

"I told you, I don't remember. I closed my eyes, and then I opened them. So I guess I slept."

A pause. "I had dreams. The old ones, like I haven't had since I left."

The Fell house wasn't a great place for sleeping. I'd never again had dreams anywhere else like I had here. I suspected my sisters had bad dreams, too—or maybe it was just Dodie who had dreams. What Violet saw was different and so, so much worse than a nightmare. What she saw didn't always end when daylight came.

"I haven't had mine yet," I said, "but I will."

"I don't want to hear about your dreams," she snapped. "They're probably filthy, you perv."

"There's only one perv walking in these woods today, and it isn't me."

"Oh, it's definitely you. Do you think Violet will get anywhere?" Dodie asked.

"I think she'll terrify whoever she has to terrify, yes." I hadn't missed Violet's steely big-sister glare this morning, the kind that could wither your self-esteem with a single look. I'd learned early to dodge that glare.

"Can we turn around now? I'm hungry again."

"Soon, you pathetic child."

Behind me, I heard her snap a branch. "I'd rather be a pathetic child than a perv."

Yes. We could do this all day.

Through a break in the trees, I caught a glimpse of a chain-link fence. We'd reached a property line, it seemed. "Was the fence there twenty years ago?" I asked Dodie.

"No. It doesn't look old," she replied.

We got closer, and through the diamonds of chain link I glimpsed more scrub, the gleam of sunlight in an empty lot. A soda can, a beer bottle, and a used condom. Dodie wrinkled her nose.

I wedged my boot into one of the chain-link diamonds and pulled myself up.

"Where are you going?" Dodie asked.

Instead of an answer, I swung a leg over the fence and wedged my boot in the other side.

"I'm not climbing that fence." Her voice rose.

"It isn't even high."

"I'm not doing it."

"Wait there, then. I'll be right back." I had swung my other leg over, and I jumped easily to the ground. I couldn't see any buildings around me. I didn't think I had ever been this far behind the house.

"Vail," came Dodie's voice when I took a step. "Don't. Come back."

I stopped. Damn it.

I knew that tone in Dodie's voice. It meant she was scared. That was the kind of childhood we'd had, that I knew exactly what my little sister sounded like when she was scared.

Damn it.

I turned back and wedged my boot into the fence again. I paused at the top before I jumped down, looking around from the higher vantage point.

That day—that terrible day—there had been police everywhere. Their footprints had cut swaths through the new snow, left deep holes in the drifts. They'd gone through these woods, calling Ben's name. We could see by their tracks that they'd made lines, thatching the back woods with the marks of their heavy boots. One of them had most likely stood in this very spot on that day, looking for my brother.

What had that long-ago policeman seen? He'd maybe thought that the white snow was an advantage. If the missing boy—or his body—was nearby, he had a chance of glimpsing Ben's blue T-shirt.

I stared around me until my eyes watered and my hands went numb on the fence, searching for details. Any detail at all. Anything. *Show yourself*, I begged him. *Show yourself.*

Why did landscapers get to see my brother? Why them and not me?

Just for a second. The sight of him. I would have given anything. *Anything.*

Finally, I swung down, my feet thumping in the damp earth. Dodie moved next to my shoulder, so close that her arm brushed mine and I could hear her breath.

"What do you think he's waiting for?" she asked.

I scrubbed a hand over my face, brushing the water from my eyes. This—these woods, this hill—this wasn't the right place. Ben wasn't here. This wasn't where he wanted us, needed us, to go.

"We started in the wrong place," I said. "The police search doesn't matter. It was all over by then."

For once, Dodie didn't argue. Instead, she said, "Where do we start?"

I knew the answer now. "We have to go back," I said. "To the beginning."

10

VIOLET

I took a booth at the Pop-Top Diner, ordered a coffee, and spread out my newspaper. Time to catch up with the news of Fell while I waited for Detective Pine.

A quick perusal showed a town that looked unremarkable on the surface. A public hearing had been held on a proposed zoning change on East Avenue, which would allow a disused church to be torn down and repurposed for apartments—the dullest news story imaginable. Only at the bottom of the short article did it mention that the church had a haunted ceiling beam, from which two priests had hanged themselves eighty years apart, and if the beam came down, no one was quite sure how to dispose of it.

Fell was a creepy little town.

On page three of the paper, a small group of students from the Fell College of Classical Education—a tiny, privately owned school that taught many a useless subject—had protested on campus two days ago. However, as all their protest signs were in Latin, no one was sure what they were objecting to. When asked by the paper's reporter, a protester said that the poltergeist in the library—which threw books from the shelves and knocked over students' chairs—was keeping them from studying, affecting their grades. The school, they said, refused to hire an exorcist, and they had had enough.

I flipped the page. There had been a smattering of arrests at the Sun Down Motel, the dive motel I'd driven past on Number Six Road on my way into town. The Sun Down was apparently a hot spot for drug dealers and prostitutes, and the police had broken up a drunken party the night before. "No one was hurt," local cop Alma Trent was quoted as saying, "except for one person who fell into the empty pool. He'll be fine. And we think the ice machine was damaged."

At the bottom of the page, tucked into the corner, was a snapshot of a pretty young woman holding a toddler and smiling for the camera. *Nine years later, still no leads in Caldwell murder,* the headline said. A young wife and mother named Cathy Caldwell had been found stripped and murdered under the South Overpass in 1980, and her killer had never been found.

I was still looking at Cathy Caldwell's face—something about it was so terribly sad—when a shadow fell over the paper.

I looked up. The man who had taken the seat across from me was in his early sixties. The top of his head was a shiny bald pate, and a bushy beard—wiry white mixed with the last few remnants of brown—covered the bottom of his face. Two bloodshot brown eyes stared at me with the power of laser beams, as if seeing through my skull. He wore an old flannel shirt, and his hands, folded over my newspaper on the table, were knotted and thin, like rope that would never fray.

"It's really you," he said without preamble. "The Esmie girl."

I blinked at him. "Yes, it's me."

"The oldest one, or the youngest?"

Dodie and I both had dark hair, so I could see why he wasn't sure. "The oldest," I replied. "My name is Violet. You're Detective Pine?"

The man snorted. "Not Detective anymore. I'm just Gus now. And I remember all of your names."

The waitress came by—she and Gus were on a first-name basis—and while Gus ordered lunch, I refolded the newspaper. When she asked me what I wanted, I was going to refuse, but then I remembered the sparsely stocked kitchen at the house. I ordered scrambled eggs and toast.

The waitress left, and I looked at Gus's face, trying to remember if I'd seen it that day. He'd have been somewhere in his forties then, and he'd probably looked different, but I'd remember those eyes, wouldn't I?

Oddly, what came into my mind about the police that day was feet. Lots of heavy boots, some of them crusted with snow from the searches outside. One man's shiny wing tips. I realized with a start that I must have kept my gaze down, staring at the floor. I hadn't looked into any of the men's faces—that's why I couldn't remember one.

"So," Gus said, ignoring my rude scrutiny. Apparently, neither of us was going to mention the fact that he was meeting me about an old case when he wasn't a detective anymore instead of sending someone still employed by the Fell PD. "You have information for me on your brother's case."

His gaze told me he didn't believe a word of it. He probably terrified people with those laser eyes, but those people weren't me. When you see the dead on a regular basis, people who are alive stop intimidating you.

He was right to distrust me, though, considering I was lying. "I'm willing to trade information," I hedged.

"Uh-huh." He was still skeptical. "Tell me why you're back in town after all this time while I eat. I'm hungry. You're paying."

I didn't argue. I waited while the waitress put our plates in front of us. Then I said, "Why we're back in town is none of your business."

"We?" Gus popped a french fry into his mouth. "So it's all three of you, then. Just the kids, because your parents are dead."

I picked up my fork, annoyed at myself. That had been a stupid slip. "How do you know my parents are dead?" Neither of them had died in Fell.

"Word gets around in this place." Gus took a bite of his club sandwich. "Keep talking."

I shrugged, poking at my eggs and deciding how much to tell him. "Okay, yes, we're back. We're going to solve our brother's case." I glared at him. "Since you couldn't do it."

The shot glanced off him with barely a *ping*. "Why now?" he asked.

"It seemed like the right time."

Gus put his sandwich down. "That's a lie." His gaze traveled my face, and then he sighed. "I spent the first few years of my career in Albany. I got married, started a family. I came to Fell because I thought a small town was safer. It seemed like it would be easy." He smiled, which made the creases on his face deepen. He was handsome in his way. "I wanted quiet, and I suppose I got it. No one shot at me. But I ended up with different nightmares than I'd had in Albany." He took the newspaper, folded it back so the article about Cathy Caldwell was face up. "This here," he said. "I saw you reading this. I worked this case. I worked the others, too."

"What others?" I asked, though I wasn't surprised. Some deep, dark part of me knew there would be others.

"Murders," Gus said. "Disappearances. Suicides. Fell has more than its share. In the last few years before I retired, someone killed a schoolteacher and left her on the construction site where the Sun Down stands now. Victoria Lee's boyfriend killed her while she was jogging and left her in the bushes. And there was Cathy Caldwell, who left a three-year-old son behind. We might have investigated better, except that we also had the disappearance of the motel night clerk on our hands, as well as everything else."

"Everything else?" I asked.

Gus was relishing this in a grim way. "Cases that should add up, but don't. Things that shouldn't have happened, but did. My first year here, we found bones in one of the graveyards that didn't belong there. They weren't part of any grave or in any of the burial records. Someone had buried them—badly, because they eventually came up out of the ground—without permission. When we had the bones examined, they were a hundred years old." He shook his head. "Did someone take a hundred-year-old body from wherever it was hidden and then bury it? Why? We never solved it. The next year, a girl at the college disappeared while she was studying in her dorm. Her book was open on the desk, the lamp on, a cup of tea sitting there. The tea was full, as if she hadn't had the chance to sip it. Her shoes were neatly side by side in the hallway outside the door, which was open. The shoes just sitting there, as if she'd lined them up. No one saw her leave. No one ever saw her again."

Vail would have his theories about that one. Most people thought his alien abduction cases were nuts. I reserved judgment, because I was too busy seeing the dead and getting locked up in mental hospitals to form a serious opinion.

"And then there was your brother," Gus continued. "Are you telling me that you and your siblings came back to Fell after all this time at random? Do you expect me to believe it? You think I'll just swallow that story like a dummy who hasn't lived in this town?"

"My brother's ghost has been sighted on the grounds of the house," I said. "There. Are you happy?"

Gus nodded. "Okay. Now we're getting somewhere."

I'd underestimated him. He was good—not good enough to find Ben, but good. "He wanted us to come home, so we came." I scooped up a forkful of eggs and ate them. I was more relaxed now that I'd told the truth.

Gus blinked, and when sadness crossed his expression, I knew what he was thinking—that Ben appearing as he did meant that he was definitely dead, that he'd died the day he disappeared or shortly after. It was the extinguishing of the faint hope that he'd somehow turned out okay. I knew the feeling. "You think his body is on the grounds, then?" he asked.

I shrugged. "Don't ghosts usually appear where their body is left?"

"I wouldn't know."

No. Ghosts, in fact, had no particular ties to where their physical remains resided. There was no winning pattern I'd seen in the dead over the years, no unbreakable rule. I'd seen the dead in their homes while I emptied out their belongings, but I'd also seen them in other places. The woman in the Long Island house had appeared to me as young—probably her favorite memory of herself—instead of the old woman she'd physically been when she died, and she'd died in a hospital. Ghosts gave no comprehensive answers, only inscrutable messages accompanied by more questions.

Except *Come home.* That message had been very clear.

"Well, I could ask around. Try to organize a search," Gus said.

"You searched the day he disappeared. You all did."

"We must not have looked in the right places." He had eaten half of the sandwich. The other half, neatly sliced, still sat on his plate. He had eaten only a single french fry, but he picked up a napkin and wiped his hands as if he was finished. His tone was all business. "It wouldn't be official, but I could call a few of the guys I know, ask them to lend a hand."

"No." The thought of cops in the house again—all those feet—was sickening. "The house is ours." After a beat of silence, I lamely added, "Er, I appreciate the offer."

Gus shrugged. "So what, then? What did you bring me here for?"

"How about the case file on my brother's disappearance? I want to start with that."

For the first time, Gus looked startled. He hadn't looked like this when I mentioned ghosts. "You don't want to read that."

"In fact, I do want to read it."

He shook his head and cast his gaze over my shoulder, avoiding my eyes. "There's nothing in it that will help you. You were there that day, weren't you? You called, we showed up and looked. We found nothing. We failed. End of story."

"I don't remember all of the details," I said. "It was a weird day. I can't ask my parents, because they're dead. So I'd like to read it."

"It's a file on an open case. You can't read it. There are rules."

As if the two of us sitting here, discussing this, wasn't skirting the rules. "I'm going to get access to that file, Gus. With or without your help." I'd pay off Bag Eyes at the front desk, whatever he wanted. It would be good use of the money my parents left. Hell, I'd sleep with Bag Eyes if I had to. I wouldn't even make him buy me dinner first if it meant finding Ben.

Gus still looked perturbed, but he was thinking it over. He scratched the side of his nose. Behind me, I heard the door to the diner swing open and closed, and the bell chimed as someone came in.

"Okay," Gus said finally. "Here's the thing. That's an old case, a cold one. No one's working it anymore. The Fell PD only has so much storage room."

My hands went cold. Was he saying that Ben's file had been thrown out like so much trash?

"They destroy old files sometimes," Gus was saying. "They're not supposed to, but they do. Nothing I could do about it. But when I retired, I didn't want them destroying the cases I worked. I can't explain it except to say it felt like they were going to erase all my work. It wasn't right. So I took a few of my old files with me when I left."

"You took police files?" I was shocked, even though the only knowledge I had of police work was from TV. "Can you do that?"

"Technically, no, I absolutely cannot do that," Gus replied, unperturbed. "But I did it years ago, and no one stopped me, and no one has brought it up since. So as far as crimes go, I'm gonna say it was a victimless one. Are you gonna argue with me?"

I had no answer to that. Who was I to argue with a detective about what a victimless crime was? If the Fell PD couldn't keep track of their files, that was their problem.

"Fine," I said. "Where are the files now?"

"In a secure location."

"Is that cop-speak for something?"

"It's a place known only by me." Gus seemed annoyed now. "It's locked up tight."

"Okay. Can I go to this secure location?"

"Not alone, you can't. I store some private things there. Valuable things."

"Okay, then, come with me."

Gus shook his head. "I won't go. It's too hard for me to look at that old stuff. Personal stuff. Too many memories."

This was getting frustrating. Something about this was upsetting him, and it was keeping me from what I wanted. "So what's the solution? Tell me what to do."

"I won't go with you, but someone I trust will." Gus nodded to someone behind my shoulder, and a man entered the booth, dropping into the seat beside him. He was big, wearing a white tee and a worn baseball cap. He pulled Gus's plate over and picked up the second half of the sandwich.

I stared at the man, who was suddenly horrifyingly familiar.

"You can go look at the file," Gus said. "My son will take you."

The man took a bite of the sandwich and spoke with his mouth full. "Hi," said Bradley Pine.

11

DODIE

I took a shower after the hike through the woods, washing the mud, sweat, and chill from my skin. I used the hallway shower, because I couldn't stand the idea of even entering my parents' bedroom, let alone using their en suite. So I used the bathtub-shower I'd used through all of my childhood, standing naked under the spray.

I put my hand on the cool tiles, looking at their white-and-Tiffany-blue swirl pattern as a memory bubbled up. Me sitting in this bathtub, the warm water up to my chest, hugging my knees and crying as I stared at these same tiles. It had happened more than once. I hadn't known I remembered it until now.

How old was I in this memory? Young. Possibly before Ben. Ben was a late baby—I was six when he was born, Vail eight, Violet nine. Our parents were strangers to each other by then, and Dad was rarely even home.

Looking back on it as an adult, it was surprising that my parents had stood each other's company for long enough to create a final, unexpected child. Then again, based on my disappointing personal experience, such an act can take ten to fifteen minutes. Maybe they tolerated each other for a quarter of an hour and the result changed all of our lives.

In the memory, I was crying after a nightmare. I was tired, terrified. I'd escaped from my room. My childhood was harrowing, but not because of any human villains—evil teachers, neighbors, priests, or the other ghouls who preyed on children. The ghouls of my childhood were under my bed, under the water. That water smelled so terrible, and it was so cold. When I escaped it, I'd sit in the bath, crying as the hot water ran in the tub so no one could hear how scared I was.

I stared at my fingertips on the tiles. The water had come less frequently after Ben arrived, though it still came. It never came on the nights he crawled into bed next to me, warming me with his little body. Ben had changed everything.

We'd adored him, all of us, even Mother. It was so easy to do. As a baby, he'd bobble his bald head and blink at us with his wide brown eyes. His arms would fly up and he'd crow with pleasure when he recognized us. I still remembered the feel of him cradled in my arms, his little legs kicking in his pajamas as he made a happy chuffing sound. I remembered the feel of the trusting skin on the top of his head against my lips.

There was no question of caring for our little brother once Ben arrived. Mother only needed to care for him for the few hours a day that we were in school, and then we fought to look after him. For afternoons, weekends, holidays, and summers, Ben was ours. We looked after him together or separately. We fed him, changed him, bathed him, played with him, read to him. We held him all night when he had a fever and cleaned his vomit when he had the flu. We held his arms as he learned to walk and taught him the letters of the alphabet. He liked games, goofy songs, and bedtime stories. The sweetness and light of our little brother made the bad dreams as wispy as smoke.

A Box Full of Darkness

I turned off the water and grabbed a towel. Ben had even had a good effect on our parents, at least for a while. Dad had come home more often. Mother had been sweet and affectionate with Ben, more so than she'd ever been with any of us, and we didn't even resent him for it. We adored him too much. When Mother had drifted her attention away from him after a few years, distracted as she always was by something more interesting than her children, we were happy about it. It meant we got more of him to ourselves.

But at first, she'd been as in love as we were. I still remembered her holding him swaddled in a blanket, directing us as we put his room together. Vail had been sent to the attic to retrieve the old crib, which had been put away after I'd outgrown it. Violet had dug out the worn baby blankets we'd all used.

Steam filled the bathroom. I didn't want to put my old clothes back on, so with the towel wrapped around me, I opened the door an inch and put my face to the gap.

"Look away, Vail," I shouted in case he was out there. "I'm coming out."

There was no answer, so I gathered my clothes under my arm and swung the door open. I stepped into the hall, turning toward my room.

I stopped.

On the dusty floor were fresh, wet footprints, leading away down the hall. They were the size of the feet of a six-year-old child.

Vail lay all the way down on the floor of the hall, pressing his cheek to the scuffed hardwood. He looked like he was taking a nap. He stared long and hard at the footprints, careful not to touch one.

"We should photograph this," he said at last. "I brought my work camera."

I'd found him downstairs, fussing with the TV, which had stopped working again. Now he squinted at the footprints, angling to see them under the light. There had never been a question of not believing me.

"If you want to do it, then do it quickly," I said, squeezing the collar of the bathrobe I'd put on. "They'll dry."

"Get a lamp."

He got up, and we gingerly stepped over the footprints as I unplugged a lamp in a nearby room and he got his camera from his bedroom.

Was I frightened? I supposed I was. What I mostly felt, though, was vindication. Even without the account from the landscapers, I'd felt Ben's presence in this house. It could have been wishful thinking or the power of the bad memories this place held. The footprints told me I wasn't as crazy as I thought I was.

"They're drying fast," Vail said, winding the film in his camera and attaching the flash. "No time to set up a tripod. Let's do it quick."

I plugged the lamp into a nearby outlet, took the shade off, and turned it on. I held it above the footprints. I'd done enough modeling shoots to know what a fill light was. This was rough, but it would have to do.

Vail squatted, bracing himself with the easy balance of an athlete, and took one photo, then another. The flash popped loudly and the bright light glistened on the fading footprints.

"Did you hear anything?" my brother asked, stepping forward and winding the film again. I followed with the lamp.

"Nothing. I was in the shower."

"What were you doing in there?"

"I beg your pardon. What do you think I was doing in the shower?"

He sighed, a deep, put-upon sound. "Were you talking to yourself? Saying anything?" he clarified. "Singing? Crying?"

He said it so matter-of-factly I couldn't speak for a second, wondering if he knew about the crying I'd done in that bathtub. Then wondering if he'd done the same thing. "No," I managed. "None of those things."

"Did the lights flicker? The water?"

"No."

"Did you see any bright lights?"

"No."

"Did you feel any temperature changes?"

I was being interrogated like one of his UFO people. Well, that was fair. "No."

"I didn't notice anything, either. You can see the toe prints. You can see which way he was going."

Ben's round little toe prints, right there on the floor. I wished Violet had been here to see it. "What do you think it means?" I asked.

"He liked to escape from the bath."

I remembered Ben's squeals of delight when he'd escape bath time, one of his harmless games. He'd get out and run, and the next thing you knew, you were chasing a naked boy, trying to grab him while he was slippery as a fish. "He loved that game," I said.

The flash popped again, and Vail straightened. He'd gotten all the shots he could. "It might just be a memory. But he also could be directing us somewhere."

I put down the lamp and we contemplated the footprints, which were almost gone. They began in the middle of the hall in front of the bathroom, as if Ben had been placed there from above, soaking wet. From there, they traveled in a straight line away from the landing behind us, in the direction of the bedrooms, before they stopped, as if Ben had been lifted up again. It was uncannily like he'd been set down by aliens, then beamed up. That was why Vail had asked me about lights.

I knew that Vail believed, at least partly, that our brother had been abducted by aliens. I didn't think so myself, and it was easy to make fun of Vail for it, to think of him as credulous or pathetic.

But even though I didn't believe what Vail did, I envied him for that belief. The thought of Ben being taken into an otherworldly ship was more comforting than the thought of the other, more mundane, more garden-variety evil things that could have happened to him.

These footprints, though—they weren't the product of alien abductions. They were made by Ben, and Vail was right: He was trying to tell us something.

"Where is he sending us?" I asked, pulling my robe more tightly over my chest.

"They don't lead to his bedroom, or away from it," Vail said. We glanced at the closed door of the room that had been Ben's. His things weren't in there anymore; we had cleaned them out at some point. Had we finally believed he wasn't coming back? I remembered Vail and Violet hauling Ben's small bed down the stairs to get rid of it while I hid in my room, unable to watch. We'd had to dispose of his clothes, his sheets. I remembered staring at his soft-bristled hairbrush in the bathroom every morning for at least a year, until one morning it wasn't there anymore. I still didn't know who had finally moved it, but my money was on Vail.

"Then where is he leading us?" I asked. "My bedroom? Mom and Dad's bedroom?" The prints didn't point to Vail's bedroom, and they might point to Violet's if you used a lax interpretation of their direction.

"You didn't see or hear anything strange in your room last night?" Vail asked.

Except for the water? Its cold, dirty depths threatening to close above my head as I lay in bed? No, sir. Nothing strange except for that rosy piece of my childhood. I shook my head.

"We didn't sleep in Mom and Dad's room, and we haven't gone through it," Vail said. "He could be implying . . ." He trailed off.

"What?" I asked. Every room in this house had been searched

when Ben disappeared. Every drawer, closet, under every bed. Was Ben telling us there was something to look for that we had missed?

Vail went still and quiet, his body tense. He tilted his chin back and pointed. I looked up.

Right above the place where the footprints ended was the door that led to the attic.

12

VIOLET

Bradley Pine ate half of his father's sandwich like it belonged to him, then started on the french fries. There was a reason Gus had only eaten half of his lunch. He'd been saving the other half for his son, who he'd been expecting from the first.

"I believe you two went to high school together," Gus said. "You should know each other."

I struggled to come up with something to say. Bradley looked the same as he had in high school, yet different. He'd thickened, much of his teenage muscle turning to bulk, though he was still obviously strong. The edge of a blurry, badly inked tattoo snaked over his biceps from under the sleeve of his T-shirt. The handsome face I'd mooned pathetically over was still good-looking, though the cheekbones were less sharp and there were crow's-feet at the corners of his eyes. He was clean-shaven, his dark blond hair cut short and neat under his baseball cap. His brown eyes fixed on me with a complete absence of curiosity as he chewed.

"Hi, Bradley," I said.

"Hey," he replied, and put another fry into his mouth.

That seemed to be all he had to say, so I turned back to Gus. "You set this up," I said.

Gus crossed his arms. "I don't meet strangers in diners. So I brought my son."

"And he just happened to be free?"

"Bradley is between jobs right now. He has a lot of spare time."

"What did you think I would do? Mug you? You don't even know me."

"You're damn right I don't," Gus shot back. "Do you know how many people have showed up wanting to talk about the Ben Esmie case in the last twenty years? Zero. No one at all. It's too weird that you showed up now, and I don't trust anything in this town. A good cop calls for backup before going into a situation he isn't sure of, so that's what I did. And it was a smart thing to do, since you've been talking about ghosts."

Bradley seemed to have no problem being spoken of as if he wasn't in the room. He also didn't react to the ghost comment. He devoured the last fry on the plate and sat back, wiping his mouth with a napkin.

"I didn't sign up for this," I argued to Gus. "This is my business, my family's business. I don't want a babysitter."

"Not a babysitter," Gus said. "You might find him useful. Someone should. Ever since he moved back home from Vermont, I can't find a single use for him. Until today." His eyes twinkled with an evil gleam. "He's between wives, too."

That finally got a reaction from Bradley. "*Dad.*"

"I'm just saying." Gus unlaced his arms and spread his hands in an innocent gesture.

"Oh my God." I scrubbed a hand over my face. This was the last thing I needed.

"You take him with you, or you don't read your brother's file," Gus said.

I turned to Bradley. "What do you think of all of this?"

Bradley dropped his napkin onto the plate. "I got lunch out of it." Then he declared, as if he was doing me a favor, "I'll help you out."

I had a moment of double vision, in which I saw Bradley in high school, overlaid like a double exposure. He'd been tall, built, good-looking—everything that was popular with high school girls. If he'd declared, in his offhand way, *I'll help you out* to my sixteen-year-old self, I would have been speechless with excitement. I—the neglected and unseen girl whose only friend had died—would have lived on those four words for weeks, like a camel crossing an emotional desert.

I crossed my arms like Gus had just done and stared current-day Bradley down. "Do you know my name?"

"Sure." His gaze darted away, uneasy.

"Do you? Say it, then."

"Uh." Bradley looked up at the ceiling, like my name would be written there. His father had just said my last name a few seconds ago, but apparently it hadn't registered. Nothing about me had ever registered with him.

"Jesus, son," Gus said, disgusted, when the silence went on too long.

"We went to high school together," I said. "Do you remember that?"

Bradley shrugged. "I guess."

"Name one thing you remember about me," I snapped. "One."

He narrowed his eyes at me, and I finally saw a glimmer of thought somewhere in his concrete skull. "You were weird," he finally said.

"Everyone in Fell is weird," I shot back. "You'll have to be more specific. Try again."

"You were weirder than the rest of them," Bradley finally said. "You and your siblings. Everyone thought you were crazy. Your brother never talked. He was a swimmer."

"A diver," I corrected him. "And you beat him up twice."

Bradley shrugged. "He probably deserved it."

I looked to Gus. "You want me to work with this?"

He grinned back at me. "It isn't about want, honey. It's about choice. You don't have one."

The files, apparently, were being kept in a storage unit that Gus rented. I probably shouldn't have left my car behind, but I didn't know where the storage unit was, and I had no patience for driving around Fell, following Bradley. I was sure he would drive off and abandon me, Gus or no Gus.

So I got into Bradley's rusty blue Pinto. He got into the driver's seat, his big bulk filling the space. As I fastened my seat belt, I noticed a baseball glove tossed on the back seat. It was way too small to fit Bradley's giant hand.

"You have kids?" I asked him.

"Two," he said as he started the car. He didn't question why I was asking. "I see them every other weekend."

"I know that feeling," I said.

He didn't answer, only drove out of the parking lot and made a turn on West Common Road. I didn't even know why I'd tried to make conversation. I was invisible to him all over again. He seemed to have forgotten I was there.

I was in a time machine. A hellish, god-awful time machine that sent me back to high school.

I risked a glance at him as he drove. Old jeans, tee, baseball cap pulled low. His belly was starting to thicken in a way I should probably find unattractive. I informed my teenage self that we were driving in a car with Bradley Pine, but she had nothing to say about it for once. We might be over him.

Our route took us past Fell High, and I watched it go by out the window. The building was over a century old and had originally been intended as a private hospital. Its Gothic spikes and stonework were modeled on Notre Dame and looked like a terrifying birthday cake. I'd been miserable there. No one at school had cared when my little brother disappeared. I hadn't graduated, because after Ben, my family had shredded like so much soggy cardboard. No fireworks, no drama, just a mushy end to something that hadn't been worth much in the first place. We'd moved away two years after Ben vanished, when I was seventeen.

"That's our high school," Bradley said.

For God's sake. "I'm glad you remember something," I snapped.

He let out a heavy sigh. "Look, I don't want to do this, okay? Let's get this over with as quick as possible."

"Bradley," I said, "you are divorced, unemployed, and living at home with your father. What else did you have to do today?"

"I need to rake leaves," he replied, as if I hadn't insulted him.

I stared at him. "Fine, then. Give me the keys to the storage unit and go rake leaves. You'll never hear from me again."

He gave me a look like I was impenetrably stupid. "If I go home and rake leaves, Dad will see me. He'll know I left."

"Surely your superior intellect will find a way around this seemingly insurmountable problem."

He frowned. "What?"

"You'll figure it out," I nearly shouted, exasperated.

"You seem mad," he pointed out. "Why? Did we date in high school or something?"

I felt myself tipping over the edge. It was the sight of Fell High that had done it. The memory of going there every day with the pain of Ben an open wound, infected and blistering. Of no one noticing. The muffled, dark silence of it all, as if I was the ghost and not the people I unwillingly saw.

"You didn't care," I said, and I wasn't talking about my old crush on him. That had burned away like ashes. "You didn't care about my brother. No one did. He was six, and something really bad happened to him. He was alone. You didn't care then, and you don't care now. And you still think that makes you better than me." I picked up the baseball glove from the back seat and held it up. "You have children, for fuck's sake. What if it was this kid who died all alone?" When he was silent, I continued. It felt good to take my anger out on him, like cleansing fire. "You think you're still a big deal. You're not. None of us are. I'm going to find my brother, and I'm not apologizing for it. I don't care that you don't even know my name. You can either help me or get out of my way. Rake leaves if you want. Or don't. *I don't need you.*"

I smacked the glove against the side of his head, because that felt good, too. Then I tossed it into the back seat again.

Bradley straightened his hat, which had fallen askew when I hit him. He kept his eyes on the road.

"Okay," he said.

We were silent for the rest of the drive.

Bradley produced a ring of keys from his pocket when we parked in the gravel parking lot. Gus had given him the ring, which had a few keys attached to it alongside a yellowed piece of paper fastened with Scotch tape. Bradley thumbed through the keys with painful slowness. I tried to take the ring from him, but he snatched it away from me, closing his big fist over it. "No way," he said. "Dad's orders."

So I waited as he started over and thumbed through the keys again. The storage unit place was a line of ugly concrete sheds with roll-up doors fastened by padlocks. There was a tiny office at one end, dark and empty. The place seemed to have no name, and the only sign displayed a phone number in bright yellow letters. There was no one else here. A few hundred yards away, cars sped by on the two-lane road that fed from the highway.

"Nice spot," I said, eyeing the rusty, sagging chain-link fence and the half-dead weeds beyond it.

"Dad is paranoid," Bradley said. "There's stuff he won't keep at the house."

"Why not?"

"His divorce from Mom was ugly. She still owns half the house, so he can't lock her out. He won't pay for a lawyer to sort everything out. He says lawyers are crooks. He thinks Mom will snoop through his things and tell on him."

"How long have they been divorced?" I asked.

"Twenty-six years." Bradley held up a key. "It's this one."

He got out of the car and I followed, my feet crunching on the gravel of the parking lot. The air smelled like a mix of fresh autumn, gasoline, and something vaguely rotten, like food gone bad.

"Which unit is it?" I asked, jogging to keep up with his long, swift strides.

He held up the paper taped to the key ring. It had a number written on it in marker. "Seventeen."

This place was eerily still, with no sign of human life anywhere, and I was reminded of the houses I cleaned for a living—a space full of abandoned things, some of them belonging to people who were dead or moved away, people who would never pick them up. I'd dealt with storage units plenty of times, either cleaning them out as part of my work or dropping items off from an emptied house. They were quiet, dead places, but they had never given me the chill up my spine that I felt right now.

Damn this town. Even the storage units were creepy.

Bradley used his key to unlock unit number seventeen. He bent to yank up the rolling door, but it stuck at first. He gave it a few massive tugs, and then it lifted with an angry groan as his shoulders flexed. I could reluctantly admit that it was useful to have a little muscle on this errand.

A Box Full of Darkness

The interior was dim, and the sunlight winked out as I crossed the threshold. Bradley was already inside, and his body posture was tense, his jaw tight as he looked around.

"See?" He pointed to some of the objects in the dim light. "Dad's old stereo, which he paid a lot of money for. He doesn't want Mom to have that. A box of china my grandma left him, which he thinks is worth money. An antique table they got as a wedding gift that Mom wants to have in her house. Dad doesn't want it, but he's hiding it from her. And—" He stopped speaking as he squinted at the writing on the side of a cardboard box.

"Fuck," he said, and gave the box a kick with the toe of his shoe. It wasn't a hard kick, but the box skidded across the dusty floor, the sound of it loud in the silence. "I'm going to see if any of these other units are unlocked. Maybe there's something good to steal," he barked, and walked out.

I approached the box, deciphering the faded writing. *Wedding photos*, it said.

It seemed that Bradley Pine and I had had similar childhoods, at least in some ways.

I heard a *clang* as Bradley worked out his anger by yanking on the door of the next unit. He would be occupied by his tantrum for a few minutes at least. I wished I could follow him and take out my fury at my parents by clanging on metal doors until I felt better, but I had work to do.

Gus had helpfully labeled two of the boxes *Fell PD*, so I dragged those off the stack and opened them. There were yellowed files in here, and I squatted and walked my fingers through them, looking at the meticulous labels typed up by some long-ago secretary at the Fell PD. *Anderson. Archer. Campbell. DeVries.* Gus had taken a lot of files from his old job. It was surprising that he hadn't gotten in trouble for it.

There was another *clang*, this one farther away, then another. I felt a chill down my back, as if someone had dripped ice water on my spine.

I froze and looked at the open door, which was a square of bright light. My heart sped up in my chest. Something wasn't right.

"Bradley?" I called.

Another *clang*, and he swore. He wasn't far. There was no one else here. There was no need to feel like I wanted to get up and get out of here. In my mind's eye I pictured that door rolling closed, leaving me in the dark. The click of the padlock locking into place. The way the air in here would quickly get stale and hot ...

The back of my neck felt tight. I had to focus on what I was doing here, focus on Ben. I looked back down at the box, walked my fingers through the folders until I got to *Esmie*. Ben's file. I tugged it out of the box, feeling how light it was. There wasn't much here.

Gus had stipulated that I could read the file, but I couldn't take it with me. I'd agreed. I pulled the papers from the file folder, folded them, and shoved the square into the back pocket of my jeans. I tucked the empty folder back into the box.

Bradley had gone silent.

"Bradley?" I called again, and then everything happened at once.

"Hey!" Bradley shouted in a deep tone of surprise. "This one's open." There was the loud sound of a door being rolled up.

I put my hands on my knees to rise, then froze as something passed the edge of my vision. A pair of feet, clad in sneakers that had once been white but were now dirty and falling apart. They shuffled through the dust with a soft sound. I saw the frayed hem of old jeans, a young man's slender legs as he came toward me.

My throat closed, my mouth filling with spit. I flinched back, scrambled to rise.

Dimly, I heard Bradley's voice. "What *is* that? What the—" And then he started retching.

I overbalanced. An icy hand gripped the back of my neck, the fingers digging hard into my flesh. I opened my mouth and tried to scream.

A voice spoke in my ear, a low, harsh rasp that vibrated through my skull and down my spine.

"Sister sent me," it said.

And then there was nothing.

13

VAIL

Dad left first. Of course he did. After Ben disappeared, Dad disengaged from us—as if he'd ever been much engaged in the first place—and one day, barely three months later, he was gone. If there was a note or a goodbye, I didn't remember it. I didn't remember any of us grieving him, even Mom. We were too busy grieving Ben.

Eventually, we got a postcard from Spain. I remembered that. That fucker. I'd hate him forever, and I'd die proud of it. There are times when blood bonds are meaningless, when holding on to your hate is an achievement to boast of. To my last breath, I'd never forgive him for being so shallow, so selfish, for walking away from us. I was utterly incurious about what his own pain or struggle might have been. It didn't matter. Long before he was dead—dissipated into noxious vapor somewhere in Europe—my father was dead to me.

I'm very good at holding on to things. It's one of my talents.

My throat tried to close as I looked at my little sister, standing here in this dusty attic with me. Tendrils of her dark hair had escaped from her ponytail and trailed around her delicate face. She looked fragile in the beams of light from the grimy window. The sight made me angry at our father all over again, made me want to spit in his grave, if he had one. It was one of those random, unreasoning bubbles of rage that surfaced at unlikely moments, aimed at someone so long dead that they would never know. If Dad had failed me, he had also failed Dodie, who needed a father more than I did and should have had one. He had failed all of us.

Dodie blew out a breath, aiming it upward to blow the hair from her eyes.

"Bloody 'ell," she said in a terrible affected English accent. "It's a mess, guvnah. Ain't it?"

Dodie only made jokes like that when she was wearing thin. Goofy jokes and silly accents were her tornado warning. When she was a girl, this kind of thing preceded tears or a sinking into dark apathy. Sometimes one after the other. Dodie was the moodiest of us, which was saying something, and this day—this entire task—was draining her faster than it was draining me. Especially with what we were looking at now, in the attic.

My hands opened and closed at my sides, and I took a breath. Who had been looking after Dodie all this time? No one.

I'd pulled down the attic door, unfolding the steps attached to it. Dodie had changed into jeans and a T-shirt, the hem of which she'd tied at the waist. We'd climbed up, and now all I wanted was to somehow get Dodie back down those steps before she became untethered and floated away.

"I forgot," Dodie said softly, using her normal voice now. "I forgot that we put all of his toys up here."

I'd forgotten, too, and even now, the memory was too hard to fully recall. Ben was a playful kid, and he'd loved games—he had puzzles, board games he made up the rules to, blocks, toy soldiers, coloring books, watercolor painting kits. In theory, he was supposed to keep all of his toys in his room, but in reality, he'd left them everywhere in the house. You'd wake up haunted by harrowing dreams, and then you'd nearly trip over a paint-by-numbers set and a drawing in which Ben had swapped all the colors around.

After he disappeared, his toys were still everywhere. *Everywhere.* As the days dragged on, turning into weeks, it became agony. Cleaning up Ben's toys meant we knew he was truly gone. Not cleaning them up meant we believed he would be back to play with them again. Both options were torture.

Eventually, we'd boxed them up and put them in the attic. Whose idea was it? Was our father gone by then? I had a numb memory of dismantling a wooden train set and putting it in a box. We'd disposed of Ben's other belongings—the small bed from his bedroom, his clothes. But we hadn't had the heart to get rid of his toys, so we had moved them up here.

The train set was here in the attic, out of the box now and set up in a tidy oval. The train sat on its track, waiting. Everything else was out of the boxes, too—puzzles and stuffed animals and coloring books. Even the old dolls passed down from Violet's and Dodie's childhoods, which Ben had played with. Everything was scattered and set up, as if a child played up here every day.

The thought that crossed my mind at the sight was, *Maybe someone is playing a trick on us.* I'd seen deception in VUFOS. Someone could have broken into this house, set everything up to make it look like Ben was here. There was plenty of time to do it and no one to catch them.

None of us had seen our brother. The landscapers could either be in on it or paid off. One phone call, and the three Esmie siblings showed up, no questions asked.

I'd noticed myself that the house wasn't dusty enough. But why would someone call us back here like this?

The people who faked abductions for VUFOS usually wanted attention, which was tied to money. Some wanted one more than the other; some wanted both equally. Some people just wanted to feel important about *something*, even if it was for a crazy thing that not many people cared about. Getting the attention of a handful of UFO investigators was more attention than they'd ever had in their life.

There was no one at our old house looking for our attention or our money, at least not yet. My mind went over the angles, and then I looked at Dodie again. Her breathing had gone shallow. Maybe someone just wanted us to feel that deep, bloody slice of pain.

"Go back downstairs," I said, my voice calm.

"He was here," she said in reply, her gaze fixed on something. I followed it and saw that a small rubber ball was lazily rolling into the corner, losing momentum as if someone had abandoned it a moment ago. It made no sound.

A trick, I thought. There had to be a way. If someone had years without interruption, they could use magnets, strings, traps to fool us. I hadn't heard noises from the attic since I'd been here, and you couldn't lower the steps and leave without making a lot of noise. My gaze shot to the window, which was dusty and shut, the only view out of it of the trees that Dodie and I had walked through this morning. Had this been set up while we were out of the house, searching the back property? Or before we arrived?

Why do it at all?

We had money, all three of us—plenty of it now. Mom came from money, and Dad hadn't had enough access to it to waste it all away. Mom's money had bought this house when they first married. Mom's money had gone into a trust fund for each of us that we got when we turned eighteen. It was enough that I could do unpaid work for VUFOS and Dodie could get occasional modeling gigs and Violet could clean houses, and we didn't have to worry where the rent came from. We'd lived frugally for the first years, making the trust funds last until Mom finally died, when we got the rest of it.

Money could motivate most people to do just about anything. But if this was a trick to get money, it was an elaborate one. I couldn't see the point of it, at least not yet.

I looked at Dodie again. There was no part of my little sister that believed this was a trick. No part at all.

"Go back downstairs," I said again, more gently.

She shook her head. "Don't clean it up, Vail." Her tone was arguing, as if I'd suggested it. "Don't take pictures. We'll wait for Violet to get back. She'll know what to do. She'll—"

"Shh." I pressed my fingertips to her elbow. "Go downstairs."

"He wants us to see something. He led us here."

I looked around again at our little brother's toys. The watery footsteps—could someone have faked those, too? The ball had stopped rolling and was wedged in the corner. Nothing moved or made a sound. I could see no message, no pattern. Just a child's playthings that announced, *I am here.*

I wanted to believe it. If it was really Ben, was that what he was trying to tell us? That he was here?

My gaze caught on something and I stepped forward, picked it up. A glider made of balsam wood in the shape of an airplane. It was a kit in which you took the pieces of balsam and slid them together, the slender parts fitting into the notches in the other pieces. Ben had put it together, but he'd done it wrong, with the wings upside down, opposite of the tail. "It won't fly," I'd explained to him as I'd gently pried the pieces apart again, trying not to break the thin wood. "If the wings and the tail are opposite like that, the airplane won't fly."

Ben had watched my hands as they worked, and then his gaze had trailed away, bored. He was rarely bored, but mechanical things did it. He was the unusual little boy who had no fascination for play dump trucks or police cars or fire trucks. The airplane, with its painted stripes and painted windows for pretend balsam wood passengers, interested him not at all.

"You'll see," I'd told him. "When we fly it, you'll see."

That was the morning of hide-and-seek day. I'd taken the plane apart, but we hadn't reassembled it. Ben's interest had moved on, and we'd left the pieces in a pile and played other games instead.

A few hours later, my little brother was gone forever.

I picked up the airplane where it sat now, on top of a dusty box. I remembered picking up the pieces and packing them away, my head throbbing, my eyes watering.

The airplane was assembled now. I ran my fingertip over the wing, which was assembled the wrong way. Then down to the tail.

I held the airplane that wouldn't fly, listened to the rush in my ears, and tried to breathe.

In the kitchen, I took the milk from the fridge, then opened the cupboard, looking for the chocolate Quik I'd bought. I poured two glasses of milk and found a spoon. My hand had almost stopped shaking.

Dodie dropped into a kitchen chair, her cheeks flushed and her eyes bright in a way that was a danger warning. "He was *there*," she said. "Ben was *there*, Vail. He was there."

I spooned chocolate into her glass of milk and stirred.

"I never thought—I never." She shook her head, her gaze far away. "I thought he was gone. I thought he'd blinked out into nothingness, that I'd never see him again. For the rest of my life. Until I *died*."

"You might not see him." I kept my voice level and careful. I put her glass in front of her on the table. "Drink this."

"I'm going to see him," she said, her voice hushed. "His little face. The smell of his hair. Do you remember the smell of his hair?"

"Of course I do."

"I believed it was over," she said. "I thought that this was my life now. Ben was gone, and this is my life. What if that isn't my life?"

"Drink your milk," I said. There was no point speculating about tricks, not when she was in this mindset. I'd talk to Violet about it.

"You believe he stopped existing, when you know the things that Violet can see?"

Dodie took a deep sip of her chocolate milk, so she was listening to me at least a little. Her throat worked as she swallowed, and the flush on her cheeks faded. I should probably find something for her to eat that wasn't pâté. "Violet sees shadows, ghosts. Like old sepia photographs. People who died a long time ago. And Violet stayed here last night with us, and she didn't see him." She looked at me, her gaze focusing from wherever it had been. "He showed himself to *us*, Vail. Not Violet."

I nodded, sipping my milk. I had to maintain the illusion that this was a normal conversation. If I caught any of Dodie's excitement, it would feed back to her and she would start to spiral. There would be tears. Or she'd pick up that glass of milk and smash it in sudden anger. Where the hell was Violet? She was better at calming Dodie than I was.

I was still trying to think of the right thing to say when Dodie reached into the back pocket of her jeans and pulled out crayons, dropping them onto the kitchen table. Three of them—red, yellow, blue, all well used. They clicked softly as they landed. I felt a brief spurt of outrage that she'd picked the crayons up, but I swallowed it. Dodie could not be yelled at right now.

"I thought you didn't want to touch anything," I said in a level voice.

"He wanted me to take these," she said, her tone a challenge. She gave me a look that dared me to argue with her.

"All right," I said.

"I'm going to leave them here." Her hand hovered over the crayons, and I could see that it was shaking, just like mine had been. "Don't *touch* them."

I shrugged like it was no big deal. "Do what you want. I'm done with this for now. I'm going to see if I can fix the TV signal."

A Box Full of Darkness

My little sister's hand wavered for another moment. Her gaze dropped, and then she glanced at the wall clock, which had stopped working sometime in the last twenty years. "I don't even know what time it is," she mused.

"Go have a nap," I advised her. "I promise to come get you if Violet comes home with important news."

"I suppose I could sleep." She rubbed a hand over her face, then pushed back her chair and stood. "I didn't sleep well last night."

She'd told me that already, but I nodded as if this was news. "Then nap," I repeated.

She walked to the kitchen door, then paused. She seemed to consider her words before she spoke them. "You're not leaving?" she asked.

It was the same tone I'd heard from her on our walk this morning. Dodie was scared. I held her gaze with mine, picked up my chocolate milk, and swigged from it as if nothing bothered me. "Nope," I said.

She nodded. I heard her steps ascend the stairs.

I put my glass down, then scrubbed both my hands through my hair as I exhaled hard, feeling the scrape on my scalp. I couldn't look at the crayons on the table.

One day. We'd been here one day, and already Dodie was about to crack like a raw egg, her yolk spilling all over the floor. Either I'd lost my ability to keep her tethered, or this situation was particularly bad. Probably both. I needed to talk to Violet about it.

Where the hell was Violet?

It felt like the house was breathing, waiting for me to do something.

I needed to be busy, or I'd crack like an egg, too. And one of us needed an unbroken shell.

I left the crayons behind and walked to the living room to fix the TV.

14

VIOLET

"Oh, man," Bradley said, putting his hands on his knees and hanging his head between them. "I think I'm gonna barf again."

I stared down between my feet at the gravel of the parking lot as my head spun, the blood throbbing in my neck. "Please don't," I said.

"Oh, man," Bradley said again.

We were sitting on the curb at the edge of the lot, our legs sprawled out in front of us. Two police cars and an ambulance were parked in front of the storage units. There were no sirens or flashing lights, because except for the fact that I'd passed out, this wasn't an emergency. The body inside the storage unit had been dead for a long time.

I lifted the damp cloth in my hand and pressed it to my forehead again, trying to still my rotating brain. The ambulance was here for me, not for the dusty corpse Bradley had stumbled on. Apparently, after throwing up, Bradley had found me passed out cold, and then he'd used a brick to smash the window to get into the small office and call 911.

I'd woken up in a stranger's lap. The paramedic had pressed the cloth to my forehead and taken my pulse, my blood pressure. He'd asked me to count fingers and name the president. Behind him, a cop car had pulled up to the other storage unit, and then a second one had joined it, like two silent beetles. The cops spoke in low tones, punctuated with crackles from their radios.

Now Bradley and I sat like two forgotten children while the grown-ups took over. The officers had taken a statement from both of us, then told us to wait for instructions. One of them was trying, with no success, to track down the owner of the storage units to discuss the window Bradley had broken.

The cool breeze brushed the back of my neck and I pressed my hand there, remembering the icy grip I'd felt right before the darkness.

"What the fuck?" The words burst out of Bradley like he couldn't contain them. He sprang to his feet, paced back and forth. "I mean, what the *fuck* was that, right?" He stopped, looked at me. "Right?"

Most people—normal people—weren't used to the dead. They didn't see ghosts. Bradley was one of those normal people, and to cut him some slack for once, he'd just seen an actual corpse. Anyone would be a little worked up.

I pressed my hand harder to the back of my neck and closed my eyes. I saw the dead with some regularity, but I had never had an experience like this. I'd never felt one of the people I saw. Heard them. I'd never passed out. Even I, the freak of nature, felt fear low in my belly. Something was very, very wrong.

Sister sent me.

I shuddered, forced my eyes to blink open, to take in the sunlight. I took a breath.

"What happened to you?" Bradley asked. He dropped to the curb next to me again. "You passed out, but you didn't see—that thing. Why did you faint?"

The spinning in my skull was slowing, replaced by a wince of pain that quickly drained away. Now I felt tired, not just from the aftermath of fear but because of this entire situation.

"Hey, Violet," Bradley prompted me. He knew my name now, because he'd heard me give it to the paramedic and the police, complete with spelling.

And here we were—back at this moment I'd had so many times in my life. The moment when I chose not to tell someone the truth. Telling the truth had landed me in a hospital, made my daughter hate me. I lied to get along, lied to appear normal, like I had with Tess, my old employer. I lied, and I lost jobs, marriages, and friendships anyway.

And this? This was Bradley Pine. Why did I care what he thought of me? He hadn't learned my name until fifteen minutes ago. Screw him. I was tired.

"It was a man, right?" I said. "The body. A young man in jeans with frayed hems. White sneakers, worn and dirty."

Beside me, Bradley went very still.

"There was a backpack, too," I said, because when the hand had grabbed the back of my neck it had imparted some ghost of memory, imprinted it into my skin. Another thing that had never happened before. "A camp stove. He was living in the empty storage unit when he died. He was . . . a vagrant, I think." Faded memories twisted through my brain like dissipating smoke. "He was young, twenty or so. He had pills. He'd traded for them? Stolen them? That part is unclear. When he took them, he died." It hadn't been intentional. He wasn't suicidal. He'd just wanted to feel high, then fall asleep. He'd taken all the pills at once instead of one at a time, thinking it would make the high stronger. As he'd spiraled down, he'd realized he'd made a mistake. Too late.

I lifted my gaze and looked at Bradley's pale, shocked face. I hadn't told the police any of that, only that I'd suddenly felt faint. You know, to appear normal.

There went another friendship. Yet again. And I didn't even *like* him.

"I see ghosts, Bradley," I said, severing the last of it. "I've always been able to see them, when they show themselves to me. The man you just found—I saw his ghost. His spirit. His undead entity. His revenant. Got it?"

Bradley stared at me, his brown eyes fixed on me. Then he stood up and walked away.

My stomach roiled. Disappointment mixed with fear. I hadn't even told Bradley about the hand on my neck, the words in my ear. Or Sister, because I had never told anyone about Sister.

He'd walked away anyway. I'd told him enough.

Sister sent me.

I had the overwhelming urge to call Lisette. I ached to hear my daughter's voice. To hear her say anything at all, even that she hated me. The need of it was like a living thing. I needed to talk to Vail and Dodie. I needed to get to my car and get home.

Bradley's sneakers came back into my line of vision and stopped as he stood in front of me. "Are you okay?" he asked.

I tilted my head back to look up at him. He was squinting at me from under the bill of his baseball cap, his expression unreadable.

"Like, physically," he said. "Are you hurt?"

I shook my head. "No. I'm fine."

He nodded, then lifted his ball cap and ran his hand over his hair. "This fucking town, man. I hate it here."

I nodded.

"I had a pet turtle when I was eleven." Bradley put his cap back on. "I let him out to wander in the yard, and the neighbor's dog got him. Can you call him up? I want to know if he's mad at me."

It took a second for that to sink in.

"Oh my God," I said. "You asshole."

"What?" He was doing a good job of acting serious, but then a smirk twitched the corner of his mouth. "It's important."

"You are such an absolute idiot. How do you manage to get your pants on in the morning?"

"I get 'em on." When I dropped my gaze again, he tapped me with the toe of his sneaker. "Did you get your file from Dad's unit? Tell me you stole it."

"I would never," I said.

"Sure you'd never. I'm hungry."

"Again?"

"Yeah, again. I threw up my sandwich, remember?" He tapped me with his toe a second time. "I'm done with this parking lot, Violet, and so are you. Screw what the cops said. They want to prosecute me for that window, they can deal with Dad. Let's get out of here."

Incredibly, I spent the next hour at the Turnabout Diner, eating hamburgers with Bradley Pine and not talking about ghosts. By the time I went home, I was almost sane again.

15

DODIE

I stared at the ceiling of my childhood room. My temples throbbed. My eyes felt heavy in my skull, dry and swollen. The light was fading behind the curtains in the window. Had I slept? I must have. I felt sick.

There were voices downstairs. Vail and Violet. So Violet was home, then. I heard the heavy fall of Vail's footsteps, his deep, familiar voice. "Damn it, Violet. You'd think—" The words became indistinct again. I listened to the hum of my brother and sister talking, listened to the soft breathing of the house. Listened for the sound of water, but it didn't come.

Words from the conversation below drifted up again. Violet: "Is she sleeping?" Vail: "Yes."

I didn't move. When Violet's footsteps climbed the stairs, when she walked down the hall, I didn't move.

There was the soft creak of my door opening.

"You're not asleep," my big sister said.

I choked the words out. "Go away."

Her tone was bitter. "I'm home, if you care."

"I don't. Go away."

"Don't you want to know what's in Ben's police file?"

My temples throbbed harder and my throat tried to close. "No. I don't."

"Jesus, Dodie."

I was staring at the ceiling, not looking at her, but I could feel her eyes on me. I wanted her to stop looking. I wanted her to go away so I could be alone in the dark.

I didn't want to know what a few pieces of paper said about my dead brother. I'd thought I wanted to know, but I was wrong. It had been a mistake to come here, because I didn't want to know anything at all. I wanted it all to go away. I watched spots dance in front of my eyes and thought about what kind of person I was that I wouldn't want to know such an important thing. Important information. As if information could make any of this better.

"So fucking dramatic," Violet said, and the door closed again.

Good. Let her and Vail take care of it, whatever it was. I couldn't do it. I'd never been able to do it. I'd never been able to do anything.

Except get my little brother killed. I could do that.

I knew Ben's favorite hiding places. He was a little kid; he was easy to outsmart. When we played hide-and-seek, Ben always hid either in the back of Vail's closet or the cubby under the main stairs. That final day, when Ben had suggested the game, I'd decided to mess with him. I'd pulled Vail's dresser across his closet door so that it wouldn't open. Then, as Vail counted loudly down from ten, I'd hidden in the cubby under the stairs myself.

I beat Ben to the hiding spot. I was faster than a six-year-old, smarter than a six-year-old, wittier than a six-year-old. What a fucking achievement.

My little brother's footsteps had approached barely a minute after I tucked myself under the stairs, slowing and hesitating. "Dodie?" he'd whispered.

"Sorry," I'd said, trying not to snicker too loudly. "This spot is taken."

Ben had paused, and in the kitchen, Vail had finished counting. Ben's footsteps scurried up the stairs.

I'd smiled to myself in the dark because I knew he was going to his second place in Vail's room. He'd strike out there, too. A successful prank all around. Ben would have to find another hiding spot.

His footsteps hurried up the stairs, and that was the last I heard of him, ever again.

I had tried a thousand times over the years to strain my memory of those last footsteps. Had I heard Ben go down the hall? Go into any of the rooms? Had I heard a door open or close? Had I heard him come back down the stairs? Or had his footsteps simply stopped at the final step? My brain thrashed it over and over. It made no sense. If Ben had stayed upstairs, where had he hidden? If he had come back down, why hadn't I heard him? Could he have hidden and come back down later, after I left my hiding spot? Where had he gone?

It didn't matter where he had gone. Wherever it was, he had died there. It wouldn't have happened if I had let him hide in one of his favorite places. If I hadn't taken the spot under the stairs—if I had let Ben have it—then I would know where he was. If someone had to die that day, it would have been better if it was me.

I let the memory bubble up, let it burst at the surface and spread its toxic stench over me, let the acid eat at me. A single impulsive choice had changed my life forever. I could have slid out of my hiding spot and given it to Ben. I could have come out and chased him up the stairs, scooping him up in my arms instead of letting him go. I could have done so many things, but I hadn't.

Had Ben died hating me?

The thought ripped me open from my throat to my belly, and I lay there helpless. I seethed. If Ben had hated me, it was nothing compared to how much I hated myself. I had never hated another being as much as I hated me.

I wanted to do nothing but sleep.

I'd never sleep ever again.

I rolled over, smelled the musty scent of my childhood pillow, and closed my eyes.

He was warm.

Curled up against me in his familiar way, a ball of heat against my stomach and chest. I flung my arm tighter over him and instinctively inhaled against his hair, the tender scent of his scalp. Baby shampoo and a little boy's skin, clean and funky at the same time. The best smell.

I pressed my cheek to the top of his head. He squirmed against me, his hand clasping my fingers and squeezing them. The water never came when Ben was here. He'd climb into bed with me, and we'd both be safe, so safe. Nothing could go wrong when we were like this. I felt my heart thump against his back.

"Dodie," he said.

I opened my eyes.

My little brother whispered in my ear, his breath hot. "Dodie. Find me."

I sucked in a gasp as icy water rushed over the bed and into my empty arms. I pushed up before it covered my face, launching my body off the mattress. In the doorway—what was it? A shadow? It looked like—

Slipping in the icy water, I scrambled out of bed and crashed through the doorway, running after my little brother.

16

VAIL

Dodie was screaming.

I was awake and out of bed before I fully registered what the sound was. I staggered to my bedroom door as a crash sounded in the hall, followed by a hard thump. My little sister screamed again, then again, the same word. "*Ben!*"

It was dark. I slapped the wall, looking for a light switch. Down the hall, another door opened and Violet's voice shouted, "Dodie?"

I smacked the switch in time to see Dodie run to the landing, then start down the stairs. She screamed again, and then she tripped, her feet sliding from under her as she clutched the railing. She twisted, holding on to the railing for a second, and then she let go.

Violet flew after her, calling her name. I descended to see Dodie sitting on the bottom step in pajama pants and an old sleeveless shirt, her arms wrapped around her knees. A red mark flared on her skin where her elbow had hit the floor. Her dark hair was a feral mess, her eyes wild. She gave an agonized wail, then dropped her head and started weeping, her shoulders heaving.

Violet and I exchanged an alarmed look. Violet tied her robe snugly around herself and lowered to the step next to Dodie, putting an arm around her shoulders. Dodie was definitely not herself, because instead of pulling away, she leaned into Violet, shuddering as she wept.

I moved past them on the stairs and stood in front of Dodie, where I squatted on my haunches in my sweatpants and tee. With her head down, I couldn't see her face. "What happened?" I asked her, my voice a rasp.

I didn't think she would answer. She seemed lost somewhere, folded inside herself. She was the only one of us to have outbursts like this as a child. Dodie could spit anger, weep, or laugh herself to tears when the mood struck her, while Violet and I never could. Violet always felt too responsible to let go, and I simply shut my feelings off, flipped them like a fuse switch. Part of me had envied Dodie's wild ability to scream.

Violet patted Dodie's shoulder awkwardly, then patted her back. She didn't seem to know what to say, either. We Esmies were bad with physical comfort.

Dodie lifted her chin enough to speak. "I felt him." The words came out in a gasp, and Violet's hand stilled. "I *felt* him, Vail. I *felt* him. There was so much water." She looked down at herself, brushing a hand over her shirt, which was dry. "I felt him," she repeated to herself.

I reached out and took her wrist, pressing my fingers to the pulse there beneath the tissue paper of skin. Dodie's flesh was freakishly cold, but her pulse was racing, and I dug my fingers gently against the delicate bones as if I could pry the truth from them. "Tell me," I said.

She inhaled shakily, her head still lowered. "He was in my bed. And then he ran out the door and down—" She closed her eyes. "He said my name. And 'Find me.'"

So Ben was playing a game, then. I knew his games. I kept my excitement down by force of will. "Where did he go?"

A Box Full of Darkness

Dodie pointed past us in the direction of the dark kitchen, the dark living room.

I met Violet's gaze briefly again, then stood. I turned and walked into the darkness.

The kitchen was silent. Nothing moved. I didn't reach to the wall for the light switch. Hide-and-seek was always better played in the shadows, where the darkness gave more places to hide.

In the faint glow of moonlight through the kitchen window, I could see a gleam on the top of the stove, the flat surface of the kitchen table. A glass Violet had left on the counter after she drank some water. I listened for a rustle, a breath. Where could a little boy hide in here?

I had been It that day. I had been fourteen, and we'd drawn straws, and I'd drawn the short straw, which meant I was It. I was It now. The silence felt like a held breath.

"Ben?" I called softly. "Where are you hiding?"

Silence.

"I'll find you," I said, my voice falling into the croon I'd used twenty years ago, a singsong lilt I had never used since. "It's only a matter of time."

I couldn't hear Dodie's sobs anymore. I was back to that day, the snow falling past the windows in huge wet flakes, the chill in the air because this house never got truly warm in winter. The smell of woodsmoke coming from a neighboring house. The blanketing silence that came with heavy snowfall, as if the entire world was hushed.

I bent and opened the lower cupboards, one by one, my hands sure in the dark. Those were easiest for a six-year-old to climb into. He could push aside some stale boxes of cereal, some dusty old pots that no one ever cooked with, and curl up. But he wasn't there.

Still crouching low, I checked under the table. Then I moved to the pantry and opened the door. "Ben?"

Nothing. Empty air, the handful of canned goods I'd bought, a stale smell of old floor wax. No Ben.

You're failing, I thought. *You won't find him in time.*

I left the door open and turned.

I hadn't found Ben in time. I was It—I was the one who was supposed to find him, but I hadn't. He'd fallen somewhere, or gotten trapped, or hit his head, and the one who was supposed to find him never had.

All of this was my fault. All of it.

I left the kitchen, still finding my way easily in the dark. I paused at the cubbyhole under the stairs, which Ben had loved to hide in. Dodie had hidden there that last day. I knew from my initial reconnaissance of the house that the cubby had been stuffed with a box of old junk, but I checked it anyway. My hand slid over the box, over its edges. There was nothing else in there. I closed the door and turned to the living room.

There were more corners in here, more pitch-black spaces a little boy might hide in. The living room was large and oddly shaped, and the furniture didn't fit into every corner. I touched the back of the sofa, feeling my way. I crouched to look beneath a side table. I called for my little brother again.

Failing. You are failing. Again. Like you've failed at everything.

I'd been a diver for a while, after Ben was gone. I had the build for it, and people said I was pretty good. It was something to do. It took time before I realized that all I wanted was to crash into the water and break my neck, every single time I jumped.

Diving felt different after that. I started to think I might do it—dive into a shallow pool, or an empty one. Dive off a bridge, or from a window. Execute perfect form on the way down.

I quit diving.

When I stood, I realized I could see my hand when I held it up.

It was hours from dawn. The light was bright, white, unnatural. There was no window in this room.

A Box Full of Darkness

Do you see lights? I'd asked Charles Zimmer in Sacramento, just a few days ago.

And his answer: *Yes. They're blinding, right in my eyes.*

Light flared, and I flinched back. From the pitch-darkness, now I could see everything—every corner of the room as bright as an operating theater.

I'd dreamed this so many times as a child. Dreamed it over and over again in this house in the middle of the night. The light from nowhere, someone standing over me. The tall form peering down, staring at me, its face in shadow. The figure stared at me, and I couldn't move—

"Ben!" I called out, but he didn't answer.

Something flitted beside me, and I turned. A shadow, long and thin. An arm reached out like a whip and a hand gripped my throat, icy and raw. The thing pulled me toward it. It was as real as any physical hand I'd ever felt, bones and hard flesh, cruel tendons twisting the thumb and digging it into the soft spot below my jaw. I felt the scrape of a ragged nail.

"Wake up," the thing said in my ear, its voice a rasp.

I gasped as it squeezed harder, as the light flared in my eyes.

"Wake up," it said again, and this time I could feel its breath, smell something rancid and undead. My stomach turned as I reached a hand down and grabbed for something, anything.

The hand, its fingers mere bones and skin, wrapped tighter around my throat as the thing leaned in. "Wake—"

I spun, swinging my arm with all of my strength, the power and precision I'd once used to slice into the water. My arms were long, and my aim didn't miss. Precision like an arrow, that was what you needed to be a diver. I hit with everything I had.

I hit something corporeal—there was no question there was a grisly thump. The grip on my throat loosened. I swung again, and I hit it—whatever it was—again. There was a cold clicking sound, and the hand let go.

The lights went out. The only sound was the hiss of my breath and the clatter of the vase as the broken shards of it dropped to the floor.

Darkness, and then a light went on—the overhead light this time, its familiar jaundiced yellow. Violet stood in the doorway, Dodie behind her.

"Did you see it?" My voice was hoarse as I spun in place. I scrubbed a hand over my throat, over my chilled skin. "Did you see the lights? I hit it. Did you see where it went?"

My sisters didn't answer. Violet's gaze was fixed past my shoulder. Dodie looked there, too, and her hands went to her mouth.

I turned. In the glow of the overhead light, I saw the wall, papered in a pattern of cream and soft blue. The colors were marred with red letters scrawled in two words. A red crayon—from the attic—lay discarded on the floor.

The three of us were silent as we read those two words over and over.

WAKE UP.

17

VIOLET

The vase Vail had broken had been a wedding present for our parents. At least I thought it was. I had a recollection of Mom telling me not to touch it when I was fascinated by the light refracting through the crystal. "When you get married, you can get your own," she'd said. Hadn't she? We were never supposed to touch anything in this house anyway.

I swept the shards into a corner and left them there.

We were all relatively sane in the morning, which was remarkable. Vail had receded into silent brooding, slouched in a chair he'd pulled away from the kitchen table. My thoughts were thin with lack of sleep, but my energy was powered by a red mist of rage. Anger, for me, had never needed a specific target. It was simply a constant of my entire adult life.

Dodie was oddly calm. She had always gone quiet after one of her outbursts of emotion, as if she'd been drained from a spigot, but this was different. She rummaged eggs from the fridge and scrambled them, dumping plates in front of Vail and me. She made toast and coffee. I had never seen my little sister cook before, though she lived solo so must be able to create some kind of sustenance. She couldn't live on cigarettes and Melba toast alone, like she did in my imagination.

None of us mentioned the words scrawled on the wall in the living room.

"All right," Dodie said, pulling her chair up and picking up her fork. She was wearing baggy cotton pants—possibly men's—and a turquoise top with a bow tied on the top of each shoulder. She had pulled her black hair into the messy twist on top of her head I'd seen before, and she had dabbed dark makeup around her eyes. She didn't look like the same Dodie who had curled up in her bed yesterday, refusing to talk to me, or the same Dodie who had collapsed, weeping and screaming, on the stairs. "Tell me what's in Ben's file," she said. "I'm ready."

Vail glowered at her from beneath his dark cloud, his arms crossed over his chest. I let the red mist of anger swirl through my brain at the thought of Ben's file. Then I looked down at my plate and realized I was starving, so I started eating.

"Well?" Dodie asked, picking up her fork.

"Why don't you just read it?" Vail finally asked. He hadn't started eating, but I'd seen his gaze flick down to the eggs and away again. He'd give in. We Esmie children had the habit of eating food whenever it was offered because we never knew when we could scavenge more.

"I don't want to read it," Dodie said. "I want you to tell me what's in it."

My mouth full, I aimed a glance at Vail. Dodie seemed calm, but she'd had a worse night than both of us. We didn't want to upset her again. Vail held my gaze for a second, then shrugged. The message was *Too bad*.

"You might be angry," I warned Dodie.

"I never get angry," my little sister replied.

"You burned my dolls when you were six," I shot back. "Lit them on fire right in the backyard."

"Did I?" Dodie asked airily, though her gaze darted to Vail. "I don't believe I recall."

I didn't miss that look. I turned a wrathful glare on my brother. "That was you?"

Vail rolled his eyes. "Why would I burn some stupid dolls?"

"It was your *idea*," Dodie said, giving the lie away.

"It was a suggestion," Vail argued back to her. "No one made you take it. You did it on your own."

"Because Violet provoked me. I wouldn't have burned her things if you hadn't told me to."

"I didn't tell you to do anything. It was just an idea. I didn't think you'd actually do it, you lunatic."

"Well, well," I said with dark calm, scraping up the last crumbs of egg with my fork. "I liked those dolls. I'll have my revenge on both of you, have no fear."

Dodie shot an accusing look at Vail. "Now look what you've done. She'll put arsenic in our tea when we're eighty. No one does revenge like Violet. You know full well she can wait that long."

Vail picked up his fork and finally dug into his eggs. "I don't plan to live to eighty, so that won't be a problem."

"You most definitely won't live to eighty, dear brother," I said with threatening sweetness. "I'll make sure of it."

Dodie slapped her palm lightly on the table. "Tell me what's in the file, one of you. I *hate* reading."

Vail was eating, the bastard, and he didn't speak. So I took a drink of half-cold coffee and I told her.

It didn't take long. The file was enraging, but it wasn't very thick. Dodie listened, every part of her body going still.

"You're right," she said when I finished. "I'm angry. Do you have a plan?"

"Of course," I replied. "I always have a plan."

"Does it involve arsenic?" she asked.

I shrugged. "Not at the moment. But if I need to use it, I will. Think about where we can find some, just in case."

I made the phone call from the kitchen. It was the only phone in the house, which was unfortunate because it was placed in the middle of the wall with nowhere to sit next to it. To make a phone call—which was rare for us—one had to stand awkwardly like a soldier on parade, posture upright, legs apart. No leaning or sitting allowed.

Dodie had wandered off, but Vail stayed in the kitchen, washing the dishes in the sink and listening in. I'd had to pull a phone book—turned nearly to dust—from under the counter to get the number. Luckily, former detective Gus Pine had lived in Fell with the same phone number since roughly the fall of the Roman Empire.

"Hello?" came his gruff voice when he picked up.

My voice was calm. "You bastard," I said. "Now I know why you didn't want me to read that fucking file."

"Ah, the Esmie girl," he said. "Such ladylike language. I guess I didn't get rid of you."

Get rid of me? "Never," I replied. "I'm still here."

"I told you not to read it. Family shouldn't read those things. It never solves anything, and it never goes well."

"I'm not just family," I said as Vail clanked dishes louder than needed in the sink, his controlled anger matching mine. "Apparently, I'm your suspect. All of us were."

It had been typed into the file by Gus himself.

> Interviewed the three remaining children. All are teenagers. Hard to pin down, but something seems off.

A Box Full of Darkness

A few lines down:

> The oldest daughter, Violet, is rumored to be sick in the head somehow. Note to speak to any local doctor who has seen her. Mrs. Lydia Thornhill, neighbor, said that Violet sees things that aren't there. Mrs. Thornhill says she has never seen Ben Esmie in person. Follow up on possibility that the oldest daughter harmed her brother and the others are covering it up.

"I was just doing my job," Gus argued. "No one else was home when he disappeared except for the three of you. What was I supposed to think?"

I remembered being numb that day, thinking, *This isn't happening, it can't be happening.* The days, then weeks, then years of guilty agony over my baby brother. "I don't care what you think. I didn't murder my brother, and neither did Dodie or Vail."

"If I still thought you killed him, would I have let you read the file?"

"Yes, because you hoped I'd give something away." What I couldn't figure out was why he'd insisted on sending Bradley with me instead of observing me himself. Bradley was hardly a Sherlockian detective genius.

"Have you found anything?" Gus asked. He'd dropped his world-weary attitude and sounded curious.

"You think I would tell you if I had? I'd rather eat glass."

"You said your brother's ghost is in the house. Have you—"

"I'm asking the questions," I said. Behind me, Vail had finished the dishes and was standing in the edge of my line of sight, vigorously drying his hands. I wasn't going to tell Gus Pine about Ben crawling into bed with Dodie, about lights that only Vail saw, about the words scrawled on the living room wall. Words that meant nothing to us. Unless one of us was lying.

On the phone, Gus turned cranky again. "Well, if you're not going to tell me anything, then I don't have all day. What do you want?"

"I'm not finished with my investigation. I'm just getting started. I want information, and you're going to help me get it."

"You saw the records I have. I told you—"

"I don't want police records," I interrupted. "I can see that not only were you incompetent, but your theories were insulting. What I want today is hospital records."

"We checked for your brother's medical records at the time. He didn't have any. At least, not that we could find."

Heavy lead threatened to settle in my stomach. He'd just given me a big piece of the information I wanted, and it wasn't good. "Did you check Fell Hospital?" I asked.

"Of course we did." He paused. "Let me guess. You want to double-check my work?"

"It seems reasonable," I shot back. "But if Ben has no records, then I want my parents' records."

"I can't get you that."

"They're dead, so yes, you can."

"You think I run the hospital?"

God, he was being a pain in the ass. "I think you're as old as God, and you know everyone in town, so you can call someone and get those records for me, yes."

"You're crazy," he grumbled, his tone telling me that my assumption was absolutely right.

"Yes, crazy. Just as your insightful investigation file says," I replied. "Did they give you a psychology degree along with your Deputy Dawg badge? 'Something seems off' is going to crack the case wide open, I'm sure. Any day now. It's only been twenty years." Next to my shoulder, Vail laughed softly, darkly.

"Something *is* off, since you're home because you think there's a ghost," Gus snapped, but there was no bite in it. This was Fell, the town of graves where they shouldn't be and a missing girl's shoes placed neatly outside her dorm room door. Fell, which had swallowed my little brother whole like a ravenous monster, like a great white whale. Fell, where twelve-year-old girls fell dead next to the train tracks, where I'd found a book about how to draw pentagrams to summon demons tucked neatly on the back of a shelf in my middle school library, where there was that tree that everyone knew not to go near and that bus stop that seemed to go nowhere, where the pool at the local motel never had water in it. Fell was where your childhood night terrors had a taste and a smell.

"You owe me," I said to Gus, thinking of that file. Those words: *the oldest daughter harmed her brother and the others are covering it up.* He should pay for writing those words, even in a file that was locked in a haunted storage unit for no one to see.

"I'll make the call," Gus said.

"Thank you. And I want one more thing."

His tone was sarcastic. "Yes, Your Majesty?"

"I want Bradley to come with me." The words surprised me as they left my mouth. I hadn't planned to say them. "Have him meet me at the hospital in half an hour."

"You can have him." Gus agreed to this one quickly, probably because he wanted Bradley out of his hair and was counting on Bradley to report back to him as a spy. "He's eating cereal in his Jockeys right now, but I'll make him get dressed."

"For the love of God, please do," I said, and hung up.

Vail watched me with his arms crossed, his look thoughtful. "Remind me," he said softly, "never to cross you." It was halfway between an insult and a compliment.

"Don't ever cross me, Vail," I said, but I just felt tired. My shoulders sagged.

"Mom's and Dad's hospital records," Vail said. "You distracted him with all of that business about you being a suspect, you being angry about it."

"I am angry about it."

"But that doesn't have any bearing on what you wanted," Vail said.

I hesitated, and then I shrugged. "You read the file." Our gazes met.

> Mrs. Thornhill says she has never seen Ben Esmie in person.

Further down on the page, Gus had written more notes:

> Parents can't supply a photo of the missing boy. After much questioning, no photo of him seems to exist. At the age of six, the boy was not enrolled in school. There are no family photos in the house, no pictures of either parent or any of the children. We can find no one outside the family who can supply a detailed description, no teacher, doctor, dentist, or babysitter. We can find no one to describe Ben Esmie except for his parents and the three siblings who were present when he disappeared.

I knew what Ben looked like. He had brown eyes and light brown hair. When he disappeared, he was wearing a blue T-shirt, navy blue pants, and white socks. I knew because I'd helped dress him that morning. I'd tried to get him to wear shoes, but he'd refused. He didn't like wearing shoes in the house, because they made too much noise and because he liked to play the game of sliding along the polished hardwood floors. I worried that he'd get splinters in his feet or step on a wayward nail.

A Box Full of Darkness

When he hid from us that last time, he'd been so quiet I hadn't even known in which direction he'd gone.

So we didn't have pictures of him. So what? We weren't a picture-taking family. None of us had owned a camera growing up. There were no family portraits on the wall, like normal families had, and if there had ever been a photo from their wedding, my parents would have thrown it in the garbage.

We can find no one to describe Ben Esmie.

Gus had said there was no hospital record for Ben. And he was right—Ben had never gone to school.

Why? Why hadn't any of us questioned it? I must have known he was old enough to be enrolled. It must have crossed my mind—crossed all of our minds. Why hadn't Mom and Dad sent him to school? Why hadn't my siblings and I asked about that or enrolled him ourselves? Had we wanted him to ourselves so badly? Had we worried that if he left the house for the real world, he'd never come back again?

The thing about doctors, dentists—that *had* to be wrong. Had Ben never seen a doctor? Had he never gotten his smallpox shot? I had the scar on my arm, and so did Dodie and Vail. Ben had never broken a bone or gotten an infection, but he was a rambunctious little boy. He had to have seen *someone*.

My parents were selfish and secretive. They hadn't told the police about Ben's medical records for some reason that had died with them. But everyone had one record, so I would start there.

I wanted the record of the day Ben was born.

18

DODIE

Vail found me in the upstairs hallway, facing the closed door to our parents' bedroom. "Want to watch cartoons?" he asked me. "Violet's going out."

I was tempted. Cartoons were my favorite—not in childhood but now. As a full-on grown-up in the year of our Lord 1989, they were my favorite TV, and Vail knew it. I wondered if that was why he'd gone to the trouble of setting up the TV. I hadn't seen him watch anything yet.

"Not now," I said reluctantly. "We have work to do."

Vail looked at the bedroom door, and his voice was stony when he said, "I'd rather watch cartoons."

"So would I. But Vail, there are words on the living room wall. That's going to dampen the mood in there."

A look crossed his face at the mention of the scrawled words, as if a thought snagged in his mind. Then he sighed.

"The detective's report was right about the lack of photographs in this family," I continued. "Of paperwork. I know our parents were neglectful, but the three of us *were* born, and we do exist.

Ben existed, too. I already know there's nothing in any of our bedrooms and nothing in Ben's bedroom." I had already looked in Ben's room, which should have been upsetting but had instead made me numb. Ben's room was completely empty, all of his furniture gone and his toys moved to the attic. It was a blank cube with nothing of my little brother in it anymore. We wouldn't find answers there.

"There has to be a document somewhere," I said, nodding toward our parents' door. "That's the only room I haven't searched."

"Which means," Vail said, the words dragging, "we have to go in."

"Correct."

After last night, I should be a mess. I should be sobbing in a corner or—more likely—getting in my car and driving back to New York.

Instead, I felt clear. More clear, in fact, than I had in years, as if a hangover had lifted. It had to do with the feeling of Ben next to me, the smell of his precious head. Despite the horror that had come after, the grief that had left me sobbing, all I could think about this morning was that after twenty years, he'd said my name.

He'd told me to find him. So I wasn't leaving.

I had no idea whether Vail believed it was really Ben. Maybe he did. My brother looked tired this morning, lines of concern now creasing his handsome face because he was still in *look after Dodie* mode. *Make sure Dodie doesn't crack up* mode. He didn't know yet that he didn't have to do that anymore.

I would go through our parents' old room to look for photographs and paperwork that they might have hidden from us. I'd do it with or without Vail, but I'd rather have him there.

Without letting myself overthink, I grasped the knob and pushed the door open. Then I stepped inside.

I didn't know what I'd expected. More writing on the walls, maybe, or some other ghoulish display. What I found was a few pieces of furniture covered in dust cloths. Grayish sunlight coming through the windows. The silence of an uninhabited room.

I tugged the dust cloth off the bed, then another off the dresser. There were no dust cloths in any of the other rooms in the house when I got here. Vail had removed them, I realized. He'd gone through the house, preparing it for Violet and me to arrive. But he hadn't come in here.

Behind me, I heard Vail follow me into the room.

The bed was stripped, and the top of the dresser was empty. When Dad left—he was the first—he'd taken all of his belongings. He hadn't even pretended that he'd be back.

After he left, the rest of us had stayed for a while, and then we'd dispersed one by one. At seventeen, Violet had gone to a waitressing job at a resort in Long Island, where she'd lost herself partying and met her future husband. Vail had thrown himself into the competitive diving circuit, staying with teammates or a rotation of girlfriends when he wasn't traveling.

At fourteen, I had stayed with Mom. We had moved to Long Island. She'd used her looks and her air of inherited wealth to make a brittle circle of friends. She'd done luncheons and taken up bridge like a rich woman, though privately she'd hoarded every penny. She'd started to drink in earnest.

At sixteen, I ran away to New York, where I waited tables and saved up money to pay for a modeling portfolio. Mom didn't come after me to bring me home.

Mom had eventually died in her small apartment in Long Island from a fall down the building's stairs, accelerating her process of drinking herself to death. She hadn't pretended that she'd ever come back to this house, either.

Our parents' clothes were gone, my mother's jewelry, my father's ties and watches. I thought of my childhood clothes, still in my dresser drawer in my room. I'd only taken two suitcases with me when we left. What did that say about me? I wondered.

I opened one empty dresser drawer after another, while Vail searched the nightstands. "Why didn't we ever have photographs?" I asked, thinking about how I stole strangers' photos to put in my room alongside pictures from magazines.

"I don't know," Vail said. "Part of me is happy about it. I don't want to see what we looked like then, do you?"

"Probably not." I ran my hand over the inside of a drawer, in case my mother had added an ingenious hidden lining. She hadn't. "The memories aren't good ones, I admit. But who gets married, has children—especially ones as good-looking as we are—then never takes a picture of them?" I pulled open another drawer. "Honestly."

Vail crouched to peer under the bed, folding his large frame into a surprisingly nimble squat. "If Mom had kept her papers and photos in the apartment she died in," he mused aloud, "then Violet would have found them."

"I don't remember Mom being pregnant with Ben." I confessed it like a shameful secret. I'd been afraid to speak it aloud before. "I have not one memory of it. Nine months. I don't remember doctors' appointments or a big belly. I don't remember her telling us a little brother was coming. I was only six, and I try not to think about it, but that's strange, isn't it? It isn't right. I should remember something, shouldn't I?"

"I don't remember, either." Vail stood, then ran a hand through his hair. "It makes no sense, Dodie. It's my literal life. My childhood—years and years, day in and day out. I was there. And my memories are jumbled and strange, out of order. Nothing makes sense."

"I don't know whether my dreams were real or not." It was easier to confess in this room, in which our past was so dead and empty, like a vacated husk. "I dream of cold water, but I swear I feel it. It's so real. Ben was real. I don't need a photo or a piece of paper. He was real."

"Then who was he?" Vail's voice nearly cracked, and I turned to look at him. I had never seen my brother, the most solid and implacable person I knew, look so uncertain and broken, so tired. "We have to face the possibility, Dodie."

I licked my lip. "What possibility?"

"You know what possibility. That if Mom didn't give birth to Ben, then he came from somewhere else. From someone else. That we don't know who he really was. That he wasn't ours."

"Stop it, Vail. He was ours."

"In the ways that mattered, yes. But biologically? Scientifically? I don't remember Mom being pregnant, either. I remember bringing the crib from the attic—"

"While Mom held Ben in her arms," I said. "I remember that, too. But why didn't we prepare the crib before the baby was born? We'd have had months to prepare, but we didn't set up his room until he was already here."

Vail looked around the room, distraught. "Why don't I remember? It's driving me crazy. These are big things, important things. I was eight. Why don't I remember Ben being brought home? I swear to God it's this house, Dodie. It messes with your head."

He was right. I'd never had trouble with my memory like I had when I lived here. In New York, I didn't wonder whether my dreams were real, or believe that I was drowning in bed, or lose entire memories of important events. Outside this house, I might not remember everything, but my life wasn't a half-finished quilt with patches missing, with worn-out holes.

All of it—the dreams, the lost time—had seemed normal to me as a child because it was all I knew. I didn't ask questions about my little brother appearing suddenly one day or the fact that we didn't take pictures or send Ben to school. Everyone older than me seemed fine with it, so I assumed it was the way the world worked, when I thought about it at all.

Vail opened the closet door and walked inside. "So what do we know?" he asked, his voice muffled in the closet. "Let's start with that. We both remember setting up Ben's room when he was a baby. Mom was holding Ben. Dad wasn't there."

"Dad was definitely not there." I closed my eyes. "It was summer. School was about to start. I worried about the baby being too hot. I remember putting cool cloths against his skin."

"I don't remember that." There was a shuffling sound in the closet. A cardboard box came flying out. It skidded across the floor, obviously empty. "Fuck it, there's nothing in here. Not even a grocery list or an old receipt. It figures."

"What do you remember?" I asked. "About when Ben was born. What else?"

My brother emerged from the closet, his cheeks flushed with frustration. "Dad was away—I remember that clearly. I was angry about it. I remember waking up sitting in a chair next to Ben's crib because I'd fallen asleep there, and Ben was hungry, so I gave him a bottle, and I was mad because neither Mom nor Dad was there to look after him."

Bottles of milk. I remembered those, too, which meant that Mom hadn't breastfed Ben. Plenty of women didn't breastfeed, but it was another nugget of information dug out of my memory. "So what happened, then?" I asked. "Mom just... *stole* a baby? Why would she do that?"

"Maybe someone gave him to her," Vail said. "Maybe Ben was abandoned."

I tried to picture our mother finding a swaddled baby on our doorstep, like something from a nursery rhyme, and bringing him into the house. Mom had no sisters or brothers who could have given her their offspring. "Did she go to a hospital and take a baby?" I asked, incredulous. "Or an orphanage? Do orphanages exist? Did she adopt a baby without telling us? My head hurts."

"And where was Dad in all of this?" Vail asked. "Did he know Mom had either stolen or been given a baby? Was he in on it? Was Ben his, maybe, and not hers?"

That was a possibility. Maybe Dad had impregnated a girlfriend, and Mom had taken the baby in. "She never said anything about it, even after he left," I argued. "Mom *hated* Dad. You'd think she'd mention that she was raising his mistress's offspring."

Vail looked frustrated again. "This is the first time I've ever wished that my parents weren't dead."

"Same. I'd do a séance, except that I'm afraid one of them wouldn't leave when it was done, and I'm happier with them on the other side of the veil."

"It's odd that Violet hasn't seen either of them in this house yet." He looked around. "This room doesn't feel as haunted as the rest of the house does, either. Even in death, they abandoned us. What assholes."

"They wouldn't dare come back," I said darkly. "Even after dying. They wouldn't dare."

Vail put his hands on his hips, some of his exhaustion evaporating in his indignation. His shoulders went back, and he looked like the conquering athlete, even in his ancient jeans and flannel shirt. "Dodie, this is a dead end. I'd trash the room, but they didn't leave anything to trash."

I turned for the door. "Whatever. I'm done with them. Do you want to watch cartoons now?"

He followed me into the hall and closed the door behind him. "I have a better idea."

"Oh?" The old habit of following my big brother's bad ideas kicked in. "Please tell me it involves getting out of this house."

He passed me and paused at the top of the stairs. "It does."

"Then don't keep me in the dark, stupid. Tell me."

Vail pulled a key from the back pocket of his jeans and held it up, pausing for dramatic effect.

I lifted an eyebrow, waiting.

"I found this under a planter on the Thornhills' porch," he said. "They're not home, remember?"

Oh. I smiled. This was my idea of fun, and he knew it. "Hell, yes," I said. "Let's go."

19

VIOLET

"Did you know that Plainsview has a strip club?" Bradley asked as we walked from the Fell Hospital parking lot toward the doors. "It opened last year. It's only thirty minutes away. I might go tonight."

"Why are you telling me this?" I asked. "And why are you wearing that shirt?"

Bradley shrugged. I reached the door first, and he made no move to open it for me. "I'm making conversation. And this shirt is comfortable."

I gave him a sour glance as I opened the door. I didn't hold it open for him, either, instead letting it start to swing shut in his face. He grabbed it without comment.

He was wearing the same jeans and ball cap as yesterday, but he had switched to a sleeveless shirt. A muscle shirt, I thought it was called. It was gray, and his arms were bare in the brisk September sunshine. It wasn't even hot out.

The tattoo I'd glimpsed on his biceps yesterday was on full view now. It was Snoopy on his doghouse. It was badly done.

A Box Full of Darkness

"I have so many questions," I said, looking away again. "I don't want the answers to any of them."

Like the rest of Fell, the hospital was both old and ugly. The ceilings were low, the floors yellowed, the air heavy with unpleasant smells. This was a building that vividly remembered World War Two.

I'd never been here before. We hadn't broken bones as children, us Esmies. We didn't play hard enough for that. Vail had dislocated a shoulder once, and I had cut my chin deeply enough to leave a small scar, but that was all. Dodie had sailed through childhood without a flaw.

There was a quiet hum of busyness in the hospital, the crackle of announcements over the speaker system, low conversations. I led Bradley to a front desk labeled INFORMATION. A fortyish woman sat behind it, wearing glasses on a chain around her neck.

"Can I help you?" she asked, giving me a narrowed look.

Bradley stepped around me to talk to her. "Hey," he said. "How are you?"

Glasses Chain blinked at his biceps. I didn't know whether she was pondering his slightly seedy masculinity or, as I had, was wondering why Snoopy was there, and why half of his face was blurry. "I'm fine," she replied.

"We need to find Joan Sleeter," Bradley said. "Can you tell us where to go?"

The woman lifted her gaze, just a little too slowly, to his face. "Do you know Joan?"

"She's expecting me," Bradley said.

Glasses Chain lifted her phone. "She's the assistant to the administrator. I'll have to call her."

"You do that," Bradley said.

As the woman dialed and spoke on the phone, he glanced over his shoulder at me and waggled his eyebrows. "Dad told me who to ask for," he said.

"What name should I give her?" the woman asked, cupping her palm over the phone and leaning over the desk.

"Bradley Pine," he answered her. I was completely forgotten. "Gus Pine's son."

"I could have handled it," I grumbled, after the woman had directed us to the third floor and waved us on.

"Yeah," Bradley agreed. "But you're not wearing this shirt."

I pushed the button for the elevator. "Do you always use your biceps to get what you want?"

"It's worked since high school," he replied, and I let loose a reluctant laugh.

The elevator doors opened, and we both paused as we looked into its tiny parameters, badly lit by half-dead fluorescent lights. "Should we take the stairs?" I asked.

"It's only two floors." He didn't sound much more confident than I was, but he stepped inside. "It'll be fine."

It should have been amusing, the two of us silent in the elevator, listening as it creaked upward through the depths of the building. Normal people would laugh it off. But this was Fell.

"Is this place haunted?" I asked Bradley in the silence.

"That's a really good question," he replied.

The doors slowly opened, and we stepped into a soulless hallway, the waxed floors silent beneath our feet. There were far-off voices, but no other sign of humans. The hallway arched off both left and right, with no indication of which direction we were supposed to go. I picked left and started walking.

"You should apply," Bradley said as he followed me.

"What?"

"To the strip club. I bet they'd hire you. I'd pay to see you naked."

He was being annoying, but I knew he was doing it on purpose this time to distract both of us. To make us feel more normal as a chill crept up the back of my neck.

"You don't have any money," I shot back, playing along.

"Fine. I'd spend Dad's money to see you naked."

"Gus doesn't have enough money for that." It was definitely cold up here. Someone had turned the air-conditioning up high. There was a door at the end of the corridor, the only exit.

"We should have gone the other way," Bradley said.

"I don't think the other way is any better. Besides, people work here all day, every day. How haunted can it be?"

"Pretty haunted," was his reply. "Violet, let's go get a sandwich. I'll even buy."

I put my hand on the door and turned to him. "We're doing this," I said. "It's for Ben."

"What are we doing, exactly?"

He didn't know. We'd talked about his shirt and his biceps, not my little brother or the terrible night I'd had last night. I'd told Bradley almost nothing at all.

"Your father's file said that there were no medical records for Ben," I explained. "No photos, either. No dental records. He didn't go to school. According to the records, it's like Ben didn't exist."

Bradley frowned. "That can't be right."

"No, it can't. Ben existed. If he existed, he had to be born, right? And if he was born in Fell, it would have been here."

"So we're looking for a birth record." Bradley rubbed his chin. He hadn't shaved this morning, and it made a raspy sound. "Your mother didn't have anything?"

"Nothing. I got a complete catalog of her belongings when she died. There was no paperwork. But it gets stranger. I have no memory of my mother being pregnant."

"Wait. What? So—"

The door opened, bumping both of us back. A man in a white coat and horn-rimmed glasses—presumably a doctor—came through. "Excuse me," he said curtly, and walked past us down the hall toward the elevator.

I looked at Bradley. "You saw him, right?" I whispered, because for a minute, I wasn't sure. Who wore horn-rimmed glasses anymore?

"Yeah," Bradley said. "Violet, what's going on? You think your parents stole a baby?"

"I don't know anything," I hissed back. "That's why we're here. Let's do this quick."

I opened the door and walked through before I could second-guess myself, before I could turn and leave. It didn't matter that all signs pointed to this being a normal hospital on a normal day. Something was wrong. I'd spent too many years seeing the impossible—and paying the price—not to believe my own instinct.

That voice in my ear from yesterday. *Sister sent me.*

She couldn't be here. She wasn't capable of it. Then again, she'd never sent anyone after me before.

I knew why my gut had told me to bring Bradley with me.

We had gone the wrong way. This was a ward, with a nurses' station, corridors cluttered with equipment, orderlies coming and going. Three nurses in blue scrubs stood at the nurses' station, two of them talking quietly, one of them writing on a clipboard. Doors opened from the corridors, presumably to the patients' rooms.

Most people, I knew, hated hospitals. The smells, the fluorescent lights, the reminder of sickness and death. I didn't feel fear or hatred, only tired resignation. This was all too familiar to me. Invisible weight settled on my shoulders, and I felt my teeth try to grind. I took a breath and made myself relax.

I took a few swift strides to the nurses' station and spoke to one of the chatting nurses. "Excuse me. Hi there. I'm looking for Joan Sleeter."

The glance she gave Bradley and me was the incurious kind that only a nurse is capable of. It said *I don't know who you are, and if you're not my problem, I truly don't care.* "Oh, the admin wing," she said. "You went the wrong way at the elevator. You can get there through that door, then take a right." She pointed to a large set of double doors at the end of the corridor, sizable enough to easily wheel a bed through, as all hospital doors were.

They swung open, and an orderly pushed a man in a wheelchair through. A nurse passed them, going the other way, leaving the ward.

The nurse was wearing a starched white uniform, not the blue scrubs of the other nurses. Her hair was tied up tightly at the back of her head. The doors closed behind her.

I had paused too long. Bradley spoke up at my shoulder. "Thanks," he said. I felt his palm on my upper back, urging me forward.

I looked around. The incurious nurse had already turned away and was talking to her colleague again. Everyone else in here looked normal. Didn't they?

The orderly pushing the man in the wheelchair.

The elderly woman walking slowly down the hall, wheeling her IV stand, a bathrobe over her hospital gown.

The nurse passing at the end of the hall, wearing scrubs, a disposable coffee cup in her hand.

I turned back to the nurses' station, looking for the nurse who had been writing on a clipboard. She was gone.

Had she walked away while my back was turned? Or had she been there at all?

"Violet." Bradley's hand nudged me more forcefully. I started walking toward the doors the nurse had gone through, my steps slow.

"Nurses don't wear uniforms anymore," I said. "The ones that look like a white dress. With nylons. That kind."

"Um," he said. "Interesting."

"They don't," I insisted. "You didn't see her, did you? Shit, shit, shit."

My hands had gone cold, and it wasn't because of the overused air-conditioning. It wasn't even because of the ghosts, at least not entirely.

Ninety days. I'd spent ninety days in a mental treatment facility. My marriage had fallen apart. I had moved out, had been served divorce papers from Clay. He had Lisette and had begun the motion for custody. His reasoning was that I was mentally ill, and my hallucinations were scaring our five-year-old daughter. I wasn't able to care for her, the papers said. I was an unfit mother.

It's just an assessment, I was told. *Get an assessment, and then you can argue that you're perfectly sane. Then you'll get Lisette back.*

So I'd gone. It was just an assessment. But the assessment took days, and then they injected me with something that relaxed me and made me feel drunk. It had loosened my inhibitions, and I'd started talking.

I'd ended up in the hospital for ninety days while they treated my *dissociative episode, cause unknown.*

When I got out, I had lost custody of my daughter.

We approached the doors. Bradley pushed them open. The nurse I'd seen wasn't in the corridor ahead, but that didn't mean anything. She could have turned a corner or gone through a door.

Think, Violet, think.

I wasn't there anymore, back at that place. There was no assessment. I wasn't about to lose Lisette, because I'd already lost her years ago. Lisette wasn't mine anymore.

Who was that nurse, and what was she doing here?

Were there others?

Bradley steered me, just like the orderly had steered the man in the wheelchair. He put his hands on my shoulder blades and steadily urged me forward. He made no comment that I seemed suddenly unable to function.

A Box Full of Darkness

Another orderly passed us in the hall. Then a woman in a skirt and blouse. Then a young man, tall and thin, his hair messy as if he'd just gotten out of bed, wearing pajamas.

I was cold, so cold.

"Bradley," I whispered, "what do you see? Who do you see?"

"Keep walking," he said.

"That boy," I insisted. "Do you see him?" There was something familiar about the teenager in pajamas.

"Sure," Bradley said.

"You don't."

"Violet. *Keep walking.*"

He studied a sign on the wall, then steered me right, down a different corridor. This one was quiet, dim. There were no people. He stopped me in front of a door. He knocked on it politely.

"Come in," came a woman's voice from inside.

Bradley looked at me. His expression gave nothing away. Then he said, "I don't know what the hell's going on right now. But get your shit together, Esmie, so we can get out of here."

I grasped the words like a drowning woman grabs a life jacket. "Go screw yourself," I said back, my voice shaky.

"I do that every day," Bradley said matter-of-factly. "In the shower most mornings. It helps to clear the pipes because divorce is shitty. Now let's go talk to this lady."

I wiped clammy sweat from my forehead and nodded. "Fine, you pig."

He opened the door, and we walked through.

Joan Sleeter, at least, was real. She was about sixty, with a short perm as hard as a helmet and an ill-fitting sweater on. She didn't bother with introductions or greetings before she started in.

"Gus Pine found my daughter at the bus station and returned her home when she tried to run away in '81," she said, her voice the hard kind that hinted at how much she dealt with in her job every day.

"That's the only reason I took his call and agreed to this. But I don't like it. I don't run the records department, and I don't know what's going on."

Both of them looked at me. I was supposed to speak, to say something. To make this happen. I had come all this way. Instead, I froze.

There was a soft shuffle in the corner behind my right shoulder, a flicker of movement. I saw blue-striped cotton from the corner of my eye. Pajamas. The boy from the hallway was standing right there, and as I listened, he shuffled forward, closer to me.

I stared forward, refusing to look at him. *Go away*, I thought as sweat broke out on the back of my neck and my stomach turned. *You aren't really there. Go away.*

"Well?" Joan Sleeter asked.

The boy came closer, so close I could feel a chill on my upper arm and in my ear when he leaned to whisper into it. "Sister sent me," he said.

Darkness clouded the edges of my vision. I was going to pass out again. I dug my nails into my palms to fend it off.

From somewhere far away, Bradley slung an arm around my shoulders, tugging me into his side. He smelled strongly of Speed Stick deodorant. "Joan," he said, "my girlfriend here, Violet, just needs a quick favor."

The darkness receded, though the boy didn't move. Bradley's touch made the urge to pass out fade, though I was still rigid and sweaty, my voice gone.

Joan said something, but I didn't hear it because the boy was whispering again.

"She thinks you're crazy," he said. It was a normal voice, a teenage boy's voice, except for the fact that no one else could hear it and it was as cold as ice slicing into my ear. I stayed rigid under Bradley's arm.

"Her little brother died young," Bradley was saying. "A long time ago. Maybe you heard. It was tragic. Violet would like any record she can find of her brother. You know, as a memento. To help her move on."

He was good. It was a good story, told smoothly. The thought was far away as the boy kept talking, his voice burrowing into my brain.

"She thinks you belong here," the boy said. "Because you do, don't you? You should be locked up because you see things. You can't take care of yourself. Maybe she'll give you an assessment. Just an assessment, right? Just an assessment."

I flinched, hard, and Bradley noticed. He and Joan were still talking. He tugged me closer, and his hand went to my temple, pushing me down so my head was on his shoulder. "It's okay, honey," he said, as if he was comforting me. "Don't be upset."

"I suppose I could make a call," Joan said.

"Could you?" Bradley asked.

"Get out of here," the boy hissed in my ear. "Go home. Before they assess you. Before they find out how crazy you are."

My stomach turned. I gave a low moan.

"There, there, honey," Bradley said.

"Take a seat in the hall," Joan said. "I'll call the girl in Records. Just one phone call. That's all you get."

"Sure, sure," Bradley said, and as he turned me, I flinched again. But the boy was gone, his whispers silenced.

There was a bench in the hall, Joan's makeshift waiting room. It was deserted. We sat down.

My knees were shaking, and so were my hands. I leaned forward, my elbows on my thighs. Bradley was silent.

"A teenage kid in pajamas," I said after a moment, my voice quiet in the empty hall. "About seventeen or eighteen. A boy. Dark blue pajamas with white stripes. He's tall, stringy. Five-eight, five-nine, maybe even taller. Dark blond hair, curly, worn short at the sides and longer on top. Brown eyes. He's been dead awhile. Why does he look familiar?"

Next to me, Bradley went unnaturally still. I stared at the floor.

"You saw him?" he asked, and I heard fear in his voice, a low hum under the words.

"He was talking to me." I kept my gaze down, rubbed my palms together. "He was standing right there in the office, telling me to leave. But it wasn't really... him, in a way. I'm starting to understand that now."

"Then who was it?" Bradley asked.

"There was a ghost in my bedroom when I was growing up." I rubbed my palms harder, squeezing them, squeezing back the fear. "A... hostile one. Angry. Evil, maybe. I don't know how to describe it. She hated me. When I left that house, when I left Fell, I left her behind. But she's still here. She's sending messages through the others, I think."

I sounded absolutely objectively crazy. I sounded like one of those people who hallucinates, hears voices. One of those people who wander the streets, shouting. That guy who said a dog made him kill all those people. Someone like that.

Someone who had no business raising her daughter.

Someone who should be locked up. Again.

Bradley was frozen still, and he wasn't touching me anymore. He'd get up and walk away, leave me here. I wasn't going to blame him. If I were him, it was what I would do.

After a long silence, Bradley said, "You saw Martin Peabody. We went to high school with him."

I wiped my clammy forehead, racking my memory for the name. It was faintly familiar, but there was no face attached to it. "He was our classmate?"

"Tallest kid in school," Bradley said. "He was six feet by senior year, skinny as a rail. Blond, curly hair. No one else looked like that. Quiet kid, no friends, didn't talk much. That has to be him."

My stomach roiled, sour liquid boiling over itself, and I wiped my forehead again. "What happened to him?"

"He ate his father's shotgun three weeks after graduation," Bradley said. "No one knows why. He didn't leave a note."

I made a choked sound. I'd been gone by then. I'd left Fell before graduating—on top of my other failures, I was a high school dropout. When Martin Peabody killed himself, I was in Long Island, waiting tables and probably trying coke for the first time. I hadn't remembered Martin at all.

Fell was a cursed town, but it had its everyday tragedies, too. The kind that had nothing to do with the supernatural. The kind that weren't mysteries, unless you counted the mystery of what had been happening inside quiet, friendless Martin Peabody's head that day.

You could leave Fell and get away from the ghosts, if you really wanted. But anywhere you went, you'd still find the usual kinds of sadness, like the kids who wanted off the ride and eventually decided today was the day.

As always, I thought of Lisette. I wanted to touch her, feel her hair. She hated when I touched her anymore.

"Here's the thing, though," Bradley said. Some of the fear had left his voice, though not all of it. "Martin didn't die in the hospital. He died in his bedroom. So why is he here?"

"They aren't tied to their place of death," I explained. "I've seen people where they died. I've also seen them in their homes when they didn't die at home. I've seen them in other places. I've seen them in different stages of life, sometimes young, sometimes old. They've never spoken to me until now. The one in my bedroom . . . I don't think she died there. She died somewhere else. I don't know how I know. I just do."

"Are they in graveyards?" Bradley sounded curious now.

I shrugged. "I don't know. Probably. I don't hang out in graveyards." I twisted to look at him. He was sprawled against the wall, his knees carelessly wide. "Why are you still sitting here, helping me? Can't you tell I'm crazy?"

He blinked once. "I have so many questions, though. Can you talk to them? Can you ask Martin stuff if he comes back? There's stuff I want to know."

"It doesn't work like that," I said, though I didn't really know anymore, did I? What was happening was nothing like it had been in the past. I had thought I had it bad when I saw the occasional dead person, silent and polite. Now I was wistful about how easy those days had been.

"Ask him what it's like to be dead," Bradley said. "Ask him if there's God. Ask if Jesus is real. Does he have the beard and the long hair, like the pictures they show in Bible school? What's he like?"

I glared at him. "I'm going to the ladies' room." I stood up.

"They're good questions," he argued.

"I'm too tired for religion or philosophy right now, Bradley. And I have to pee."

"Fine," he said, defeated. He pointed back down the hall. "I saw a sign that way."

I turned and started walking. I caught sight of the restroom sign and aimed for it. There was no one else in this hallway, but at the end of the corridor, people walked by, going about their business. Nurses. Orderlies. Two doctors, walking and chatting. The nurses wore scrubs, not decades-old uniforms. I had been reduced to checking every person I saw, verifying if they were alive.

As I put my hand on the ladies' room door, a woman paused at the end of the hall and watched me. She was young, pretty, slender. Unlike with Martin Peabody, I recognized her almost immediately, even though I had never met her. I had seen her picture in the newspaper I'd read in the diner, right before I met Gus Pine.

I stood for a moment, looking at her. I could have sworn she saw me, too—truly saw me. I felt no harm coming from her, only sadness. I paused there, taking her sadness in.

I had no idea if I could talk to her, or if I could, what I would say.

Maybe that I was sorry. Maybe that I didn't have answers for her. Maybe that her murder would be solved someday, by someone. But I couldn't promise that, could I? And until that happened—if it happened—the unfairness of life meant that she would have to wait for justice.

I pushed open the door and walked through it before Cathy Caldwell could follow me.

20

DODIE

"Okay, so I'm not a CIA agent," Ethan said on the phone. "I'll tell you the truth this time."

"Are you sure about that?" I was standing in the kitchen, using the annoying wall phone that didn't feature anywhere to sit. Why had we never acquired another phone line? Oh, right, because we had no friends to call.

Before we left for the trip to the neighbors' house, Vail had taken his Jeep to the FunTime Foto at the nearest strip mall to drop off the roll of film he'd taken. He'd used the first half of the roll on some UFO investigation in California, and the second half taking pictures of Ben's footprints in the upstairs hall. He'd be gone for twenty minutes at most.

While I waited for him, I was alone in the house. I realized my mistake in not going with him the minute the door closed behind him. I didn't want to be here in the silence—I needed to talk to someone. Ethan had come to mind.

You have my phone number, he'd said. *Call me if you need me, Dodie.*

Incredibly, he'd answered the phone, even though it was the middle of the day.

"Yeah, I'm sure," he said now. His voice sounded more relaxed than it had on our date. "Here goes. I ran away to join the circus when I was ten. I've been with them ever since."

"You must really like the circus," I said, deadpan.

"Absolutely." His reply was as serious as mine. "I'm not just a clown now, I'm the *head* clown. And you'd be surprised by the benefits package."

"Oh, thank God," I breathed out. "I've always wanted to meet a sugar daddy with a benefits package."

We both laughed. His laugh was low and gentle—just as nice as I'd imagined. I was irrationally glad I got to hear it.

"Don't you want to know where I am?" I asked him. "Why I left New York so suddenly?"

"If you want to tell me, yes."

I did want to tell him. In all of my years living in New York, I had never talked to anyone about Ben. Ethan was a good listener, and the fact that I didn't know him very well—or at all, honestly—was a point in his favor. If he thought I was crazy, he could hang up, be done with me with that simple motion, and I wouldn't blame him. Much.

Besides, he'd guessed about Ben already. I was just giving him the details.

So I talked. I told him about Ben's disappearance twenty years ago, about the house sitting empty, about Ben calling us back. I told him about Ben's footprints in the hall and his toys in the attic. I told him how he'd crawled into my bed last night, as real as he'd ever been. That particular memory should have scared me, but it didn't. In the light of day, it was the best memory I could imagine. It felt less like a haunting and more like a gift.

Ethan listened quietly. I couldn't see his face to catalog his expression, but he didn't hang up. Maybe he just wanted to hear my crazy story to the end.

"It's okay if you think I'm delusional," I said when I'd finished. "I understand."

He cleared his throat. "It's surprising," he admitted. "But if you're delusional, then you're sharing the delusion with your sister and your brother. That is, if you're telling me the truth."

"I'm waiting for my brother to get back from the photo place," I said, deciding I may as well pile it all on. "Then we're going to break into the neighbors' house while they're away. You can see why I only ever go on first dates."

"Yes, I see." He still didn't hang up, though. "What do you expect to find at the neighbors' house?"

"I don't know. That's the fun of it. Maybe there's a scandalous secret to dig up over there. Maybe there's nothing, and they simply went on vacation to Disneyland. I've always preferred to lose myself in other people's lives, even without their permission."

"You have strange hobbies," he said, his voice flat. "I thought mine was bad, but I feel a little better now."

"You have a hobby? Tell me."

He paused briefly. "Ah," he said, an embarrassed sound. "I play Dungeons and Dragons. I know, I know—I'm thirty. Feel free to tease me. But it's a great game, I swear. You wouldn't make fun of it if you tried it."

I blinked, gripping the phone in my hand. I had just told him about my quest to reunite with my dead little brother, my plan to break into the Thornhills' house, and he was embarrassed—truly embarrassed—by his nerdy board game. I felt a flutter behind my breastbone, somewhere in the region of where my withered, long-dead heart was rumored to be.

No. I refused to be charmed. At all.

"Dodie?" Ethan asked.

"I would love to try your game," I said gently, "but I won't be back in New York for a while. I really don't know when."

"Of course," he said quickly. "I didn't mean we should literally play it. Because you don't do second dates."

"Right," I said as the front door opened and closed. Vail's boots clomped their familiar beat down the front hall. "My brother is back."

"So you're off to do some breaking and entering?"

"Just a little bit." I made my tone light, refusing to acknowledge that I had to force it this time. "No one gets hurt."

"Okay. Have fun, Dodie. Call me again if you want to."

What did that mean? Did he want me to call him or not? I frowned. So far in life, I had spent exactly zero seconds wondering what a man wanted from me. I wasn't going to start now.

"Maybe I will," I said to him cryptically. "Goodbye."

Vail was in the kitchen now, his big bulk seeming to take up half the room. His frown mirrored mine. "Who was that? A boyfriend?"

I tossed my hair back over my shoulders, much as I would have in the shampoo ad I'd bailed on to come to Fell. "I told you, Vail. Nightly ecstasy. Someone has to provide it. I'm interviewing candidates."

Vail made a convincing gagging sound, and I pushed down the feeling that I wanted to take the words back.

"Fine, I'm never asking again," my brother said. "Let's go."

There was mail and a single newspaper on the Thornhills' front step because Vail had taken the others when he lifted the key.

The grass was overgrown by a week or two, and the planter on the front porch was black and dead. I had been excited to go on this little expedition, but now I wasn't so sure, and it wasn't just because I could hear Ethan's perplexed voice in my head.

Vail didn't seem to have any hesitation as he unlocked the front door and swung it open. He stepped inside, making his usual clatter of noise. I followed behind.

"Oi!" I called out, using the English accent I'd learned in a long-ago acting class, back when I thought I might act in something. The accent came out when I was nervous. "Anyone 'ome?"

Vail gave me an annoyed look, and I wedged the toe of my sneaker hard into the back of his jean-clad knee. He swatted me away.

"No one's home," he said, as if I was slow in comprehension. "Let's look around."

"What are we looking for?" I asked.

"Anything interesting," was his laconic reply.

I walked into the Thornhills' living room, which was packed with fussy furniture. An overstuffed sofa in a gaudy floral pattern. An overwrought side table. A glass-top coffee table that was probably a nightmare to keep clean. A floral throw rug under it all.

The room was pristine—it was obviously the "good" room, kept for company that never came. There was no way Mrs. Thornhill ever sat with her feet up on that sofa, reading a racy novel and eating bonbons. No way Mr. Thornhill spilled chip crumbs there while he drank beer.

My siblings and I had done this kind of break-in plenty of times. If one lived nearby and was stupid enough to go away for a period of time, leaving one's door unlocked or an easily opened window in reach, then an Esmie child might find their way into one's home. At first, we did it for the usual reasons—to search for money or food, neither of which was given out often at our house. Then it was simply a habit. I liked being in other people's houses. I liked looking at people's photographs, the snapshots and children's drawings they pinned to their fridge with magnets. Like I had at the birthday party, I occasionally stole a snapshot. A picture of a picnic, maybe, or a beach trip. You could keep your wedding and baby photos. Those weren't my style.

A Box Full of Darkness

It was the forbidden thrill that drew us to it, even more than money or food. There was no one to stop us, no one to say no. Our parents didn't know or care where we were. Our teachers noticed even less. Why grow morals when no one cares whether you have them or not?

I looked around the Thornhills' living room, thinking, *That isn't entirely true, is it? That we don't have morals. Because we never brought Ben with us when we snuck into an empty house. We never taught him that. We taught him songs and letters and stories and games, but not that.*

My gaze snagged on a photo in a frame on a side table. I picked it up and studied it, thinking at first that I might add it to my collection. Then I realized what I was looking at.

The photo was old—it was black-and-white. The Thornhills were younger in it than they were in my memory. They stood in their front yard, Mrs. Thornhill in a simple dress with her hair in a perm, Mr. Thornhill in his Saturday pants and white shirt. Between them stood a boy of ten or eleven, gangly and tall. His hair was clipped in a buzz cut and he stood awkwardly, his smile for the camera rather shy. Mr. and Mrs. Thornhill each had a proud hand on his shoulder.

The Thornhills hadn't had any children. Was the boy a nephew? It didn't seem like it. They stood too close to him, their hands on his shoulders too possessive. They'd kept this photo in their formal living room for decades.

I was still pondering as Vail's steps came down from upstairs. I met Vail in the hall.

"The bed is made, but there are clothes all over it," he said. "The closet looks like it has clothes missing, and I didn't see a suitcase. They packed and left on purpose, but they did it in a hurry."

"Did the Thornhills have a son?" I asked him.

He shook his head. "They didn't have kids."

"There's a photo of a boy, though." I held it out to him.

Vail studied the photo for a long moment, like I had. "That's strange," he said. "I wonder where he went."

There was a moment of weighted silence between us. Was Ben's disappearance not the only one in the neighborhood? Why hadn't anyone mentioned the Thornhill boy when all of those policemen were in our house? Why hadn't Gus Pine said anything about it to Violet or added it to the police report?

"Well, the Thornhills haven't moved out." I motioned to the furniture around me. "So it must be a vacation."

"A hasty vacation." Still holding the photo, Vail headed for the kitchen. "They didn't cancel their newspaper subscription."

I followed him into the kitchen, which had a small farm-style table covered in a gingham tablecloth. "There are dishes in the sink," I pointed out.

Vail opened a high cupboard and pondered the contents. Without a word, he grabbed a box of granola bars, took one, and handed me one.

I put it in my pocket for later. Old habits die hard.

Vail was frowning. He looked particularly off-putting when he did that, though I could grudgingly admit that he was good-looking. Women had always loved Vail, even from the time he was twelve or thirteen. Girls got cross-eyed and swoony when he was near. Violet and I got used to it early.

Vail never encouraged them. If a girl was persistent enough, he'd date her for a short while, then tell her that it was over. No matter how she cried, he never changed his mind. And those were the girls he *liked*. The rest, he fended off carelessly, like you fend off flies with a can of Raid.

"What?" he asked, looking at me and scowling harder.

Until I came back to Fell, I couldn't recall when I'd spent this much time alone with my big brother. Possibly I never had. The little sister in me was thrilled about it, but it was a fate worse than death to let him know that. "Vail," I asked in my most treacly, annoying voice, "are we bonding?"

"No," he replied, turning to open the fridge. "Hey, there's one can of Coke in here. I'm calling it."

"I think we are," I said. "I think we'll be best friends now. Let's pop popcorn and watch TV tonight. You can braid my hair."

Vail had opened the Coke and took several long, deep swallows, his throat flexing in annoyance. I knew what was coming. I ducked as he aimed the belch at me.

"How old are you, you pig?" I shouted at him. "I can smell that in my hair."

"Stay on topic, Dodie," he said, unconcerned. "The Thornhills left in a rush, and I want to know why."

"Who cares why?" I straightened and took a step back, out of the gaseous range. "Mrs. Thornhill was the one to tell the police that Violet was crazy. I hope she has food poisoning and a sunburn, wherever she is."

"There are milk and eggs in the fridge," Vail said. "It's full of food. Who goes away on a long vacation with a full fridge?"

I wiped my palms on the hips of my pants. "You think something chased them out of here. You think they saw Ben."

"The landscapers saw Ben," my brother pointed out. "Maybe the Thornhills did, too. Or maybe they saw something else. Like those lights I saw last night."

I rubbed my palms again and thought it over. If you started seeing eerie lights and ghost children at the neighbors' long-empty house, you might pack your bags and decide that a trip to Bermuda was urgent.

Then again, maybe they had seen their dead son.

"It's possible that they had a different reason," I insisted, mostly to myself. "A family member needed them for something. An emergency."

Vail shrugged. "It's possible. But we know they weren't abducted, and they aren't dead."

I felt my jaw drop. "You thought there were dead people in here? And you still brought me into this house?"

"I thought it was unlikely since their car is gone, but you never know."

"You are such a jerk. Can we leave? I don't like it here, even without dead bodies. Something about this doesn't feel right."

Vail put down his can of Coke and looked thoughtful for the first time, the scowl and annoyance leaving his expression. "You're right. This is weird. There are neighbors on the other side of us—a family with a kid."

"A kid?" I said in surprise. "How old?" There had never been other children in this neighborhood when we were young. There were children elsewhere in Fell, children we went to school with, but when we came home from school, there was only ever us, with the childless Thornhills on one side, the old lady on the other, and the empty house across the street. I sometimes thought wistfully that if I'd had even one friend as a child other than my siblings, I might have grown up slightly normal. I'd at least have had a chance at it.

"About ten, I think," Vail said, answering my question. "Their name is Chatham. We should talk to them, ask if they know where the Thornhills went."

"If you want." I shrugged. Anything to get out of this house. "I'll do the talking. People like me more than they like you."

"That isn't saying much." Vail swigged the last of his Coke.

I picked up the photo from where Vail had left it on the counter. It seemed wrong to move it, to take it, even though the Thornhills had left it behind. I walked back to the living room to put it where I'd found it.

The photo had shifted in the cheap frame, and I poked at it to put it back. I noticed something placed behind the photo and tugged it out.

A Box Full of Darkness

It was a postcard. The front showed an expanse of beach and blue water, with the words *Sydney, Australia*. I turned it over and read:

> December 18, 1968
>
> Mom and Dad,
>   I am in Australia now. The navy has stationed me here, for the next six months at least. I will not be home for Christmas or for a visit. I'm sorry I left all those years ago, but like I keep saying, I couldn't live in our home any longer. I had to go. I know you don't understand, but maybe someday you will. In the meantime, have a merry Christmas.
>
> Your son,
> Alfie

"He isn't dead," I said to Vail when I returned to the kitchen.

"Who isn't?" Vail asked.

"The Thornhills' son. There's a postcard from him. He ran away and joined the navy. He never came home. That's why we never saw him."

My brother scratched his jaw, and neither of us mentioned our relief at the idea that there wasn't another dead child to think about.

"Maybe they went to visit him," Vail said.

My gaze caught on the kitchen trash can. There was a photo in it, tossed on top of the garbage. I didn't have to pick it up to see that it was a recent portrait of the Thornhills, one they'd had professionally taken. Their son still sat in the good sitting room, but their couples' portrait was in the trash.

It crossed my mind for the first time that the Thornhills might not have been very happy all those years with their son gone.

I pictured fights, stony silences. Weeping, some of it loud, some of it suppressed into silence or covered by the running water in the bathroom, like mine. Hissed insults. Plates banged loudly on countertops. A woman's scathing voice. A man's angry roar. Maybe one or the other had left, then come back. Over and over, in a miserable cycle. Until this house was unbearable for both of them, and they had left for good.

There was no Bermuda vacation. Just a son long gone to the other side of the world, more tears, and phone calls to lawyers.

The back of my neck went cold, and my stomach roiled.

"Dodie?" Vail said.

Without answering my brother, I turned and left the house.

21

VIOLET

If you didn't count Sister—who plagued my nightmares from a very early age—I first saw the ghost of a dead person when I was in first grade. Apparently, I asked the teacher why the boy at the back of the classroom didn't have to do homework like the rest of us. When questioned about this injustice and asked who I was talking about, I pointed to an empty corner. I was sent home. My mother was furious.

Oh, what a joy it is to have a childhood in which you're a freak. To understand early that you're so unlike other people that you're impossible for them to comprehend. To learn not to trust what you see and to certainly never speak of it. To think you might be insane, and to know that if you are, you're alone in a world in which no one cares.

The dead don't show me how they died. They don't tell me their stories. It would almost be better if they did, if in my freakishness I could at least have some understanding of what made them do what they do. But they appeared in silence. Sometimes they looked at me with stark, pleading expressions, and sometimes they looked away, as if they didn't know I was there. As if my torture was, to them, unnoticeable as they went about their business.

None of them had ever spoken to me. Not until the young man in the storage unit—that had been the first. But now, as I sat on the toilet in the ladies' room at Fell Hospital with my pants around my ankles and heard the bathroom door open, I realized it had started earlier than that. It had started with the old woman back in Long Island, putting the landscapers' phone number in the middle of her bed for me to see. That hadn't happened before, either, and I hadn't paid it close enough attention. I had been too distracted by the phone call summoning me home to Ben.

Ben, who had spoken. To someone other than me.

Sister had no mercy. She gave no quarter for humiliation, which was why the bathroom door opened after I'd finished urinating and before I could pull my pants up. I froze in startlement as the footsteps came into the otherwise empty ladies' room.

Oh, Sister, I thought through the haze of terror. *I hate you so much.*

I thought it might be Cathy Caldwell who came into the bathroom, but it wasn't women's feet I spied under the stall door. It was girls' feet in a familiar pair of Oxfords.

There was no other sign as Alice McMurtry, my dead childhood friend, came into the room. The lights didn't dim and there was no icy hand on my neck. There was only Alice's footsteps. She had hated those shoes, but her mother had bought them, and Alice didn't get to pick what shoes she wanted to buy. She was only twelve. So she had obediently worn the shoes, since she had no other pair to wear to school. She had most likely been wearing them when she died. They had probably found those shoes on her feet as she lay by the train tracks all alone.

Alice's feet stopped outside my stall door, and I thought, *Sister will never stop torturing me. Never.*

"Alice," I choked out, my voice wavering in the silent bathroom.

"It's all right," Alice said. Her voice was thin, as if she was on a bad phone line, but it was hers. I hadn't heard it in so many years. I suddenly felt like crying.

I put my hand on the closed stall door. I should pull my pants up, but what did it matter? I had been humiliated so many times since I was sent home that day in first grade that it didn't matter anymore. One more humiliation could be added to the pile.

"I have to tell you something," Alice said. "I don't have much time."

I pressed my hand to the door and tried to breathe. The stall door was cool, as if it had been kept in a refrigerator.

"She wants you to leave," Alice said from beyond her death, which had happened so long ago. "She's trying to scare you. She doesn't want you here."

"Sister?" I asked.

Alice's voice dropped to a whisper, as if that word had scared her. "She's very dangerous. But please don't go."

So Sister wanted me gone. I had felt the hostility since I came here, worse than before I left. "Who put the phone number on the bed?" I asked. "If it wasn't her, if she didn't want me to come, who was it?"

"We're trying to help you," Alice said. "You can make her go away."

"I can't." The only one that had ever made me truly afraid was Sister. The fear of the others I'd seen was an old bruise now, dull with overuse. The fear of Sister was a bottomless pit, sharp and acrid, a roller coaster drop to the center of the earth. "I can't."

"You can," Alice said. "Violet, you can do anything."

My tears were hot and icy at the same time as they stung my eyes. "Alice, I'm sorry," I said. "I should have been there. You shouldn't have been alone."

"It wasn't so bad," my friend said. "It didn't hurt. There was nothing you could have done."

I thought of Ben, dying alone like Alice had, and the tears slipped free and slid down my cheeks. I couldn't remember the last time I'd cried. "What happened?" I asked her.

"I don't remember," she said. "It doesn't matter. It was fast. My time was over, that's all. We only get so much time."

I closed my eyes. This had always been here. Alice, Ben, my parents. Cathy Caldwell and the rest of them. You don't put your past behind you, no matter how much you tell yourself you do. It sits waiting, patient, until you come back. You never get very far away. Especially when you're me, and the place you come from is Fell. I would never get far away from this town.

"Tell me what to do, Alice," I said.

"This is the wrong place to look," she replied. "You won't find him here."

"Then where do I go?"

"You already know," she said. "It's all connected. He's been telling you and telling you. You have to go back to the beginning. The real beginning."

I had thought Ben's birth was the beginning. That was why I was here. Did she mean to go back further than that? How? And to where?

My hand was clammy on the stall door, my tears drying on my cheeks. I was running out of time. I could feel it. "Is he my brother?" I asked her.

Silence.

I glanced down. The shoes were still visible under the door. "Alice?" I called.

Silence, and then a whisper. "It's the wrong question. Be careful, Violet. Three of you went into the house. Only two of you will leave."

"What does that mean?"

"I have to go."

"Alice!"

The squeak of shoes on the floor, then silence.

I was cold now. I hadn't felt threatened when Alice was here, but now a chill crawled up the back of my neck. I stood, pulling up my pants in a hurry, flushing the toilet. I pushed open the stall door.

The bathroom was empty. There was only my reflection in the mirror. My face was pale and my eyes were red. I quickly scrubbed my palms over my cheeks.

I stepped forward and turned on the tap.

There was a cold breath of air, and then Martin Peabody appeared in the mirror behind my shoulder. His tall form was familiar now. In his eyes was nothing but torment.

The edges of my vision went gray. I gripped the counter as the water hissed. I fought the dizziness. I couldn't pass out again. Not here.

"Sister sent me," Martin said.

I opened my mouth, but only a strangled sound came out. Humiliation upon humiliation, it seemed. I was not only going to see a ghost while I was on the toilet, but I was now going to pass out on this bathroom floor, alone.

Still, I fought it. I felt my nails scrabble against the hard counter. I tried to make my throat work. In the mirror, Martin's hand came up. He was going to touch me, like the boy in the storage unit had. He was going to push me, grip the back of my neck the way Sister would, and it was going to be horrible, and I was helpless. This would happen over and over, and I would always be helpless.

Lisette, I thought.

There was a quick wash of sensation from Martin Peabody, as if he had brushed me with his fingertips. The sadness was icy and suffocating, and he had believed with every part of himself that it would never end, that he would feel like this forever. He had believed that to the last moment.

I dropped on weakened legs, falling to my knees, pulling away from Martin. As I went down in a dizzy spiral, my forehead knocked against the edge of the counter. The water was still running.

Not again. Not again.

The room spun. The floor came closer.

Somewhere, a door opened with a bang. Footsteps approached. This was going to get worse. Someone else was coming. There was more than one, there were too many, and I didn't know how to—

Hands gripped me, pulled me up. Big, warm hands. A hard shoulder was pressed into my midsection.

Then Bradley Pine stood up, threw me over his shoulder, and carried me from the room.

22

VIOLET

It started raining after Bradley parked his car. We ended up at Springheel Park, in the small paved lot facing the trees. The clouds rolled overhead, and in the park, I could see a family packing up their things from a picnic table, hurrying to get out of the rain.

I rolled my window down and hooked my arms over the door, resting my head on my arms. The rain was cool and soft on my cheek and my hair, soothing me. My forehead throbbed, though my clash with the bathroom counter had left only a small red mark. For the first time since I'd come back to Fell—and despite what had just happened to me—I felt oddly, perfectly calm.

"Who was it?" Bradley asked from the driver's seat. He had carried me all the way out of the hospital over his shoulder. No one had stopped him. He'd dropped me into his car and started driving, as if he wanted to get out of there just as much as I did. "Who came at you?"

"Martin," I said without lifting my head. The cold, suffocating darkness when he had touched me made me shiver. That poor boy.

What if Lisette felt that way and wasn't telling me? I needed to call Lisette.

"Did he say anything?" Bradley asked.

"Lots of things," I replied. "I don't blame him. He didn't want to do it. He just wants to sleep. What made you come in to get me?"

"You were gone too long," Bradley replied. "No one else went in or out of the bathroom. Something wasn't right about it. I got a feeling."

Rain was trickling through my hair to my scalp. It felt good, as if it anchored me to the real world. The people at the picnic table were real, I knew. They were alive, trying not to get wet. They anchored me, too.

If it weren't for Bradley, I'd still be on the floor of that bathroom, so I took a breath. "Thank you," I said. "For coming with me. For coming to get me. For getting me out of there."

I glanced up to find him looking at me. His eyebrows lifted slightly.

"How hard was that for you to say?" he asked.

"Very hard," I admitted.

He cupped a hand around his ear. "I'm suddenly hard of hearing, Violet. Say it again."

He had to make this difficult, but for once, I didn't mind. "Thank you," I repeated.

He leaned closer, his hand still cupped around his ear. "What was that? You're saying it out the window."

I lifted my head and pulled all the way back into the car. I raised my voice a notch louder, enunciating the words. "Thank you, Bradley."

He lowered his hand, looking satisfied. "You should thank me. I had to go into a girls' bathroom. Someone could have been *shitting* in there."

"I'm aware," I said. "Now tell me what Joan said. Because I assume you got an answer from her."

Bradley lifted his hat, ran a hand through his hair, and lowered the hat again. The Snoopy tattoo flexed on his arm.

"Just say it," I said. "I can take it." I already knew what he would say.

"Violet, your mother gave birth three times in that hospital. You, your brother, and your little sister. That's it."

It was upsetting. I had questions. And at the same time, I felt several pieces deep inside me fall into place at last. Our mother hadn't been pregnant with Ben. She hadn't given birth. She'd come home with a baby in her arms, and we'd gone to the attic to get the crib after he was already born. Those memories finally made sense.

Who was that baby? Who was the little boy we'd lived with for six years? What family had missed him, wondered where he was?

Thinking of that family made my head ache, so I said, "Tell me about your kids. How old are they? What are their names?"

He didn't remark on my change of subject. "Guess," he said.

"Timmy and Tommy," I said immediately. "Twins. They call the kids in school with glasses Four Eyes. Their teachers hate them."

"Not quite," Bradley said. "Lance is nine." He caught the look on my face and shrugged. "My ex chose that name. Lance is all right. We get along. I get him. It's the younger one, Amy, that I don't quite get."

"Amy?" I asked.

"She's five. I picked that name. My ex got to pick the first name, and I got to pick the second."

"I like it."

"So do I. Her head's in the clouds, though. She dreams all the time. Barely pays attention in school, just draws on the backs of her notebooks. She tells bedtime stories to us instead of the other way around. She makes up songs for her stuffed animals to sing and plays for them to put on. She has a hat with unicorn ears and a horn on it, and she refuses to take it off. Wears it to school and everything."

I leaned my head back against the seat, feeling myself smiling. "You're telling me your daughter is cute?"

"The cutest. Divorce is shit. Your kids either live with a split, or they live with two parents who don't belong together and fight all the time. I don't know what the answer is." He looked away from me, at the rain out his window. "I thought I would do it different when I grew up and got married, but it didn't turn out that way. I try to be friendly with their mother, though. I try to be nice. I don't know if it's working. All I know is that I don't want to handle it the way Dad and Mom did."

We were quiet for a moment as the rain landed softly on the roof of the car. I thought of the storage unit, the petty things Gus kept there, the box of wedding photos that Bradley had kicked in frustration.

"We can do better than our parents," I said. "I know we can. We don't have to make the same mistakes they made."

Bradley turned to look at me, his expression soft and honest for once. "Violet, we don't have custody of our kids. I got kicked out, then got laid off, and I'm living at Dad's. You're even worse. You see dead people, and your mother stole someone's baby."

I cleared my throat. "When you put it like that." I narrowed my eyes at him as he smirked. "It isn't funny, Bradley."

"It isn't funny at all," he agreed, forcing the smirk from his face.

"Maybe there was a legal adoption," I tried. "Maybe there's paperwork."

"Sure, a legal adoption," Bradley said. "That takes years, but your parents never said anything or told you about it, and they could have their own kids anyway. A legal adoption that left no paperwork in your mother's belongings or anywhere else. A legally adopted kid who was never taken to a doctor, never sent to school, and never had his picture taken."

So Bradley Pine was the clear-thinking one. How far I had fallen.

The people in the park had packed up and loaded their car. They started it and drove away, leaving us alone.

You have to go back to the beginning, Alice had said. *The real beginning.*

All we'd found since coming back to Fell were dead ends. Where was the real beginning? How could we find it?

"I'm going to pursue this," I said to Bradley. "I'm going to find out who Ben was and what happened to him. I'm going to come clean to his real family, if I can. You're off duty. Take me back to the hospital and drop me off at my car. Go back to your life and forget about all of this."

"No way," Bradley said. "I'm in it now. You're seeing Martin Peabody and dealing with stolen babies, and I'm supposed to rake leaves? Fuck it." He raised his hands from the wheel in a helpless gesture, and then he smirked at me again. "Besides, you need me, Violet. Admit it. You *need* me."

"I don't need you," I shot back, mostly by reflex.

"Uh-huh, sure. Because you love napping on bathroom floors so much."

"Okay, you were useful that *one* time."

"And when you passed out in the storage locker, and I called the ambulance?"

"It isn't going to happen again," I lied. Something bad was definitely going to happen. Probably much worse than fainting in a bathroom. This was Fell, and I was who I was, and there was Sister.

I felt a pang at not having Bradley as a bodyguard anymore, but I didn't want Bradley to encounter Sister, just as I had never wanted my siblings to encounter her. It was safest for the others if I dealt with Sister alone.

"Just tell me where to go next, and we'll go," Bradley said, obstinate as an ox.

"No."

He rubbed the bridge of his nose with a fingertip. "I've been thinking. If someone's baby got stolen, they'd report it to the police, right? Which means Dad might know about it. Or he could find out."

I felt the yawning pit of my fear of Sister, the inescapable trap of it. "Bradley, you don't understand how dangerous this is."

"You mean the ghost from your bedroom? The one that hates you? What are you gonna do, Violet? Are you gonna let her win?"

I swallowed, my dry throat flexing as I stared ahead. Normal people didn't understand this fear, the fear of Sister. I had never told my parents about her. I had never told Vail or Dodie, because Sister had always appeared to me, not them. If I didn't tell my siblings, then Sister would stay focused on me. Only me, and she would leave them alone.

In my head, that was the deal. Me for them. Come to my room, and in exchange for my silence, never go to theirs.

So my siblings didn't know what she was capable of, how she could make you curl up in the dark, crying softly, trying not to wet yourself. How I'd wake up and see her standing in my bedroom, her back to me, always her back to me. Just the shape of her, with her hate and malevolence coming off of her in waves.

My bedroom door would be shut, even if I'd left it open when I went to sleep. The curtains would drift where there was no breeze. The closet door would creak as it moved. The dresser would shuffle a few inches along the wall, making a soft scraping sound. The lamp would flicker on, then off again. There would be a hiss of breath, close, as if in my ear, even though I could see her across the room. A clicking sound I couldn't identify, cold and sharp.

And I would crouch in bed, trying not to make a sound, because if Sister noticed me—if she turned around—then she would—she would—

I closed my eyes. Was it Sister's baby who had been stolen? Was that why she was so angry? No, I had seen Sister before Ben was born. Was Sister connected to Ben at all? How could she be?

Had she killed Ben? Had Sister taken my little brother from his hiding place that day?

"Violet?" Bradley asked.

The answer was close, so close. Alice had told me so. *He's been telling you and telling you,* Alice had said.

And, *Three of you went into the house. Only two of you will leave.*

And, *Violet, you can do anything.*

"Violet?" Bradley asked again.

"Ask your father," I said, my eyes still closed. "Ben was born in 1963. We got him as either a newborn or very close to it. Our parents told us that Ben's birthday was July 31, but that might not be true, since there's no birth paperwork. If they stole a baby, why would they tell us his real birthday? My parents were liars."

Bradley was quiet.

"It was summer," I continued. "July or August. He was still drinking formula and didn't start on solid food until . . ." I put a hand to my forehead. I could remember feeding Ben solid food, but the timeline was blurry. The house always fogged my memories. "Thanksgiving? I don't know. I'll try to remember. But if he wasn't born on July 31, then the baby would have been born in June, July, or August of 1963. Not before and not after."

"Okay," Bradley said. "Dad and I will look into it. What will you do?"

I dropped my hand and opened my eyes. A headache was starting in my temples. If only two of us were going to leave the house, then something was after one of my siblings.

Unless the person who wouldn't leave was me.

If the house wanted me, then so be it. But it wasn't going to take Vail, and it wasn't going to take Dodie.

"Take me back to my car," I told Bradley. "I'm going home."

23

VAIL

My very first memories were of the figure standing over my bed.

I don't know how old I was, but the light was bright white, and at the same time my vision was cloudy, as if someone had placed a layer of gauze over my eyes. I couldn't make out details, only shadows. There was just the light and the shape standing there, looking down at me.

I remember being afraid. In the beginning, on the nights the figure came, it didn't move or speak. I'd open my eyes to the light and see it there, like a bad dream, and no matter how I tried, I couldn't move.

Maybe it was the same shadow every night. Or maybe there was more than one.

After a while, the fear changed into a tired resignation. Every time I closed my eyes at night, I knew the figure might come, that I might wake frozen in the light, and there was nothing I could do. There's nothing kids can ever do about their situations. There was no point in talking about it, just as there was no point in talking about my parents' hatred of each other or the fact that no one ever asked me whether I had done my homework, or about the time my father looked at me with a bleary, hungover gaze as if he'd never seen me before and said, "I thought I'd be a Hollywood actor. What happened to my life?" There was no point talking about anything.

Later, on the bad nights, I'd open my eyes and see the figure moving. Sometimes the light would shift, as if someone was adjusting a lamp. There were whispers, words I couldn't hear, as if there were more of them outside my vision. They never touched me, only left me frozen in terror before the light went out.

I had periods when they came frequently. Then weeks or months when they never came at all, and I'd think it was over.

One night, when I was eight, I went to bed early because I was getting over a cold. I slept restlessly, and when I woke, the bright light hurt my eyes, my head. I had the gauze over my eyes, but it seemed thinner this time.

There was only one shadowy figure, standing there, looking down at me, perfectly still. Male or female—it was impossible to tell. This one was a tall, narrow blur, and though I couldn't see its face, I knew it was looking at me. Hostility rolled off of it like a stench. I was so afraid that I stopped breathing.

It spoke for the first time. A harsh whisper, close, as if right in my ear, though the figure hadn't bent down. It just stared down at me, and somehow it spoke.

"Wake up," it said.

Finally, I screamed, and then I jerked awake in my dark bedroom. My pajamas were soaked with cold sweat. No one came into my room to comfort me. Maybe no one had heard. I lay alone for the rest of the night, curled up and silent.

Soon after that night, Ben arrived. My little brother, the only brother I would ever get. From the first, I loved him so hard I could feel it like an ache behind my rib cage. It was a feeling I understood by pure, primal instinct. Ben was mine. He was ours.

We set up his crib, and in my mind I pictured the figures standing over my brother, staring down at him with their cold hatred as his little arms and legs pumped, a helpless and defenseless baby. I couldn't stand it. At night I'd sneak into his room after the house was asleep, put my pillow and blanket on the floor, and sleep there. I was ready to fight them off in a way I had never been able to fight when they came for me.

The figures didn't come for Ben. When I slept by his crib, they didn't come for me, either. When Ben became a toddler, he'd sometimes slip into bed with either Violet, Dodie, or me, snuggling us in his sleep. I knew he was safe if he was sleeping with one of us. And when he slept with me, the figures didn't come. During the years with Ben, I saw the light only rarely.

And then, a game of hide-and-seek and Ben was gone. Unexplained. Unexplainable.

What was I supposed to think?

I'll tell you what I thought. What I *knew*. They took him. I was supposed to find him that day, but I was too slow, too lax. I wasn't on my guard. The figure over my bed had shone its light on him, put the gauze over his eyes. *Wake up,* it had said, and my little brother had been afraid just like I had been, and for once I wasn't there to help him. To protect him.

Ben had disappeared in the middle of the day, so how had they done it? Why hadn't any of us seen the light? Why hadn't I seen it? If I had seen the light, I would have done anything. I would have gladly offered myself to whatever they wanted if they would just leave Ben. But they didn't give me the chance.

After I moved out of this house, I didn't see the light and the figures anymore. I had plenty of other things to keep me awake at night—like, say, agonizing grief, heavy existential dread mixed with rage, and bleak contemplation of the future. Adulthood is fun.

Eventually, I found some books and looked up my childhood

problem. I read about sleep paralysis, lucid dreaming, and the various types of seizures. Any one of those things would explain what I'd seen as a kid, those nights with the light and the figures over my bed—but they didn't explain it to me.

I knew what my problem was. It wasn't sleep paralysis, and it wasn't seizures. My problem was fucking aliens. They had studied me, found me wanting, and had taken my brother instead. And then they'd left.

So I studied aliens, the way they had studied me.

I could work for VUFOS until I was a hundred, and it would never bring my brother back. I understood that. But my investigations were the only things that made me feel even a little bit better. People said that Violet was the crazy one, but only VUFOS made me feel sane.

When my interview subjects talked about what they saw—descriptions that everyone else in their life had scoffed or laughed at—I understood. I looked at their bedrooms and their abduction sites with dead seriousness. I wandered fields in which strange markings had appeared overnight. I investigated dead cattle. I measured electromagnetic signals and radiation. I studied flight schedules from nearby airports. I stayed awake for nighttime vigils, looking for lights in the sky where they'd been reported before. This was how the world made sense to me, and the aliens who had visited me as a kid stayed away. They knew I was onto them. When I did sleep at night, it was always in unbroken darkness.

Then I had come back to this house, and the lights had come back, and those old words from my childhood had been written on the wall. WAKE UP.

Those fucking aliens again. But what happened wasn't right. I was a grown-up now, not a kid, and I had spent years studying a lot of aliens—secondhand accounts, but still—and I knew my business.

The thing in the living room had grabbed me by the throat, which had never happened in my childhood. I had felt its fingers, which were cold and dead. It had whispered those old words, but it had sounded different. I hadn't been frozen, I hadn't had the veil over my eyes, and when I aimed the vase at it, I had hit something solid. Then the thing had vanished.

And it had had a rancid, dead smell. A stench.

I'd assumed it was aliens, but I hadn't been thinking straight in the moment. That wasn't how aliens behaved. Not to me, and not in any of the encounters I had studied. I'd been shunted back to my childhood at first, reacting like that scared little kid, but now I stood in the Thornhills' house and thought clearly about the evidence. I'd been running on the theory that the Thornhills might have been abducted, but clearly they hadn't. Why had I thought they had? Because it was a habit, the easiest explanation in a mind like mine?

You're supposed to be an investigator, you idiot, I told myself. *So investigate.*

Dodie had left, and I'd seen her walk off down the street. She was upset, but that was fine. She'd get over it, and until she did, I would work alone. As I always did.

I left, not bothering to lock the front door behind me, and strode toward home. The street was silent. A breeze gusted through, scraping some old dead leaves over the pavement and shushing in the trees around the empty Thornhill house and the abandoned house across the street. This neighborhood was a graveyard, a tomb. The rest of Fell wasn't much better.

I banged through the front door of our house like I had when I was a teenager, then took the stairs two at a time without taking my boots off.

In my bedroom, the sunlight slanted through the window, illuminating the dust motes in the air. I yanked at the box of my files and removed the lid. My fingertips touched Charles Zimmer's file—the most recent one—and then skimmed past it. Zimmer would have to wait. I took out a blank file with blank pages in it, a pen. I closed the box and picked up my camera and tripod.

> Subject: Vail Esmie
> Age: Thirty-four
> Status: Single, never married, no children
> Number of encounters: Exact number unknown in previous period (estimated at least twenty); in current period, one
> Type of encounter: Home invasion and possible study
> First encounter: Unknown, possibly 1959 or 1960? to 1971; current period 1989

In the living room, I stared at the words on the wall. They looked just as strange in daylight, though less frightening. I loaded a fresh roll of film into my camera.

> Points of entry: Two doors (front, back), numerous windows
> Time of encounters: Night (all)
> Communication from entities: Whispered words "Wake up"
> Physical encounters with entities: Assault
> Missing time: None
> Injuries from encounters: None
> Other manifestations: Lights, vision effects, smell, writing on wall
> Notes: Visitations seem to be connected to one house and have changed in nature between 1971 and 1989. Current visitations include physical assault (grab to the neck) and whispering. Visitation has left the bedroom and migrated to the downstairs living room. Visitors left writing on living room wall, using crayons left on the kitchen table. Visitation only seen by one resident of the home and not the others, though

the others were nearby. Visitors left by unseen means after the subject hit one with a vase, which broke.

I set up the tripod next to the coffee table and mounted the camera, lining up a perfect shot of the writing on the wall. I took several pictures of it. A crayon lay on the floor beneath the writing. I took a picture of that, too. And a picture of the shards of vase where Violet had swept them into a corner.

I stepped back from the camera and looked around, giving the room a critical eye. Nothing else looked moved or disturbed. How had the thing gotten in, and where had it gone after I hit it? There was no window in the living room, so where had the light come from? There was a window in the kitchen, but not in here. Violet and Dodie had been in the kitchen, but they hadn't seen the light.

I strode into the kitchen and to the window, studying the dust on the windowsill, then running my fingers along where the window met the pane. Nothing moved or wiggled. The window was locked shut, and the dust was undisturbed.

I circled back to the living room, took the camera from the tripod, and walked out the back door, making a circuit of the house. I saw no footprints in any of the soft earth below the windows. I checked each window, one by one, and found them all firmly locked, undisturbed.

I went back into the house and upstairs. I opened every door, walked into every room, checked every window. I even checked the window in our parents' bedroom, ignoring its airless emptiness. I checked my own bedroom last, giving it an investigator's eye for the first time.

The window in this room was, most likely, how they had come in when I was a child. Aliens didn't need to physically open windows and climb in, but they needed something. A sight line. It was why I hated skylights.

The window in here was undisturbed, too. Locked shut. I had never kept my window open at night as a kid, even when it was hot out. I had been trained too early not to make it easy for them to get in uninvited.

I sat on the bed, dangling the camera between my knees. The silence of the house pounded in my ears. I stared out the window, which was at the front of the house, looking across the street to where the empty house was shrouded in trees. I didn't see anything move, didn't get a rush of inspiration. I was thinking too hard.

"Damn it," I said aloud to no one after a few long minutes. Because even though I wanted to, I couldn't escape the truth. After years of studying this one subject, I knew the truth too well.

It didn't add up.

The change of location, the physical touch, the writing on the wall, the rancid smell, the lack of window. It was too inconsistent.

The aliens had finished with me twenty years ago when they took Ben. They weren't back for me now.

Which meant that what had happened last night wasn't aliens at all. It was something else.

What was it?

I put the camera down on the bed next to me and dropped my head into my hands, racking my brain. I was out of my depth here, but I knew someone who wouldn't be. I'd have to call her.

"Damn it," I said again, and then, because there was no one to stop me, "Fuck it."

Then I stood up and went downstairs to the kitchen phone.

24

VIOLET

Petey's Pizza hadn't changed since 1971. It still smelled like burnt mozzarella and sweat. The vinyl seats still stuck to the backs of your legs if you wore a skirt. The Coke was flat, the napkins felt like sandpaper, and no one really wanted to be there. There was a bored teenager behind the counter and old soda ads on the wall.

"One comes to Petey's Pizza," Dodie said, "for a certain *ambiance*. A je ne sais quoi."

Even in the nasty, morgue-like light of Petey's, I could see that my sister was beautiful. She had our father's dark eyes—Dad was an awful father, but he was wildly handsome—and expressive arches of eyebrows. Her skin was immaculate, her lashes long even without makeup. She didn't have my sullen look or the default glare that Vail and I gave everyone we met. Dodie was a lot, but unlike us, Dodie looked like someone you might actually want to know.

She caught me looking at her for a second too long. "What?" she asked.

I dropped my gaze to her top, the one with the bows on the shoulders. "I'm thinking about that shirt," I said.

She touched one of the turquoise bows with a fingertip. "You like it? I thrifted it for fifty cents."

"I believe it. Your whole wardrobe screams *I thrifted this for fifty cents.*"

Dodie waved a hand over my all-black outfit. "And yours says *I'm dowdy, yet mean.* Very expressive."

Vail scrubbed his hands over his face. "God, I hate having sisters."

"You should think about clothes more often," Dodie shot back at him, dropping her gaze over him. "Or ever. Tell me, how many fishermen died to make that sweater?"

"Barbers are a real thing, Vail," I added. "They use scissors. The technology has been around for thousands of years."

"Please, Violet," Dodie said. "Thousands of years? Cavemen didn't use scissors."

"How do you know? You're a model, not an archaeologist."

Vail lifted his head. "Shut up," he said, his voice deceptively calm. "Both of you. Shut. Up. Things are bad enough."

My gaze dropped to the table, where our emptied plates were stacked. I had told them about my trip to the hospital, about what Joan had found in the records. I had told them about seeing Alice. I told them about Martin Peabody and the reason for the mark on my forehead, though I didn't tell them what Martin had said to me in Joan's office. I'd had enough shame for one day.

"So she spoke to you," Dodie said, getting back to the subject. "Alice. Do they usually speak to you?"

My jaw tightened. Talking about this had cost me jobs, friendships, my marriage, and custody of my daughter. It had won me a stay in a mental hospital. I had trained myself over a lifetime never to speak aloud about what I saw, and talking about it now made a headache throb in my temples. "No," I managed. "They don't speak. This is new."

"It's changed," Vail said. When I lifted my gaze, I saw he was staring at me with an intensity I couldn't read. "It isn't like it was when we were kids. Something has changed."

"Ben came into my bed," Dodie added. "That's different, too, from my usual old nightmares. Why?"

Was it Sister? I was certain, now, that she had controlled Martin and the young man in the storage unit. She had somehow had them do her bidding. They had told me as much. Alice, with her warning, didn't seem to be under the same control—but did Sister control everything in the house? Was she controlling Ben? If she was, what could we do about it? There was no dispelling Sister, no eliminating her. Sister was permanent darkness. I might, if I was lucky, keep her away from my siblings.

"We have to think clearly for once," I said. It was hard to strategize in the house, which was why we were talking about this in a restaurant. At least it was a deserted restaurant, with no one to overhear our insane conversation. "We know now that Mom didn't give birth to Ben. We need to figure out who *did* give birth to him. We have to find whoever it was, and if they didn't give Ben up willingly—or even if they did—we have to tell them what happened."

"I keep coming back to the fact that our parents wouldn't have stolen a baby," Vail said. "Not because they had morals but because they didn't want the kids they already had. Why would they steal a fourth one? Why would they go to the trouble?"

"I agree," I said. "I think the baby was given to them or left to them somehow. Who would be so foolish as to give our parents a baby?"

"Mom didn't have siblings," Dodie said. She picked up a napkin and folded it into squares, her elegant fingers working. "Her parents were still alive when we were born, but they were both gone by the time Ben came."

I had no memory of my mother's father, but I had an image of my grandmother, a stern woman with a salon hairstyle and an unapproachable, vaguely angry air. She had died of cancer, we were told.

I had no idea what kind of cancer, which meant it was probably in an unmentionable body part. How embarrassing, to die of a cancer that has to do with a breast, a vagina, or an ass. Better never to speak of it, or her, again.

"Maybe our grandmother had a late baby," I said. "Or maybe there was an illegitimate aunt or uncle. What about Dad's side?"

Again, Dodie knew the answer. "His parents lived in California. He had a brother, but he always said he didn't know what happened to him. He hadn't seen his brother in years and didn't know where he lived."

"So Ben could have been the brother's," Vail said. He shrugged. "Or it was simpler than that. He could have been Dad's."

We looked at one another.

"It's the explanation that makes the most sense," I said.

The idea sat there, on the table in the middle of us, sitting on top of the messy plates, crumpled napkins, and pizza crusts.

I had no feeling about the idea of my father cheating on my mother, I discovered. No betrayal or outrage, not even sadness. No feeling at all.

"They hated each other." Dodie's voice was almost a whisper. She dropped her napkin to the table. "I don't know why they even got married. It wasn't because they were in love."

For the first time, I thought about my parents as people younger than me. I tried to picture my father proposing, my mother saying yes. Had it been hopeful at one time? Had either of them thought it would work?

Both of them were good-looking, so maybe there had been an attraction and nothing else. Mom's family had money. Dad's family, from what I could tell, were California dreamers with no money at all. Somehow, Dad had twigged on to Mom's healthy bank account and used his looks to do the rest. I didn't even know how they met, and now I would never know.

I was conceived so close to the wedding that they'd probably fudged the dates. Dad had impregnated his meal ticket, thinking he'd won the lottery. That sounded like Dad. That he'd gotten careless years into a miserable marriage was not only possible, it was almost probable.

"Mom never said anything about it," I said. "And she loved Ben."

But the theory still fit. Mom never talked about *anything* unpleasant. And Ben was an innocent baby, easy to love. Maybe by then Mom hadn't cared who Dad slept with. Maybe she had someone else, too. Maybe she'd hated all of it, but the baby—that particular baby—had made it better. Not loving Ben wasn't possible.

"We're never going to know," Dodie said. "They left us with this mess, with all of these questions, and we can't ask them *anything*. And even if we could, they wouldn't answer. They were so good at that, weren't they?" She lifted her chin. For a second, I wondered if she was going to spiral, but her gaze was hard and focused instead of wild. "What gets me is that none of it matters." She lifted her hands. "You live your whole life, and you feel all these things, you experience all these things. You learn things. And if you don't tell anyone about it, it all just dies when you die. What you know, your life, your experience, it dies when you do. It's all just—what? Electric impulses in your brain. Your memory of your whole life from beginning to end is just vibrating brain cells, and when the brain cells stop vibrating, then it never happened. Don't you ever think about that? I do."

In the back of Petey's, a phone rang. The teenager behind the counter picked it up reluctantly and took an order, reaching for a pen and writing with it, his expression annoyed.

"It's like the photos of Pompeii," Dodie continued. "Skeletons in ash. When I see those pictures, I think of how those people knew things, felt things, thought things. They had memories and important information. Every secret thing they knew disappeared forever when the volcano erupted, and those are just the people we know about. Most people vanish so completely they don't even leave bones."

"If you're asking whether I wonder what the point of life is," Vail said, "I think about it all the time."

"So do I," I said. "But not everything disappears forever. Not for everyone. Not every time."

We exchanged a look. The things I saw—had always seen—were remnants of lives, for better or worse. The last traces of Dodie's electric brain impulses, maybe. Or maybe they were something else.

"You should have called one of us," Dodie said. "When they locked you up in that hospital. You should have called Vail or me. We would have come to get you out."

I swallowed hard, remembering sitting in that room, thinking stupidly that it was the key to getting my daughter back. I hadn't called my siblings. Neither of them had known about the hospital until long after it was over and I was already out. "They didn't give me very many phone privileges," I said. "And they wouldn't have released me. You wouldn't have had the right paperwork."

Vail scowled. "Paperwork? You think I couldn't have *made* the right paperwork and made it look real?"

"Easy peasy," Dodie said.

I choked out a laugh that was supposed to be disbelieving, but when I thought about it, I didn't disbelieve it at all. My siblings would think nothing of forging whatever paperwork they needed, by any means necessary. It would be a top-shelf forgery, too. Sometimes it was useful to have next to no morals.

But I hadn't called them. For a while, when I realized what was really happening, I'd believed I belonged there, in the hospital. I'd believed I shouldn't be free. It had even been tempting to be relieved at having no choices anymore, at not having to pretend to be normal. It had taken time for anger to replace the shame and despair.

"I'll call you next time it happens, then," I said.

"See that you do," Dodie chided me. "But let's get back to this problem. Maybe Dad was Ben's father. Who was his mother?"

"Someone local?" Vail asked.

"Maybe," I said, "but Dad traveled a lot." *Business* was always the explanation we were given. *He's away on business.* Dad had no business we could discern aside from marrying Mom's money and making all of us miserable, but children don't question their parents. When you're a child, no one wants to know what you're wondering about. You shut your mouth and wonder in silence, because you don't know anything yet and no one wants to hear it. I felt a quick, hot burst of angry pride that my own daughter was a mouthy bitch.

"So she could be anyone, from anywhere," Vail said, deadpan. "That narrows it down."

"Gus Pine is looking into it," I said. "If someone's baby was stolen, they would have reported it to the police. It's a start."

"If she was local, there would have been gossip," Dodie added. "A single woman in the sixties, having a baby alone. Unless she was married." She sighed and rubbed her fingertips on her forehead. "Ugh, this is *hard*. I detest thinking. I talked to the neighbors, but they haven't lived there long and didn't know a thing."

"What neighbors?" I asked.

"The Chathams, on the other side from the Thornhills," Dodie said. "I wandered over there and knocked on their door to say hello. I gave them my most charming version of myself. There are two parents in their thirties and a daughter of around nine or ten. The daughter has an unflattering short haircut and is named Terri. The mother is a receptionist in a dentist's office and the father is a lawyer. They moved here for his job. They've been in town for eight months. They don't know where the Thornhills went. They weren't very friendly. They seemed a little spooked."

"If you're not spooked in our neighborhood," Vail said, "then there's something wrong with you."

A Box Full of Darkness

We contemplated that for a moment. Maybe the neighbors had seen a little boy at our house, or lights, or something else. Maybe they knew the reason the Thornhills had left so quickly. Or maybe they had just looked around at our dead street and our weird town. Maybe they had opened a Fell newspaper, read about hanged priests and poltergeists and Cathy Caldwell, and wondered what they had done.

"What did you tell them about us?" Vail asked Dodie.

"That we grew up in this house and we've come back to clean out our parents' things," Dodie replied. "I told them we're going to decide what to do with the house, whether to sell it or not."

"That sounds so normal," I said. "Maybe we should do that."

Vail's voice was icy. "We're not selling that house."

I nodded. Ben was in the house somewhere, so the house was ours forever. "But the clearing-out part. We don't have to sell, but do we have to keep our parents' bed? Would it kill us to get rid of the ugly wallpaper or our childhood furniture? I know we're all psychologically damaged, but when I'm in that house, I can see just *how* damaged. Maybe we could throw out some furniture and lessen the damage a little."

"Maybe," Vail said, "but what about the attic?"

Dodie looked at me, her eyes soft for once. "Go into the attic, Violet. Please. Go see for yourself."

I felt the muscles in my jaw tighten harder, felt my teeth try to grind. I'd given myself the tasks so far that had taken me out of the house. I could have sent Vail to the hospital to look for records. But deep down, even though I had come all this way to be in the house, all I wanted was to leave.

"I've been busy," I snapped.

"So have we," Vail shot back calmly, not buying it for a second. "Go into the attic, Violet. See it for yourself."

"You have to," Dodie said.

I bit my lips together, fighting it. It was too hard. I had come all this way to Fell—had given up my job, left Lisette, left everything—and now that I was here, I couldn't face Ben. I couldn't face my failure. I wasn't soft like Dodie, and I wasn't hard like Vail. I was just soft enough to feel gutted, just hard enough to be a bad big sister and a bad mother. I was the big sister, the mother, the one who was supposed to know the answers, the one who was supposed to be soft and hard at the right times. Instead of being competent, I walked a tightrope I had fallen off so many times that I was irreparably broken. I was cracked in half.

Still, I was here now. I was the big sister, the mother. I had no parents. There was no one to handle this for me. There never had been, and there never would be.

"All right," I said. "I'll go."

25

DODIE

The TV worked fine once Vail adjusted the rabbit ears until the picture was clear. We only got reception of two channels. One was showing an old Western, and the other had *Matlock*. We picked *Matlock*.

It was dim in the living room—there were no windows, and the kitchen was dark. I turned on a lamp in the corner, which gave off a familiar, sickly yellow glow. The lamps in our house growing up had been chosen for their decorative qualities, not their ability to give off proper light. Our parents weren't readers. If you wanted to read in your bedroom, you did it best by flashlight.

I curled up on one end of the sofa, pulling the blanket sitting on the back over myself in the gloom. After I sneezed the emitted dust from my nose, it was quite comfortable. I lay my cheek on the arm of the sofa and watched Matlock drive around wherever he was, intending to solve a case.

Vail sat on the other end of the sofa, making it groan softly. He dropped his boots to the floor, then put his feet up, trying to get under my blanket. Our legs battled briefly, then found a truce.

We settled in. Upstairs, Violet had gone to the attic alone, but for once, I wasn't worried. The house felt calm, as if the choke hold of fear had relaxed for a little while. Vail and I watched Matlock go to court, our faces lit by the twin glows of the old TV and the lamp. Behind us, the words WAKE UP were still scrawled on the wall.

The woman on TV had definitely killed her husband, I thought, but no worry. Matlock would ferret out the truth. I rolled over and glanced at the words on the wall, studying them for a long moment, for the first time able to stare at them without flinching in fear.

"It was Ben," Vail's voice said softly. "He wrote them."

I turned my gaze and saw that my big brother wasn't watching the TV, either. He had turned to his back and was staring at the ceiling. He was thinking.

"What did he mean, do you think?" I asked.

"I don't think," Vail said. "I know."

I frowned. "What do you know?"

Vail started talking.

He spoke of waking as a child, of alien figures standing over him, of bright lights. Of being unable to move. He spoke of how it felt when he dropped off to sleep, wondering if tonight it would happen, if tonight they would change their minds and finally take him with them.

I lay my head back down on the arm of the sofa as he spoke, watching the TV unseeing as Vail finally talked, *talked*, on and on. I blinked hard and thought that Ben hadn't been the only helpless little boy to live in this house. But Vail hadn't crawled into anyone's bed for comfort. He'd stayed in his own bed, alone.

He talked about the night the figure had spoken to him, the only time it had said words. Two words: *Wake up.*

"That happened right before Ben came," he said, his voice drifting and dreamy. He was still staring at the ceiling. "He wasn't born yet. But he knew about it. The lights, everything. He just knew. He kept them away. Until they took him instead of me."

I let my thoughts circle lazily, as if they were in a warm tumble dryer on a slow setting. The lights. The words. Ben. On TV, a commercial for Nair was on. Nair was a cream you put on your legs—or wherever—and when you wiped it off, your hair came with it. It smelled putrid. Women in short shorts were showing off their smooth legs, happy as could be. I had auditioned for a handful of razor ads, but though my legs were good, they weren't quite good enough. For a Nair commercial, your calves had to be extremely narrow, because the camera would make them look thicker. My agency told me it was best to "lead with my hair," as they put it. My hair was always a shoo-in, and although you could starve yourself into thin air, there was absolutely nothing you could do about wrongly shaped legs.

For a second, I stood outside my own life in shocked dismay. My little brother was dead, my big brother had lived with nightmares his entire childhood just like I had, my parents were dead, and my big sister was in the attic right now, looking at our little brother's toys and grieving. And I was supposed to *care* about how narrow my calves were. In my world, that was supposed to matter so much that I hollowed myself out with worry, that I wished for a different body so that more people would buy disgusting cream to wipe their hair off. If I was lucky—*lucky*—the legacy I'd leave behind in my life, the proof of my existence after the volcano erupted, would be Nair.

Wake up, I thought.

Vail had gone quiet, and I knew he wasn't waiting for me to speak. He didn't need my approval or my acceptance. He didn't even need proof that I'd heard every word he said. He already knew.

"It was water," I said. "For me. It was always water."

Vail's eyebrows twitched down and his gaze narrowed on the ceiling. "Water?"

"I wake up and it's everywhere." My throat was thick. I had never told anyone this before. "It's filling the room, rising. My bed is an island. It's dark water, fetid. Cold. I wake up trapped. I sit up against the headboard and hug my knees. I know I can't wade through it, can't swim, because if I try, it will drag me down."

My brother lifted his head and fixed his gaze on me. In his expression was growing alarm.

I felt strangely calm, talking about this. I knew I had gone into some kind of spiral after going into the attic, that I'd stopped making very much sense. I remembered feeling feverish, except that the fever was pulsing in my temples and the back of my head. It made my stomach turn and acid burn in my chest. But I felt none of that now. The fever had burned away.

"The water used to come at night," I said as Vail listened. "It was a dream, but it wasn't a dream. I think you know exactly what I mean. I'd wake up to the sound of the water, the smell. I'd pull my knees up and sit, waiting. Not moving. Because going into the water was dangerous, but also if I moved, something would notice me. Something would know I was there."

Vail waited, silent. On TV, the woman had confessed, and Matlock was triumphant. Justice was served.

"I would wait for the water to go down," I said, "and most times it would. But sometimes—sometimes it would keep rising, and then it would wash over, and I couldn't escape." I wiped an icy hand over my face. "That's what happened the other night. Ben came, and he was in bed with me, and it was—I can't describe it. I was so happy. And then the water came back."

My brother's face was stark with grief, with understanding. We looked at each other for a long time, saying everything and nothing.

"I should have protected you," he said, and the words broke my heart.

"You couldn't have," I said. "There was nothing you could do. Just like there was nothing I could do for you. Like there's nothing either of us can do for Violet."

He inhaled through his nose, then let out his breath. His gaze flicked to the words on the wall. "The lights," he said. "The water. They're connected. They have to be."

I nodded. "They have to be."

His expression went unfocused, thinking, and I knew my big brother would figure it out, just like I knew that the sun would rise in the morning and that I would never go back to modeling. "I think the timeline is the key," he said, mostly to himself.

"Vail," I said.

"The timeline isn't what we think it is," Vail said. "Not at all. It never has been."

"Vail."

He looked at me. "What?"

"It wasn't aliens that you saw the other night," I said. I bit my lip, then plunged on, hoping he was ready to hear it. "It wasn't ever aliens, what you saw back then. Maybe that theory—it was never right. What you saw was something else."

My brother's response to hearing that his life's work to this point was an illusion, a pointless waste of time, was to slowly give one of his scowls and say, "Yeah."

26

VIOLET

I had been avoiding the attic. Since Vail had told me what he and Dodie found there, I hadn't wanted to see it for myself. I thought it would be too hard. I'd opted to go to the hospital instead.

It had been, in retrospect, one of my stupider ideas.

As I pulled down the attic stairs and climbed them, I reminded myself that it wouldn't be that bad. It was just a few toys. We had stored them here ourselves sometime after Ben went missing, during the weeks and months that blurred into one long, miserable day that had no morning, noon, or night. I couldn't remember whether we'd emptied Ben's room before Dad left or after. It didn't matter anymore.

The crayons and the other things Vail and Dodie had seen were probably a hoax anyway, put on by some unknown grifter who wanted to torture us. I refused to calculate all the ways this was illogical, or the reasons why a stranger breaking into our house to torment us was preferable to the thought of Ben.

I had stuffed a flashlight into the waistband of my jeans because it was dark and there were no lights in the attic. As I climbed to the top of the ladder, I took out the flashlight and turned it on, moving it in a slow arc around the dusty space.

The Snakes and Ladders game was out of its box, a few of the pieces placed on the board. There was a half-done puzzle next to a heap of unused pieces. Dolls. A coloring book. Blocks. A rubber ball, rolling slowly into a corner as if someone had just put it down and it was slowing to a stop.

I kept my feet on the steps as my throat went dry and my temples pounded. Downstairs, I could hear the TV in the living room.

"Ben?" I said.

There was no answer. I rotated the flashlight again. My palm was sweating, my knuckles aching as I gripped it. Was that a shadow moving in the corner? What about there? Was that something outside the black window, or just a reflection of the light?

I closed my eyes briefly. *Ben doesn't frighten you,* I reminded myself. *He's just a little boy. Your brother. He's never frightened you before, and he doesn't now.*

Sister wasn't here—at least not right now. I would know if she was here.

I recognized the voices on TV downstairs. Vail and Dodie were watching *Matlock* with the words WAKE UP scrawled behind them on the wall while I explored the attic, looking for our long-dead brother. Just a Friday night in the Esmie house.

"Ben," I said again, but this time it wasn't a question. I made my legs move, made my feet take the final step into the attic.

This time, when I rotated the flashlight, I forced myself to look with the eyes of someone who had cleaned out dozens of houses. The old crib in the corner, which all of us had used—that was most likely trash, because cribs had safety protections now. If you had an old crib, it turned out, your child could wedge its head through the bars and die. How any of us made it to adulthood was a mystery. Then I pictured Alice and Martin and remembered that some of us didn't.

So the crib was garbage. There was a dusty box of baby clothes, but baby clothes were cheaper now than they had been in the sixties, so those could likely go, too. Did the puzzle have all of its pieces, and did the board game have all of its dice? They weren't worth anything, but maybe there was a daycare or primary school that could use donations, or—

There was a familiar glass tinkling sound in the dark. I swiveled the light to see that a purple velvet drawstring bag had tipped over, and marbles were slowly rolling away from it.

And just like that, my fear vanished.

My little brother. My sweet, sweet baby boy.

"It's okay." My voice was a rasp through my closed throat as I walked toward the marbles, trying to sound normal, trying to sound like I had all the answers. "Don't be afraid. I'm here. I'm right here."

The marbles rolled to a stop. I crouched next to them, then sat all the way down, crossing my legs, tucking my socked feet under the crooks of my knees. I had changed into old shorts and a stretched-out T-shirt, my hair in a ponytail. When I scooped up the marbles, they were cool in my palm. It reminded me of the feel of the stall door in the hospital bathroom where I'd talked to Alice.

"Are you scared?" I asked Ben. "Tell me what you're scared of, and I'll fix it. I'm your big sister. I can fix anything." I tilted my hand, making the marbles roll in my palm, letting their satisfying weight and coolness soothe me. My daughter had never played with marbles. How was I only remembering now how good marbles felt in your hand, how solid and smooth, how perfect? You didn't have to play with marbles, really. You just had to hold them and look at them to enjoy them.

I put the flashlight down, resting it against a box so it aimed its light at the ceiling. It reflected a diluted glow in that position that lessened the gloom, even in the corners. I watched the light glint on the glass as I let the marbles drop from one of my palms into the other.

"I miss you," I told Ben. "I have my own daughter now. Do you already know that? I didn't do a very good job with her." I tilted my hands the other way, let the marbles drop back into the first palm. "I think I used all of my mothering up on you. But you asked us to come back, and we came. I came. Tell me the problem, and I'll take care of it."

Silence answered me, but I thought he was listening. Maybe it was wishful to think so. Did it matter?

"You can tell me anything," I said to Ben, "even if it's about her." Familiar fear pricked my spine, followed by a curious warmth of relief. Sitting in the dark, talking to my dead little brother, I could tell the truth. Ben understood. If he was here in this house—if he had been here all these years—he already knew.

"I hate her," I said. "She's tormented me all my life. I wanted to protect you from her, protect all of you, and I don't know anymore if that was even possible. I don't know if it was the right thing to do. All of my decisions are wrong, but I don't know what the right ones are, and the stakes are so incredibly high." The words were coming in a rush like an exhale. "Is she hurting you, Ben? You can tell me. It's gone on long enough. We don't have to be quiet anymore. I can make it stop. If she's hurting you, I'll find a way. Just tell me, please."

There was only silence as a reply.

"I'm sorry," I said. I had said the same thing to Alice because she had been my friend, but I was Ben's big sister, and I owed it to him even more. "I should have been there. You shouldn't have been alone."

I let the marbles fall into my other palm again. Then my gaze caught on something and I stopped.

Sitting on the Snakes and Ladders board was a piece that didn't belong there. It was dark brown wood, not plastic. Closing my fist over the marbles in my palm, I leaned forward and picked it up with my free hand.

It was a wooden horse, hand carved, twice the size of my thumb. It was blocky, not overly detailed but recognizable. I ran my hand over the curves and grooves of the carving, frowning.

I hadn't played with this, I was sure. I hadn't seen Vail or Dodie play with it, either. Had one of our parents played with it as a child? Had it lain forgotten in the bottom of a box? For how long? Why had Ben taken it out now?

He had put it on the Snakes and Ladders board. He had wanted me to see it.

He's been telling you and telling you, Alice had said.

I put the horse back down. I felt around for the bag to put the marbles away so I could leave. My fingers landed on the bag and I picked it up. I pulled open the drawstring and dropped the marbles in.

Something about the bag wasn't familiar. I had played with marbles as a kid—hadn't I? I was sure I had, or one of us had. Didn't every kid play with marbles?

I rolled the bag against my palm. There was an inked imprint on the fabric, a stamp like you'd see on old bags of flour. On impulse, I picked up the flashlight and aimed it at the bag.

For a long moment, the world spun.

Everything made sense, yet nothing did.

He's been telling you and telling you, I thought again.

I had asked, *Is he my brother?* And Alice had said, *It's the wrong question.*

He's been telling you and telling you.

The answer was on the bag of marbles.

In faded ink, the logo said, *New York Glass and Marble Company. 1899.*

27

VAIL

I once dated a woman who read tarot cards. She worked in a Wiccan shop in Santa Fe—UFO researchers spend a lot of time in Nevada and New Mexico—and she read cards as a sideline. Because we were dating, she would read my cards for free. I'd listen with half my attention as she talked about my destiny, whether I was going to be rich or poor, whether I would travel far or stay home.

I didn't believe it, but she did. I knew she wanted me to believe it, too. I also knew that she used the card readings as an excuse for the two of us to be alone so she could get me into bed. It worked.

But afterward, I'd lie next to her as she slept and stare at the ceiling, thinking about those cards. It was a simple trick on the surface. Each card was about such a broad topic—wealth, travel, triumph, war, wisdom—that anyone could apply it to their own life. War? That must be about the fight I had with my wife. Triumph? I turned in an assignment at school. The cards could always be right.

That didn't interest me. What interested me was that the cards could be reversed.

Wisdom or foolishness. Triumph or defeat. Sacrifice or selfishness. A simple flip, and you had one destiny or another.

Flip a card and your life is different than it was a second ago.

Flip a card and tell your little brother to go hide.

Flip a card and walk away from your parents, your home, leaving your sisters to fend for themselves.

Flip a card and get on a plane back to Fell, so the intruders can shine their light on you again.

Flip a card and it wasn't aliens after all.

Sorry, but that's the way it goes.

I watched TV with Dodie, and we bickered about whether to watch the news or the late-night movie. Then Violet came down from the attic and stood in the doorway, pale and shaken, and I knew that the cards had flipped yet again.

There's an explanation, people liked to say when they heard about my investigations. *You're reaching. There has to be an explanation.*

There are a lot of possible explanations, I would always answer. *And one of those explanations is aliens.* They never knew what to say to that.

Violet showed us the wooden horse and the bag of marbles, and the first thing I thought of was the balsam wood airplane that Ben had never been able to assemble. I thought of his disinterest in race cars and toy trucks. It was because those things meant nothing to him. Nothing at all.

There's an explanation. Yes, there is. There are many possible explanations, in fact. Flip a card and pick one. You might not like it.

When I broke up with the tarot girlfriend, I was mean to her. I was mean to every woman I broke up with, because when I was cruel, they backed away and left me alone forever. They didn't understand that it wasn't about them, about what they had done or hadn't done, how they looked or didn't look, what they said or didn't say. It was always about the fact that without Ben, I was a shell of a person, and the only thing I truly wanted was to be left alone.

So when I broke up with the tarot girlfriend, I said, *Did you see this coming? If your cards are so accurate, did you predict this?*

She'd looked me in the eyes and said, *Vail, I predicted this from the beginning.*

I owed that woman an apology, but she would never get one. Just like all the others.

Sorry, but that's the way it goes.

28

VIOLET

Even though it was late, I called Lisette. Clay answered the phone and argued with me for twenty minutes before he finally put her on. When she picked up the phone extension in her bedroom, her voice was surly and resentful. "Yeah? What?"

My mind was spinning, my eyes were dry as sandpaper, and my stomach was trying to flip upside down. For once, anger had no hold on me. I couldn't even feel an echo of it inside my skull. I could only feel a rush of relief and happiness at the sound of my daughter's pissed-off voice.

I wasn't thinking about the attic or the bag of marbles in that moment. I was thinking about Martin Peabody, the look in his eyes, the brush of his fingertip on the back of my neck, filling me with cold despair.

"Are you all right?" I asked Lisette.

"Yeah."

"Is everything going okay there?"

"Yeah."

She wasn't going to give me anything. When was the last time my daughter had given me even the tiniest piece of herself? It had been years.

I was trying, for once. It had been years since I had done that, either.

We did a dance of strike and parry. *Is school okay? Yeah. Did you do your homework? Mostly. What homework was it? English.* She didn't ask anything about me. She never did.

"What's going on there?" I asked, still trying.

A brief pause. "Dad's watching *The Love Boat* with Katie."

Clay must have a girlfriend, then. Had this been kept from me like some careful secret? Had they thought I would explode at the news? I truly did not care that Clay had a girlfriend. I assumed he'd had more than one over the years. I did care that this woman was spending more time with Lisette than I could.

I wasn't going to explode, though. I wasn't going to be the Crazy Ex-Wife, just this once. I would glide past this news with dignity, like a ship in the night. "You like that show," I said.

"It's a stupid show." She shot the words back at me like a slingshot. I wasn't even sure she meant them.

"You always said you liked it."

"It's stupid," she proclaimed. "Dad says I have to go to bed now. I have to get up for school tomorrow."

"You're a night owl."

"I need to *sleep*."

Annoyance crept up the back of my neck and pinched my skull. This was Violet the Bad Mother, always annoyed and out of patience. My daughter knew I had a short fuse, and in the last few years, her favorite hobby was testing it, then blasting it to pieces.

"You can tell me anything, you know," I said. "You can ask me anything, too. I'll answer any question you want."

I had surprised her, but only for a second. She was too smart to trust those words out of my mouth. "Who cares?" she shot back. "It doesn't matter. You left."

"I'm only in upstate New York," I pointed out. "Not Mars."

"You left," Lisette repeated. "Dad says you did it because you wanted to. Because you didn't want to have to look after me."

I felt a flash of anger, and then a cooling jet of admiration. She was very good at this. It was a one-two punch of Bad Mother accusation and the words guaranteed to infuriate me, *Dad says*. When Lisette wanted to pick a fight with me—which was most of the time—all she had to do was use the magic phrase *Dad says*, and she'd get one.

For the briefest second, I almost gave in and gave her the fight she was looking for. Then my anger popped, the air flapping out of it like a balloon, and I couldn't. Instead, the words marched out of me, one after another, perfectly calm.

"I know I'm a bad mother," I said. "But I work hard, I'm sober, and I'm around. I ask you to stay for the weekends, but you never come."

"You're *around*?" Lisette's voice was dramatic, near tears, and I still drank it in like water. "That's how you're my mom? By being *around*? You left."

"This is important."

"Sure it is." There was all the pain and despair of a teenager in her voice. "More important than being *around*."

I blinked hard at the wall, at the faded, flowery wallpaper. Vail and Dodie had gone upstairs, ostensibly to bed, but I could hear Vail's footsteps in the upstairs hall and the water running in the bathroom sink. Vail said something, his tone caustic, and Dodie said something caustic back. Vail's steps retreated.

We were here in this wretched house, which was full of awful memories and seemingly haunted by something malevolent and cruel. We were watching TV in a room with words scrawled on the wall. Our dead brother's things were moving in the attic. Soon, we would all try to sleep as the nightmares crawled in.

I had always shielded my daughter from the worst things in life.

It was what you did when you had a child, what made you a good parent. You told your child bedtime stories about unicorns and treasure maps, not about how you lost your voice screaming your brother's name as you walked the hallways, how you only knew the cops in the house by their feet because you never raised your gaze. You didn't tell little children about Ben, about how your parents looked through you like glass, about being lonely and scared, about dead people watching you work. About Sister.

That was fair. It was right. But Lisette wasn't a baby anymore. I had been much, much younger than Lisette when I had first seen Sister standing in my bedroom. Maybe, at a certain point in time, your children craved the truth, because without it they didn't know you anymore.

"When I was your age," I said into the kitchen phone, "I lost my little brother."

There was silence on the other end of the line.

"He was six years old," I said. "He would have been your uncle, I guess. His name was Ben."

Another second of silence. Then, "Uncle Ben? Like the rice?"

It was rude, sarcastic, but I wasn't fooled. Lisette was invested. I invented this kind of rudeness. I knew it well.

"Like the rice," I replied.

"What happened?" she asked. "Was he murdered?"

The question was a punch to the gut. I thought of wrestling Ben into his clothes that morning, trying to get him to comb his hair. In my mind, I had silently decided that Ben had an accident, that he'd fallen somewhere and lost consciousness, that he'd gone quietly without knowing what was wrong. That it was just one of those things. Children died every day, didn't they? They drowned in pools or played with matches or got into a bottle of prescription pills. The thought of anyone murdering Ben was, even now, too much to bear.

"I don't know," I managed to say. "We don't know. We played hide-and-seek with him one day, and he hid and never came out, and we never found him. He died and we never found his body."

"Didn't you call the *police*?" she asked as if this had just happened, with the blithe certainty of someone who has never known this kind of pain. "Didn't they look for him?"

"Yes, we did, and yes, they looked. We all looked. We never found him."

"How could that happen? How could he just be gone?" She was in disbelief, and I had the strange double vision of being irritated and knowing that yes, I had successfully shielded her from some of the bad things in life. At least I had done that much.

"Lisette, he disappeared." I found that I was suddenly infinitely patient. "That's all we ever knew. So yes, I know I'm screwed up, but there's a reason for it. Okay? And I'm sorry. I'm sorry the bad shit I grew up with got dumped on you. You didn't deserve it, which was why I never told you this story. I thought I was protecting you. But I'm telling you now."

The words were jumbled, ineloquent. The sentences spilled like stones, rolled away like marbles on the attic floor.

On the other end of the line, there was silence.

Then Lisette said, "Why are you there now? Are Aunt Dodie and Uncle Vail there?"

Lisette had only met her aunt and uncle a handful of times. We did not do summer vacations or Christmas visits. In the way of little kids, she hadn't been curious about her aunt and uncle, who to her were distant adults, ancient, another species. But two years ago she'd seen one of Dodie's shampoo commercials, which was inescapable on TV at the time. She'd watched those commercials in fascination, going silent whenever one of them came on during *The Young and the Restless*.

She'd asked me questions about Dodie. Where did she live? Was she married? Was she a runway model like Cindy Crawford? Was she rich? Was she really that pretty? Was she in magazines?

Clay, of course, had discouraged her. He was against Lisette having anything to do with my side of the family, and Lisette's questions about Dodie probably gave him nightmares of our daughter thinking she'd become a model. He'd told her that her aunt and uncle weren't interested in her, and Lisette's questions had gone quiet after that. I couldn't argue otherwise with any honesty, and even if I believed that Lisette should be around either of my siblings, there was nothing I could do about it. It was part of the infuriating helplessness of not having custody.

"They're here." I answered her question, trying to calculate how much to say. If I told her about ghosts, about aliens, about dead childhood friends and dead suicidal boys whispering in my ear at the hospital, I would never be allowed to talk to Lisette again. "He was their little brother, too. We all want to know what happened to him. So we came here to look for ourselves and find out."

"Like, investigating? What exactly are you doing?"

"We're going through the house. Comparing our memories of what happened. I've made some inquiries in town." I made it sound routine, when in fact I'd passed out at the storage rental place and Bradley Pine had had to carry me out of the hospital like a sack of grain. So much for honesty.

"Have you seen him?" Lisette asked. "Ben?"

I sagged against the kitchen wall, my hand sweaty on the phone. Lisette knew I had been in the hospital. She knew it was because I saw things that weren't there, things that I claimed were ghosts. She had learned all of this from Clay, not from me. I never talked to my daughter about the people I saw. I never wanted her to know how crazy her mother was, how ashamed I felt. The shame weighed me down, but I was so used to the drag of it that I hardly noticed it anymore.

My daughter had never asked me about it. Not only was she asking now, she sounded as if she might believe me.

"No," I replied, the honesty a shield this time. "I haven't seen him." Despite everything, I didn't want to be the crazy woman in Lisette's eyes, the mental patient. Just this once, couldn't I be normal? For a few minutes? "It's nothing like that, Lisette. It's simply that we never got an answer, and now we've decided to look for one." I paused, then added, "Please don't tell your father any of this. I told him that this was a family visit, that's all."

"Dad doesn't know? About Ben?"

That was my marriage to Clay, right there. I had never told my own husband about the death of my little brother. "No, and there's no reason for him to know now. I have to be here for a little while, do this one thing, and then I'll be back. If you tell him too much, he won't let me talk to you anymore."

Lisette seemed to think this over. "I think you should find whoever killed Ben, then get them arrested," she concluded. "Maybe Uncle Vail can beat him up."

"Okay," I said. "Maybe. I'll be back as soon as I can. I miss you."

Annoyance now. "Jeez, Mom."

"I know, I know. I'll call. Every night, if you want."

"Not *every* night."

"Every other night, then." I really did miss her. I wanted to see her face, even if it was in its usual affected sneer, even if she was sulking or rolling her eyes. I wanted to listen to her talk about anything at all. I wanted to hear her careless, thumping footsteps in the house and the rattling in the kitchen as she rifled through the fridge. I wanted her clothes dumped on top of the washing machine and her backpack dropped in the hall. I wanted all of it. There hadn't been much good in my life, and Lisette was a whiny bitch, but she was *my* whiny bitch, my surly, curled-lip princess who flitted from sourness to white-hot rage and back again. I didn't just love Lisette, I *knew* her.

A Box Full of Darkness

And I knew more than anyone that she had every right to be angry. I hoped she banked that anger, stoked it carefully, and kept it for life.

After I hung up the phone, I stood in the kitchen, in the silence. It was late, the darkness outside the window deep and seamless, as if we were in space. Either Dodie or Vail had left a lamp on in the living room, and another light reflected down the stairs from the upstairs hall. There was a silent agreement among the three of us not to sleep with the lights out.

A closet door opened and shut upstairs with a squeak. A drawer shut in Dodie's bedroom. Vail's footsteps—even in socks, he couldn't walk quietly—sounded in his bedroom. Then a creak as his childhood bed protested as he got in. A thump from Dodie's room, probably her dropping something off the dresser.

And then, half a second later, like an echo of the other sounds, there came the staccato rap of knuckles from high up in the attic. *Knock, knock, knock.*

My breath stopped in my throat. Upstairs, Dodie and Vail went instantly silent.

The silence stretched on, beating like a heart.

"Good night, Ben," I whispered softly, then turned toward the stairs to go to bed.

29

DODIE

The car came up the driveway just after eleven the next morning. Violet had gone to the grocery store. Vail and I were bickering as we emptied the ancient museum that was the kitchen cupboards, deciding what to keep and what to trash. So far, every argument had ended in trash. Vail had filled two garbage bags and dumped them in the backyard.

"This kitchen needs new wallpaper," I said, fixing my ponytail and glaring at the awful paper we'd had to look at growing up, a pattern of twined flowers and fussy stripes that some housewife thought was pretty back in the forties.

"Yeah," Vail said. His back was to me as he stared at the top shelf over the sink, where we'd found decades-old rags and a bar of soap furry with dust. He was wearing an old gray T-shirt and hadn't shaved again this morning. He put his hands on his hips and tilted back, peering.

"It's ugly," I said.

"Yeah," he said again. I thought he wasn't listening, but then he said, "Do you want to go now?"

"Where? The wallpaper store?"

Vail looked at me, and we had the same thought, which passed between us. We were the grown-ups now. If we didn't like the wallpaper, we could just change it. This was our house. We had money, a car. There was no one to stop us. The freedom was heady.

"Let's go," I said.

He was reaching for his keys when we heard a car in the drive. "That isn't Violet," I said. It didn't sound right, and she hadn't been gone long enough.

The car that had parked in front of our house was an unfamiliar Cutlass. As I stood on the porch, watching, the driver's door opened and a woman got out. She was fortyish, with glasses and dark blond hair tied in a bun. She wore a neat skirt and blouse. She opened the trunk to retrieve something, but she paused when she saw me.

"Good afternoon," she said, surprising me with her crisp English accent. "You're one of the sisters, I suppose."

I felt myself scowling at her. What sisters?

"I'm going to guess that you're Dodie," the woman said, as if I'd spoken. She bent into the trunk and took out a heavy briefcase. "Based on your clothes."

I glanced down at myself. I was wearing bell-bottom jeans—very old and thrifted—and a T-shirt I'd tied in a knot at the waist. The shirt, also thrifted, was red and had the name and logo of a tire shop in Rochester, New York, on the front. I had bought it because it was comfortable and cost twenty-five cents. Was she insulting me or paying me a compliment?

I was going to tell her to go away—I was in no mood for strangers—when Vail came onto the front porch behind me. "You said you weren't coming," he said to the woman.

The Englishwoman slammed her trunk. She turned to us, the briefcase in her hand, her feet in their practical flats braced on the driveway. "No. I said it would take some time, Vail," she replied calmly. "Not that I wasn't coming. I was busy."

"Not that busy, obviously," he argued.

"My plans changed. Are you going to introduce me?"

"Vail," I said, "what is going on?"

He glanced at me, as if he'd forgotten I was there. "This is Charlotte Ryder," he said, as if I should know that name. "I've met her in my line of work."

I glared at him. "You mean the aliens?"

"Aliens are Vail's specialty, not mine." The Englishwoman—Charlotte—stepped onto the porch. "Vail," she chided, "you didn't tell your sisters?"

"Well, now they know," he said, his tone annoyed. Without another word, he turned and went back into the house.

I narrowed my gaze at Charlotte. She looked back with calm regard.

"I see his social skills haven't improved since I saw him last," she commented in her crisp accent.

"What do you want?" I asked her.

"He called me," she explained. "He asked me to come. He said there's a manifestation in this house that he can't identify. I'm a parapsychologist."

"What's that?"

"I study psychic phenomena." She sounded like an English nanny explaining to a dense child. "For a living. I have degrees in science and psychology. I also teach parapsychology. If you would like a copy of my résumé, I'm sure I can produce one."

I crossed my arms. "So you're a ghost hunter?"

She looked at me with curiosity. "Do you believe there's a ghost in this house?"

I bit back a laugh at that. "If you want to catalog everything that's wrong with this house, you'll be here for a decade."

"I don't have quite that long to spare," she replied with cool politeness. "But as I've checked in at the local motel—horrid as it is—and I've already paid for the night, I may as well make use of my time and look around as Vail asked me to do, don't you think?"

I hesitated. There was nothing wrong with her that I could put my finger on, but I had the instinct to turn her away. In all of my memories, I couldn't recall a stranger ever coming into our house.

Our parents never entertained. We never had friends over. There had been no dinner parties, birthday parties, or friendly drop-ins. No relatives. The only time strangers had come into our home was the day the police had come to search for Ben.

This house was our misery, but it was our inner sanctum. No one else was allowed in.

Yet Vail had invited her. I stood there arguing silently with myself, my arms crossed, as Charlotte waited, finally becoming restless. Before I could decide, Violet's car pulled into the drive behind Charlotte's.

Violet got out and hefted a paper grocery bag onto her hip. "Who's that?" she asked me, as if Charlotte wasn't a sentient being.

"Vail invited a ghost hunter here to investigate," I replied.

Violet went very still. Her face blanched and her knuckles went white on the grocery bag. Charlotte could get all the degrees she wanted, she could drive around with her briefcase, asking questions in her accent, but she would never know as much about ghosts as my sister did.

Violet and I exchanged silent thoughts. No, we weren't going to tell her. We didn't tell people about Violet. Not now, not ever.

"Really," Charlotte said. "I understand the distrust, I do. But if you're truly not going to let me in, please hurry the decision along."

Violet stepped onto the porch. She had regained her composure, and her expression was her most familiar one—dark brows lowered, eyes blank, corners of her mouth turned down. It was an expression that said *Don't fuck with me*, and it worked on most people. She usually wore it in public, which was why people called her a bitch.

"Sorry," she said to Charlotte. "I'm Violet, and this is Dodie. Our brother didn't tell us about you."

"So I've gathered," Charlotte said.

"Come in." Violet opened the front door and held it for her. "How much has Vail told you?"

Charlotte set her briefcase down and looked around the front hall. "He said that this is your family home, that your parents died, and that you're here to clean out the house. He said that there's a manifestation that he can't explain." She turned to us. "He described it to me, but I'd like to hear from both of you, as well."

Violet made a sound in her throat that was vaguely derisive. She walked down the hall toward the kitchen. Charlotte followed Violet, and I trailed behind.

Vail was in the kitchen, cleaning out cupboards again.

"How do you know Vail?" Violet asked Charlotte, as if Vail wasn't in the room. She put the grocery bag on the table and began to empty it, setting the items together like a display.

"We've crossed paths over the years," Charlotte replied. "We know the same people. We've referred cases to each other."

"Rarely." Vail didn't look away from the dented cans he was pulling from the cupboard.

"Of course," Charlotte said. "I'm aware that you only contact me when under duress, Vail. And yet I must reiterate that you called me here."

Vail glared at her.

"Well, well," I said, breaking the silence. "Charlotte, don't tell me you're one of Vail's heartbroken conquests."

"I am not," she said in a tone that allowed no argument. She turned back to Vail. "Colorado wasn't my fault," she said to him, her voice gentler.

Vail's throat worked. He seemed to be wrestling with what to say. "I know," he said finally.

"It wasn't yours, either," Charlotte said. "Not every case goes the way we want it to."

"I know," he said again.

"Good. Then tell me what's going on here. Show me what you can." They seemed to have forgotten Violet and I were in the room.

I looked at Violet. She looked back at me, her eyes wide.

Vail closed his eyes and scrubbed a hand over his forehead. "I told you on the phone. I thought it was a visitation, but it didn't follow the usual pattern. It was in a different room, there was no window for the light source, and it grabbed me. A physical touch, and I know I didn't imagine it because I broke a vase on it. It spoke in my ear. It wrote on the wall."

Charlotte nodded. "I'll want to see that. Go on."

"There were footprints." Vail dropped his hand. I could see how tense he had been, how it was wearing on him. "I took pictures, but they're still being developed. Things have been moved in the attic. Last night, there were knocks in the attic."

I had heard those, too. As I lay in bed, hoping for sleep. They had been soft, almost friendly, like a good night from Ben. I'd waited, but they hadn't come again.

"All right," Charlotte said, her voice calm, as soothing as the cold aloe I used to put on my sunburned shoulders. I understood, then, why Vail had called this woman. Why he'd called someone, anyone.

We thought we were handling this, but we weren't. We were too close to it, and all three of us were crazy. We needed someone dispassionate. A professional. Preferably one who talked like the queen. We needed Charlotte.

"I'll just take a look around and get started," Charlotte said. "I'll be as unobtrusive as possible." She gestured to the ransacked cupboards. "Is there a possibility of tea in any of this? A kettle?" When we gave her blank looks in reply, she said, "Never mind, I'll do without. Could someone direct me to the writing on the wall?"

"I'll do it," I said.

"No." Vail shook his head. "I'll do it. Charlotte, get your briefcase. Come with me."

30

VAIL

In some ways, Charlotte had changed, but in others, she hadn't changed at all. When I'd last seen her in Colorado, she'd had the same cool manner, the businesslike poise. The difference now was in her eyes and the barely perceptible sag of her shoulders. Even after Colorado, her shoulders hadn't looked like that. Something had happened that had made her sad. Maybe more than one thing. Well, she could join the club.

"Your sisters are nice," she said politely as she carried her briefcase into the living room, following my lead.

"No, they're not." My sisters were many things, but no one used the word *nice*. One of them annoyed the shit out of me and the other one bossed me around. Then, for kicks, they'd switch places. I could hear their voices in the kitchen—low, hissed whispers overlapping each other. They were talking about us, no question.

Charlotte didn't argue the point. She was staring at the wall, with the words WAKE UP scrawled in crayon. Her gaze went to the crayon still on the floor, to the shards of glass swept in the corner. "Your manifestation did this?" she asked.

"Yes," I replied. "I already took pictures. You can take your own if you like."

That was the usual procedure with any investigation, whether hers or mine. Get out the camera, the tape recorder. Get out the electromagnetic meter, the infrared lens. Take pictures, record the interviews from the witnesses, record your own notes as quickly as possible. Dates, times, names, as if you're a cop. Document, document, document.

The goal of every investigation was proof. No one believed in this thing you spent your life on. Everyone made fun of it, or they thought you were a con artist or a fool. In defense, you became a cross between a detective at a crime scene and a scientist. You became Sherlock Holmes. You became the fingerprint analyst and the blood analyst and the detective figuring out which window the killer had entered through. You employed cold logic and technology, because you wanted to *know*, and you wanted other people to know. You wanted to be right. You wanted it to be real and for everyone else to think so, too. You didn't want to be thought of as the nutjob anymore, the one who is either an idiot or a charlatan or both. You wanted other people to see what you did, see the world the way you did, just once. Just once.

Charlotte didn't take out her camera, or her recorder, or anything else. She stared at the words on the wall and said, "Tell me what happened."

My throat tried to close. I flexed my hands at my sides, opening and closing my fists. "You don't want to start an investigation? That's why I called you."

"I'll investigate however I see fit. What I want is to hear you tell it."

My cheeks stung hot. No one had ever asked me this. I had done hundreds of interviews, but no one had ever interviewed me. I had talked to Dodie last night, but this was different. Charlotte was in the business of talking to people who had seen things that terrified them.

A Box Full of Darkness

I had never truly understood before how it feels to have someone listen to you without judging. People called VUFOS and Charlotte because they were crazy or because they were lying, sure. But they also called because they wanted someone to listen for once. To see them.

I talked.

I told her the events of that night, beginning with Dodie screaming and ending with me smashing the vase over whatever had grabbed me. It was only a sliver of the whole story, but where was the beginning, really? Not with Dodie screaming. Where, then? I had never known where the story began, and now I didn't know if it had a beginning at all. So I told her that one part, that one night. It was something.

Charlotte listened without interrupting. She put her briefcase back down without opening it. She stepped forward and inspected the letters closely, then crouched down to look at the crayon.

When I finished, I dropped into silence. Charlotte still studied the crayon, and it looked like she was thinking. She should have asked a thousand questions, but instead, her thoughts seemed far away.

I studied her profile, the shape of her chin, the nape of her neck where her hair was tied back. She had told the truth when she said that we knew each other through our lines of work. When someone experienced something strange—like, for example, what happened in this living room the other night—they didn't always know how to define it. Sometimes, more than one person had the experience, and they differed as to what it was. Charlotte might get called if it seemed to be ghosts. VUFOS might be called if it seemed to be aliens. If I was nearby and available, VUFOS would send me.

Charlotte and I had worked the same case only a few times. Once, we both concluded that the person was an obvious liar. Once, I had been reasonably sure the problem was some kind of ghost, so after I called Charlotte in, I had bowed out.

In Colorado, a man claimed that something was tormenting him. *Tormenting* was the word he used. According to his account, the thing—he had not seen it except from the corner of his eye—followed him to work and back, rang his doorbell, tapped his windows. It stomped on his roof and dug up the garden. He claimed that this entity had dogged him for years, though in recent months, it had gotten worse. His doctors could find nothing wrong with him, except that he might be crazy.

He'd talked about this problem to a retired college professor who lived down the street. The professor had known someone who knew Charlotte, who agreed to come assess the situation. Then Charlotte had called VUFOS, who called me.

Charlotte and I had spent seven days in the man's house, going over every inch of it, including his garden. We kept vigil at night, waiting for the sounds to come on the roof or at the windows. We shadowed him to work and back. In all that time, we saw and heard nothing unusual.

The man insisted that the thing knew we were there, so it was being quiet to make a fool of him. This was entirely possible, so Charlotte and I stayed as long as we could, hoping to help him. Then we both had other commitments, so we left.

Twenty-four hours after we left, the man took his gun from the safe in his basement and killed himself with it. He didn't leave a note. Since he lived alone, he wasn't found for several days.

Charlotte was right. Colorado wasn't my fault, and it wasn't hers, either. The man could have been deluded, psychotic. He could have had some other mental problem I wasn't qualified to diagnose. He could also have been tormented by something that waited until we left to start up again, and he only had one way to escape it. There are always several possible explanations, and that was one of them.

"What happened to you since Colorado?" I asked Charlotte.

"Did something happen?" she asked, not looking up.

"I can tell."

She hesitated, but only briefly. "My dad died." She stood up, brushing her skirt into place.

Charlotte had learned about parapsychology from her English grandparents on her father's side, who had pursued famous ghost-hunting cases in the twenties before they retired to obscure country life. Her father had fought in World War Two, then moved to America with his wife and daughter. On one of those long, sleepless nights on vigil in Colorado, Charlotte told me that as a teenager she had lived with her grandparents back in England, before both grandparents died in the early seventies. I had inferred that she had some kind of problem with her parents. But her sadness now at her father's death was different.

I'm sorry was the accepted line I should say. Also *That's too bad, He's in a better place, Time heals all wounds,* and depending on the kind of death, either *At least he didn't suffer* or *At least he isn't suffering anymore.*

"Did you hate him?" I asked her.

"Only sometimes," she said.

"I hated mine all the time."

She gestured to the writing. "This wasn't aliens," she said. "You know that. You have a ghost in your family home. What am I missing?"

It was hard to breathe, but the words came out anyway. "Ben was my little brother. He died twenty years ago, when he was six. He was playing hide-and-seek. We never found him. My sisters and I are here because our little brother is haunting this place."

Were her eyes always this kind, this sad? I thought maybe they were. It was why I looked into them as rarely as I could. But our gazes caught now, and I let myself sink for just a second, let her dark lashes and inky pupils take me in.

"Oh, Vail," she said, the two words soft and heartbroken.

There were too many thoughts in my skull, pressing over each other, trying to explode, one after another. There were always too many thoughts, so many that I never got any silence, so many that I could never speak quickly enough to catch one, so I didn't try. I wanted to tell her everything in that moment, but I didn't know where to start.

"I need help," I said, my voice a rasp. The first time I had ever said those words.

Charlotte stepped forward and put a hand on my cheek. Her touch was cool and soft, her fingers slender. She smelled like clean clothes and something faintly flowery.

She leaned up and gently kissed my lips, then pulled away. My thoughts went quiet.

"Show me the rest," she said.

I nodded. "The attic."

"The attic," she agreed. "Lead the way."

31

VIOLET

"What are they doing up there?" Dodie asked.

We'd heard Vail lead Charlotte upstairs to the attic, then nothing. Dodie was standing in the kitchen doorway, leaning toward the stairs, trying to catch the vibration of a sound.

"Leave them alone," I told her. "Let them work."

"Are you sure they're working?" She glanced back at me, then waggled her eyebrows. She was trying to annoy me, and she was succeeding. No one could annoy like Dodie could.

"Get your mind out of the gutter," I said, even though I knew I should ignore her.

"My mind lives in the gutter," Dodie shot back. She listened until a footstep sounded from the attic, and then she jumped away from the doorway. "They're just talking," she reported. "Boring." She turned to the mess on the kitchen counter. "I'm going to finish this."

I picked up my purse. The walls of the house were closing in on me. "I'm going out."

"Where?" Dodie asked.

"None of your business." This meant *I don't know*, but I didn't tell her that. Instead, I walked out the front door.

A breeze was blowing, warm and surprisingly gentle, carrying the scent of dying vegetation and asphalt. No cars passed on the street. I stood in the driveway with my keys in my hand and closed my eyes.

Images came back to me, moving behind my closed eyelids like snippets of film. Vail at thirteen, lying on his bed reading a book on a winter afternoon, his brow furrowed, his legs impossibly long, sprawled over his comforter in the snowy gray-blue light. Me bickering with Dodie as I braided her hair, the dark strands sliding over my fingers. My mother's perfume, the scent of which lived in the satin lining of her best wool coat. My father putting his hand on the top of my head when I was small, the only memory I had of him touching me with affection. Walking to school in the rain. Scraping my knees in a playground somewhere—school? A park?—and watching drops of blood soak into my torn tights. Sleeping next to a noisy fan in the heat of summer, waiting for the sun to come up again. The cold shock of a Popsicle on my tongue.

Sister wasn't the only memory that made up my childhood. There were other memories, too.

I opened my eyes and looked back at the house. A bird was perched on the roof, large and plump, its silhouette black against the sky. As I watched, it ruffled its inky feathers out, then preened the feathers with its beak. Was it a raven? A crow? I didn't know the difference. Maybe it was something else. I wondered if it had a nest up there, if it was part of a flock or if it was alone. If it lived there or was just passing through.

I had never seen the ghost of an animal, I realized. Not ever. Maybe they knew better than we did how to let go.

Gus and Bradley Pine's house in Evergreen Heights was just like every other house on the street, an unremarkable box made of brick topped with shabby aluminum siding. The shutters had been painted blue over a decade ago. Cedar trees—plants of the lowest possible maintenance—lined the sides of the yard, with a maple tree in the center. The leaves on the lawn, I noted, were in a pile. Bradley had done his assigned raking.

When I rang the front doorbell, Gus answered. He wore old army pants and a gray sweatshirt. He grinned at me, showing his yellowing teeth through his bushy beard. Without a greeting, he shouted back into the house: "Violet's here!" Turning back to me, he said, "You could have called."

I rolled my eyes in answer. "Just let me in."

"Gladly." He stepped aside and waved me into a well-worn living room, complete with deep sofa upholstered in plaid with matching chair, both aimed at the TV. He may as well have hung a sign that said BACHELOR'S RESIDENCE. It smelled weirdly of man in here, a sweaty, mustardy miasma I wasn't used to. Vail only smelled like soap.

Bradley appeared from the hall, buckling his belt and pulling his shirt over it as if he'd just dressed. "Thank God," he said to no one, jamming his feet into his shoes and taking my elbow. "Dad, Violet and I are going out," he announced, hustling me toward the front door.

"Stay for a coffee." Gus was still grinning as if he'd said a joke.

"No way, old man." Bradley pushed me onto the porch and slammed the screen door in Gus's face.

"Don't let him eat yogurt!" Gus shouted after us through the screen. "It goes straight through his guts!"

Bradley opened his car door and folded me in bodily, like a cop arresting a dangerous suspect. "Hurry up."

"Okay, okay. God." I leaned away from the door when he slammed it and waited for him to get in the driver's seat.

Bradley backed out of the driveway at top speed, twisting to see out the window behind him.

"Where are we going?" I asked when we were at the stop sign at the head of the street.

"Fuck if I know," was the answer.

So he wanted to escape his house as much as I had wanted to escape mine. We drove in silence for a while, and I found that I didn't mind his company, the quiet, or our aimless route. I turned off my thoughts and watched the scenery out the window.

No one would call Fell beautiful—laundromats and variety stores were no one's concept of urban utopia—but it was familiar to me. We passed the Fell College of Classical Education, which looked like a leafy visitor from another world, its elegant Victorian buildings clustered around a cobblestoned square, out of place among the squat, ugly buildings that made up the rest of town. A rich man's long-ago dream. It looked peaceful, but I also remembered the poltergeist in the library and Gus's story of the girl who disappeared from her dorm, her cup of tea left cooling on her desk.

When we came to the South Overpass, I remembered that it was the place where Cathy Caldwell's body was found. "We're leaving town," I said.

"I just want to drive," Bradley replied.

We turned onto a two-lane road lined with trees. After a sign that said we would eventually get to Albany if we drove long enough, there was no other indication of where we were. Bradley's shoulders relaxed. I wondered what had happened, whether he'd argued with Gus or had a disagreement with his ex-wife. Maybe living with his father wasn't going well. Maybe one of the kids was sick, or maybe he was worried about money since he was out of a job. I was uncomfortable with the idea of Bradley Pine having feelings.

He ruined my momentary softness toward him by saying into the silence of the car, "I think we should have sex."

I couldn't help it—I laughed. "Where?" I asked him. "My house, which is haunted as shit? Yours? You want to do it on the plaid sofa with your dad in the next room?"

He swore in frustration, his knuckles white on the wheel. "There's a motel."

"Have you *seen* the Sun Down?" I asked. "It's the creepiest place in town, and that's saying something."

"Violet, come on. You know you want to." This was said, for once, without Bradley's usual unearned confidence. It was just a fact.

"Bradley, it isn't happening," I shot back. I ignored the question of whether I wanted to sleep with him. Part of me did, but it was the part of me that had made similar bad decisions, like snorting cocaine up my nose or sleeping with Clay the first time. "We'd hate each other after. It wouldn't even be good."

He looked perplexed, his brows drawing down. "What does that mean?"

"The fact that you just asked that question means I'm right."

"What?"

"Forget it."

"I just think it would clear the air," he said, as if this was a valid argument.

"Wow, that's flattering," I commented.

"What?" he said again.

I pinched the bridge of my nose with my thumb and forefinger. "No, Bradley. The answer is no."

"Whatever." Then, "Dad made some calls. There aren't any cases of stolen babies. No closed cases, and definitely no open ones. He says your father probably screwed around and your little brother was his."

"That's the theory we were going with, too," I said. I told him about the attic, the marbles.

Bradley, as always, questioned nothing. "It's reincarnation, maybe," he said. "He was another kid before. The *National Enquirer* writes about reincarnation, but it's always Elvis being reincarnated, or... Actually, just Elvis."

"Ben was a real baby," I said. "I fed him, I changed him. So did my siblings. I know what ghosts look like, and he wasn't one. He was real."

Bradley nodded. "Reincarnated people are real."

"But reincarnated people are born," I argued. "Ben must have been born, but we don't know to who, or how my parents ended up with him."

"Maybe it doesn't matter," Bradley said.

"Of course it matters." I waved my hands in frustration. "That's what this whole thing is about. Finding out who Ben was, finding out what happened to him. Because they're connected."

"Who cares where he came from twenty-six years ago?" Bradley argued back. "What matters is where he came from the first time. That's what the marbles mean. That's what he's trying to tell you."

My temples throbbed and my eyes stung. *He's been telling you and telling you,* Alice had said. *You have to go back to the beginning. The real beginning.*

How long ago had my little brother really been born?

"Has anyone written a history of Fell?" I asked.

Bradley shrugged. If there was ever a person disinterested in history, it was Bradley Pine. "Who knows? One of those nerds at the college probably has."

I looked at him, and our gazes caught for a second before he turned back to the road and sighed, flicking his signal on.

"Yeah, I get it," he said. "I'm turning around."

32

DODIE

"It's time for me to tell you the truth," Ethan said. "I'm a Russian spy."

"Are you?" I leaned against the kitchen wall and twisted the phone cord around one index finger. I had meant to tidy the kitchen, truly I had, but it was so boring, and I got distracted. The phone was right there on the wall. I took a chance, calling Ethan in the middle of the day, and he had picked up. He told me it was his day off. From what, I still had no idea.

"If I'm lying, you'll never know," he said.

"Spies get days off?" I asked.

"No one can work all the time."

"I see. So now that you've told me, do you have to kill me?"

"That depends. How many CIA operatives do you know?"

"None, since apparently you aren't one."

"Then you're safe for now. How is the search for your little brother going?"

I leaned my shoulder against the wall, feeling tired. "Ethan, you're going to think I'm crazy. That we're all crazy."

"Dodie," he replied, his voice oddly gentle, "if I was going to judge you, I would have done it by now."

"I don't understand why you're asking. Why you even want to know."

"Because you seem sad."

I stared at my feet.

"That's the only reason," Ethan said into the silence.

I thought about Ben in my bed the other night, his warm body against mine, and then... "I think he died a long time ago," I said. "Even longer than we think, do you understand? Further back in the past."

There was a beat of silence. "How long ago?" Ethan asked.

I bit my lip. "It depends how old this house is." The logic rotated slowly through my brain, like an old clock being wound. "He lived in this house—I'm sure of that. He died here. But he didn't die the day we played hide-and-seek." I shook my head. "Or maybe he did, but I mean—"

"I understand."

I laughed softly. "Are you sure about that?"

"Okay, it's confusing. But I understand what you're getting at. You think that your life with Ben wasn't his first life. That he lived another time, before he lived with you."

I lifted my gaze from my feet as my eyes watered. Never mind how crazy it was—something about that sounded so inexpressibly beautiful. To be given more than one life, to never truly die—there was a reason some religions believed it. Because thinking of it any other way was too hard. "There's a bag of marbles in the attic from 1899," I said, "so it would have been sometime after that. But I don't know when."

"And you don't know how old the house is?"

"No. If there was something in our mother's papers about the house, Violet would have seen it. And there are no papers left in our parents' bedroom."

"Maybe there are municipal records."

"Violet went out. She'll probably find out." Violet was out investigating, and Vail was in the attic with the ghost hunter. My big brother and big sister were taking care of everything, as usual, leaving me to be the useless one. I had no experience with this like Vail did, no brains like Violet. All I'd ever had to do in life was look pretty and bite my tongue in public in my best attempt to be charming. No one expected anything much of me at all.

I ran my palm down the wall, looking at the ugly wallpaper.

"You don't have to have all the answers right now," Ethan said, as if reading my mind. "I don't think that's what Ben wanted when he called you home."

"He asked for us to make it right."

"No, he didn't. He said, *Come home*. That isn't the same thing. Maybe he just wanted you there, Dodie. Maybe he just missed you like you missed him."

I pressed my palm to the kitchen wall and closed my eyes. "He told me to find him when he was in bed with me." I could still hear those words in his familiar little voice. *Dodie. Find me.* "What does that mean, then? Something was done wrong, and it has to be made right. That's the only way this makes any sense."

"No," Ethan said. "It isn't."

Ben's warm body in the bed with me. It was the water that interrupted us, that chased us out of the room. Then, downstairs, something vicious and cold had grabbed Vail and whispered in his ear.

If I could live here, could feel Ben in bed with me every night, would I ever leave? I'd give up anything, everything for that. Wouldn't I?

Did he want me to?

"Where are you right now?" I asked Ethan.

"In my apartment," he replied. "In the Lower East Side. It's tiny, but it's cheap. It came with a pullout sofa, so that's what I sleep on every night. I sit on it when the sun is up, then lie down on it when the sun goes down. This thing is so heavy that I don't think it will ever be moved out of this building. I don't even know how anyone got it up the stairs."

I smiled to myself, picturing it.

"So I have a single room, a tiny kitchen, and a bathroom. The main room is my bedroom, my living room, my everything room. I own two plates, four forks, and a plastic bowl with a beer logo on the side. I don't know why a beer company would make a bowl, so don't ask. I can hear my upstairs neighbor every time he pees, and my downstairs neighbor smokes a cigarette every hour, on the hour, that comes up through my vents. The garbage truck arrives, very loudly, at six o'clock every Wednesday morning. My parents live in a nice house in suburban Maryland and think I'm insane to live here. They tell me regularly that I'll regret coming to New York, but it's been over two years, and I don't. I keep waiting for the regret, but it never arrives."

At his words, I missed New York with an ache deep in my body, emanating from my bones. "My apartment has faulty fuses," I said. "You can't plug in a lamp and a curling iron at the same time."

"Sounds perfect," Ethan said.

"It's sweltering in summer," I said.

"Oh yes," he agreed. "I fill a bowl with ice water and put my feet in it. That's the only thing that helps on the worst days."

"I do that, too. I can use a fan in summer, but only if I unplug everything else in the apartment."

We both laughed.

"It's too quiet here," I said. "Too quiet and too creepy."

"You have to be there for a little while," Ethan said. "Then come back to New York. And when you do, will you have lunch with me?"

"Lunch?" I asked, surprised at how stung I felt. "Don't you want a second date?"

"I do, but you won't say yes to a second date."

"I haven't said yes to lunch, either."

"You don't need to go on a date," Ethan said reasonably. "But everyone needs to eat lunch sometime."

After I hung up, I looked around the kitchen, feeling useless again. Then I saw the girl out the window.

It was the neighbor girl—Terri, I remembered. Terri Chatham. An unfortunate name, and the girl had an unfortunate haircut, but otherwise she had seemed sweet. She was walking along the tree line behind our house, looking like she was woolgathering. Wasn't this a school day? Why was she walking around alone?

It was none of my business. I picked up a dusty can of tomatoes—honestly, when had anyone in this house ever eaten canned tomatoes?—and then I saw the second figure.

It was quick, a shadow flitting between the trees behind Terri. Terri didn't notice. She kept walking. As I watched, the shadow flitted behind her again, as if following her from a distance.

The can banged down on the counter as I grabbed my coat. The hair stood up on the back of my neck. I strode to the back door and was hurrying toward Terri before I formed a complete thought. *Get away from her, whoever you are. Whatever you are.*

The girl lifted her gaze and caught sight of me approaching, and I remembered to rearrange my face into something approaching pleasant. "Hi there!" I called out to her, an approximation of a friendly, neighborly greeting. "I'm Dodie. Remember me?"

Terri smiled back at me. "Hi."

"Hi, Terri." I was close to her now, and I resisted the urge to grab her by the arm or by the shoulders to move her along. Every alarm instinct was clanging in my gut. "Why aren't you in school right now?"

Her brow crinkled. "It's Saturday?"

"It is? Well, what do you know." I looked around, taking note of the trees. I didn't see the shadow again, but I could feel it. There was definitely a bad smell in the cool air. "I had no idea. But since it isn't a school day, let's do something fun."

Her brow crinkled further, though she looked—pathetically—a little hopeful. "You and me?"

"Sure," I said. "Anything you want." Since I was bad at subtlety, I pointed away from the trees, in the direction of the road. "Something that way."

"Oh, well. Okay?" She didn't seem convinced that I was telling the truth. "I was walking, but I was thinking maybe I might ride my bike."

"Bike riding sounds delightful," I said with more force than was necessary. Something that took place on the road, complete with mode of transportation to escape whatever was in the trees? Yes, indeed. "What fun."

The look on Terri's face reminded me that I should never reproduce, something I was already fully convinced of. I was scaring her a little.

"Want to come?" she asked me. She must truly have a dearth of friends.

"I don't have a bike, dear," I replied.

"I have an extra," Terri said. "I got a new bike for Christmas, but I don't like it as much as my old bike. So now I have both."

I couldn't remember the last time I rode a bike. Vail had taught me to ride when I was six, watching and—of course—laughing every time I fell off. The only bike we owned was Vail's, because Violet and I had no interest in physical activity. When Vail had started teaching Ben to ride on that same bike, he hadn't laughed at him.

But my gaze flicked to the trees, where something was definitely moving. Something dark that I didn't like at all. I'd have to make a sacrifice.

"All right, show me this bike of yours," I said to Terri. "I'd love to take a ride."

33

VAIL

Charlotte took her time in the attic. In her briefcase, she carried the basic tools of her trade—a radio-wave scanner, a camera with flash, a portable tape recorder with microphone. She told me to sit in the corner in silence while she worked, not to speak, not to tell her anything else about Ben or his connection to the house. It was best if she worked blind.

The toys had been rearranged again. The bag of marbles was gone—Violet had brought it down with her—and the crayons were still scattered in the kitchen and the living room, but the rest of Ben's toys were here. A teddy bear with black-button eyes sat on top of a Jack-in-the-box with its lid closed. The balsam wood airplane with the upside-down wings was on the floor in the corner, as if briefly played with and discarded. The board games and puzzles had been put back in their boxes, but the boxes lay on the floor. A left rubber boot and a right sneaker lay side by side. No matter how many times we reminded him to clean up, Ben was always a messy little boy.

I lowered myself to sit on the floor, my back to the wall, my knees bent, as Charlotte took items from her briefcase. She made no comment on my little brother's ghostly mess. I closed my eyes and imagined I could hear Ben, breathlessly telling me something scattered that was very important to him in the moment. I pulled the teddy bear into my lap.

"Don't touch anything," Charlotte scolded me softly.

"Too late," I replied.

We weren't going to talk about the kiss. She had never done that before, and I had never asked her to. We didn't have that kind of relationship. I couldn't have said why she did it. All I knew was that her lips had been cool and soft, and the memory of it soothed a small part of my jagged edges in this attic. Maybe that was why she had done it. Maybe a kiss doesn't need any other reason than that the person receiving it simply needs it.

"Do you recognize all of these things?" Charlotte asked after another moment. "Is there anything here that strikes you as strange or out of place?"

The bag of marbles from 1899 wasn't familiar to me, but I didn't tell Charlotte about those. It was best if she wasn't influenced by anything else that had already happened. "I recognize everything," I said without opening my eyes, talking to the darkness behind my lids. "I know every piece in this attic. We had to box it up and put it up here when we started to understand that he wasn't coming back."

"The mismatched shoes?" Her voice was gentle but businesslike. The voice of a doctor who knows you're scared of the answers to her questions.

"Definitely Ben," I said.

"Has anything been moved or rearranged since you were here last?"

"Everything," I replied. "Everything has moved around."

"But nothing is destroyed." I heard the click of her camera as the flash hit my closed eyelids. I hadn't taken photos up here because in those first upset moments, Dodie had asked me not to. I was glad I had called Charlotte. Someone needed to take over this investigation.

"Ben didn't destroy his toys," I told her. "He played with them, but he didn't wreck them."

"These are well used." Another click, another flash. "Did he ever play up here before?"

Before he died, she meant. "No. No one came up here until we had to store his things. We got rid of his other things eventually, but not the toys."

"His bed?" she asked. "His clothes? His furniture?"

I choked the word out. "Gone."

A moment of silence behind my closed eyelids in the dark. It had seemed like the best idea at the time, because none of us could inhabit the space with his things anymore. Maybe it was wrong, but even now, I wasn't sure of that. Looking at Ben's pillow or his soft, well-worn pajamas today would kill me.

When the unimaginable happens, you make the best decisions you can, and you never know if they were the right ones.

Charlotte spoke again. "So it isn't the space that draws him but the toys. He followed his belongings up here. When you took the crayons downstairs, he followed them and used them. He loved these things, and he loves them still. You were right not to get rid of them. He didn't want you to."

Jesus, this was hard. I kept my eyes closed, kept breathing through the sharp pain in my chest. I stroked the soft head of the teddy bear, feeling the fur against my palm. "Some of these things were ours first," I said. "We handed them down. The bear I'm holding was Dodie's, and she passed it to Ben. Other things, we bought for him."

"These toys were his life," Charlotte said softly. "His favorite things. Where they go, he goes."

My throat choked closed. When I could speak again, I said, "What are you getting at?"

"Your revenant is a little boy," she replied. "He has always been a little boy. That's why the toys are so central to what's happening. He has never been a man."

I opened my eyes and looked at her. "What do you mean?"

Charlotte was putting her instruments back into her briefcase. Her businesslike motions calmed me a little. "When did your parents buy this house?" she asked. "Or is it an ancestral home?"

I shook my head. "They moved here after they married and before Violet was born." I did the math in my head. "Around 1954. Why?"

"I'd like to go downstairs, please. I'm finished here. I'd like to see the bedrooms, since the manifestation appeared there as well."

"Charlotte."

Her look was all cool English imperiousness. "Vail. You called me all the way here. Do you want my assistance, or don't you?"

I bit back my retort and stood.

"Which bedroom do you want to see?" I asked when we had descended the attic stairs.

"Dodie's, since your brother appeared to her there."

I had been trained from childhood not to enter my sisters' bedrooms or face immediate execution, so I opened Dodie's door for Charlotte and stood back. "Be my guest." I didn't hear either sister in the kitchen downstairs. I wondered where they had gone.

Charlotte took out her spectrometer and went into Dodie's room. We went down the hall like that—Dodie's room, then our parents' abandoned bedroom, then Violet's room. Ben's empty bedroom. Charlotte used the spectrometer in each room but didn't take any more photos, even in Ben's room. She also didn't take notes.

When we got to my room, I leaned against the doorframe and watched her. Charlotte took silent note of my VUFOS file boxes, the few clothes in the open closet, the slanted ceiling, the messy twin bed. If she had any comment about being in my bedroom, she didn't say it aloud.

Instead, she turned a dial on her spectrometer and rotated in a slow circle, staring at the output screen.

"Does that thing actually tell you anything?" I asked her, unable to bear the silence any longer.

"A little," she said without looking up.

"I always wondered if it was just a prop."

"It isn't a prop," she replied icily. "It measures electromagnetic waves."

"And?" I didn't want to admit I was curious, but I couldn't help it.

"There are peaks and valleys on this floor," Charlotte said. "The readings are all over the place. Very low in the master bedroom, and high in your sisters' bedrooms. It's rather unusual. I haven't seen readings quite like this since a case I worked in Vermont—an abandoned girls' boarding school. I don't know what haunted that place, and honestly, I hope never to know. I was happy to get out of there as soon as I could."

I crossed my arms. "So my house is haunted."

"You already knew that," was the irritated reply. "Have you seen any manifestations in this room?"

I scratched an eyebrow with one finger, letting my gaze drift to the wall. "I saw lights over my bed when I was a kid. Figures standing over me. The words 'wake up.' It hasn't happened since I've been back."

"The same words written on the wall downstairs."

"Yes."

There wasn't a flicker of disbelief in Charlotte's voice. "Such riveting psychological insight into your character," she said. "I suddenly understand you better."

"Don't get used to it," I shot back.

She almost smiled. Almost. "Dodie saw water. You have seen lights. Has Violet seen anything?"

The words stopped in my throat. I wasn't ashamed of Violet, and

I didn't think she was crazy. But her story was hers to tell, not mine. "Violet sees things sometimes," I settled on saying. "But not in this house."

"Are you sure about that?"

I frowned, because I wasn't sure. At all. We had never talked about our nightmares in detail growing up. What had Violet seen that she hadn't told us? If she'd kept silent, how bad must it have been?

"You're getting at something, Charlotte," I said. "You've seen everything you need. Just tell me what you're thinking."

Charlotte looked pensive. She really was pretty, with her elegant jawline and her tilted-up chin. If you liked that sort of woman. "I am reminded of a case I consulted on some time ago," she said in her best English lecturer's voice. "A family bought a house in Tennessee that they came to believe was haunted. The children saw figures in the shadows, and the littlest child—she was only three—claimed that something came in her window at night."

I nodded. "Go on."

"The girl's bedroom was on the ground floor. The window wasn't tampered with, but the little girl had persistent nightmares about someone coming in the window. She said it was the mailman. That was very odd, to be certain, but the girl always described it the same way, as if she was sure. The mailman was coming through the window." She shook her head. "It could be written off as a child's recurring nightmare except that the two other children in the house saw things, too. And the parents heard scrabbling, thumps, something being dragged on the floor. One of my colleagues investigated it. He was baffled, and he called me."

I waited. Despite my impatience, I could admit that she was a decent storyteller.

"I come across many hoaxes in my line of work," Charlotte said, with a knowing look at me. "It was possible that this was one of them. But before he called me, my colleague discovered that a murder had taken place in that very house, fifty years before the family bought it. The teenage girl sleeping in the main-floor bedroom was murdered one night, her body left on the floor. Whoever did it came through the window. The case was never solved."

I wanted to make a scathing remark, but the words wouldn't come.

Charlotte put the spectrometer down on my bed and opened her briefcase again. "The case, alas, had to be left a mystery. I'm sure you're familiar with the feeling. Did a mailman commit the murder of the teenage girl? No detective will reopen an old investigation based on the nightmares of a three-year-old child fifty years later, so we will never know. Perhaps the little girl was simply having a recurring dream. Perhaps she had seen the street's mailman one day and her mind fixed on him. Perhaps she had been coached by her family, or had picked up on a conversation somewhere about the murder. Or perhaps, as she slept at night, she was witnessing the murder that had taken place in her bedroom before she was born. And she was witnessing it over and over again."

Something moved on the edges of my mind, made a hollow sound like an elongated knuckle tapping on the glass of a skylight. A thought and a memory in one.

"The police wouldn't look into the family mailman, but you would," I said to Charlotte. "And you did."

She nodded. "Of course I did. The mailman whose route included their home was nearing sixty and close to retirement. He lived alone with his wife because their grown children had moved away. He did not seem like a person who would sneak out at night to terrify a child. That's all I know."

"There are many possible explanations for what I saw in this room," I said. "And one of the explanations is that I saw something that happened here. Something that happened to Ben."

"And yet this isn't Ben's bedroom."

Yes. It was. I was suddenly sure it was.

This had been Ben's bedroom the *first* time.

I moved to the bed and sat down. I put my head in my hands, my elbows on my knees. I stared at the floor between my feet.

Where did you go, little brother? Where did you go?

It was fucking terrifying, but the first thing I felt was grief. I had spent my childhood in my little brother's room before he was born. This stupid room, with the slanted ceiling that I banged my head on—*this* was Ben's room. All these years, and I had never known.

What had he seen before he died the first time? Had he seen lights? Someone standing over his bed? Had he heard those words, "Wake up"? Was that why he wrote them on the wall?

Charlotte broke into my thoughts with her cool, crisp accent. "I recommend an exorcism," she said.

I lifted my head from my hands. "I'm not *exorcising* my little brother."

"Not him." She waved a hand. "Please think clearly, Vail. You need to exorcise the other entity in this house. The one that grabbed you. The one that wrote on the wall downstairs."

Now I was confused. "Ben wrote on the wall downstairs."

"That does seem possible, but the evidence tells me otherwise. You said your little brother was six. Could he write?"

I stared at her, lost. "What?"

"Could he write?" Her voice was patient. "He would have been learning at that age. Some children take to writing faster than others. But the words on the wall downstairs are perfectly formed, and they are written in a straight line. They don't look like a child's lettering. And we've just established that Ben was never an adult."

I shook my head. "He could—he knew some of his letters. His name." I didn't add that Ben was a slow learner because he wasn't enrolled in school. He learned reading and writing from his siblings, and the three of us weren't exactly disciplinarians. We didn't try all that hard to teach him.

The fact was that when he died, Ben was a slow, sloppy reader, and he could barely write at all.

I had been too blind to see it. But I would know Ben's handwriting, such as it was. And his handwriting wasn't on the downstairs wall.

Charlotte took a small, slim book from her briefcase and handed it to me without a word.

"What's this?" I took the book from her.

"It's from the attic. It was propped up against a box."

The book was yellowed, its few pages bound between delicate covers. A children's book called *Fairfield Rabbit*. On the pastel green cover was an ink illustration of a fat rabbit with chubby cheeks and kind eyes, his ears flopping. The rabbit wore a striped waistcoat. The book looked very old.

"This wasn't in the attic," I argued. "I've never seen this before."

"And yet it was there today," Charlotte said.

I opened the cover and turned to the title page. The book was published in 1904. Written in ink on the corner of the page, the words faded with over eighty years of age, was an inscription.

To Edward Whitten, from his sister Anne. On his fifth birthday. August 3, 1905.

The handwriting was neat and straight. Schoolroom handwriting.

"Edward Whitten," I said aloud. The words hung in the air of my bedroom, seemed to bloom in the dusty emptiness. The knuckle in my brain tapped again, as if the name was a memory.

I looked up and locked gazes with Charlotte. "Who is Anne Whitten?" I asked.

Something screamed.

I dropped the book and gripped my temples. The scream wound higher, stronger, reverberating in my skull. Charlotte dropped to a crouch, her hands over her head. Her mouth was open. She was screaming, too, but it wasn't her scream in my head. It was something else.

There was a footstep in the hall, heavy and angry. It was the thing that had grabbed me in the living room. It was screaming, and it was coming.

I grabbed Charlotte's instruments and shoved them into her briefcase. Then I grabbed her by the arm and pulled her from the room, toward the stairs. She sagged in my grip, disoriented. I dug my fingers in harder and pulled her down the stairs behind me.

Another step sounded in the hall behind me, and another. The scream wound on and on, in no need of breath.

Charlotte stumbled, but I kept her moving, getting behind her and pushing her down the front hall toward the door. Gripping her shoulders, I sidled past her and twisted the knob, kicking the door open. Then I shoved her past the porch and into the front yard.

The scream went silent. Charlotte fell to her knees in the grass, gasping. I dropped her briefcase beside her and spun to look at the house.

In an upstairs window, a shadowy figure moved, brushing one of the curtains. Then it was gone.

I watched for another moment as the ringing slowly subsided in my ears, but nothing else moved.

"Vail." Charlotte's normally calm voice was a rasp. She stood, trying to brush the dirt from her knees.

"You need to get out of here," I told her. "You need to run from this place. Right now."

Her skin was ghastly gray, her eyes wild. "What was that?"

"I don't know."

"It was screaming." Charlotte rubbed her palms over her cheeks, as if reassuring herself she was still here. "It was screaming, but it wasn't. It was like it was screaming inside me. I could feel it. It was like it touched me."

A Box Full of Darkness

Could it follow us from the house? Could it come out here? Was it still in there, walking the halls?

It had started when I said the name Anne Whitten aloud, as if it had been waiting to hear its name.

"You need an exorcism," Charlotte said sharply. I turned to see that she had regained most of her composure. Splotches of angry red splashed her cheeks. "Either that, or burn the house down to get rid of that thing."

I shook my head. I would never burn the house down, no matter what lived inside. Not my little brother's house, the only place he had ever lived.

"I've seen exorcisms work," Charlotte said as she picked up her briefcase. "You can call it a banishment, if you prefer—it removes the religious aspect. But there's a ritual."

"Chants and burning sage?" My tone was harsh. "Ouija boards? Séance circles? You think those things will work on *that*?" I gestured to the house, which was unnaturally still now. Silent. The curtains in the upstairs window didn't move.

I didn't believe in exorcisms. I didn't believe in séances, either, or tarot cards, or psychics. Bigfoot or cryptids. After a decade of chasing shadows, I didn't believe in any of it.

I didn't even believe in aliens anymore.

With the echoes of that scream in my head, it was all so fucking clear.

My voice was eerily calm when I said to Charlotte, "I think you should go."

"*You* called *me*," she reminded me, her voice icy. "But don't worry. I have no desire to go back into that house."

"Go," I said again. "Leave Fell. Don't even stay tonight at the motel. No one stays at that motel." I had never been to the Sun Down, so I shouldn't know that—but of course I did, because why would this town ever leave me alone? It was too much to ask. "Drive as far as you can, then stop and stay somewhere else. Just drive and keep driving."

"Thank you for the advice," she clipped out. "I intend to take it."

"You aren't much of a ghost hunter," I pointed out.

Her shoulders straightened. "Vail," she said, "kindly go fuck yourself."

I heaved in a breath. "I'm sorry." Of the people in my life who deserved an apology—and there were many of them—Charlotte topped the list. "You came when I called because you're a good person. You gave your advice. Now you have to trust that I'll do what I have to."

She hesitated, her jaw working. Then she said, "You're going back in there."

"No," I said.

"You're lying."

"Yes, I am."

"You can't." There was a final note of pleading in her voice. "You're a fool."

"I know. But I'm not running away and leaving my sisters to go in there alone."

Charlotte's gaze moved uneasily to the house, then away again. "I can't help you, Vail. I want to, but I can't."

"I know." My voice was as gentle as I could make it. I was sorry I'd dragged her into this, sorry I'd put her in danger, but I had, and what was done was done.

I watched her get into her car, watched the driver's door slam, watched her turn the key. Watched her leave the driveway. Watched her lights disappear down the street. And as I watched, I thought over and over, *To Edward Whitten, from his sister Anne. To Edward Whitten, from his sister Anne.*

I wondered if Edward Whitten had lived long past his fifth birthday, when his sister had given him a book as a gift.

I wondered why Anne Whitten was walking the halls of my family home, screaming when she heard her name. There was one way to find out.

I turned without hesitating and walked back to the house.

34

VIOLET

I had never gone to college—that went without saying—and neither had Bradley. We both felt out of place on the campus of the Fell College of Classical Education, with its air of quiet contemplation, its dedication to the study of topics no one used in everyday life. A noticeboard in a hallway of the administrative building featured information about the Marcus Aurelius Society (*not* the Marcus Aurelius Study Group, which was entirely different, according to the note's writer). Another note stated that a debate about the relative merits of fourteenth-century popes would be held on Tuesday night. The attendees, the note warned, were to be civil this time.

Bradley's muscles were of no use to us here, even if he'd had them on display. It was up to me to approach a bespectacled student and ask if there might be a history of Fell anywhere on campus. The kid sent us to the library, across the quadrangle. We only saw three other students as we walked, all of whom gave us a wide berth. Fell College wasn't known for its large number of attendees.

The library was small, dusty, and dim. The librarian gave us a glare that could have singed metal, but when she heard our request, she called over another bespectacled student, this one a blond boy with too-big metal-framed glasses and a fading pimple on his chin. The kid, who was probably eighteen and would have been crushed immediately under my ass if I sat on him, gave us a haughty look. "Yes?" he asked, his voice as icy as a nobleman's.

"Take them to the Local Literature room, Farley," the librarian said.

Farley gave her a shocked look. "The Local Lit room is for students only."

"The library is for students only," the librarian corrected him. "The Local Lit room is supposed to be for local residents who ask to use it. No one has ever asked."

"You have a records room that no one ever uses?" I asked.

The librarian gave me her glare again, and I flinched. "Just because it isn't *used* doesn't mean it has no *purpose*. Farley, please let them in." She handed Farley a key. "You have one hour," she said to us.

Farley led us in annoyed silence down one hall, then another. He stopped at a door that said FELL LOCAL LITERATURE—RESIDENTS ONLY and inserted the key. "In here," he said.

The room was the size of a large closet, with a single stuffed bookshelf and a wooden chair in the corner. Placed beside the chair was a floor lamp. The whole atmosphere was that of a disused attic, crossed with a police interrogation room.

"I can tell you don't teach interior decorating at this college," I said.

That made Farley mad, which was satisfying. "What are you even doing here?" he asked us. "You can't possibly need research because you're writing something."

"Hey," Bradley interjected. "I can write."

Farley looked him up and down. "When was the last time you tried it?"

"You guys don't write so great yourselves." Bradley pointed to the motto engraved on a plaque above the door. "That's not even in English."

Farley looked at the plaque and his cheeks went red. "That's Latin. *Vincit qui se vincit*. It's the college's motto."

"Yeah, well, you can *vincit* your way out of here, Pimple Face," Bradley said. "Get lost."

The kid hesitated. "You're my responsibility. I should probably stay."

Bradley crowded him until he stepped back, out of the doorway. "Bye," Bradley said, then swung the door shut, turning the lock. "God, I hate nerds."

"How many nerds did you bully in high school?" I asked him.

"All of 'em," was the reply.

"That's what I thought." Since I didn't see a light switch, I turned on the lamp. It had a hundred-watt bulb that made the room brighter than the surface of the sun. I squinted and tilted the bulb toward the wall, which made it flicker before it settled down again. "Let's get this over with." I walked to the bookshelf and began studying the titles.

"I'll supervise," Bradley said, dropping into the room's only chair. He leaned back, tilted his head against the wall behind him, and closed his eyes.

The books were a collection of pamphlets, essays, and maps about the city of Fell. All of them were originals, and some dated as far back as the 1850s. There was a musty old memoir by a long-dead, long-forgotten city councillor, published—seemingly by himself—in 1912 and bound so cheaply it was falling apart. I turned the loosening pages carefully, hoping for something juicy, but the book seemed to be a collection of the man's complaints and grievances about other city councillors and everyone else in town, especially anyone who had crossed him. I couldn't help but aspire to achieve that level of pettiness by the end of my life. Robert R. McCannon was my new role model.

"You don't have to stay," I said to Bradley when I realized I'd spent twenty minutes perusing the weird collection on the bookshelf. Bradley's eyes were still closed, and he seemed to be napping. "I'll come out when I'm done."

"Nope," he replied without opening his eyes. He must be bored, but I realized he was staying in case Sister sent another one of her otherworldly messengers after me. It was strangely chivalrous. I wondered how many dead people I might see wandering around the FCCE. Did people die here often?

"Make yourself useful, then," I said to Bradley, handing him an old map. "Hold this open under the light."

He unfolded it and angled the lamp, and we both stared at it. The map seemed to date from around 1900, which predated even the FCCE. Some of the ink was sun faded, and the edges were worn.

The spot where the FCCE campus now stood was only farmland on the map. I oriented myself by finding the main road in and out of town, which now led to the interstate. I traced my finger along the main streets, trying to picture what Fell might have looked like in 1900.

"Yeah," Bradley said. "This is definitely Fell."

He pointed. Along the edge of the map was a line I knew was Number Six Road, near where the Sun Down Motel now stood. Off the edge of Number Six—the road wasn't named on the old map—was a square labeled *Graves—Unknown*. It was marked with small *x* marks in careful handwriting.

"There are a lot of cemeteries," I said. "For such a small town at the time, Fell had a lot of dead people."

"Like I said," Bradley agreed. "It's definitely Fell."

My eye moved to the spot where my neighborhood should be, where our house should be. I saw only open land on the map, with a tidy label written on it: *Whitten Estate*.

I felt a chill up my back, one that—for once—had nothing to do with ghosts. It was those two words, *Whitten Estate.* The name sounded right somehow, familiar, as if I'd overheard it years ago and had forgotten it until now. Like I'd known a Whitten at some point and couldn't remember from where.

"Whitten," I said to Bradley, taking the map from his hands. "They might have built our house, or part of it. The house is old enough. It's a start."

"Looks like they own your whole neighborhood," Bradley said. "At least, they used to. The whole thing was one lot."

"So what happened?" I asked. "They sold it off?"

Bradley shrugged, then sat back in his chair. I squinted at the map in the harsh light. On the Whitten Estate, near the edge of the grounds, were more small, careful *x*'s, though these were unlabeled. Graves unknown?

I refolded the map and looked through the rest of the shelves, hoping to find something that contained the name. If the Whittens had an estate in Fell in 1900, then they were a rich, important family at the time. Someone must have mentioned them, or some Whitten must have felt himself important enough to write papers or memoirs. Then, it seemed, they'd had some kind of downfall, which led to the estate being broken up. Someone must have noticed that, too.

Where were the descendants of the Whittens now? If the family left Fell, where had they gone? Was there any way I could track down their descendants? If so, would any of them have any old documents from their ancestors?

It was a start. I glanced at Bradley. He had picked up the memoir of Robert R. McCannon and was leafing through it. "This guy was a dick," he remarked.

"Remind you of anyone?" I asked, but the insult didn't have much venom in it. Harping on Bradley was becoming more of a habit than a passion at this point.

"Ha ha," Bradley said, deadpan. "This guy keeps mentioning 'the honey-sweet, innocent countenances' of his teenage daughter and her friends. I'm not sure what a countenance is, but I think this old guy might have been a piece of shit."

"You're likely right." I picked up another book, but it was written in 1968. We were already living in the Whittens' house by then. Still, I leafed quickly through the pages in case the book mentioned the name.

"The map said Whitten, right?" Bradley turned another page. "This guy didn't like them, either. He dishes the dirt right here."

"What?" I put down the book I was holding and held out my hand. "Give it here."

My gaze quickly scanned the page. Robert R. McCannon was talking about the prominent families of Fell, and how he—according to himself—played the part of trusted confidant and adviser to all of them, beaming his wisdom on them (and, presumably, on their teenage daughters).

> I spent many evenings with the Whitten family, one of the founding families of Fell, now much diminished in size as well as in prominence. Successive generations of Whittens had suffered misfortunes, such as death by shipwreck, fire, and wasting disease. Many of their children did not live to see the age of five. Some said that the misfortune was earned by the family's coldness and pride, and I could not disagree.
>
> I tried to give counsel to the family in the hopes of turning their fortunes around, but Henry Whitten refused to listen. When his daughter, Anne Whitten, died by her own hand in 1907 at the age of twenty-one, it was a truly sad day, as she was the final heir. Her younger brother, Edward, had died in a childhood accident a year earlier.

My hands were ice. My stomach turned.

A little boy dead in an accident. His older sister.

Sister.

I found you, Sister, I thought, my terror mixing with my inescapable triumph. *I found you at last.*

"Violet?" Bradley stood behind my shoulder. His voice was tight with concern.

"I'm fine." And, though my heart was beating hard and cold sweat was beading on my neck, I was. Sister wasn't here, and neither were any of her emissaries. For once, she wasn't breathing down my neck, waiting for her chance. She was gone somewhere else, she didn't know what I was doing, and while her back was turned, I had finally found her.

Maybe Sister didn't win everything. Not every time.

The doorknob rattled, and an alarmed knock sounded. "What are you doing in there?" Farley's voice called out. "Your time's up. What are you doing?"

I unlocked the door and opened it. Farley's face was flushed, and he looked past me, directly at Bradley. "You weren't supposed to lock the door," he said.

Bradley shrugged, unconcerned.

"You better not have taken anything from the shelves," Farley continued in his annoying drone. "Everything in this room is the property of the college."

I stepped in front of him, blocking his view of Bradley. I gave Farley my haughtiest glare. Clay called it my Bitch Glare, but that didn't matter. I never had to care what Clay thought about anything ever again.

Farley's gaze rose to my face, his eyes locked with mine, and he paled.

"We don't steal from libraries," I said in my iciest tone. "We came here to research. We're finished now."

Farley nodded. He was worried. He was supposed to supervise us, and he'd left us alone in here. Too bad.

"You've been most helpful," I said in the sarcastic tone that actually said *I will cut your head off and drink your blood if you don't obey me.* "We're leaving now. Step aside."

The kid stepped out of the doorway and back into the hall. I strode off in the direction of the front entrance without a backward glance. I heard Bradley fall into step behind my left shoulder.

I'd given Bradley a mere few seconds, but I knew it was enough time. When we were out of earshot, approaching the front doors, I asked softly, "What did you take?"

"The map," he whispered back. "I figured it was what you wanted."

He was right. The map would do just fine.

I pushed open the doors, walked out into the cool air of the parking lot, and smiled.

35

DODIE

I was, to put it mildly, not an athlete. Some models did aerobics or jogging to stay thin, but most of us used the time-honored methods used by our model ancestors of decades past. If starvation, cigarettes, and fishy diet pills were good enough for the girls in the fifties, then they were good enough for me.

So I was out of breath before Terri and I had gone a block on our bikes. The bike Terri had lent me—the one she got for Christmas and didn't like much—was a five-speed, the kind with a high seat and low handlebars curled like horns that you had to lean onto. It made a loud, somewhat-satisfying whizzing sound as I rode, but the seat was so hard that my nethers began screaming. Within moments, I hurt in places that I hadn't previously known existed, or usually refused to acknowledge.

Terri rode ahead of me, ignorant of my pain. She seemed delighted to have a companion for this ride, even a companion as old and decrepit as I was. She talked as she pedaled, while I wheezed as quietly as I could. Luckily, she didn't seem to need me to respond.

"We can go to the creek," Terri said. "I'll show you the fort I made."

"No creek," I said, thinking of the shadow in the trees. "Let's go toward town."

"I'm not allowed to go downtown," Terri said. "But there are lots of good spots in the neighborhood."

"Aren't there other children around for you to play with?"

"There are no kids in this neighborhood, and none of the girls at school want to come over. Were there kids here when you were growing up?"

"No, there weren't. None at all."

Terri was incurious about this. I followed her around a curve in the road, feeling the trees recede behind our backs and remembering how there were no children here for us Esmies to play with, even if we had wanted to. Only Violet had had a friend, Alice McMurtry, who I had thought was boring. I'd felt bad for thinking that when Alice died. Alice had been around Terri's age, and now I was thinking about Terri lying lifeless next to the train tracks. I pumped harder on my pedals to stay close to her, nearly hitting her rear tire with my front one.

Terri slowed next to a curb, then got off her bike. "There's a hollow tree this way," she called to me, leaving her bike sprawled as she hurried away.

I got off my bike, wincing, and followed her. I had no interest in a hollowed-out tree, but I said, "Fine. Don't you have any siblings?"

"No," she called back.

How did one live without siblings to drive one crazy day in and day out for one's entire childhood? I suddenly felt fond of my dullest days growing up, which I spent drawing, reading a line or two of a book at a time, or simply lying on my bed, staring out the window at the sky while Vail and Violet bickered down the hall. I was even nostalgic about Violet hogging the bathroom and Vail emitting various gases on me whenever possible.

The tree Terri showed me was indeed hollow, as advertised. "How nice," I said politely as she showed me the hole, where she sometimes stashed treasures for the purpose of retrieving them later.

"There's a hill I like to bike up as fast as I can," the girl said. "It's steep. Want to try?"

Just the thought made me wince. "Maybe another time."

"How about the old graves? Have you seen those?"

The sweat trickling down my back went cool. "Pardon me? Graves?"

"You haven't seen them?" She seemed surprised. "Didn't you say you grew up in this neighborhood?"

"I didn't go outdoors very much," I said. "What do you mean, *graves*?"

Terri's eyes widened, and she looked pleased as she realized she could show me something I'd never seen before. "They're really old," she said. "They're back where we came from, behind your house."

I hesitated. "You mean in the trees?"

"Yes." She was walking back to her bike, so I had to follow. "I'm sorry I went back there, but no one lived in your house. I didn't think anyone would mind."

"I'm not angry," I assured her. "I just don't think it's safe."

"But it is. There are bugs, and it's muddy after it rains, but there aren't any wild animals or anything." She picked up her bike. "The graves are old, and they're really neat."

Neat. I did not think that going back to the trees, toward that shadow, would be neat.

But graves? I had no idea there were graves back there, and neither did my siblings. The police who searched the grounds for Ben hadn't talked about graves, and they weren't in the police report.

Vail and I had walked through those trees, and we'd seen nothing.

This girl wasn't lying. That much I knew. If I sent her home, I couldn't find the graves by myself without hours of searching. To find them, we had to go back to where I'd seen the shadow.

Terri was waiting, so I nodded. "It has to be quick. And don't stray far from me."

She smiled. She thought I wanted her to protect me, not the other way around. "All right."

She pulled to a stop between our houses and got off her bike again. She hurried across the grass in a line as straight as an arrow, heading for the trees where we'd met.

I followed her, half jogging and looking from side to side. We entered the trees at a different spot from where Vail and I had walked. Terri seemed to know exactly where she was going. She wove along a path only she could see, stepping over fallen branches.

I felt cold and sweaty, but that could have just been because of the exertion. When I glanced behind us, I didn't see a shadow.

"I hope this cemetery isn't for family pets or something," I said. Was it getting darker, or was I imagining it?

"It isn't pets," Terri assured me. "It's the Whittens."

"What's the Whittens?"

"They're people. It's their graveyard."

She stepped over a fallen branch and pointed to a space clear of trees. Brush and weeds had been roughly pushed aside in some places, obviously by hand.

At first I couldn't see anything, but when I stepped to one of the cleared spots, I saw a stone. It was a flat headstone, dirty and tarnished.

"There are a dozen of these," Terri said. "I haven't found them all, I don't think. They're all Whittens."

I looked at the stone between my feet, then stepped to the next one. I understood it now. If the police had come here in their search for Ben, they wouldn't have seen these stones if they were covered in dead brush. The graves would have been deep under the unbroken snow.

I crouched down to read *Nathaniel Whitten, Dearly Departed, Beloved of God and His Family, July 7, 1848–October 29, 1889.*

I kept walking, using my feet to flatten the grass, and found another Whitten, and then another. One of the stones listed three names, all babies born a year apart. Next to them was their mother, who had died at age fifty-one.

How was it possible for a family to just bury its members in the woods for years? Was that legal? Perhaps this had been a cemetery at one time, though there was no church for miles. Maybe it had been private land. Whitten land.

I pictured a family living here for decades, maybe a hundred years or more. Burying their dead in the family plot instead of at one of the city's cemeteries. Your father would be here, and then your babies, and eventually yourself. None of you would have to leave, to be buried near strangers.

I had no idea where my father was buried, and my mother was scattered in Long Island Sound.

"This one's at the edge," Terri called to me. "It's the only one over here. I don't know why."

I followed to where she'd cleared a space. *Anne Whitten, 1886–1907. RIP.* Anne Whitten wasn't beloved, by God or by anyone else. She had died at twenty-one.

The wind picked up, sending veins of cold over my skin. I glanced around into the trees, looking for a shadow.

"Dodie?" Terri said beside me. "It's getting cloudy. I think it might rain."

The words *Anne Whitten* scraped the back of my brain, pulling at something old and barely remembered. Something I thought I knew.

"We should go," Terri said, but I ignored her. I moved to another grave, away from Anne's, toward the center of the plot. I gently pushed the long grass aside.

A Box Full of Darkness

Edward Whitten. Beloved Child. August 3, 1900–September 22, 1906.

"Ben," I said, the word surprising me and coming out in a whisper. It was almost a sob.

I heard Terri ask, *What?* But it was an echo far away. I heard the wind in the trees and the cries of the birds overhead, the rustle of the tall weeds. A car's motor, somewhere far off. The pounding of my own blood in my ears, the blood I reluctantly carried from my forebears, the blood I shared with my siblings.

Beloved Child.

He had died at six years old.

I felt a rush of love so hard it made me choke. It was followed by a rush of fear. The water flowing over me, icy and dark, pulling at me, dragging me down. Over and over again, night after night, the water coming, always coming. Always hungry to pull me under and never let me go.

Me as a child, sobbing in the bathroom in fear, running the bathwater to get warm, hoping that no one—that *it*—wouldn't hear me.

"Dodie?"

I turned to Terri. She was pale with alarm, her eyes wide as she watched me. It struck me that she was so small, so alone. Defenseless against the shadows in these trees. Alice McMurtry had died by the train tracks years ago, and now she haunted Violet in the ladies' room of Fell Hospital, forever a girl.

"Terri," I said, making my voice as gentle as I could manage, "do you ever have nightmares?"

"No," she replied, but she was lying.

"It's all right," I said. "I have them, too. Mine is about water rushing over me in bed. Cold, dirty water, trying to drown me under it. Horrible, isn't it? I've had the same dream many times. My siblings have different nightmares, but they dream, too."

The girl next door pinched her lips together, as if biting back the words. I knew the feeling.

"Hanging," she said, the word barely a whisper over the rising wind. "Someone hanging in my room. A shadow."

I nodded, as if this was something I had expected to hear. "That's a nasty dream. Did you ever have it before you moved here?"

Again, she bit her lip, as if afraid to speak. If you were too loud, it—she—might hear you. Terri shook her head.

"All right, then." I didn't have it in me to give her a fake smile or a line of bullshit, not here and now, but I could try to reassure her a little. "I'm going to see what I can do about that. Let's get you home."

"You can fix it?" She stood rooted to the spot as the first drops of cold rain began to spit down. "You can make it stop?"

I didn't understand everything. I didn't believe I ever would, or could. But standing here over these graves, I understood so much more than I ever had before. What I now knew made me panic just looking at her, thinking of her alone in her bed at night, just like I had been. Just like Vail and Violet had been.

No child should be alone and frightened in bed while something watched them. It wasn't normal. No one had stopped it for me, but I wasn't a child anymore. I could stop it for Terri.

If I had Violet's and Vail's help, we could stop it together. I'd show them these graves, tell them about the shadow I'd seen in the trees. We'd come up with something to do about it. We'd find a way.

I had believed it was just our house. But the Whittens had owned more than that, hadn't they? They had owned this land, at the least.

I remembered the old photo in the Thornhill house, the postcard from their long-gone son. *I'm sorry I left all those years ago, but like I keep saying, I couldn't live in our home any longer. I had to go.*

How many kids had lain terrified in their beds over the years? How many had had nightmares they didn't understand? It would go on forever if we didn't stop it.

"I'm going to try," I said, to answer Terri's question. I held out my hand to her. "Let's walk back to your house together, and you can go inside."

"Will you be all right?" she asked uncertainly as she took my hand and we started to walk.

"I'll be fine," I told her. "It's just a little rain."

I watched Terri go inside her house, watched the door close behind her. I was about to turn when the door opened again and her father came out.

Charles Chatham—that was his actual name, according to his own introduction—was near forty, with the reassuring belly and beginning jowls of a successful husband and father. He was wearing an NYU Law sweatshirt, and his hair was receding at the temples. Likely, he looked in the mirror each day and despaired over his vanishing youth, the fact that he hadn't become a rock star or an astronaut as he'd dreamed of. He had no idea how girls like me would have done anything, absolutely anything, to have a father like him—one who was home, one who cared even a little, one who paid enough attention to give the stranger who had gone bike riding with his daughter the glare he was giving me now.

"What were you doing with Terri?" he asked, getting straight to the point.

"She's lonely," I replied, serving honesty with honesty. "She shouldn't live in this neighborhood. You should move."

"Move?" He looked offended, but I saw the glint in his eyes. He'd already thought about it, was possibly even planning it.

"Look around," I said, waving to the dead neighborhood under the gray sky, the desolate half-constructed lot across the street, the uncanny silence. "Can you honestly say you like it here? It's a bad place for kids. Terri is all alone here, and she rides her bike alone. She walks in the woods alone. She should live somewhere with other kids on the street. Somewhere safe."

Charles hesitated. He wanted to posture as the all-knowing dad, the authority figure with all the answers. But he didn't have all the answers to this, and he knew it. I waited for him to admit it. He couldn't admit it to Terri, but he could admit it to me.

"What do you know that I don't?" he finally asked.

I thought, again, that I would have done anything for a father like him. I would have given anything at all.

"This isn't a good place," I told him. "This neighborhood, this town. Terri shouldn't be here. You moved here for a job, didn't you? Take a different job and move away. Quickly. Do whatever it takes. Bad things happen to children in Fell. To adults, too."

He tried to scoff, but couldn't quite make it believable. "You live here," he pointed out.

"I was born here," I replied. "I had no choice. You do. Terri has nightmares here. She doesn't have them anywhere else."

He looked startled. He likely knew about the dreams, but was surprised I knew, too.

"Do you have somewhere you can take her tonight?" I asked him.

I thought he would scoff again, but again he thought better of it. "I might."

"Do it," I advised him. "Take a trip. I don't care where you go." Before he could speak, I said, "Go for a few days if you can. Terri can miss school. You're the dad—figure it out. Just get your family out of here, because it won't be safe. By the time you come back, it'll be over."

"What will be over?" he asked.

"Whatever we're doing," I replied. "Someone should end it. So we'll end it."

Our gazes locked for a moment. Then Charles said, "I hate this place."

A Box Full of Darkness

I nodded. "You should. Some of us sprouted here, like mushrooms. But that isn't you. So go."

His jaw worked for a second, and then he gave a stiff nod.

As he turned to go back in the house, I called out, "One more thing."

He turned back. "What is it?"

"I'd appreciate it if you'd leave your garage unlocked. I promise, whatever I borrow, I'll pay for. Even if it gets broken."

"Jesus Christ," he said, and the front door slammed behind him.

But he was going to do it.

The rain was spitting harder now. I turned on my heel to go home.

36

VIOLET

Vail was in the living room when I got back to the Fell house, sitting on the sofa with his booted feet on the cushions. He was reading a *Life* magazine with Frank Sinatra on the front. He gave me a glance and went back to his reading.

"She isn't here," he said.

"I didn't know you like baseball," I said. He was wearing a long-sleeved baseball-style shirt, white with navy blue sleeves, with the number 22 on the front.

"I don't," my brother replied, his eyes still on his magazine. "It's just a shirt."

"You weren't wearing it when I left."

"I changed my shirt."

"Why?"

"I felt like it."

"Why do you have that shirt if you don't like baseball?"

He finally looked up at me, his annoyance prodding him away from the magazine. "Violet. It's just a shirt."

I shrugged, the gesture feeling hard, tight in my shoulders and my back. I had been so brave when I left Fell College, but now I was afraid again. Afraid and angry. If Sister ever hurt Vail, if she touched a hair on his stupid head, I would kill her. I didn't care that she was already dead. I'd dig her up from hell and kill her with my bare hands.

Vail was either unaware of or uninterested in my turmoil, because he looked at his boring magazine again. "She's not here," he repeated.

"Who? Your ghost hunter?" She obviously wasn't here, and her car was gone from the driveway. "Dodie?" Dodie's car was here, but it was possible she was sulking in her room.

"No." Vail turned a page, the sound loud in the silence. "Anne Whitten."

A noise left my throat, or maybe it was just a breath. Vail looked up at me again and our gazes locked, for real this time.

"You know who she is?" I asked.

Vail dropped the magazine and sat up. He picked something up from the coffee table and held it out to me without a word.

It was a children's book. Small, slender, and old, with a rabbit on the cover. I flipped it open and read the inscription. *To Edward Whitten, from his sister Anne. On his fifth birthday. August 3, 1905.*

Her handwriting, faded and neat. Sister's handwriting. I didn't know how I knew, but I did.

The marbles in the attic from 1899, the year before Edward Whitten was born. They were new when he was a child, and he'd played with them.

Her younger brother, Edward, had died in a childhood accident a year earlier.

I dropped the book back on the table, unable to touch it anymore. Vail didn't pick it up again, either. "She died in 1907," I said, unable to speak Anne's name. "She committed suicide. The year after he died, age six."

Vail's jaw worked, and he nodded.

"She was older than him," I went on. Everything made so much sense now. A crazy kind of sense, but still sense. "She was a teenager when he was born."

"Like us." His voice was low.

"Like us. But older. She was fourteen."

My brother's gaze moved to the words on the wall. I wondered what had happened in this house while I was out, what Charlotte had found. What Vail was thinking about as he stared at those words.

"She killed him," I said.

"I know," he replied.

We were silent. Nothing happened. I had said the words aloud, and nothing happened.

"Did your ghost hunter find that book?" I asked.

Vail nodded. "In the attic. Then Anne Whitten came down the upstairs hall, screaming, and I got Charlotte out of the house."

"Screaming?"

Vail's expression went hard. "It wasn't good. I could hear her walking, and when I left the house, I saw her in an upstairs window. Charlotte is never coming back."

"Some ghost hunter," I said sourly. I couldn't help it.

"I told her the same thing."

"And how did she take it?"

"Not very well."

Vail's gaze stayed on the wall as he spoke again. "I came back in to look for her. For Anne. I shouted. I banged open all the doors and the closets. I yelled at her to come out, but she didn't. I think she leaves this house sometimes. Her presence isn't here. But where does she go? She's gone."

"For now." The words were automatic. Sister could leave, but never for long. Never for good.

Vail looked at me again. "How many times have you seen her?"

The words stuck in my throat, because I'd had a lifetime of not speaking about Sister. Then they came, like painful shards. "Too many times to count."

"Since you were a kid?"

"Yes."

I dropped into the chair. My brother didn't say anything stupid, like *Why didn't you tell me?* He was Vail. He knew why.

"What does she do?" he asked instead.

"She used to stand next to my bed with her back to me. Nothing else, really. That was all she needed to do."

He nodded.

"Did she hurt you?" I asked him.

He gave an annoyed scoff. "As if she could."

I opened my mouth to argue, to tell him that Sister was more dangerous than anyone could know. Then the silence of the house hit me again. "Where's Dodie?"

"Gone," Vail replied.

"Gone where?"

"I don't know. Violet, we have to talk about this. We have to focus."

"Gone where?" I repeated. A pulse was starting to pound in my neck again, the panicked pulse that always had to do with Sister. "Vail. Where's Dodie?"

"I don't know." He sounded irritated, and I wanted to shake him. "She was gone when Charlotte and I came down from the attic."

"Her car is here."

"So she walked somewhere. Violet, focus."

There was no focus. There was nothing in my head except the moment twenty years ago when I first realized that though we were all looking for Ben, he hadn't made a sound. No giggles, no clumsy shuffles in his hiding place. Just nothing. Nothing at all.

"Where's Dodie?" I nearly shouted.

In the kitchen, the phone rang. The sound was shrill in the silent house. Vail rose and walked to the kitchen, where I heard him pick up the phone. "Hello?"

Lisette, I thought. My panic spiraled. No one else had the phone number. It had to be—

"Hold on," Vail said, and then he shouted, "Violet, it's for you."

I was already on my feet, half running to the kitchen. I snatched the receiver from his hand. "Hello?"

"Where is she?" Clay's voice was an angry shout on the other end of the line.

"Clay?"

"Where is she?" he shouted again. "Where's Lisette? What did you do to her?"

"What do you mean, where is she?" I shouted back at him. "She isn't here. She's staying with you."

"She said she was going to her friend's for a sleepover last night." Clay was furious. He rarely got truly angry, and the rage in his voice made my panic spin harder. "She didn't come home this morning, and when I called, there was no sleepover. She left last night."

Oh, God. I looked out the kitchen window, where the sky had darkened and rain had started coming down. "Where the hell did she go?" I shouted at Clay. "You're supposed to look after her! You're supposed to keep track!"

"This is your fault!" he roared back. "What did you tell her, Violet? Some load of bullshit about ghosts? Did you tell her to come to you? What did you promise her? You said something to her, I know it. It's just like you. You fed her a bunch of your crazy lies, and she believed you, and now she's gone."

"I didn't tell her anything." My panic had blurred into rage. It was just like Clay to blame me for his own mistakes. It must be so convenient, having a crazy ex-wife with a fucked-up life. He used me as a human garbage can so that he'd never have to be responsible ever again. "I didn't promise her anything. She's your responsibility, Clay.

You wanted custody, didn't you? You're supposed to be *so good* at this. So where is our daughter?"

It was petty, childish. It was beneath both of us. Lisette was gone, and we were sniping our old hurts at each other, our fruitless accusations from years ago. We were selfish and stupid, and I couldn't help it, and neither could he.

"You're a bitch," Clay shouted over the phone. "You're just trying to undermine me with her every chance you get. Well, it won't work, Violet. You're nuts, and Lisette knows it. You may have gotten her to buy your lies this time, but you'll let her down. You always do."

"Violet," Vail said behind my shoulder, but I ignored him.

"Where could she have gone?" I asked Clay. "Who saw her last? She can't drive yet. Does she have any money?" Had she hitchhiked? I thought I might throw up with fear.

"The money is gone from my wallet," Clay replied. "I had less than a hundred bucks in there. I can't believe she would do this. She didn't say anything. What the hell did you say to her?"

"Violet," Vail said again. He reached a hand out, but I swatted it away.

"We have to call the police," I said to Clay. "There's no other option."

"It's been less than twenty-four hours," Clay shot back. "They won't do anything."

"Still, we have to call them," I argued. "We have to talk to someone, make them see—"

Vail's big hand yanked the receiver from me, while his other hand pushed my shoulder. "Clay," he said into the phone, "she's here. I just paid her cab driver."

Clay yelled, and Vail kept talking—*She'll be fine, I don't know, she just got here, we'll take care of it.* I barely heard. I ran to the front door, which Vail had swung open while I was on the phone. I got there in time to see a taxi's taillights driving away.

My daughter stood in the doorway, a backpack in her hands. Her hair was in a messy ponytail and her face was pale.

"Mom?" she said, her voice shaking.

I strode to her and swept her up. I didn't care that she was fourteen, that I couldn't remember the last time I'd hugged her, the last time she'd let me. I put my arms around her and buried my face in her shoulder, which smelled like sweat and drugstore body wash and Lisette.

She hugged me back, for a brief moment like the little girl she had once been. She hugged me like Ben used to. Then she remembered herself and squirmed, moving her hands to push me away. "Mom," she said again, this time in protest.

I let her go, and she walked toward Vail's voice in the kitchen. I followed.

"Hi, Uncle Vail," Lisette said when she saw him, her tone suddenly shy.

Vail gave her a brief up-and-down assessment, decided she was unharmed, and said, "Lisette." He held out the phone receiver, stretching on its curly cord. "Tell your father you're not dead."

"Do I have to?" she asked.

"You do," he replied, his voice gruff.

My daughter sighed, dropped her backpack, and took the phone from him. There would be more arguments, more accusations. Clay would shout at all of us, including Vail. I didn't know why Lisette had come all this way, or how she had done it. We still didn't know where Dodie was. We still had the problem of Sister, of Ben.

But for just one moment, all I thought was, *Lisette is here.*

Those three words. Just for one moment.

It would have to be enough.

37

VAIL

Lisette, it turned out, had taken money from her father's wallet, taken a city bus to the nearest bus station, spent most of the cash on a ticket to downtown Fell, and then taken a taxi. Since she had spent the last of her money on a bus station sandwich, I'd had to pay the cab when it pulled into the driveway to drop her off.

She couldn't explain her reasons. Her father asked her over and over on the phone—*Why? What got into you? Why would you do that?* Lisette's answer was that she didn't know, she wanted to, she wasn't sorry, she hated him. The last was shouted through tears.

I didn't ask her why she'd done it, and neither did Violet. What was there not to know? Lisette was rebellious, she was thoughtless, she was impulsive, she was selfish. She was yearning for some independence, which she had romanticized in her mind until she sat alone on a Greyhound bus full of strangers, her stomach rumbling, unsure where her mother's house was exactly or how she would get there. She'd started to get scared then. Adult independence had its dark side.

She'd used a phone book in the bus station phone booth to find the Esmie house, then taken a taxi with an empty wallet. She didn't have to say that if it hadn't worked out at the end of the taxi ride, she would have simply run instead of paying the fare.

She was an Esmie.

As if to illustrate this point, after Violet and Lisette finally hung up with Clay—thus turning the dial down on the drama—Dodie walked through the front door, her hair wet from the rain and her expression unconcerned. She toed off her sneakers, and they made a squelching sound.

"Where have you been?" Violet shot the words like bullets.

"Out," Dodie said. She caught sight of Lisette, and I could have sworn her face grew paler. She didn't look unconcerned anymore.

"Hi, Aunt Dodie," Lisette said, straightening a little from her hunched-in-anger position at the kitchen table.

Dodie gave her a strained, silent look. Then she turned to Violet. "*That*," she said, pointing at the girl, "cannot stay here."

Lisette recoiled.

"Knock it off, Dodie," I said.

"What's wrong with you?" Violet hissed. "It's raining, and it's getting dark. Lisette is staying the night. We'll figure out how to get her home tomorrow."

That had been part of the drama. Clay—I did not fucking like that guy—had demanded his daughter be returned to him as soon as possible. Packing her off alone wasn't an option, and if Violet drove her daughter home, it would take all night, and she would be leaving the house. We weren't done here.

Clay could drive to Fell to pick Lisette up, but he'd have to take days off from work. Why couldn't Violet fix the problem she had created by tempting Lisette to run away in the first place? And so the argument went around and around. I leaned silently against the kitchen doorway and stayed out of it. I had never been more sure of my decision not to have any romantic attachments or any children. This kind of shit was simply not my thing.

"She can't stay the night," Dodie said again, as if Lisette wasn't in the room.

Lisette looked hurt and confused. She probably thought that Dodie was taking a personal exception to her, but I knew better. It was the house that Dodie was worried about. Lisette, in this house. At night.

"Where do you suggest we take her?" Violet argued back. "The motel?"

We all knew we weren't taking her there. Lisette looked even more confused. "I want to stay," she said, her tone as stubborn as Violet's ever was.

"It isn't ideal," I said. All three women turned to look at me—I hadn't spoken in a while. I shrugged. "We didn't plan it, but she's here now. Night is falling, and none of us is leaving. We can keep arguing, or we can make a plan. I know which one I'm game for."

The silence was heavy. The only sound was the rain, which was falling harder outside. My niece, more perceptive than I gave her credit for, shouted into the pregnant air between us, "Someone tell me out loud. I want to know what's going on."

Violet pressed her fingertips into her eye sockets, as if trying to massage the worry out of her brain. "Vail is right," she said. "Let's regroup. I'll pull together something to eat. Dodie, take Lisette upstairs and help her get changed and washed up. Vail, you can either help me or just stand there being useless, like you usually do. We regroup in half an hour."

Dodie still looked worried, but resigned. Lisette's brows drew down, probably because she was being assigned a guard, as if she was a prisoner. But when Dodie motioned to her imperiously, she pushed her chair back and stood. She picked up her backpack and followed her aunt up the stairs.

"Dodie will tell her everything," I said to Violet when they had gone, their footsteps banging down the upstairs hall. "Are you ready for that?"

Violet took a carton of eggs from the fridge and put them on the counter. "Not in the least," she said.

"It's an untenable situation," I said. "What did you say to her on the phone?"

"Nothing." Violet pulled an old pot out from the cupboard and ran water into it. "I swear it, Vail. I told her where I was and why. I told her that Ben died a long time ago. I'd never told her that before. I thought it was time she knew the truth, or part of it. I didn't ask her to come. I didn't make it sound like an adventure. The last thing I want is for her to be here." Her hand shook as she reached for the tap, and she twisted the water off with force it didn't need.

I ran a hand through my hair, thinking. Violet was probably a bad parent—it would be surprising if she wasn't. We hadn't exactly had good role models. But she would never have asked Lisette to come here, to this house. Never.

"All right," I said, not willing to dig any deeper into what might be happening in Lisette's psychology. "But it's an untenable situation, like I said. What do you plan to do?"

Violet's voice was low, her gaze on the stovetop as she turned on the gas. "I'll take her home tomorrow. I have to."

"No," I said.

"I have to," she said again.

We were here for Ben. Was Ben more important than Lisette? Was Lisette more important than Ben? Neither sounded right.

"If you go," I said, speaking the truth, "you won't be back."

"Yes, I will. I'll be back as soon as I can."

"Which won't be soon enough."

She slammed the lid onto the pot and glared at me. "What do you want from me, Vail?"

"You can't leave here tomorrow," I said, "and Lisette can't stay here a second night."

"God, no. No. I won't risk it."

I looked at the fear in my sister's eyes and nodded. "So we rest up tonight, and we finish this tomorrow. Before night falls again."

She shook her head, but I saw the thoughts behind her eyes, fighting with the fear. "If I don't get Lisette back to Clay tomorrow, he'll call his lawyer. He probably already has. I'll lose all the visitation I have. I'll lose—"

"Violet." My voice was ice. "This ends. Do you understand? We waited too long already, all of us. He had to call us home because we failed him, and then we ran. This ends. We end it."

My big sister searched my gaze, took a breath, and then she nodded.

38

DODIE

I hadn't seen my niece in—how long? A while. She'd been Terri's age or so. Now she was almost as tall as me, though not as tall as Violet, and she would never be as tall as Vail. She had Violet's thick, unruly hair, though it wasn't quite as dark and had chestnut in it. She had Violet's cheeks and her sulky mouth, but her eyes were her father's. At least, I assumed so, since I could barely remember what Clay looked like. I had only met him once, and he hated me.

"Take a shower," I told her when we were in Violet's room, her backpack deposited on the bed.

"Why?" Lisette asked.

"Because you've been on a bus." I suppressed a shudder. "I'd prefer to burn your clothes, but that isn't practical, so we'll have to make do."

She gave me a glare that was pure Violet, and then she let out a gusty sigh. "Fine."

"The bathroom is this way." I led her down the hall and pointed inside. "There's a towel. You can use my nice shampoo and conditioner. And for the love of God, brush your hair. I'll wait out here. Don't take too long."

"I don't need you to babysit my shower."

"And yet here I am, giving you no choice. Now go."

She made an impressive display of closing the door just a little too hard, then turning the lock loudly before clomping around in the bathroom. It was truly bitchy and well done. I liked her already. I might have no use for children, but teenagers were my kind of people.

I stayed outside her door as she showered. Vail and Violet talked softly in the kitchen, and then they were quiet. I listened for sounds, footsteps, anything that wasn't the rain. The hair on the back of my neck didn't rise. I heard nothing except the normal sounds of a house.

When Lisette finished, I escorted her back to Violet's bedroom and sat on the bed with my back to her while she dressed. "This is stupid," she said as I heard clothing rustle. "Do you think I'll run away again?"

"It would be convenient if you would," I replied. "But no, I don't think you will."

"Don't you want to know how I got here?"

"I'm not curious in the least." No one had told me, and I didn't care to ask.

"I shouldn't have come."

"Are you expecting me to disagree?"

"Don't worry, you don't have to put up with me for long. I'll go home tomorrow."

I sighed. She was almost—almost—as dramatic as I was. I turned around to see her dressed in jeans and an unflattering T-shirt, her damp hair hanging bedraggled as she shoved her belongings miserably into her backpack. Her eyes were red.

"Put that down and sit on the edge of the bed." I gentled my voice. "Please."

Lisette dropped the backpack with a thump and sat.

"I'm horrible," I said as I slid across the bed to sit cross-legged behind her. "But I have top-shelf shampoo and conditioner. Admit it."

The bottles in the shower contained the very best, most expensive brand. My hair was my livelihood, along with my hands.

"It's pretty nice," Lisette admitted.

"Of course it is." I put my fingers into her hair, combing out the strands. "I also make excellent French braids." I sorted her hair into pieces, and she sat still without protest. "Now," I continued, "I'm going to braid, and I'm going to tell you a story. You're going to sit and listen. When you decided to come here, you decided you were an adult. So I have no choice but to tell you the truth."

I saw her shoulders tense, but she still didn't protest, and she didn't pull away.

I braided her hair, and I spoke. I told her about Ben, about the day he disappeared, the lack of footprints in the snow, how we'd shouted ourselves hoarse looking for him. I told her how he'd called us home. How we'd come, and we'd found Ben, but we'd found something else, too. Someone else. A thing that had taken Ben, that was still in this house, that was sometimes a shadow in the woods, following a ten-year-old girl as she walked. A thing that kept the neighborhood children away.

Lisette didn't speak. She didn't argue, even when I told her that Ben's original name was Edward Whitten, and he'd died in 1906.

"I know it isn't a happy story," I said as I finished the braid and tied the end with Lisette's hair elastic. "But you see why we're worried for you, especially your mother. You see why we don't think you're safe."

Finally, she spoke. "Dad says ghosts aren't real."

"Men say a lot of things," I replied. "They don't know as much as they think they do."

"Mom is crazy."

"Is she?"

She squirmed in annoyance under my hands as I tucked away errant pieces of hair. "Don't ask me. I'm asking *you*."

"I didn't hear a question." I could do this all night. "If you think Violet is crazy, then why are you here?"

She paused, and then she said, "It was either this or school."

I fell a little bit in love with her.

"Coming here was stupid, in case you were wondering," I told her calmly. "Stupidity runs in the family, because what you did sounds like something I would do. We came to this house before you did, and we aren't leaving, so we're in no place to judge. But now my siblings and I have to worry about you as well as ourselves."

Lisette twisted, placing her palms on the bed to look back at me. She wasn't on the verge of crying anymore. "What's going to happen?" she asked with a child's certainty that I'd know the answer.

I adjusted the last loose strands around her face. She really had lovely hair. "If I had to guess, Violet will take you home to your father tomorrow."

"And leave you here alone?"

"Not alone," I corrected her. "Vail is here."

"But what's going to happen?"

For the first time in our conversation, I decided not to tell her the truth. I didn't tell her that I had no answer, that I wasn't sure that even Vail could protect both of us from whatever haunted this house. I didn't tell her that I didn't think I would get to go back to New York, and that the thought made me sad, because for the first time in my life I had things I wanted to do. Things I was looking forward to.

I didn't tell her that from the moment I answered the phone and heard Vail's voice on the other end of the line, part of me had believed that I wouldn't get past this. That my story, such as it was, was beginning its last chapter. There would be no more chapters after this one.

Instead of telling her all of that, I asked, "What would you do if it was your little brother, trapped in this house? Your little brother who asked you to come home?"

She didn't have an answer for that, and neither did I. So we went downstairs to dinner.

39

VIOLET

When Lisette heard that she was to sleep in my room with me, she argued, because of course she did. My God, could that child argue. It was like living with fourteen-year-old Dodie all over again, and once had been more than enough.

She wanted to sleep in our parents' bedroom—the master bedroom—by herself. I told her she was sleeping with me. I'd put up with my parents' bed if I had to, but Lisette would not sleep alone.

It didn't matter that Dodie had explained the dangers of the house to her. It didn't matter that Lisette was a selfish child who had run away from home and was in a heap of white-hot trouble, that she'd cost us my paltry visitation rights, that she was putting herself in danger and making the rest of us deal with it. She argued until I wanted to put her out in the rain or scream. Or both.

Vail finished his dinner—hard-boiled eggs, toast with butter, cheese, and apples, all things I'd cobbled together from the fridge—and pushed his chair back, picking up his empty plate. "I wouldn't sleep alone, myself, if I didn't have to," he said in a bored, flat voice.

A Box Full of Darkness

"The thing in this house is nasty and it hits hard, especially at night. But you do what you want. I'm going to watch TV."

Lisette watched him, her face pale, as he washed his plate and left the room. I watched her try to imagine what kind of thing would make Vail admit he was afraid.

"Fine," she said to me after a moment. "We'll sleep in your room."

Lisette watched TV with Vail for a while, and then she came up to my room and changed into her pajamas. Her arguing seemed to have exhausted itself, because she slid into the bed with me without a word, keeping a chilly foot of space between us.

I turned the lamp out. We lay on our backs in the darkness.

"I'm sorry I screwed everything up," she said after a moment.

I could only be honest. "It was already screwed up."

"I'll talk to Dad. I'll tell him that I—that I want to see you. That I came here to see you and Uncle Vail and Aunt Dodie. That you didn't tell me to come."

I had no answer to that. Maybe it would make a difference and maybe it wouldn't. Maybe I wouldn't get a chance with Lisette until she was an adult, if she would even speak to me by then.

"Why did you do it?" I finally asked her.

"Dad wouldn't have let me come," she replied. "He says I shouldn't be around you, but he never explains why. He would never have said yes to me coming here, so I didn't ask. And when you told me about your brother, I just thought ... I don't know." Her voice went thick as her throat closed. "I don't fit in anywhere. I don't have many friends. I don't do sports or theater at school. I thought that I wanted to know where I come from. I thought it would help."

She sounded so lost. When she was a child, I'd sometimes wondered if my ability to see things could be passed down to her. But she'd never shown any signs of it, and I wasn't going to ask her now. I knew the answer.

Lisette wasn't talking about not fitting in because she saw ghosts. She was talking about not fitting in, period. She had wanted to see her family, to find out if she fit in with us, because she was a teenager, not a so-called psychic.

"I know that feeling," was all I could think to say. "I understand."

"Aunt Dodie braided my hair," she said. "She's so pretty. Can I see her and Uncle Vail more when this is over? Can we visit them more often? Please?"

I did feel a bolt of fear then, cold and icy. Because I didn't want to promise things to her that I couldn't deliver. And Alice McMurtry had said that one of us wouldn't leave this house.

"If it's possible," I hedged, "then I'll make it happen. I'll do everything I can."

That seemed to mollify her, at least for the moment. She rolled over with her back to me, and with the resilience of the young, she fell asleep.

I didn't sleep. I lay awake. This was my room, Sister's room. Maybe Lisette would have been better off in our parents' room after all. But Sister had appeared everywhere lately—downstairs when Vail hit her with a vase, then walking the upstairs hall in daylight. Screaming.

If I knew Sister—and I did—she hadn't been screaming in fear. She was angry. The thought of my daughter here while Sister was angry made me sick. If Lisette had insisted on sleeping in my parents' room, I would have gone with her. I wasn't going to let her out of my sight.

When I was sure Lisette was sound asleep, I rolled over and put an arm around her. She slept on without stirring, so I moved closer and held her more tightly.

Sister would have to tear me to pieces if she wanted Lisette. And she was welcome to try.

A Box Full of Darkness

"Mom?"

The voice was soft, but I woke up right away.

I didn't know what time it was in the dark. Lisette had pushed up to one elbow, staring at something I couldn't see.

"Did you hear that?" she whispered into the silence.

I strained, but I heard nothing. "No," I whispered back.

Her body tensed against mine. "There it is again."

I squeezed her, but she squirmed against me, trying to free herself from my grip. "Baby, no," I said.

"It's him!" She broke away from me easily. "It's Ben, Mom! I found Ben!" She slipped from the bed and was gone.

I rolled out of my side of the bed. I didn't see Sister's familiar form or feel cold. The furniture wasn't moving and the curtains weren't juddering. I registered all of this as my feet hit the floor. "Lisette!"

There was no answer.

I slapped the light switch, but nothing happened. The darkness was thick, the air heavy with silence. My siblings didn't make a sound.

"Lisette!" I called again.

In the bedroom doorway, I held my arms in front of me. How was it so dark? We'd kept lights on every night since we came back. Who had turned them off? Had the power gone out?

I shouted this time. "Lisette! Vail! Dodie!"

No answer.

I shuffled into the hall, my bare feet sliding with caution on the hardwood floor. I braced a hand on the wall and took a few steps. Where would Lisette have gone? To one of the other rooms? Downstairs? I heard no footsteps, and it made me frantic.

I opened my mouth to shout again, and something brushed my legs.

I flinched, but then I recognized the touch and the sound of small footsteps. A child had run past me, his body brushing the fabric of my pajama bottoms. Ben.

Fear mixed with something else, overwhelming and warm, flooded me. "Ben?" I called. I bent, then lowered to my knees, the way I had always done for him, to be on his level. "Ben? Honey?"

His footsteps were just out of reach. I leaned forward, my arms out in the dark.

"Ben, come here," I said. I heard the pleading note in my voice, and I didn't care.

"You have to find me."

His voice was so clear, so normal. Right there. Ben, a few feet away.

I wasn't in this dark hallway anymore. I wasn't chasing my daughter or chasing ghosts. I was fifteen again, and the world wasn't all right, but it was more all right than it would ever be again. I hadn't known how little time I had, that the next time, or the next, would be the last time I'd see my little brother.

Ben's feet moved as he came closer. I could make out the shape of him, the familiar outline of his face just out of reach. I could see his eyes. He was looking at me, and his expression was sweet and sad.

"Annie is angry," he said.

I flinched, because the mention of Sister could still do that to me, even now. "I know. It's my fault."

"She says I ruined everything," Ben said. "She couldn't get married because of me. What does that mean, Violet?"

"I don't know, Ben," I said softly. "You didn't do anything wrong. Not ever. Come here." I moved forward on my knees, but he took a step back.

"I told her I was sorry," he said.

"You have nothing to be sorry about," I told him. "Come here. Please. Please."

He didn't move. I wanted to get closer, but I didn't want to chase him away. He was as fragile as a wisp of smoke, barely here at all. In the shadows, I watched him frown, thinking. Then he smiled.

"Violet," he said, "you're my big sister."

"Yeah, honey," I replied. "I am."

He turned and ran, and I didn't have time to call after him, to get up and run, because in the dark I heard a familiar clicking sound and a low hiss that made terror beat its wings inside my skull.

Sister was here.

I felt her before she kicked me. I had shifted my weight when she caught me on the left side of my rib cage, sending me off-balance. I rolled and she kicked me again in the kidneys, making me bark with pain. My head smacked against the wall.

"Get out," she hissed, an angry voice that scraped my brain. "Get out."

I felt for something, anything to hit her with. I could see only a shadow in the dark, the familiar figure that had stood at the foot of my bed when I was a child. On the edge of my perception, I heard a shout.

Lisette, I thought.

I kicked at Sister as hard as I could. My foot hit something unrecognizable, cold and soaking wet. Water splattered to the floor.

I was screaming, the sound coming out of me by instinct, unfiltered. I kicked at Sister again and missed, then missed again. Hot tears ran down my face. Her foot swung at me and I rolled away, just out of reach.

As I scrambled to get my feet under me, an icy hand gripped the back of my neck. I went still. The sound died in my throat.

There was nothing but yawning darkness, frostbite cold, spiraling inside my mind.

I fought it. I made my voice work, even though my body wouldn't move. "I hate you so much," I whispered to the ghost who wouldn't leave me alone.

Sister hissed in a breath. Her fingers dug in, merciless on my tendons, my nerves, the bones in my neck. She was going to break me. She had infinite strength. More water dropped to the floor.

"I hate you, too," she said in my head, and one of us screamed. Maybe it was me.

A light came on. Its yellow glow on the floor surprised me, and then Sister's grip vanished from my neck. I looked up.

My daughter stood in the glowing doorway of Ben's bedroom, her eyes wild, her face pale. She held a lamp in her hand. Her gaze fixed on Sister, the horrifying sight of her, and I knew she felt the cold and she heard the clicking, heard Sister's icy breath. No one but me had ever seen Sister in the flesh.

Lisette stared, and I watched her jaw set. Her arm drew back. Then she threw the lamp at Sister so hard it smashed against the wall.

40

VAIL

I went to bed in my clothes. Instinct, probably, because something must be up. Anne Whitten wasn't going to stay this quiet.

Since I didn't expect to sleep, I lay on my back, staring at the ceiling, my hands laced behind my head. Did I think about Charlotte? Maybe a little. The kiss she'd given me had faded to the periphery, but I thought about her story of the little girl and the mailman. I understood now why she'd told that story. Mostly, I hoped that Charlotte had gotten out of town all right, and that she'd kept driving until she was as far away as she could get.

There was a soft murmur of voices from Violet's room, and then silence.

When I woke, I was curled on my side and a warm body was climbing into bed with me, sweet-smelling and achingly familiar. I curled around my little brother and gathered him close, digging my nose into his warm skin at the collar of his pajamas.

"Ben," I said.

He squirmed to get comfortable. I heard him breathing, felt the rise and fall of it.

"It's okay, Vail," he said.

He'd said this because I was crying, my tears soaking soundlessly into the cotton of his pajamas.

"No, it isn't," I said. "I'm sorry. I'm sorry."

"It's all right." His voice was truly Ben's. His palm patted the back of my hand, and I knew that he was truly my little brother, even though that wasn't possible, even though Ben hadn't really been Ben. Or maybe he had. It didn't fucking matter.

"I failed you," I choked out.

"I was hiding," he said. "I came back for you, but I had to leave, so I'm sorry, too. I didn't want to go, but I can't stay."

"Please," I begged him. "Please stay. I'll do anything. Please."

There was no reply, and I sobbed into his neck. Because we both knew the answer.

How was his skin so warm? Was I crazy? His hair tickled my face. He breathed evenly, in and out, and I counted each breath like a prayer. It didn't matter who he was, who I was, where we were, or what year it was. It didn't matter where we had been or where we were going. It only mattered that he was my brother. I held him tight for as long as I could.

When he was gone again, it felt like my chest had ripped open, like my guts were spilled on the floor. I lay exhausted, still smelling his scent. And then a familiar white light came on above me, glaring down over the bed.

"Wake up," a voice said.

I'd researched sleep paralysis, and I knew what it was supposed to feel like. I tried to flex my hand on the blanket, but nothing happened. Sleep paralysis, but I wasn't asleep at all.

"Wake up," the voice said again. A woman's voice in a harsh whisper, excited. The same voice that had spoken those words to me before I hit the thing with a vase.

Somehow, I moved. I was in a dream state, myself but not myself. I wasn't moving my own body, onto my back to look up, and when I spoke, it wasn't words that I planned to speak.

"Annie?" I said. "What is it?"

The figure above me wasn't an alien. The light wasn't light from a UFO. It was a woman of about twenty, her hair pulled back and her face a pale moon. I had the feeling that I had heard her screaming only a few hours ago, heard her walking toward me down the hall, but right now she was just a woman. In her hand she held a lamp with a glass cylinder, and the light it gave off was weak and yellow, not blinding white light at all.

"Wake up," she said again. "And don't call me Annie."

"Sorry," I said. "I'll remember next time."

"Fine. Now get up. I want to show you something."

My hand came up and rubbed my eyes. I was small, sleepy. Confused at being awoken from my dreams. "Something in the middle of the night? What is it?"

"You'll like it, I promise," Anne said.

I hesitated. I wanted to make Annie happy, but something felt like it might be wrong. "We'll get in trouble," I hedged.

"We won't if you sneak out quietly like I tell you to."

"But why?"

She went rigid, and I knew she was getting angry. My throat went dry. She was always so angry with me. I was about to tell her I'd do anything she wanted when she spoke.

"Do you remember the place where they're building a cellar?"

I nodded. They had tried to build a cellar for extra storage, but the hole they dug in the ground kept filling with water. They couldn't keep it dry, so they gave up. I'd been strictly forbidden from exploring the still-open hole, because it was dangerous.

"I remember," I said.

"Well, there's ducks living in it," Anne said.

I started to get excited, forgetting my fear, forgetting the rule that I wasn't supposed to go to the cellar hole. "Ducks?"

"A whole family," Anne said. "Including babies."

"Baby ducks?" This was the most exciting thing I could have imagined. Somewhere in the back of my mind, I remembered that baby ducks were born in spring, not in autumn, like now. But I ignored it. Maybe ducks could be born in September, too.

The only way to know for sure was to see for myself.

I sat up. "Can we go now?"

"Yes, we can," Annie said, "but you must be quiet. There's no time to change. The ducks might be gone by the time we get there. You could miss your chance to see them."

"I'll be quick," I promised. "And quiet, too. Should I put on shoes?"

"It isn't far," my sister said, which meant that she didn't want me to wear shoes, so I didn't. I slid out of bed and stood in my bare feet. "I'm ready," I said. "Let's go."

When I landed on my knees on the floor, I was no longer crying. Cold moonlight shone through the window. Someone screamed down the hall, something crashed, and my own scream was already coming, bursting from my chest. The word that came out of me was *No*.

41

DODIE

This time, I was looking down at the water from above. It was inky black and still. A cold moon was reflected on the surface.

It had never been like this before. My feet were cold.

"Where?" I asked, because I was looking for something—something I was excited about. Birds? Ducks. I was looking for ducks, but it was fall, and it was the middle of the night, and there were no ducks in the water. Of course there weren't. There never had been.

"Look closer," said a voice.

"I want to go back to bed," I said.

"They're there." The voice was hideously familiar from somewhere in the depths of my brain. "Look closer."

When the water came, I curled into a ball with my head in my hands. I didn't run. It was cold, but only for a second. It covered my mouth and nose, but only for a second.

I stayed curled in a ball as the water washed over me, on and on. *This isn't so bad*, I thought. *It doesn't even hurt. Why have I spent all of my life so afraid of this?*

Someone screamed, and someone else shouted, so I uncurled and pushed my way out of the water. I moved slowly, because I didn't really want to leave. There was no hurry. Everything was going to be just fine.

I pushed off with my feet and rose to the surface, letting myself float. My hair swirled around my head. I kicked my feet, the movement languid in the water.

Finally, I broke the surface. It was dark out except for slices of moonlight through the window. I saw the moon, with clouds moving over it like they did in the movies, the kind where werewolves or vampires were about to come out. I was in my room, standing barefoot on the floor next to my bed. The bedside clock said it was 3 a.m. I was dry, and in the hallway a door banged open. Something smashed. Was that Lisette? She was screaming. Then Vail's voice, anguished in a way that turned my blood cold. Vail *never* sounded like that.

I banged open my own door. Light shone up from the downstairs hall onto the stairway landing. The door to Ben's bedroom was open, the light on inside. Lisette was helping Violet up from the floor of the hall. There was a thin line of a cut on Lisette's cheek, leaking drops of blood. Vail's bedroom door opened and he stood there fully dressed, swaying as if drunk, his eyes red. We all looked as if we'd just awoken from a nightmare; then I realized that we had.

I spoke to Lisette, who was brushing dust off of Violet with shaking hands. "What happened to you?" I asked her. When she gave me a look of confusion, I touched a finger to my cheek.

Lisette touched her face and looked at the blood on her fingers. "I broke a lamp." She looked at the shards scattered around her bare feet. "She had Mom. She was grabbing her. She—" Lisette pulled in a ragged breath, and Violet put her hands on her shoulders.

"It's all right," she said softly. "She's gone."

Lisette's gaze rose to meet Violet's. "I saw her," she whispered. "She was real."

A Box Full of Darkness

Violet's expression shifted. I recognized that look. It was the look that said that someone was in very, very big trouble.

I glanced at Vail, but his gaze was unfocused. He barely seemed to be following.

I turned back to Lisette, keeping my voice calm. "Why were you in Ben's room?"

"I saw him." Lisette turned pleading eyes to her mother and spoke to her as if she'd asked the question. "I thought I did. He was in the hall. He told me to find him, and I went into the room, but he wasn't there."

Violet didn't answer, and Vail still didn't speak, so I explained to Lisette. "He liked to play hide-and-seek. It was one of his favorite games."

Violet blinked as if waking up. She swiped her sleeve under her eyes. She still looked furious, and I knew it wasn't at Lisette.

"Fucking Sister," she said, her voice controlled.

I flinched back, steadying myself with a hand on the doorway. The voice I'd heard—*Look closer. Look closer.* The voice leading me to the water. She was here? Had she been here all our lives? How did Violet stand it?

Vail finally spoke. "She came to him in the middle of the night." His voice was low, hoarse from shouting. "She held a lamp in her hand and shone it in his eyes in the darkness. She said, *Wake up.*"

The words on the wall downstairs. The words Vail had heard in his ear. The light he'd seen at night as a child, the figure he'd thought was an alien.

"She got him out of bed," Vail continued. "They had started to build a cellar, but the hole they dug kept filling in with water. Nothing kept it dry, so they gave up. They couldn't fill the hole in, so they left it there. They told Edward not to go near it, not to swim because it was dangerous."

Water. My head spun. I thought I might be sick.

"Anne told him that she wanted to show him something," Vail said.

"Ducks," I said.

He turned toward me. Our gazes locked.

"Ducks," Vail agreed.

"She led him out to it in his bare feet." I finished the story. "She drowned him there."

I watched Vail's expression change, and I knew he was remembering what I'd told him of my nightmares about water. He bent and rested his palms on his knees. I had never seen my brother so undone before.

"It happened in this house," he said. "It's still happening in this house."

Lisette's gaze traveled from one of us to the other in turn. "Who was she?" she asked, her voice with an edge of shrill fear in it, barely contained. "Who *is* she?"

Again, it was me who answered. "Ben's sister. Anne."

Lisette stared at me, and I was struck that she was so young she could still be shocked. "His own sister killed him? Why would she *do* that?"

"I don't know, honey," I said. "But Ben is buried in the old family plot behind the house. I found his grave there today. His name was Edward. His sister, Anne, is buried farther away."

"She died by her own hand." This was Violet, her voice low. "That's what it said in the book I found."

I remembered Terri's dreams of someone hanging in her room. But that wasn't in this house. Was Anne haunting other houses? How many?

"The Whittens owned the land around here," I said. "This house, the family plot, the land the Thornhills' house is on, the land the Chathams' house is on—"

"The lot across the street," Vail said. He had straightened again and regained his composure, though he still looked like he might be sick. Our gazes locked, and then he looked at Violet.

"What lot across the street?" Lisette cried. "Could someone just tell me? You three never say *anything.*"

Find me, Ben had said to me.

I thought of the Thornhills' long-lost son, who had run away from home. *I couldn't live in our home any longer. I had to go.*

I thought of Terri, having nightmares alone in her room.

The Whittens had owned all of it. They'd poisoned all of it. Then they had all died, and when none of them were left, their precious land was parceled off, and the rest of us lived on their haunted ground.

My siblings and I finished our silent conversation. Then Vail spoke.

"Violet," he said, "is Sister in this house right now?"

Violet paused, then shook her head. "No. I would feel if she was."

"Right." Vail sounded a little like his old self. "She comes and goes from here. I've noticed that she wanders, and if the Whittens owned all of the neighborhood, then she likely goes wherever she wants. No one has ever lived in the lot across the street. Someone tried rebuilding it and abandoned the project. So now I'm wondering, what are the odds that the house across the street has a cellar under it?"

Something tugged behind my rib cage—fear, but the feeling of a long-lost memory, the same feeling I'd had when I saw Anne's name on her gravestone. I had told Terri's father that we would end this, and I had meant it. "I'd love to know," I said. "Let's go look."

"I'll get dressed," Violet said.

"Oh my God." Lisette looked around at us again. "You're going to an abandoned house in the middle of the night when there's a ghost walking around? You're doing this?"

"Yes, sweetheart," I answered her. "We are."

42

VIOLET

The Chathams' house was dark and empty. There was no car in the driveway. Dodie told us that she'd urged Mr. Chatham to take his ten-year-old daughter out of the neighborhood, at least for the night. Apparently, he'd taken her advice. He'd probably lived in this neighborhood long enough to want to leave anyway.

He'd also, at Dodie's request, left his garage door unlocked. The sound of Vail pulling it up was loud in the silent night, but no one was around to be awakened. The rain had stopped, leaving the ground mushy under my sneakers. The air was still wet, like a hanging blanket.

The garage at our house had nothing in it—no toys, bikes, tools, or old junk. Our parents had parked their nice cars in there to get them out of the weather, and that was all. We didn't have a childhood with a dad tinkering with his car on Sunday afternoons while our mom got messy in the garden. We didn't even clear our own driveway in winter—hired landscapers did. The landscapers hadn't come on the day Ben disappeared, and the driveway had been thick with untouched snow.

The Chathams were different. Their garage wasn't a museum, it was a jumble. There was a rough workbench with a toolbox on it, some sports equipment, two gas cans, and several boxes labeled *Christmas* and *Old Toys*. Vail found the overhead light bulb and pulled the string, and the space was illuminated with harsh yellow light.

I glanced at Lisette. She had cleaned the blood on her cheek where a fragment of the smashed light bulb had grazed her. It was a minor scratch, but it made her look different, less like a little girl. She was coming with us on this nasty errand. I wasn't leaving her alone in the house. She wouldn't agree to it, and she wasn't safer there anyway. She was safer with me.

Still. "Stay close to me," I couldn't help but say. "Don't stray, and if I tell you to do something, do it. Okay?"

She nodded. Her expression was carefully composed not to show fear, but she had just seen Sister full in the flesh, and her hands hadn't fully stopped shaking. "This is crazy," she said, aiming the comment at all three of us.

"It was either this or school," Dodie shot back, giving her a raised eyebrow. How Dodie was the most composed of us, I had no idea.

Vail picked up a baseball bat and gave it an experimental swing. Since he was wearing a baseball shirt, it made him look oddly boyish, except for the fact that he was over six feet tall and his shoulders flexed gracefully under the cotton. He hadn't told us exactly what had happened to him before the dreams woke us all up, but something new was etched in his features, even though otherwise he was the old Vail again. "When I hit her with the vase, I felt impact," he said, his gaze on the bat as he hefted it.

"She kicked me," I said. "And she can grab. Her grip is hard."

Vail nodded. "She's sturdy for a ghost. If I hit her once, I can hit her again."

Dodie wandered into a dark corner, and I heard clinking. "I'm only planning on self-defense, if needed," she said. "I'll stay behind you, Vail." When she turned around, she had one of Mr. Chatham's golf clubs in her hand, a relic of an abandoned hobby. "This will do."

"What if she isn't there?" Lisette asked.

Vail swung his bat again. "Then we look for her in the other houses, or in the woods. If we have to, we'll go back to our house and wait. She has to turn up sometime."

I found a dirt-crusted garden shovel and felt immediately better when I had it in my hands. When I looked at Lisette again, she had picked up a hand-sized hatchet that someone had used to cut down dead tree branches.

"There's one more thing," I told them. "I don't think Anne was Edward's sister. I think she was his mother."

They all turned to me.

I swallowed. "I saw Ben. Just—just for a moment. He said that Anne was angry that she couldn't get married because of him."

Vail lowered the bat. Dodie made a small sound of distress.

"He said he was sorry," I added. "He said I'm his sister. I thought it was just an endearment, but now I think he was telling me that I'm his sister as opposed to Anne, who isn't."

"She had an illegitimate baby as a teenager," Vail said. "It would have been shameful for Anne back then. Shameful enough that her parents would pass the baby off as her little brother."

I nodded. "I've been thinking about it. Anne was the sole heir. Then she had a son, who would have been the heir after her, if he was legitimate. But he wasn't, so he was passed off as her brother. When that happened, Edward became the family's male heir."

"He usurped the inheritance," Dodie said. She held the golf club at a jaunty angle, as if she was a woman without a care on her way to a round of golf. "The secret was bad enough, but the cover-up disinherited her for her brother."

"She would have lived the rest of her life a spinster, financially dependent on her family," I said. "Her parents were ashamed of her. Her home life was probably terrible. When she was pregnant, there was nothing she could do about it. She was trapped. She hated Edward, and getting rid of him would solve all of her problems."

"Jesus," Vail said softly.

She had killed her son, and a year later, she had hanged herself. Was it remorse, I wondered? Maybe she was just crazy. But I had been called crazy enough times in my life. I had believed it myself. I, of all people, knew that crazy was more complicated than it seemed.

"I wonder who Edward's father was," Dodie added. "She was only fourteen when he was born."

I shook my head. "We'll never know. They kept it secret, and now they're all dead." The knowledge of Edward's parentage, of Ben's original father, had died with the Whittens. Ben himself had never known. His father's identity was vibrating brain cells, like Dodie had said. Ashes at Pompeii.

Lisette spoke up. "I hope he died horribly." Her cheeks were flushed with anger. "The father. I hope he died in really bad pain." She was thinking about having a baby at her age, I knew. So was I.

Someone, as Vail said, had tried to rebuild the house in the lot across the street. When we were kids, the house's cracked windows were shrouded in dirt, the weeds were waist-high, and there were missing shingles on the roof like punched-out teeth. In a normal neighborhood, an abandoned house like that would be a magnet for kids and teens, daring each other to break in and commit acts of vandalism. None of us Esmies had ever set foot on the property.

In the years we'd been gone, the house had begun to fall down. The roof had caved halfway when a tree had fallen in a storm. In the brief burst of construction, the tree had been cut down, its roots dug up. The long-ago lawn had been dug up, too, and most of the lot was now deep ruts of dirt, softened to mud by the rain and cradling thick puddles. Weeds had taken over. They had probably planned to tear down the old house and build a shiny new one, but early on they had given up and driven their construction machines away, leaving overturned earth, a half-ruined building, and a single torn tarp, flapping in the remains of the wind.

Comically, the front door was locked. None of us wanted to risk climbing through the jagged glass of the windows, so we circled to the back, our feet squishing in the mud, in search of the back door. This was locked, too, but the wood was soft and black with mold. Vail kicked it hard with the sole of his boot, and the wood cracked. A second kick, and a third, and the frame gave way and the door groaned open.

It was still dark, so there was no light coming in through the half-destroyed roof. I switched on the flashlight I'd taken from Mr. Chatham's toolbox, gripping my shovel in my other hand. We filed into the house.

We were in the kitchen. Rain had collected under the peeled linoleum floor, which gave spongily under my feet. Something smelled bad. There was furtive scurrying in the walls and the corners, and the wiring from the old stove was exposed, frayed and eaten through. The door of one cupboard had rotted off, and there was an abandoned nest inside.

Our house should look like this, I thought, *or close to it.* We'd had landscapers, but no caretaker or maids. That was my decision. I could have hired someone, but I couldn't bear the thought of strangers in our house, of strangers possibly finding Ben or what was left of him, in whatever state he was in. The house was Ben's grave, which made it sacred ground.

So we didn't sell it, we didn't tear it down, and we didn't hire strangers to clean it out. Yet I hadn't seen evidence of a single rodent, even in the attic.

Maybe Sister scared even the rodents away. Yet still, a window should have broken, or the roof should have leaked rain. Something in all those years.

"It's cold," Lisette said.

I raised the flashlight beam to see that she was right. The air was frosting gently with our breaths.

Dodie poked at the nest in the cupboard with her golf club. "What a mess," she commented. "They didn't even get as far as to tear this heap down." The tarp flapped on the roof with a sharp sound, making her jump. "Hurry up, would you, Vail? I'd like to get out of here. Preferably before this demon house eats us all alive."

Vail was out of range of my flashlight beam. He had walked through the kitchen as if he lived here every day. I heard something thump in the next room, then a doorknob rattling. The tinkle of glass.

"The carpet's soaked in the living room," he called back to us from the dark. "It isn't just the rain."

I bent my knees, doing an experimental flex, and I felt the kitchen floor give alarmingly beneath my feet. The wood was rotten. "There's water below," I called back. "Under the foundation."

"It's why they couldn't build." Vail sounded calm. "Why they gave up. They thought they could fix the problem of the water under the house because it makes no sense. We're not on a high water table in this neighborhood. But it's as wet in here as if we're on an underground lake. They likely had a plan to fix the drainage, but had to abandon it."

"The water problem was here when they originally tried to build the cellar," I called out to Vail's disembodied voice. "Why do you—"

"Jackpot." Vail ignored me. "I found the basement door." A thump. "It's locked."

"There's a *basement*?" Lisette said. "It must be soaked."

Who locked it? I thought but didn't ask.

There was a crack as Vail hit something with his baseball bat. "I can't break it," he called out. "Dodie and Violet, come here."

We found him around the corner, aiming one of his powerful kicks at the basement door. I handed the flashlight to Lisette and hefted my shovel with both hands. "Vail, get out of the way."

We took turns—me with the shovel, Dodie with the golf club, and Vail with his boots and Lisette's hatchet. It took much longer to break than the back door had. The basement door seemed to be made of something stronger, and the lock was tight. I stared at it and felt sudden cold certainty. *Sister, I've found you.* My ribs and kidneys still throbbed with pain where she'd kicked me.

"Should we have called a priest or something?" Lisette asked.

As if in reply, there was a thump in the basement, the sound deep below the house, on the other side of the door. Lisette's hand grabbed my arm, her fingers digging in.

"No priests," I said.

"No priests," Vail agreed. "Some things you have to do yourself if you want to get them right."

"If she's going to kill me, could she please get on with it?" Dodie complained. "It would be easier getting into a bank vault." She gave the door another hard swing with the club.

Finally, the wood frame gave enough for the lock to splinter. Vail kicked the door in. Lisette aimed the flashlight beam into pure, inky darkness. The only thing we could see was a set of rotten wooden stairs descending into blankness, as if the world ended here.

Lisette lowered the beam, and I could see that the stairs didn't end in a black hole. They were sunk into water at least several feet deep, the surface glassy and still in the beam of light.

My breath fogged as it left my lips.

For the first time in this wild expedition, I hesitated. I did not want to go down there. I didn't want Vail and Dodie to go down there. And I definitely didn't want my daughter going anywhere near that water.

Vail swore, his voice a rasp. He turned to Lisette and handed her the hatchet. "Keep this," he told her. "I'll take the bat."

"You're going *down*?" Dodie's voice sounded as panicked as I felt.

Vail didn't even flinch. "It's what we're here for." He picked up the bat. "I'll go first."

I grabbed his arm. "Wait."

Vail stopped, turning.

"Do you remember Ben's fourth birthday?" I asked him.

He nodded. "Yeah, I do."

"We baked him a cake." I blinked down at the black water at the bottom of the stairs. The cake had been chocolate, the kind from a mix in a box. We'd baked it together in the kitchen. Where were our parents that day? I didn't remember, and it didn't matter. The best memories of my life didn't include our parents.

Had that really been us? Had we been kids, cracking jokes and insults as we baked a cake for our little brother? Kids who weren't thinking about their nightmares? Kids who didn't know they would someday end up here, riding waves of anger and grief into the dark?

I didn't know what I wanted. I tore my gaze away from the water and looked into Vail's eyes.

"It wasn't all bad," Vail said, his voice soft.

I nodded. The cake had been really good in the end. We'd baked it perfectly. Then we'd all devoured it.

"Can we do this?" I asked Vail.

He raised his gaze to the ceiling as he gave my question a moment of serious thought. He let out a slow breath, rolled his shoulders, and tensed his jaw.

"Yeah," he said, looking at me again. "We can."

Then he started down the stairs.

43

VAIL

The water rose over my boots, my ankles, my calves as I descended. It was icy cold, and the surface was uncannily still, except where my body made it ripple. When I glanced down, I saw the reflection of something oily on the surface. The air was freezing, and I could smell something—probably more than one thing—that was rotten and dead.

I lifted the bat above the water's surface as my knees, then my thighs sank into the water. I didn't know where the stairs' bottom was, so I slowed in caution. I didn't want to slip.

Behind me, I heard Dodie say, "Screw it," then sloshing as she followed me. Violet told Lisette to stay at the top of the stairs and hold the flashlight. Lisette didn't argue.

I admit I winced when the icy water seeped to my waist, but I gritted my teeth and tried to adjust. My feet edged forward and found only floor. "This is the bottom," I called out.

Lisette aimed the flashlight ahead of me, and I waded into the flooded basement. I couldn't see anything floating on the water's surface. I also couldn't see the walls, because it was so big down here that the beam didn't reach them. It felt like I was in an endless underground cavern.

Behind Dodie, there was more splashing as Violet followed us down.

"Anne Whitten!" I let my voice boom as I rested the bat behind my neck, my hand ready on the handle. "I know you're here. Come out, you coward."

At the edge of the darkness, something splashed.

I stopped, and Dodie came close behind me. I could hear her ragged breathing. She bumped into my back, and I realized she had turned so that we were back-to-back. The best position if you don't want to be surprised.

"Do you see her?" Dodie asked.

"No."

We waited. I looked behind my shoulder and saw that Violet had made it to the bottom of the stairs, shovel in hand. The water was higher on her because she was shorter than me. She pushed forward, the water parting around her.

"You all right?" I asked her.

She looked at me, and then her eyes went wide in panic. It took me a split second to realize she wasn't looking at me but at something past me.

Under the water, something slithered over my feet.

I shouted, but Dodie was louder. She screamed, and then she staggered, as if something had crashed into her legs. The golf club fell from her hands. She jerked as if something pulled at her. I didn't have time to spin and grab her before she fell and disappeared under the water.

The thing under the water slithered over my feet again, and I kicked it. I dropped the bat and plunged down where Dodie had sunk, groping under the water. There was nothing—just icy emptiness where my sister had been. My numbing hands scrabbled over empty floor. I felt Violet submerge next to me, her hands searching, too.

My breath ran out. I bobbed up and gasped, ignoring Lisette's terrified cries, and plunged again.

This time, I felt a calf. A knee. One of Dodie's arms flung toward us under the water, and together Violet and I wrenched upward, pulling Dodie into the air with us.

"Fuck," I shouted as I spit out foul, dark water. We had all dropped our weapons. "Lisette, be quiet," I shouted to the wailing girl at the top of the stairs. "We're okay. We need the light."

Lisette got under control enough to aim the flashlight again. "Mom?" she called out.

"I'm fine," Violet managed.

Dodie was shivering. "It grabbed me."

"I felt it," I said.

"She's down here," Violet added, pushing her soaked hair back from her face. "I saw her."

I waded toward my floating bat, then the golf club, then the shovel. We regrouped, shivering. A splash of water came from one of the dark corners of the room. "Not good enough, coward!" I barked at the thing that was in the basement with us. "Try again!"

I waded farther out. Lisette's light moved in my path. Dodie and Violet, armed again, followed behind.

There was a hiss of breath in the darkness.

"Yeah, that's right," I said. "We're coming for you."

"Vail, you're making her mad," Violet warned, her teeth chattering.

"So what?" I took another step. The water got colder the farther we got from the stairs. "I've been mad for twenty years."

The floor became uneven, and my toe hit something hard. A piece of metal. A remnant of old furniture, maybe. Had someone tried to put a furnace down here? They must have been insane.

Something bumped my leg. "Watch out," I warned the others. "She's under the water again."

Dodie jabbed into the water with her club. Water dripped from the ends of her long hair, making circles on the surface. "She pinches the backs of your knees and hits your ankle. Puts your feet out from under you. She's fast."

As if on cue, something gripped my ankle—cold, hard fingers made of bone. I kicked hard, then stomped down with my other foot. If it was bone, I could break it.

I thought I felt something beneath my boot, but my feet were numb. A soft clicking sound came from the darkness, then another hiss.

"I felt her that time," Violet said. "Circle up."

We moved back-to-back again, keeping still, holding our weapons ready.

"Mom?" Lisette called from the stairs.

"Hold on, honey," Violet called back. "We're almost done."

"Wake up," a voice said, coming from everywhere and nowhere, making my nerves seize in instinctive terror. "Wake up, Edward. Get out of bed."

Lisette shrieked.

We waited for Sister to say something else. My rage burned, replacing the fear, hot and healthy, cleansing. I would never let it go. I would hate Sister until I died.

The Whittens were tragic. Whatever had happened to Anne Whitten to get her pregnant at fourteen was lost to time, and it was sad. Her whole life story was sad.

I was going to kill her anyway.

The silence was cold, tense. The water lapped around my waist. I couldn't feel my legs.

"Violet?" I said when the silence had stretched too long.

"Yes?"

"I need to tell you something."

I heard her let out a shaky breath. It plumed in the cold air.

"That time Dad gave you five dollars for your tenth birthday? I stole it."

There was a splash as she smashed her shovel down on the water's surface. "I *knew* it."

Behind my other shoulder, Dodie laughed.

"You swore it wasn't you." Violet's tone was dark.

"I lied," I said. "I bought comic books with it."

"How did you even know where it was? I hid it."

"It was in your dresser drawer, under your underwear. I mean, come on. It was the most obvious hiding place."

Dodie laughed again, and Violet shouted, "You went in my *room*?"

"Violet," Dodie said, "we went in your room all the time."

"True," I said. "If we're going to die down here, then I guess you should know."

"*You* can die down here if you want," Violet snapped. "I don't plan to."

Dodie's teeth were chattering. "If this is our last moment, then I want you both to know that Mom liked me best."

"No way. It was definitely me," I shot back.

"Shh," Violet said. "I can hear her now."

A hiss came from the darkness, and we went quiet.

"I want to show you something," Sister said. A shadow moved, tall and thin. It came from one direction, then another, flickering. I tensed. "Wake up. *Wake up.*"

I lunged forward and swung the bat, but hit only air. Dodie started to stumble but grabbed my arm, steadying herself.

"Sister," Violet said.

I turned. Violet was frozen still, her face a mask of terror. The shovel shook in her hands.

"Sister," she said again, and then she rushed past me in a splash of dark water. She raised the shovel to hit something—I couldn't see what it was. The flashlight moved. There was a strange thump, and then Violet dropped the shovel. And then, without another sound, she was simply gone.

"No," Dodie moaned. "No, no, no." She lunged forward to where Violet had disappeared and reached down into the water. "Vail, help me. She's—"

Something bumped hard into my legs, and I staggered. I braced myself to rebalance, and it hit me again. Sister was trying to drag me under.

I kicked her. Then I plunged my arms into the water again, submerging, looking for Violet.

It was pure darkness under here. I forced my numb hands over the floor, searching, searching. An icy, bony hand landed on the back of my head, pushing me down.

I jerked, jamming my elbow back, then flipping my position under the water and kicking her off me. Her hand lost its grip, her fingernails raking my scalp in stinging pain. I kicked her again, then pushed up for breath.

"Vail!" Dodie shouted. "Over there! Toward the stairs!"

Something thrashed beneath the oily surface of the water behind us. I regained my balance again. My bat floated by me, and I grabbed it as I waded as fast as I could through the water, Dodie beside me.

Violet's hand flew out of the water, then sank.

"Mom!" Lisette screamed.

I pushed toward the spot where the hand had gone under, then reached into the water again. Hands grasped at me—real hands, human hands. I gripped Violet and pulled up with all my strength.

There was resistance, because something was dragging her down. Something powerful. Sister had a grip on Violet and refused to let go.

I moved my leg under Violet and levered myself up. Dodie had grabbed her, too, and was leaning back with her full weight. We pulled her toward the stairs.

Violet's face broke the surface of the water, and she gasped in a breath. She was dragged under again.

We pulled, Dodie and me. I dove down and pushed Violet upward. She broke the surface and gasped again.

Dodie picked up her club, gripped it in both hands like she was holding a stake, and stabbed it down into the water, hard. Violet squirmed as the grip on her loosened. Dodie stabbed down again, and I pulled Violet toward the stairs.

"Go!" Dodie screamed, stabbing down again. There was the sound of her hitting something solid. "Hurry!"

Violet flung an arm around my neck, and we were almost to the foot of the stairs when she was yanked out of my grip. She lurched onto her knees on a lower step, her hands grasping for purchase on the rotting wood of the stairs.

I turned to find Dodie struggling, slashing with the club. I took a step back, holding out my hand, and she grasped it hard. I pulled. I still gripped the bat in my other hand.

There was a long hiss, a click, and something rose out of the water.

She was oily black, an inky shadow. A wretched smell came from her as she pushed up. She was between me and Violet, with her back to me. She was fixed on Violet. I had never seen my sister's face like that—blank with terror, helpless. She stared into Sister's face transfixed, and then she tried to scramble up the stairs.

Sister took a step toward Violet, reaching an arm out, a bony hand.

I let go of Dodie's hand and gripped the baseball bat with both hands. I swung with all of my strength. There was a *crack* as the bat connected with the back of Sister's skull.

Sister reeled, snapping around, raising her arms, but Dodie was faster. She hit Sister just as she swiveled, the golf club catching Sister's jaw.

Sister screamed.

Behind her, Lisette scrambled down the stairs and reached out to Violet. In her hand was the hatchet. Violet took it.

Before Sister could turn again, Violet stood, grasped Sister by her lank, slimy hair, and swung the hatchet.

Again. And again.

There was no blood. Sister stopped screaming. I held her icy bones while Violet kept swinging. In the end, it was like breaking an old, dead twig.

Sister's head rolled into the water and sank. No bubbles rose to the surface.

The rest of her body collapsed, and then it was gone.

44

DODIE

**New York, New York
One year later
September 1990**

When I first came to New York, I spent a lot of time in Central Park. I had taken a waitressing job to pay the bills, because I had no modeling work yet and I wasn't old enough to get my trust fund. I lived in a tiny apartment with two awful roommates. We hated each other. I loved it. It felt like home.

Still, I was broke and Central Park was free, even though it was dangerous, so on days when the weather was nice and I had an unscheduled hour, I'd go. I'd walk, or I'd lie on the grass of the lawn and stare at the sky. No one knew or cared where I was. I didn't matter. I didn't *want* to matter. I wanted to be no one.

"You're pretty," my first agent said to me frankly after she'd signed me. "I have this shampoo thing here, you'd be good for that, but we could market your face. You'd have to learn to smile more."

"No, thank you," I told her politely. "Hair is just fine."

She looked doubtful. "It's just a shot of the back of your head. You get that, right? It's a start, but—"

"The back of my head sounds great," I said.

I watched her try to discern whether I was being sarcastic. I wasn't. "You'll never make it big with shampoo. You know that?"

"I'm counting on it," I replied.

She never understood me. That was fine.

I did show my face eventually, of course. In a commercial, you smile for the camera, then turn, raising your arm and letting your hair run over it. "You look good," one director said to me, "but you're not warm. Try for warm."

In Central Park, no one cared if I was warm.

So when I came back to New York after my siblings and I killed Sister, and I started looking for a new apartment, it made sense that I ended up on 107th, with the park outside my window. The elderly landlady warned me that the park had a lot of "those people." I didn't care. When I saw the joggers, the dog walkers, and the creeps going about their business, this was the first place I'd lived that felt like home to me, even with the banging radiators and the crooked bathroom door that you had to force closed. It felt like I belonged here, like it was mine.

That was the first change I made. The second change came when my agent learned that I was back in town. She called me, and partway through her shouted lecture, I hung up. I never called her again, and from the moment I hung up that phone, I never again thought about whether my hands were pale enough or what the size of my calves was.

The third thing I did was by far the hardest.

First, I had to track down Nadia, my fellow model, and ask her where she lived. Then I went to her building and stood outside. I tried to look casual, as if I was expecting a friend to come out any minute. People bought it. It helped that models lived there, so I looked like I belonged.

I didn't see the person I wanted, so eventually I chatted up a nosy neighbor and found out where he worked. Fifteen minutes later, I walked into a record store on Lower Broadway. The bell above the door jingled.

Ethan looked up from where he was standing behind the counter. When he saw me, he went very still. "Dodie?"

I cleared my throat. "Hello, Ethan."

He blinked, then looked around, as if panicked. A man with a graying ponytail was browsing records in one corner. A kid in a ball cap was pocketing his change and leaving, brushing past me to get out the door.

"You're back in town," Ethan said.

"I am." I let my gaze take in his tall frame, his dark tousled hair, his glasses. The flush on his cheeks. I shoved my hands into the pockets of my belted wool coat. "You work here."

"I'm the manager." Immediately, he pinched the bridge of his nose and closed his eyes, his cheeks going more fiery red. "Oh, God, that sounded bad."

I smiled. The man with the ponytail paused his browsing and glanced at us.

"You have my number," Ethan said when he dropped his hand. "You could have called."

"I wanted to see what you do for a living," I replied. "The truth this time. And I think . . . I wanted you to see my face. A phone call wouldn't do."

"So you tracked me down?" he asked. "Why?"

I was sweating under my coat. I was so nervous that I clenched my hands into fists inside my pockets and reminded myself to breathe. I'd never been this terrified in my life, and that included the moment that Anne Whitten's murderous ghost pulled me under black water, her bony hands dragging me down.

I hadn't thought I would get this next chapter, but I had been

A Box Full of Darkness

wrong. I hadn't died in that basement, the same place Ben had died, with Sister pushing me down. I'd walked out of there instead. This was my chapter, and I planned to take it.

The ponytail man was listening avidly, his eyebrows rising. Good for him.

"I want to know if you'll go on a date with me," I said to Ethan.

"A second date?" he asked, surprised.

"Yes, a second date."

Our gazes caught, and I didn't know what he saw, but slowly, he relaxed. His shoulders lowered. The panic left his face. His cheeks were still a little red, but he smiled.

"I'm happy to see you," he said softly.

"I'm happy to see you, too." I meant it.

We looked at each other for another long moment. Maybe this would work, and maybe it wouldn't. There was no way to know, but I was going to try. Not because I needed to or because I was supposed to. Because I *wanted* to. I wasn't used to wanting things, to hoping for them. Apparently, it started now. In this chapter, I was a woman who had things to do.

The man in the ponytail said, "Say yes quickly, son, before she changes her mind. She's a looker."

I bit my lip. And I waited for an answer.

This morning, I had put on my favorite work outfit: black pants, spiky black heels, black turtleneck, red lipstick. Dramatic? Yes. The men I worked with loved it. They said it gave the right first impression.

Ethan—as he told me on our second date—was not only a record store manager but also a part-time musician, playing bass with his band at obscure bars on Saturday nights. He knew someone who knew someone else, and by our sixth date I had heard about an independent record company in a rented office in SoHo that was in need of a receptionist. The job was one of precarious stability and strange hours for a company running on pennies, with pay to match. No sane person needing a paycheck would rely on it.

I got it, of course, even with no experience as a receptionist. Their standards weren't very high. I answered phones, kept schedules, and made coffee. The partners who ran the place were two fortyish men with rumpled sport coats, raspy beards, and bloodshot eyes, who somehow worked both all the time and never. The schedule made no sense. The musicians were younger than me and hit on me regularly, and some of them smelled truly terrible. Boxes of records were stacked randomly behind my desk. People cared greatly about T-shirts. There was absolutely no money. It was the first job I ever had that I loved, and I never wanted to leave it.

After work at least once a week, I'd walk to Lower Broadway to pick up Ethan as he closed the store, and we'd explore the city. We'd eat fifty-cent noodles or catch a second-run movie. We'd wander thrift shops while sipping milkshakes. We'd buy secondhand books. We'd read the scandalous movie titles on the porn posters in Times Square. We'd talk about everything and nothing. We'd hold hands like teenagers. Sometimes he'd kiss me in a doorway, right there among the stacks of garbage and the crazy people. Then we'd go home.

The phone on my desk rang as I was putting on my coat at the end of the day, and because I was in a generous mood, I answered it.

"Dodie," came my big sister's voice. "I finally caught you."

"I'm just leaving," I said. "Can this wait?"

"No, because you're never home."

"Not never." Ethan and I got in late on the nights we ended at my place. I never checked my messages because I was too pleasantly distracted by then. The tall, quiet ones are apparently the most devastatingly talented.

"Never." Violet was very sure of this. "I need to talk to you. Give me five minutes."

I rolled my eyes, though she couldn't see me. I regretted ever giving her my number at work. "Go."

"Lisette wants to come the weekend before Christmas," Violet said. "She wants to see the Brooklyn Bridge, the World Trade Center, and the Rockefeller tree."

"Violet, those things are *boring*. No one in New York does those things."

"Lisette wants to see them, so you'll take her." She used the Big Sister Voice of Dire Threat.

"Fine. But we'll also go shopping. And don't blame me if she hates it."

"She won't hate it. You'll have to pick her up at Grand Central. I'll give you her train time. And don't leave her waiting."

It was only September. "I can remember to pick up my niece three months from now, yes."

Violet didn't notice—or chose not to acknowledge—my sarcasm. She continued with a list of instructions, from what to feed Lisette to making sure she wore her mittens. I looked at my nails and barely paid attention.

Lisette's visits to me in the city, when she slept on my secondhand sofa, were a new thing. Lisette had a wild, independent streak, and the supervised trips to New York were her parents' compromise so that she wouldn't pull a stunt like she had last year. The deal was that Lisette got to spend a weekend with her glamorous aunt—me—and in return, she did her best to behave. So far, it seemed to be working.

"Did you get all of that?" Violet asked on the phone.

"Yes."

"You didn't."

"I absolutely did. If Lisette is giving you so much trouble, why don't you send her to Vail's?"

"I already am. At Thanksgiving."

I laughed. "Does she think she's getting a turkey dinner?"

"No, she thinks she's getting toast and canned tuna. Which is what Vail will be eating."

Lisette probably wouldn't mind. She was used to the menu at the house in Fell. She had spent two weeks there in the summer, just like Ethan and I had.

If you had ever told me that I would spend summer vacation in Fell, of all places, I would have thought you were crazy. But Vail had worked hard fixing the house up. He'd gotten rid of most of the old furniture, and he'd finally stripped the ugly wallpaper in the kitchen. It was almost nice there now. It helped that the ghosts seemed to be finally gone.

I had told Ethan about Ben, about the Whitten children. What we'd done. Ethan had paled, but he said he understood. For weeks after that, I expected to get no answer when I called him. I expected us to be over. Who would put up with that kind of madness?

But incredibly, he'd kept answering my calls and going on dates with me. He'd come to the house in the summer and seen it for himself. He said he understood me a lot better after he spent time in Fell.

He also said he had a cousin who was in an expensive rehab and an uncle with a gambling problem, so ours wasn't the only family with secrets.

"Are we done?" I asked Violet. "I have to go see my boyfriend and have some actual fun. You should try it sometime."

"I have fun," Violet said.

"No one in Vermont," I declared, "has fun."

"God, you're such a snob," my sister shot back. "Goodbye, Dodie."

I grabbed my bag and ducked into the ladies' room. I changed into jeans, sneakers, and a thrifted sweater with a pattern of Queen of

A Box Full of Darkness

Hearts playing cards. I believed it was incredibly fashionable, and no one could tell me otherwise.

I rubbed off my red lipstick and tied back my hair. I was in a hurry now. Ethan was waiting. New York was waiting.

By the time I walked out the front door and onto the street, I was smiling.

45

VIOLET

Warren, Vermont

I hung up the phone on my office desk harder than necessary. God, my sister was annoying.

There was no one in the empty office to hear it. I only had one employee, and I had sent her home at five. I had stayed later, updating the schedule book and calling contractors, but now I was officially finished for the day. I had turned on the answering machine. Tomorrow's appointments were set. I could go home.

But there was no one at home in my small chilly apartment, so I had called Dodie about Christmas instead. Christmas, which was three months away.

I had become a worrier, a planner. When had that happened?

I sighed out a breath and stood up, listening to the pops in my shoulders and back as I stretched. Since I had moved, become a business owner, and become—as much as possible—an actual mother. That was probably when.

After we killed Sister—I still loved hearing that phrase, and repeated it often in my head—I had gone back to Long Island. I had assessed how much money I still had from Mom and Dad. Then I had made Tess, my old employer, an offer to buy her business.

She said no. She wasn't ready to retire, she said. Also, she added, my plan was guaranteed to fail, because no one would hire "a company run by a former mental patient."

So I left Long Island—I hated it there anyway—and moved to Vermont. I started my own estate cleaning business there, one that was most certainly run by a former mental patient. For good measure, I hired as cleaners other former mental patients, along with ex-cons and people out of rehab. Because, apparently, that's how petty I can be.

It worked just fine. Mental patients and ex-cons are glad to get work, and they don't ask for much. Some of them flaked, others tried to rob me or screw me over, but not as many as you might think. People who aren't mental patients screw each other over on a regular basis anyway, so why not give someone a chance? It gave me some satisfaction to hire people no one else wanted. The work wasn't too hard, and the customers were dead, so they didn't notice if you showed up late or hungover every once in a while. They also didn't notice if you pocketed a few things from their house. I didn't ask.

As for customers, there were enough. People die everywhere.

It worked for me. I made money, and I didn't have to clean the houses myself anymore. I didn't have to find myself face-to-face with the dead quite as often. I'd had enough of the dead to last me a long time.

Why Vermont? There were a lot of reasons. It was a fresh start. It was a few hours' drive to Fell to visit Vail. It was a long bus trip for Lisette to visit, but my adventurous daughter liked long bus trips. The fallout with Clay after the Fell incident was nasty, but Lisette was fifteen and headstrong, and she wore Clay down to get more time with me. I got her once a month and for three weeks in the summer, and in a few years, she'd be an adult. She was already looking at colleges in Vermont.

Aside from all of that, it was nice here. Harsh winters were fine with me, as was the lack of population. I still had my ability to see the dead, but I didn't think about it as often as I used to. I would never think that my ability had gone away, but it was calmer here, in the middle of nowhere.

The only exception was when I'd driven through a small town called Barrons on my way somewhere else. In Barrons, I had gripped the wheel and accelerated past the limit as icy dread seized my bloodstream. I didn't look right or left, not wanting to know who—what—I might see out the window. I didn't calm down until Barrons had vanished behind me. I would never go back there.

Now I put on my flannel coat and picked up my desk phone again. Dusk had settled outside the window of the two-room office I rented in downtown Warren. An eye doctor rented the office next to me, and a psychic had the space downstairs, with an entrance to the street. I truly hoped, for her own sake, that she was a phony.

I dialed the other reason for Warren, Vermont. He picked up right away.

"Yeah?"

"Bradley, do I ever have fun?"

There was a pause as he tried to figure out what I was getting at. He picked the dirty option. "Violet, I have the kids. We can't do that tonight."

"Not that kind of fun. Another kind. Any other kind."

He sounded happy that he had an answer. "Oh. Sure you do. Remember when we took the kids to Tall Tale Gardens?"

We'd done that a few weeks ago, on the last weekend of summer. Bradley had his kids, and we had taken them to Tall Tale Gardens, a local children's park that had playgrounds, cheerful music piped over speakers, a high school kid in a Winnie the Pooh costume, and climbable statues of storybook figures like Humpty Dumpty and the Big Bad Wolf. Lance was too old for it, but he'd had fun anyway, mostly because the younger kids had flocked to him and because we'd fed him junk food. Amy had had so much fun that she'd cried when we finally pried her off Humpty Dumpty at dinnertime. She'd fallen asleep sixty seconds later in the car. It had been a good day.

"I knew Dodie was wrong," I said.

"Why," Bradley asked with the logic that he was often capable of, "do you ever listen to Dodie?"

"I don't know. Do you have the kids at Thanksgiving?"

"No. I'm going to see Dad in Fell."

"Okay, I'll go with Lisette to Vail's." I didn't mind trips to the Fell house anymore. Vail's renovations were nice. The ghosts were gone. On the last trip, I'd made time to visit Alice McMurtry's grave and put flowers on it. Then I'd visited Martin Peabody's grave and done the same. Finally, I'd located the grave of the unknown man Bradley and I had found in the storage unit. He'd been cremated and given a small plaque by the city. I had put flowers there, too.

I didn't know how Sister had wielded power over them, how she'd made them do her bidding. I would never know. But none of them had appeared to me again in my visits to Fell. I could only hope that with Sister gone, they were forever at rest.

"I'm glad you'll be in Fell," Bradley said. "I need someone to talk to besides Dad."

"You can stay with us if you'd rather get away from Gus."

"Vail hates me," Bradley pointed out.

"He does," I agreed.

"If we get married, he'll be mad."

"Good thing we don't have to worry about his feelings because we're not getting married."

Bradley made a *ha* sound that said he didn't believe it. "We'll see."

"Never," I said.

"Next year," he replied, confident.

This was how it was. I gave myself credit that I hadn't given in right away. I made Bradley wait months, but I had my reasons. I needed to get my life together, and so did he. While I wrapped up my life in Long Island, Bradley had moved out of Gus's; rented an apartment half an hour from his kids in Vermont, where he'd lived before the divorce; and gotten a job as a supervisor at a wool factory.

Still, Lisette came first for me, and if she didn't like Bradley, I would have been done with him. But in a completely upside-down turn of events, Bradley Pine and my wild-child daughter got along just fine. They liked the same soapy TV shows and bad action movies. Bradley had taught her the basics of driving this summer, even though he wasn't supposed to, and had let her practice in his car. Bradley knew about the ghosts, about what happened with Sister—things Lisette hadn't been able to tell her own father—and it didn't spook him.

Lisette hadn't spent much time with Bradley's kids yet, but to them, Lisette was the coolest person on the planet. She'd probably warm up, since they fed her ego.

Still, I wasn't going to marry Bradley Pine. The idea was insane.

"Forget about that," I told him. "Let's do something fun tonight. Let's take the kids for a movie and ice cream."

"I'm sorry, what did you say?" Bradley said loudly. "Did you say a movie and ice cream?"

A chorus of shouts behind him said that they'd heard him.

"A movie with popcorn," I said, matching his loud tone.

"What did you say?" He gave a dramatic pause. "Did you say a movie with popcorn?"

More shouts.

This was going to be so, so good. I knew it.

"I'll pick you up in ten," I said. "Be ready."

46

VAIL

Fell, New York

I was never leaving this house. I knew that now.

Not that I couldn't—I could. I could leave Fell, too, if I wanted. But where would I go?

So I stayed. My sisters left to start their lives over, to at least try to find their happiness. When they left, I knew that I wouldn't find my happiness by leaving. I'd find it by staying.

Besides, there was a lot of work to be done.

The house, for one. The dusty furniture, the old linoleum, the wallpaper. I did most of the work myself, only hiring someone when one person couldn't do a job alone. I got books and magazines from the library and taught myself how to do most of the things I needed. I had time and patience. I also had a trust fund I had barely touched.

I painted the walls. I mowed the lawn. I raked the leaves. I got proper cable hooked up, and when the bill came, I paid it. I paid the phone bill, too.

A Box Full of Darkness

On weekend mornings, I haunted garage sales, looking for furniture. I'd rather have someone else's old furniture than ours.

My Jeep was a rental, so I returned it and bought a car from a used car lot on the edge of town. It cost eight hundred dollars and came with free rust on all the doors.

As the months went by, I watched the weather get cold, then wet, then hot. Then cold again. I relearned the sound of rain on the roof of this house, the creak of snow under my boots when I stepped outside to shovel after a snowfall. My tools began to pile up in the garage, so I installed a workbench and kept my rusty car in the driveway. I emptied my parents' bedroom and threw out their bed. I cleaned the disused stove and actually used it. I raked more leaves.

In winter, the cold drafts in the house came from the old windows, not from ghosts. Damp spots came from leaky sinks, not from Sister dripping water on the floor. I sealed the windows and fixed the sinks. Nothing walked in the upstairs hallway. Nothing screamed. I scrubbed the words WAKE UP from the living room wall.

Sometimes, on rainy afternoons, I'd go to the attic and sort through Ben's clothes and toys. I got rid of the puzzles with half the pieces missing and other broken toys. I donated the stuffed animals he'd barely used. When it got too hard, I'd come downstairs again. Ben was okay with that, I felt. He didn't need me to hurry. He knew I was here for good and that I wasn't going to leave him alone again.

One day, I put in a call to the city, complaining about the construction site across the road. I said that it was hazardous, especially the basement, which was full of water and had a terrible smell coming from it. I said that as a concerned neighbor, I thought something should be done.

A few weeks later, the city sent an inspector. He got out of his car wearing thick work boots, put on a hard hat, and went into the house. He came out thirty minutes later, walked across the street, and knocked on my door.

I let him in and gave him tea.

"I checked it out," the inspector told me. "There's no water in the basement. But it's wet down there, and you're right about the smell."

"No water?" I asked, raising my eyebrows as if this surprised me.

He shook his head. "It was there recently, though, and all the way to the ceiling, based on the water marks. And the mud down there—my God. No wonder you complained. No kid in the neighborhood should come near that place."

I didn't tell him that since Terri Chatham's family moved away, there were no children in the neighborhood anymore. "That's interesting," I said. "When I looked, it was full of water. What did you see in the basement?"

"Not much." The inspector sipped his tea. "Just what I could see with my flashlight, because I didn't go all the way to the bottom of the stairs. The steps are rotted, and the mud looked—well, they don't pay me enough to replace my boots, so I wasn't about to walk in it. It looked like if I sank down, I'd never get out."

"A distressing thought," I agreed.

"Whatever's down there is definitely rotten," he said.

I thought about Sister's head rolling off her bony body and falling into the water, and I smiled.

The inspector didn't notice. He was deep in thought as he scratched the back of his head. "The question is what to do. There's a city bylaw about having contaminated soil on your property. I think if we invoke that one, we can get the owners to act. They live in Texas, apparently. They tried to move here, but I guess they didn't like it, so they didn't stay long. And they can't sell the property as it is, obviously."

I nodded. "Obviously." *Contaminated soil,* I thought.

"If the water problem comes back, that's an issue." He had warmed up to his topic. "It sure is strange why there was so much water down there. But I've lived in Fell for five years, and I see a lot of strange things. I'll get an expert to come take a look, but I'm not hopeful we'll get an explanation. The best we can hope for is that the owners will tear down the remains of the house and fill in the basement."

I nodded. "That suits me just fine."

He looked at me, obviously curious but not willing to ask. "No one has complained about that lot before."

"That's because this house was empty," I told him. "But I live here now, and I'm staying."

"By yourself? No wife, no kids?"

"I'm a bit of a loner, I guess."

"To each his own. I guess you have plenty of room." He stood up. "Have a nice afternoon, Mr. Esmie."

I watched him cross the street and get back into his car. When he looked back and noticed me, I waved.

I didn't spend all of my time on the house. I was at the library in downtown Fell a lot, not just for renovating magazines but for everything else. I checked out detective novels and history books. I sat in the records room, reading old newspapers, learning about my town. There was a job board on a wall near the checkout desk—a corkboard with index cards pinned to it advertising help needed. From one of these, I called a landscaping company and picked up work. I weeded, mowed, mulched, and shoveled. I didn't care about the hard labor or the early hours. The money was good, and it was mostly paid in cash.

"You're big enough," the foreman said to me on my first shift, "and you don't look drunk. You got a driver's license?"

"Yep."

"Is it real?"

"Yep."

"Then I don't even care what your name is, honestly. I just care that the work gets done."

Landscapers, it turns out, can gossip like nobody's business. I learned about every house we worked—who was divorced, who was cheating, who was maybe going broke. I also learned how to keep an immaculate lawn, a talent I'd never had to have in my life of wandering.

I made a trip to city hall one day for land records. It was late November, after the leaves had left the trees bare but before the first snow, when the sky was stark gray and the air biting cold. I pulled the deed to our house and checked the property line. I compared it to the map that Violet had stolen from the FCCE. I had returned the map to the college myself, when I made a visit to the Local Literature room and slipped the map back where it belonged. But I had photocopied the map at the library first.

I made pencil marks on my photocopy, noting exactly what we owned. Our property stretched behind the house into the trees where Dodie and I had walked, which was why no one had ever built back there. At the back edge of the trees was a lot the city had marked *Undesignated*.

The undesignated land matched up with the spot on Violet's map, marked with small *x*'s, that was for graves unknown.

I put in a request to the city that the undesignated land be recognized as part of the Esmie property. If no one contested it, the land would be ours.

There were forms to fill out, of course, and bureaucracy to wait for. But I had nothing but patience and time.

No one cared about an empty plot of land, forty feet by forty feet, in backwoods Fell. The Thornhills had gotten divorced—landscaping gossip said their marriage had been miserable for years, if not decades, since their son ran away—and neither of them lived in the house while their lawyers argued over who would get it. The house the Chathams had rented hadn't found another renter, so it sat empty. The lot across the street had no one, of course. I had most of the neighborhood to myself, at least for now.

A Box Full of Darkness

The city didn't care about the land, either, so eventually, with the help of some money to move things along, a line was redrawn on a piece of paper in the bowels of city hall. I now had ownership, with no interference from the city, of the Whitten family graveyard and my little brother's grave.

When I got the notification in the mail, it was the first time I'd wept since Ben had disappeared from his spot beside me in my bed.

Dodie visited in the summer, bringing her boyfriend, Ethan. Dodie had never had a steady boyfriend before—no man, including me, could tolerate her for very long—and I hadn't known what to expect. Ethan was quiet, kind of dorky, and he seemed to actually like my little sister. (To each their own, as the inspector had said.) Dodie really liked him, and God knew I didn't want her to move back in here with me, so I tolerated Ethan as much as I tolerated anyone, and I mostly left him alone.

Violet, of all the men she could have chosen on this planet, had ended up with Bradley Pine. I loathed Bradley Pine. The few times we met, he tried to be nice to me, because apparently he'd mellowed since high school and had no recollection of beating me up. I was not a personable man at the best of times, and I definitely wasn't personable with Bradley Pine. Violet would have to deal with it until I changed my mind.

Lisette, though—I liked Lisette. She was turning into a perfect cross of both of my sisters, incorporating their good and bad traits, which should have annoyed me but instead pleased me greatly. Apparently, she was nonstop trouble most of the time, but when she was in Fell—when she stayed in this house—she was relatively calm. She was comfortable here in a way that she wasn't anywhere else. She laughed more, and there were fewer screaming fights. She slept deeply. She belonged here, though she was too young to know it yet.

She was, deep down, a creature of Fell, of this house, like me. Which fit, because someday this house would be hers.

She would do a lot of wandering before then. She would live a lot of life in other places before she came back. The house would be here when she was ready. I had nothing but patience and time.

Even before I had the property line changed, I began making regular visits to the Whitten family plot. I used my new landscaping skills as well as the tools I'd bought. It took weeks of sporadic trips to clear the weeds and the underbrush, to sod and plant grass. I wanted to clear it before winter hardened the ground and hid the headstones.

I had to clean the headstones, too, even Sister's. It bothered me at first, that she was buried here near Ben, but then I stopped caring. Sister didn't matter anymore, if she ever had. She was inconsequential. I did the bare minimum to clear her grave, then ignored her. It was too much trouble, even, to dig her up and move her, preferably to a garbage dumpster or to hell. I had better things to do.

On my way back from one of these outings, I saw a black bird fly overhead. It landed on the roof of the Esmie house, which I was approaching, and seemed to settle in. It looked like a raven, maybe even the same one I'd seen before. It seemed to be alone. I wondered if it lived here or if it was just passing through.

A book at the library on my next visit said that ravens eat most things, but prefer meat, so the next time I saw the bird—on my way home from grave tending—I left some raw chicken out on the porch. An hour later, the bird was gone, and so was the chicken.

The next day, I heard voices on the street outside. When I looked out the window, three children rode by on bikes, calling to one another and laughing. They rode down the street and disappeared, but I thought I could still hear their voices.

A Box Full of Darkness

It took me an embarrassingly long time, but eventually I remembered the roll of film I'd turned in when we found Ben's footprints in the upstairs hall. I had completely forgotten about it. I dug the slip of paper from my wallet and drove to the FunTime Foto at the nearby strip mall to pick up my pictures. The old man behind the counter—he was eighty at least—took his sweet time and made sure to lecture me about how late I was, but eventually he handed me my photos.

I looked at them when I got home, when I was sitting in the half-finished living room with a mug of hot tea.

Ten of the photos were of the upstairs hall. There was water on the floor—it glistened under the camera flash and the light from the lamp Dodie had held over my shoulder as I took the shots. In my mind's eye I saw the footprints, the impression of Ben's toes, but it was blurrier on film. What showed there might be footprints, or it might not be. A skeptic would know that they could have easily been faked. An outside observer would have doubts. I had none. I put the photos aside in an envelope to keep.

The rest of the photos—the first part of the roll of film—had been taken just before I came to Fell, at Charles Zimmer's house in Sacramento. I remembered standing in his cold white house, taking pictures of his bedroom, his skylight. Making notes in his file, which I still had in a cardboard box in my childhood bedroom.

None of those photos had turned out. They were white with overexposure, and a few of them were grayish-white, as if taken in fog. I frowned at them. There was nothing wrong with the camera or the film roll, since the photos of the hall were fine. Why hadn't these ones turned out?

I tried to put the pictures away and forget about them, but I couldn't. I went upstairs, pulled out my box of VUFOS files, and found Charles Zimmer's phone number. I dialed it from the phone in the kitchen.

There was no answer.

I gave up listening to it ring, hung up, and called Dave Teller, my contact in VUFOS's California office. "Vail," he said excitedly when I told him who it was. "Are you coming back to work for us? You know we're begging for you to—"

"No," I told him, as I'd told him before. "I'm done."

He sighed. "What do you want, then?"

I told him about Charles Zimmer, how I'd left the file unfinished. "Someone should check on him," I said. "When we talked, he was pretty distressed, and he didn't answer when I called."

"Probably just wasn't home," Dave said, "but let me make some inquiries and call you back. You're right, someone should pick up that file."

He called half an hour later, when I was hauling trash to the curb. I barely caught the phone before he hung up.

"Vail, you might get a call from the Sacramento police," he said. "I gave them your number."

I gripped the receiver harder. "What's going on?"

"Turns out Charles Zimmer didn't come to work one day three weeks ago. His family was worried about him, so the police did a check. His house is empty. He's gone."

I stared at the stripped kitchen wall. I was amazed, in a way, that I could still feel surprise.

"He's a missing person now," Dave continued. "Looks like he didn't take anything with him. His bank accounts haven't been touched. The cops don't know if it's foul play or, you know, suicide. Maybe he did it somewhere and no one has found him yet."

Colorado, I thought.

"You said he was distressed." Dave was still talking. "I told the police you said that. They might want to talk to you, is all."

"All right," I managed to say. "Thanks, Dave."

"If you want to come back, call me. We need you."

After I hung up, I stood with my hands at my sides as I clenched and unclenched my fists. There were many possible explanations, I reminded myself. There always were.

I had the sudden urge to call Charlotte Ryder, who was the only person who would understand how I felt in this moment, what it felt like to fail over and over, what it felt like to seek and never to know.

I didn't call her. Because what could she say that would make it better? Nothing made it better.

That was why I was done.

The idea came to me slowly, over time, as I worked or landscaped or read in the library or cleaned graves. It started small, but soon it grew. Bigger and bigger.

It bothered me, actually. It shouldn't have—I should have been able to forget it. But it was like a cold, when you know it's coming on, when your throat gets sore and you think, *Now what?* You hope maybe you're mistaken, but you're not, and every day it gets worse.

It made me so irritable that I bought a spiral notebook and wrote it down. Then I woke up early and wrote more. Stayed up at 2 a.m., writing in the notebook.

I put the notebook away, tried to forget about it. I was busy. I had no time for ideas.

But it wouldn't die. It grew and grew. One of the landscaping guys had bought a computer for his son, hoping it would help his son improve his grades, but his son never used it. I offered to take it off his hands for a hundred bucks.

I set up the computer in my parents' old bedroom, which I had redone. It was nice in here now, with a tidy bedspread on the new bed and a desk by the window where the breeze came in. I divided my sleeping time between this room and my old bedroom, Ben's bedroom. But I used the desk often to pay bills and keep paperwork.

The computer took up most of the desk. It took me a while to set up as I consulted the instruction book over and over again. Then it took more time to figure out how to use it, but eventually, I got it.

In December, with snow outside much as it had been on the day Ben vanished, I sat at the desk and powered the computer on. It whirred and clanked as it woke up and came to life. Then it beeped, and I entered the commands I'd learned to log in and open WordPerfect.

It had a lot of memory, this thing. You could edit, unlike a typewriter. You could put all of your work on a floppy disk and save it. You could take that disk with you anywhere.

Still, before I started, I went back to the spiral notebook. I had the idea for a story about a boy detective who is also a time traveler. He is sent from one time to another every six years, something he has no control over. Wherever he is, six years is all he gets, so he has to do the most good in the time he gets each time.

In each time and place, he tries to solve a mystery. To make friends. To learn.

Victorian England. Cleopatra's Egypt. Prohibition Chicago. The boy spends six years in each place, having adventures and solving crime before he has to leave.

My problem was that I hadn't found a name I liked. He wouldn't be called Edward or Ben. I had written two pages of possible names, first and last, trying to find exactly the right one before I started.

I looked at those pages now, then picked up a pen and added to them. More names, then more. And then I had it.

I had the boy's name, first and last.

I had the name my little brother would have in his next life, the life where other people got to enjoy him, to love him, just like I had.

It was perfect.

A Box Full of Darkness

I looked at the balsam wood airplane with the upside-down wings, which I had taken down from the attic and placed on the desk where I could see it every day. I ran my finger along its smooth, fragile wood. In the drawer next to me, in easy reach, was a small wooden horse and a bag of marbles.

I turned to the screen, to the blinking cursor, and started writing.

ACKNOWLEDGMENTS

Writing this book was an intense experience. I should probably thank the team of people who made *The Witcher 3: Wild Hunt*, which I played whenever I needed a break. The number of hours I have spent on that game will never be spoken of. Let's just say I'm undefeated at Gwent.

In the real world, I want to thank my wonderful editor, Michelle Vega, and my wonderful agent, Pam Hopkins. Claire Zion, for being in my corner when I present inexplicable ideas and pitch them as books. Danielle Keir, Elisha Katz, Jessica Mangicaro, Craig Burke, Tawanna Sullivan, and the rest of the amazing team at Berkley. Every copy editor who has worked on one of my books and pointed out my many errors. You all turn a jumbled Word document into a real book, and I'm grateful.

For my brother, David, and my sister, Nicole: I promise we're not the Esmie siblings. (We're much better-looking.) Molly and Stephanie read an early draft, as they always do, and gave me suggestions, support, and their priceless friendship. Thank you to my husband, Adam. And thank you to the readers, booksellers, librarians, reviewers, and fans who read my books. I appreciate you beyond words.